. . . From Chapter Three . . .

Aiden tightened his hands into fists. "There can never be anything between Lily and me. There can never be anything between *any* woman and me."

"You don't know what will happen," Lucas reminded him. "The other Guardians were good men who didn't realize what was happening to them. You do! You have a lot more information to help you control the situation. And you are doing an amazing job of handling the side effects. Give yourself some credit. Go back to The Oracle. Deal with what's happening. Alec and Kane will help you—I promise. But it's not going to help you to run away from it. Or from her."

"This isn't about—" Aiden cut himself off. He raised his hands and placed them on either side of his head, responding to a feeling that he was being overcome by several strong emotions all at once—anger, stress and pain.

Strangely enough, despite his pain, the confusion cleared for a split second and he became acutely aware of what was causing all this: *someone was trying to send him a message!* And immediately he got his answer.

"What is it?" Lucas asked him, recognizing Aiden's obvious distress.

Aiden, feeling as if all the blood was draining from his head, said, "It's Lily . . . she's in trouble!"

MORE FROM MEN OF BRAHM HILL

&

ALSO FROM CHRISTINE WENRICK
AND RED TREE HOUSE PUBLISHING

THE CHARMED TRILOGY

In a modern world of paranormal adventure, discover a woman with a truly unique gift and a hero fighting for one last chance at salvation.

Leaving Lily Behind

Men of Brahm Hill

Book Three

Christine Wenrick

Leaving Lily Behind

PRINT - ISBN 13: 978–0-9860450-1-1
E-BOOK - ISBN 13: 978–0-9860450-0-4

Red Tree House Publishing, Seattle, WA
Contact: ChristineWenrick@RedTreeHousePublishing.com

Cover design by Whitney Maass, Mill Creek, WA
Contact: WhitneyMaass@gmail.com

Editorial by OPA Author Services, Scottsdale, AZ
Contact: Info@OPAAuthorServices.com

Printed in the United States of America
March, 2016

Dedication

A special thank you

to the man who breathed life

into one of my favorite heroes.

PROLOGUE

Brahm Hill
Just east of Athabasca River, Alberta, Canada

Aiden opened his eyes to a night sky filled with remarkable beauty—beauty he could appreciate despite the incredible pain he was currently feeling. He blinked a few times, each simple, involuntary movement sparking a shooting pain in his temples that ran down his spine as he lay there against the frozen ground staring at the blue moon above him. Blink, blink, blink, more pain followed, and still he focused on the thin clouds that appeared to be speeding past the oversized orb faster than what should be possible. Blink, blink, the quiet . . . He couldn't hear a single sound around him, almost as if someone had hit the mute button on the entire world.

How the hell did he end up here, flat on his back, in the first place? It was as though his brain had been wiped clean and his senses numbed. Then, slowly, sound started to penetrate his consciousness once again. Shadows appeared in his peripheral vision, clashing with one another in front of pillars of flames reaching like hands into the sky. But he couldn't get over the beauty of that moon, at least not until a more beautiful sight came into view above him, commanding all of his attention.

A woman.

A *beautiful* woman with the brightest green eyes.

"You're going to be all right," she assured him, her tone projecting absolute confidence as she bent down and brought her face closer to his. He liked the sound of that voice. Actually, her tuneful voice was the only sound that didn't currently offend him.

Without a second thought, he reached up to touch the line of her jaw with his fingers. Her skin was soft, her expression stilled, elongating the moment between them. "Don't move," she warned him, closing her hand over his.

Don't move?

With those words a single memory clicked into place for him and no two words seemed more wrong. *Don't move?* The sound of metal weaponry clashing, male-laced curses and angry growls suddenly became louder and louder until they blared in his ears! He remembered he and this beautiful woman were in the middle of a supernatural battlefield, engaged in the fight of their lives. So the instruction to "not move" was insanely counterintuitive. If he didn't move they would probably both die. Moving was exactly what he *needed* to do . . . just as soon as he could get his damned legs to cooperate.

"You're in shock," the beauty said, her eyes at first appearing green, now evolving through several goldish hues, beautiful colors that he could only attribute the change to the light from the moon. "Just take it slowly. I've got us covered."

"Fuck! He was a Guardian!" Shouldn't *he* be the one concerned about whether or not they were covered instead of debating the color of her eyes? Aiden blinked harder, trying to jog his memory. Surely he would remember the minutes—seconds even—before *this* woman, one of the most beautiful females he'd ever laid eyes upon, knelt over him and assured him he would be all right.

She began to shake him out of the trance he had fallen into. "Aiden? . . . Aiden!"

"How do you know my name?" he asked her, totally confused about whether this woman was a stranger to him or someone he was intimately familiar with. Because she *was* the type of woman he would want to be intimately familiar with.

The beauty didn't answer his question but he became aware that all the sounds of war had begun to slow down around them. In contrast, the throbbing he had been feeling turned into a raw pain that shot through his right leg as if it had suddenly awakened from a deep sleep and burst into fire. 'Aw, fuck,' he thought, 'don't tell me the pain I'm feeling was from the bite of a Lycan. If it is, I'm screwed!'

Aiden reached for his leg, but her hand stopped him. She was gentle, but she used enough force to leave little doubt that she was not going to let him inspect the wound. "Lycan . . .?" he asked.

She shook her head. "You were struck by a lance. You've lost a lot of blood, but you're going to be all right. You'll heal quickly."

"Why do you say that?" Aiden asked with an equally visceral shake of his head. "I am human."

Her hand went back to his shoulder, those incredible eyes of hers sparkling like jewels. "We both know why. You're more than human."

Aiden focused his gaze straight to her. "Tell me your name."

She glanced quickly around her and then returned her mesmerizing gaze to him. "Lily. My name is Lily."

"Lily . . ." he repeated quietly, then asked, "How do you know—?"

"Aiden!" Fellow Brethren Guardian Zane Merrick shouted at him as he stood among dozens of bodies littering the bloody battlefield, his long, curved sword lodged in the body of an unmoving Lycan at his feet that now, in death, was returning to human form. Zane's ragged breathing was rough from the exertion of battle, so rough that Aiden could hear his friend's blood spiking within his veins. He removed the blade from the inert body beneath him and Aiden watched as blood dripped from his sword to his feet. "Get away from him!" Zane shouted at Lily.

Aiden felt her hand immediately lift from his chest at Zane's bellowed command. She appeared confused at first, seemingly caught off guard. Then she recovered from whatever hesitation she was feeling and directed a look of utter defiance toward Zane.

"I must go," she said, that look somehow warming instantly into a genuine smile when she gazed back down to him. Then she disappeared from his view entirely, just as quickly as she had entered it.

"Wait!" Aiden called after her, and it seemed to take him forever just to roll onto his side. When he finally did, shattering pain raced up his leg from toe to thigh, but somehow he was still able to move his legs. Slowly, hesitatingly, he rose to his feet and searched what was left of the battle scene around him. Torn up earth, the scent of fresh death, and the glow of fire in the night met his searching eyes as Nightwalkers were being sacrificed into the fire he had earlier sensed was somewhere nearby.

"We need to get you out of here," said Zane as he rushed up beside Aiden, curling his arm around his friend's shoulder to serve as strong support.

"What was that about?" Aiden asked in his most critical-sounding voice. "She was just trying to help."

Zane snorted, ignored the question, and asked in return, "Can you walk?" Aiden nodded and started to move his leg forward, but glancing down at his damaged limb he realized that the task of walking would be easier said than done. His thigh had been slashed deeply by someone's blade, and with even the most subtle movement he had to grind his teeth together to keep from screaming . . . but he kept moving.

As the two warriors limped by the body of the Lycan Zane had killed, Aiden scanned the field one last time to see if he could find Lily again. But she had simply disappeared. "Why can't I remember anything? What the hell happened?" he asked, to no one in particular.

A tired look spread across Zane's face. "Trust me . . . if you have no memory of this night, then both you and the Lycan got off easy."

CHAPTER ONE

"Aiden, I wish I had better news. But the fact is you're not responding to the treatments as I had hoped. At this point, I'd say there is an eighty percent certainty that the vampire blood transfused into your system will take over your human system. It's just a matter of how long the process will take."

"But I feel better than I have in a year. Surely you're wrong."

"I'm not wrong."

Aiden Rowan's less than encouraging verbal exchange with Dr. Li that morning continued to echo in his head as he made his way inside The Oracle's grand lobby, the home he shared along with other hybrid-humans training and fighting for the organization known as the Brethren. The rather discouraging diagnosis which offered little in the way of hope or solutions to stopping his slow transition into a vampire should have warned him he was about to have a bad day, possibly his worst since coming to this place more than nine years ago. But for some reason, the thought hadn't occurred to him, until . . .

"Aiden, hold up!" head guard Sampson called to him. "Elder Lambert has asked to see you immediately. He is in his office."

Aiden frowned. He was seldom summoned privately to the Brethren leader's office. "Did he say why?"

The guard shook his head but, showing a small smirk, added, "Find Kane. He's asked to see you both."

Aiden closed his eyes in a long blink and then rolled them upward, exhaled a heavy sigh and asked, "What's he done now?"

Sampson chuckled softly, his shoulders visibly shaking with amusement as he turned back toward the secured elevator that would return him to the Elder's offices on the top floor. "I think the easier question is: what hasn't Kane done?"

Aiden snorted in wordless agreement.

"Hey, you're the one who decided to be BFF's with the guy."

"That was before I knew he was a Shifter!" Aiden shot back at Sampson as the elevator doors slid closed in front of the guard, but Aiden's sarcasm held no scorn. Kane had really been a good friend to him over the past year, when few others wanted to be after word of the highly dangerous blood transfusions he'd participated in spread throughout The Oracle. But trouble always had a way of following Kane. And, unfortunately, Aiden was usually standing right next to him when it did.

Aiden pivoted to his left and headed toward the first floor corridor off the lobby, which he knew was the most logical place in the building for a man to disappear when he didn't want to be found. The long hallway was a never-ending series of doors leading into at least a dozen various sized banquet rooms and small, odd spaces within the century-old former Bavarian-styled hotel. In only a few seconds, his sensitive ears picked up a familiar voice coming from one of the old phone booths that lined the corridor, relics of the days when the building was host to many meetings, formal gatherings, and the like.

"I think this is the perfect place," the disembodied voice said. "We're comfortable, and you are simply too irresistible in this short skirt." That slow, sexy drawl was definitely Kane. The seductive timbre of his voice was followed by the sounds of passionate kissing and, soon, some very hard breathing. As The Oracle's only Natural Shifter, Kane caused trouble on a good day and mind-blowing chaos on a bad one. The small, curtain-fronted phone booth where he currently had some beauty stashed before lunch (when she was probably supposed to be somewhere else), was an example of a good day . . . a Tuesday.

"Pecker . . .," Aiden mumbled to himself before stopping in front of the velvet curtain that concealed its occupants.

"Very irresistible," Kane continued. Then sounds of more kissing, and Aiden had had enough. "No one's gonna find—"

"Kane . . .," Aiden interrupted, making his presence outside the curtain known to the clandestine lovers. However, Aiden wasn't prepared to hear the woman behind the heavy drapery respond with an awkward gasp, something between a screech and an exhaled breath, as if she had been bitten by something poisonous. Still safely concealed by the curtain that was now beginning to shudder from the frantic action going on behind it, she scrambled around, making all sorts of strange sounds.

"What?" Kane growled at him as he drew back the curtain just far enough to reveal his head, obviously holding the drape closed as best he could.

Aiden tried to restrain the broad smirk that had erupted in spite of his mood, but he couldn't manage a solemn face, considering how ridiculous Kane looked there on his knees, with his rumpled, messy black hair and handsome face framed by the twisted curtain. "Am I interrupting?"

Kane shot him a cold glare in return that said 'you know you are'.

Suddenly, without warning, a small, honey-blond bundle of energy burst through the curtain and crashed against Aiden's chest so hard he thought she was going to fall back smack-on-her-ass. Instinct took over as he reached his long arms around her and pulled her firmly against himself to save her from an embarrassing spill. The woman's palms flattened against his chest—and he felt an instant charge under their contact. The sensation surprised him. Then her head popped up and the biggest green eyes Aiden swore he would ever see in his lifetime made contact with his and widened in even further panic.

No! It couldn't be.

"Lily . . .?" Aiden swallowed thickly, surprised that an actual sound came from his throat as he said her name. It was her, the woman Aiden had not been able to get out of his head since the first night he saw her three weeks ago at Brahm Hill—and every single morning since after she appeared at The Oracle to assist Dr. Li in the labs, and with his testing. Except for this morning. She wasn't there this morning when Dr. Li had given him that disturbing news that he wouldn't be able to stop the process of Aiden transitioning into a vampire. Now he knew why; she was busy kissing Kane in a goddam closet!!!

His hand moved from her back to her shoulder, in-advertently bumping her sloppy bun and nearly spilling all of her honey-blond hair onto his hand. But somehow it managed to stay tethered to its vulnerable pins. Aiden's heart seized in his chest, his body instantly stiffened as he tried to tamp down a fierce jealously that had arisen within him in the instant of recognition. "I didn't know it was you," was all he could think to say. Then, suddenly, he felt cold, very cold. He could feel a darker side—*darker instincts*— pushing forward, and it was stressing him to the point that he feared he couldn't hold them back.

Lily's expression faltered as she continued to stare up at him, little creases forming between her brows. To Aiden, she appeared to be praying to be anywhere else in the world other than in his arms. That bothered Aiden, too, and his body responded by tightening further. This freaking gorgeous woman felt so perfect in his arms—so 'right'—that he just wanted to slowly kiss up and down the column of her throat and massage his fingers along her thighs until he heard her sigh. Then he realized that he had just listened to his best friend doing that with her . . . *to her*. How was he supposed to deal with that?

Simple. He just kept himself perfectly still and said nothing.

"Aiden . . .," she stuttered, hesitantly, as if she had no idea what additional words would follow.

Jealousy and frustration were continuing to surge through Aiden's body at the sound of her voice, and he knew immediately. He just knew! This was what he had been working so hard to control now for the entire three weeks since he'd met her—it was the want, the need, the dominance he felt every time Lily Abbott was close to him. Since the transfusions, he had spent the last year practicing being nothing but in control. Yet this strong, beautiful, and he just knew, passionate, woman had blown all that up in a second. She was absolutely the last person Aiden would want to hurt but if he didn't stop touching her, right this second, he couldn't promise himself that he wouldn't do just that. He reflexively yanked his arms from around her so quickly that she awkwardly stumbled back from the surprise of it all.

"This had better be good, buddy," Kane grumbled as he finally rose to his feet, straightening his shirt over his jeans.

"Excuse me," Lily said before turning to escape down the hall in a sexy skirt that Aiden often suspected she wore under her lab coat in Dr. Li's offices. The slim-silhouetted skirt showed off her toned legs. *Legs* that Kane just had his hands all over! It crushed Aiden and infuriated him all at the same time. Every instinct inside him wanted to punch his friend in the jaw and demand, 'why her'? But he knew why. Lily was new to The Oracle, unattached and pretty, perfect prey for the lascivious minded Kane.

Aiden hadn't said one word of his attraction for her to Kane, or anyone. He much preferred to observe the world, and hold onto his private thoughts instead of sharing them.

"Well, hell. Look at that," Kane said, staring after her as Lily reached the end of the hall, then turned and disappeared from their view. "You scared her off."

Aiden swung back to Kane angrily, his private thoughts shouting something about "Lily perhaps being embarrassed at being caught in a closet with the Oracle's resident gigolo". But when Kane replied, "That's a bit harsh," (albeit, evenly, without the slightest hint that Aiden's words actually bothered him) Aiden realized he'd verbalized his thoughts aloud.

"If I didn't know better, I'd say you had a thing for the fair Lemon—," Kane quickly cleared his throat—"I mean Lily— yourself."

Aiden simply responded with his hardest scowl while Kane continued. "No, of course not. That would be ridiculous. You're far too tall for her. What's the rule? 'Never date someone who's less than half your height plus seven inches?' Or maybe that's 'date someone less than half your age plus seven years'. Either way, you've got a good foot on her, buddy. It won't work. You need to be an even six feet, like me. Not too tall or too short."

"You're an asshole," Aiden replied with a surprising amount of restored calm before turning on his heels and heading back down the corridor. "Come on. Alec wants to see us."

Kane blew out a hard breath and quietly asked himself, aloud, "What have I done now?"

"That's what I'd like to know," Aiden replied sourly, "because evidently I'm in trouble by association."

Kane quickened his steps until he was even with Aiden, which was not easy to do, given Aiden's excessively long strides. "You seem a bit off this morning. All week, actually. Are you sure you're feeling OK? Maybe you should go see—"

"Kane . . .," Aiden replied with implicit warning not to push him further.

Surprisingly, Kane seemed to listen to his warning and was silent most of the way down the corridor . . . most.

A few seconds later . . . "I haven't seen you respond to any woman like that since the transfusions."

Aiden remained silent and continued to march forward until Kane grabbed at Aiden's arm and swung him around to face him, stopping both of them in their tracks. "Hey, you know what I'm asking you here. Are you drawn to her? I mean . . . drawn to her in a way you shouldn't be?"

But Aiden didn't say a word, feeling he had to be careful what he admitted, even to his best friend. His silence seemed to frustrate Kane. "I'm not your fucking doctor, man. You can tell me the truth."

"I would tell you if there was a problem," Aiden replied with perfect, even resonance. He just knew it wasn't the truth. Dr. Li had been right. The symptoms he was experiencing from his vampire blood transfusions, symptoms of anger, dominance and jealousy, were getting worse. He just didn't want to see it. The foreign vampire blood in his veins—blood he volunteered to take—was beginning to take over his human system. And he had only himself to blame.

"Man, this was a bad day," he thought.

CHAPTER TWO

Entering her sixth floor private room, the only escape she had, Lily managed to shut the door behind her without slamming it, even though all she really wanted to do was to grab the closest object—any object—and throw it at the wall! The little scene she had just starred in was downright embarrassing. Slumping back against the door, she sighed, "What were you thinking, Lily?"

Obviously she hadn't been thinking. In her defense she reminded herself that her intentions had been good, but nothing happened this morning as she had planned. After first rearranging her schedule with Dr. Li, she rushed to find Kane so she could tell him about the information she had just discovered before it was too late. Everyone at The Oracle believed that their friend and former team member, Lucas Rayner, was dead, killed the night of Brahm Hill. But Lily knew that Lucas was, in fact, still alive and, as unbelievable as it seemed, was bouncing between this world and another plane of existence. Lucas needed a friend's help soon or he risked being pulled to the other side permanently. Specifically, she knew he needed Kane's help.

But instead of warning Kane, as she had planned, she'd gotten caught in a closet with him with her skirt up, like she was some high school virgin. How did that even happen? Ugh. The last thing she had prepared herself for was Kane hitting on her, and hard! Not that she didn't realize she was attractive. She knew her strengths in that regard. But since arriving at The Oracle three weeks ago she had worked very hard at trying to make sure she was someone everyone would forget. Someone plain and unnoticeable.

Why else would she bypass her normal morning ritual of make-up, adding only the slightest hint of pink gloss to her natural lips just to keep them soft? Why would she sloppily pull her long hair up into a ridiculous bun that she still hadn't quite managed to figure out how to pin so the whole mess would stay in place? Most of the time she hid her toned body beneath the most unflattering lab coat she could find, occasionally wearing a colorful, short skirt underneath just to remind herself that she wasn't really the boring woman she showed on the outside. Her focus on her work, and her refusal to give people more than a passing glance, told everyone she was not interested in getting to know them. And it was pretty much working. No one noticed her . . . until today.

Once she found Kane she immediately went into plan mode. Unfortunately for her, Kane immediately went into *Kane* mode. One moment she was innocently talking with him in the hallway, feeling good about her chances to gain his trust and lead him someplace more private so she could tell him what she knew about Lucas with no supernatural prying ears around to overhear. And in the next few minutes she found herself in an ornate phone booth with her legs wrapped around him like a pretzel. His hands were up her skirt, caressing her thighs, while he simultaneously chained kisses down her throat. The man was literally an expert at sweeping women off their feet.

Her plan had fallen miserably apart because Lily had let herself get carried away by the moment, by how lustful and desirable Kane made her feel. He wanted her, and it felt nice. Yes, definitely nice. It was nice to feel her response to a man; it had been a long time since she had felt much of anything.

Oh, she would lust after men; there was nothing wrong in that department. But when it actually came to game time and the action rolled around, Lily would feel very little. It was strange really, kind of how she imagined an ice cube would feel inside a freezer. Normal.

Lily closed her eyes and tried to remind herself she had been ready to stop things in their tracks just before Aiden had discovered them. The level of Lily's embarrassment at being caught by Aiden Rowan surprised her. He was the one person at The Oracle who seemed to have the ability to see right through her.

Lily saw Aiden every morning when he would come to the labs for his testing—testing that was designed to raise his exertion levels so they could measure his adrenaline responses. Adrenaline was known to spike a vampire's desire for blood, and it was the truest measure of how fast Aiden's human blood chemistry was changing from the transfusions. As the newly appointed behavioral psychologist on Dr. Li's team, she was asked to observe and evaluate Aiden's responses as his treatments progressed, look for any changes. But she had to admit she found Aiden fascinating, and not only on a professional level. For such a quiet man he had a noticeably intense presence. He had no problem with being observed in only his black boxer-briefs while running on a treadmill. He was tall, confident and had the perfect, narrow hips and long legs to make even his underwear a fashion statement. The way he would steady his stride and confidently glance in her direction as he answered Dr. Li's questions seemed to indicate that she had his full attention. But he rarely said anything directly to her other than, "Yes" or "No".

"Lily, you need to fix this," she mumbled to herself. "You're new here and have professional boundaries that must be maintained with Aiden. And you still have to warn Kane about Lucas!" She straightened from the door and rushed out into the hall to find them both. Surprisingly, it took her longer to find either one of them than she thought. They didn't seem to be in any of the usual areas inside The Oracle. She spotted Aiden coming into the main lobby from the outside portico. He looked right at her, as if he knew she would be standing there.

"Aiden," she called to him. "Do you have a moment?"

He seemed to come to an awkward halt in his long strides, pulling his shoulders back and digging his feet into the floor as a hard frown slashed across his brows. "This isn't a good time, Miss Abbott."

Lily blinked back. Aiden had never called her Miss Abbott. Only Lily since the first night she had seen him at Brahm Hill. She rather liked that because it made her feel as if she was gaining Aiden's trust, which was important if she were to successfully evaluate him as part of Dr. Li's team.

"I promise I won't take much of your time. This is important." She walked directly to him and stared up at his tremendous six-and-a-half foot height, realizing his hard expression hadn't softened in any way. "I want to apologize for earlier. It was unprofessional and I'm embarrassed. That isn't like me to—"

"I'm leaving," he said, cutting her off, nearly growling as he spoke.

Her head popped up. "Leaving? On assignment?"

He nodded. "I've just received orders directly from Elder Lambert."

"But what about your testing and treatments with Dr. Li? Things have been going so well."

Aiden's lips thinned even more as he exhaled deeply through his nose, making her feel as if there was something she was missing. "That must be why Alec trusts me to go on this assignment. Or would you prefer they keep their lab rat close to a cage?"

Lily stiffened, thinking she hadn't heard him correctly. "Aiden, I know we don't know each other very well but you can't possibly think I would ever want to see you locked up?"

He raked his hand roughly through his hair, at least appearing to have the decency to regret his comment. "I don't."

"Where are they sending you?"

"You know I can't tell you that," he answered. "But I have to go. Kane is waiting."

"Kane?" Lily said with surprise as she glanced past Aiden to see Kane putting the last of their baggage into an SUV outside. "You're going on assignment with Kane?"

"Yes," he replied, slowly. "Is there a problem?"

Lily nodded rapidly. Yes, she had a big problem with it because she knew the danger Kane—and now Aiden along with him—would be facing. Trying to warn Kane was why she ended up in a phone closet with him in the first place. "Aiden, you can't go! It's too dangerous!"

That made the scowl return to his expression. "I'm trained for this. You can hardly expect me to sit back here on my heels after being given a direct order." He then turned to leave.

"Wait! Please!" she said, reaching her hand out to him as he turned away. Her fingers brushed his arm and she swore she saw him visibly pull away. "There is something important I need to tell you—both of you!"

"Both of us?" Aiden seemed to question.

"Yes, I—"

"You should know that when I return I'm going to ask Dr. Li to have you removed from my testing."

"Wh—what? Why?" Lily was visibly shocked. What was happening? Aiden had given her no clue before that moment that he had been uncomfortable or displeased with her presence at his tests. She always sat quietly in the corner while Aiden was being examined, working hard to never interrupt him or the doctor. "Have I done something?"

"I'm not comfortable . . . with you."

"You mean because of this morning? Again, I apologize for—"

"No. I never have been."

Lily swore it would have hurt less if he'd sucker-punched her with a fist to the stomach. Yet she only allowed the feeling to last for a moment, because for some strange reason she was more determined than ever to help this man—even if he didn't want her help. Drawing on a confidence she didn't necessarily feel, she placed her hands on her hips and took one step closer to him. Aiden responded by holding himself awkwardly stiff. "Dr. Li will not replace me," she warned him. "He brought me onto his team to record and monitor your treatment and progress. And that's exactly what I intend to do. So you better get used to the idea of me being in that room when you return."

"You weren't there this morning, were you?"

Lily felt sucker-punched again. Aiden's anger *was* about what had happened with Kane in the closet, and she had been naive to think the whole incident could be glossed over with a simple apology. From Aiden's perspective, she could just imagine what it said to him to see his behavioral psychologist fooling around in a closet like some ridiculous teenager, what he must think about how committed she was to his treatment. His life was at stake! She had really screwed up this time. "No, I wasn't there, and I'm sorry for that. But if you just give me a second chance you'll see I'm good at what I do—"

"And what exactly do you do?" he interrupted. "Why are you even here? Behavioral psychology? Why do I need a be-havioral psychologist, anyway? I was transfused with vampire blood, not verbally abused by a drunken uncle."

"That's not what I do. By monitoring your behavior and repeating certain exercises we can help condition you to adjust to your new life—"

"New life? As what, a vampire? I'm not a vampire. I'm not becoming a vampire! And . . . even if I were . . . I don't know any vampire who ever gave a shit about his behavior!"

Lily was speechless for a moment, mostly because this conversation—no, more like argument—was the most she had heard Aiden say in the entire time she'd been at The Oracle. She was really worried about him. This flash of temper was com-pletely unlike the man who was always so purposeful and in control. She doubted whether Dr. Li would ever agree to allow Aiden to be placed on assignment away from The Oracle, especially when he was so clearly agitated by something. She hated even to consider such dark thoughts. But how could she not wonder if what she was witnessing were the same signs the other transfused Guardians from Reese Lambert's horrendous super-soldier experiments exhibited before they fully turned? And that certainly did not end well for them. They were all dead!

"Aiden, whether you want to admit it or not, you've been through a trauma with these transfusions. I don't mean to upset you. I just want to help."

Aiden dropped his chin until she could feel his breath right there on her cheek. Good Lord, the man had a strong presence about him, especially when he wasn't saying anything at all. Strength just radiated from his shoulders and wrapped around you like an extra pair of arms. "You can't help me," he replied, surprising her with a darkness in his voice that she had never heard before. "You are the last person here who can help me."

Lily was left standing, stunned, where she stood as Aiden pushed past her and moved toward Kane, who had come in a few seconds before, grabbed a backpack from Kane's hand, and continued striding toward the front doors. She wasn't even sure how much time had passed when she finally realized Kane was standing beside her. He offered her an empathetic smile while he squeezed her arm. "This is my fault. He's angry with me, not you."

Lily begged to differ. Aiden certainly seemed plenty angry with her. "I promise I will fix this before we return," Kane continued. "Whether he shows it or not right now, Aiden needs to know there are people on his side. He needs to believe he's not fighting these transfusions alone."

That seemed to bring Lily back into the moment. "Aiden's going with you to the Northwest Territories?" she repeated, more for herself than for Kane.

Kane simply stared back at her as if asking how she would know that. When she said nothing, he turned to leave.

Sudden panic hit Lily. "No, wait, Kane! There is something I must tell you. I tried to tell you this morning!"

"Shhh . . .," he said, silencing her with a finger to her lips. "I already know . . . Do not worry, sweet Lemon. Everything will be all right."

He turned and walked out the door, leaving her standing there totally confused. Were they talking about the same thing? Did Kane already know that Lucas was still alive?

". . . *Wait,*" she thought. *"Did he just call me Lemon?"*

CHAPTER THREE

Three months later

Lily sensed immediately that she was being watched. As she stepped from the restricted access corridor, closing the airtight, steel door behind her, she instinctively felt hidden eyes tracking her every move. Whoever was watching her possibly didn't have the best intentions or they would have already made their presence known. Two things occurred to her immediately. She was not supposed to have access to this section of the labs, and the timing could not be worse. She could not defend herself in that moment nearly as well as she could have even fifteen minutes earlier. That put her at a distinct disadvantage. She made small fists to try and calm the unsteadiness of her hands, then rubbed her forehead to reduce the massive pounding of the headache she had suddenly developed. Carefully, she entered the main lab, a large room littered with of state-of-the-art equipment, and she looked about in all directions, hoping to determine where her invisible observer was hiding.

She didn't have to wait long.

"Where are you sneaking in from?" came a familiar male voice from the shadows in the far corner of the room. Lily recognized the unmistakably deep, gravelly voice before he even stepped out of the dark. Fully visible now, he smiled at her, but there was absolutely no warmth in his smile, for his eyes were narrowed to slits that concealed his otherwise attractive bright, blue eyes, and they were further framed by a pair of extraordinarily dark brows, drawn together.

"Zane, what're you doing down here? You know this area is off limits."

Zane Merrick was the one man who should definitely *not* be down in the empty medical labs at nearly midnight. He, along with Aiden, was the only other survivor of Reese Lambert's super-soldier experiments, and in Lily's opinion, there was something reckless about Zane, maybe even dangerous. It was not difficult for her to maintain a professional distance as she monitored his progress, unlike Aiden, who she had not seen or heard from him since he'd charged out of The Oracle lobby three months ago to go off on assignment with Kane.

"Ah, ah, ah . . .," he remarked with an almost teasing tone. "I asked you first."

Lily wasn't in the mood for games. "I'm here doing my job. So unless you're experiencing some health-related emergency at the moment, I suggest you start explaining why *you're* here, or I will have to call the guards."

Zane took one long step closer to her, seemingly not at all concerned with her threat to call someone. "You don't want to do that, Lily. But go ahead and call Dr. Li if you like. I'll just explain to him how I watched you come in here from that restricted tunnel that no one except Dr. Li. is supposed to have access to."

Great! Lily really didn't need this right now. The steel-lined corridor had become her escape when she felt an episode coming on. Originally built by former Elder Reese Lambert, the underground tunnel was intended to be a secret passageway off of The Oracle's sacred ground. Current Elder, Alec Lambert, had recently seen to it that the corridor was sealed off at both ends, viewing it as a potential security risk. Until now, the tunnel appeared to have been forgotten about by everyone . . . everyone, that is, except for Zane. "Not that I need to explain myself to you, but Dr. Li has given me access to the tunnel," she blatantly lied, praying Zane could not see through her deception. "Obviously, he's given me access to the tunnel or I wouldn't be able to get in there in the first place. So do you really want me to call him down here?"

Calmly, Lily then tried to move around Zane, but he stopped her by grabbing hold of her arm. "Yes . . .," he answered darkly. "I do." Lily yanked her arm back immediately, annoyed with Zane's presumptive arrogance, even if he was *right* that by bringing Dr. Li down here Lily's secret would be forcibly exposed.

What was driving Zane to push her so hard tonight? Especially when he had enough to deal with on his own. Zane and Aiden were experiencing the same difficult side effects as a result of the super-soldier blood transfusions given to them, but Lily had decided soon after meeting both men that the two were nothing alike. Where Aiden was quiet, intelligent and introspective in his actions, Zane was headstrong, defiant and calculating. Where Aiden was led by a moral compass, Zane said 'fuck you' to the world.

"Let go of me," she warned him.

"Easy, Lily. I'm only looking out for you. A woman should not be down here alone at this time of night. Things can happen."

Lily cocked her head and carefully narrowed her gaze on Zane, unsure of exactly what game he thought he was playing. "Are you threatening me? Because, I assure you, I can take care of myself."

"Oh, I know you can," he replied, his voice now barely more than a whisper. "In fact, I seem to be the only one around here who *does* know that."

"What are you getting at?"

There was that cold smile again. "I'm simply stating the obvious; that we know little about you. You show up here four months ago, charm your way onto Dr. Li's staff, and now you claim to have been given access to this high security section of the lab that no one else seems to have access to. You're efficiency at gaining people's trust is impressive. I'll give you that." Lily ignored Zane's comment and turned to make her way back to her office, trying not to give any sign that she was still fighting off some dizziness from earlier.

"I am going to call Dr. Li.," Lily warned him without so much as looking over her shoulder. "You are a patient, inside this private facility after hours, confronting one of Dr. Li's staff. You've got a big problem here, Zane. You just seem to be too arrogant to realize it."

After Lily reached her desk and sat down, she glanced up and noticed that Zane, who had followed her into her office, was responding to her last warning with a bold twitch of his lips that seemed to mirror his current contempt for the world. From her previous experiences while working with him, she had become very much aware that Zane had always worked hard at keeping his emotions in check, just as Aiden did. But tonight, he seemed not to care what Lily saw in him, which didn't make any sense. He knew that the clinical staff's eyes were on him, day and night, to observe and record whether he was responding to treatment or beginning to show signs of aggression, just as the other transfused Guardians had done before they went into the final stages of vampire transition that eventually killed them.

"Not going to give me any hint of what you're really up to down here, are you . . .?"

"Why don't you just tell me what answer you're looking for, Zane? That'll save us both time and I can get back to work."

"I don't have to tell you," he replied as he took a step closer, a step that made her increasingly uncomfortable as to how this confrontation with him was going to end. "You already know the answer."

"I'm going to give you one final chance to tell me how you got into this secured area tonight before I call Dr. Li."

When Zane didn't respond, Lily reached out to activate the webcam on her laptop that communicated directly with Dr. Li. But Zane came forward and grabbed her hand and snatched it away at the last second. Whatever his agenda, Zane was definitely not playing games with her. "Why so frosty tonight?" he asked, releasing her hand but, walking around her desk, he placed both of his palms firmly on the worksurface at each side of her, as though to trap her there. Lily, who had spun her chair around, responded immediately by pushing him back—hard! But she was surprised by how much strength she had to use to do it at a moment when she actually felt far short of full strength.

"Back off, Zane! I mean it."

"Easy," he said coming slowly toward her again, almost like a predator stalking prey. "I'm not here to hurt you. I mean, if you think about it, we know each other pretty well. I've stood nearly naked in front of you while doing those ridiculous tests." He gained back the ground he lost when she pushed him back, and now he crowded her against her desk. "I see you watching me sometimes. Do you like what you see?"

What the heck was wrong with him? Lily never watched Zane like that, and he knew it! Unfortunately, the same could not be said for the way she saw Aiden. Lily watched Aiden way more than she should or than was professional—but never Zane! He just was not acting like himself at all, suddenly exhibiting signs he never dared show before. It was almost *careless* of him.

Lily shoved him back once more, so hard that this time his head and shoulders slammed against the wall behind him. She stood up, stepped away from her desk, and jammed her forearm against his chest, noticing the surprise in his expression as she pinned him so tightly that he was having trouble breathing. "Back off—now!" she warned him one last time.

There went that slight twitch to his lips just before he replied, "No."

"Are you crazy?"

Zane's response to her question was to shove her back so violently she crashed into the desk behind her and didn't stop until she slid across the surface and slammed against the wall on the other side. That certainly didn't help her current state of dizziness, and as she recovered she found herself utterly amazed at the power he displayed. The hybrid inside Zane Merrick was increasing in strength much faster than he had let on during his last test. And it made no sense why he was revealing this to her now.

Lily popped back to her feet just in time to defend herself against his next charge. And this time she used what strength she could muster to send him flying back out through her office door and into the corridor. He crashed back against one of the glass lab windows so hard the supposedly shatter-proof glass broke into thousands of pieces with the weight and force of him. She heard him groan from his discomfort and hoped that she had finally knocked some sense into him. But instead, he came to his feet with a truly menacing expression on his face and charged at her with everything he had, and one thing became very clear.

Lily was in trouble here.

***

Aiden sat up stiffly in his makeshift bed on the cold ground, his body covered in an equally cold sweat as he noticed one more time the moon's slow descent from the dark, winter sky. The sight had become very familiar to him because of his inability to sleep. Had he managed even an hour's restful sleep that night? In the past several nights? He doubted it and his head seemed to pound even harder at his effort to recall such a simple detail. Traveling with Lucas Rayner for weeks while trying to figure out how to keep his friend tied to this dimension (instead of being pulled to an alternate one), plus simultaneously dealing with the side effects from his own recent transfusions, were starting to wear on him. His mind simply refused to stop. When Aiden was not thinking about how to help Lucas, he was thinking back to the things he took for granted in his life before the transfusions. Things like, how it felt to fall asleep truly relaxed, or to wake without a splitting headache. Or to dream; he couldn't remember the last time he'd had any sort of dream.

Quietly slipping from his sleeping bag so as not to disturb Lucas, Aiden walked to a scenic spot at the hill's edge and used his rapidly evolving night vision to capture the details of the mountainous landscape in front of him. He even cast a long glance southward toward The Oracle, which was still several hours away by vehicle. But it was the closest he'd been to his home in months.

He let out a long, heavy sigh.

In the three months Aiden had been away, he had come to realize that he missed The Oracle, and that seemed strange to him. Prior to this trip, he hadn't really stopped to consider whether or not a century-old hotel that had been converted into a hybrid-being training center actually felt like his home. But that's what it was to him—a home—because of the people there, his friends. He missed being one of the team, fighting alongside his brothers and supporting them on missions. And often he found himself thinking about a beautiful woman with honeyed hair pulled sloppily into a bun that always seemed ready to tumble to her shoulders. A woman he barely knew. A woman he'd left behind months ago and who still seemed to steal the majority of his private thoughts.

He'd hated having said those awful things to her when he'd left The Oracle. The angry words he spat at her that last day in order to push her away felt as though they had physically cut *him*. But he had to say them. Lily Abbott was just too dangerous to him then, and now. She had a way of getting under his skin with just a simple smile. And if she ever touched him, he swore his body would go up in flames the moment of contact. He just couldn't seem to control the desire he felt for her, and he hadn't been ever since the first night he'd laid eyes on her at the battle on Brahm Hill.

His severe and negative responses to her had to be from the blood transfusions. God help him, it was the only explanation. His body had never reacted to a woman like this before, especially one he had barely even touched. He was used to being in complete control, but when he was around Lily a humming energy coiled and burned through him until he felt his palms ache to touch her gentle curves, and his lips craved to taste her kiss, just once.

Aiden had believed his hunger for this woman would vanish when he left her behind at The Oracle, that with time and distance she would eventually fade from his memory. But instead, his thoughts of her only seemed to grow more and more frequent. He was starting to worry that he was becoming obsessed. Aiden had enjoyed a lot of experience with pleasing women. He loved women! Before the transfusions Aiden enjoyed passionate sex with many women, both young and quite old, which was not hard to do when you were living among slowly aging and stunningly beautiful Dhampirs. But since the transfusions, he could barely allow himself even to touch a woman for fear he might start showing the first signs of sexual aggression towards them. He refused to be the next transfused Guardian who went out of control. He didn't want to attack a woman inside a fog of sexual lust, as other test subjects had done before him. The thought sickened him.

"It's strange out there tonight, isn't it?" Lucas asked, rubbing the sleep from his eyes. The words seemed boyish coming from a man with such a hard face, emphasized by a distinctive scar on his right cheek.

"How so?" Aiden asked him.

"It's too quiet. I don't know if it's because I'm sliding between worlds or what, but when I come back to this side it feels like things are changing here—like, I feel it in the fucking air or something . . ." Aiden turned toward Lucas as his friend seemed to be considering his thoughts for a moment. ". . . that bad is somehow getting the upper hand on good, and we just can't see it yet. We can't see what's happening in front of us and in spite of us."

"I hope you're wrong about that."

Lucas shrugged his shoulders carelessly. "Fuck, I probably am. Wouldn't be the first time. Did you get any sleep?"

Aiden simply shook his head and both men were quiet for a long while before Lucas also turned his body in the direction of The Oracle, just as Aiden had done earlier. "You should go back. You've done your job here. You helped me get settled with supplies and money. I can handle things now."

"I didn't help because it was my *job*," Aiden reminded him, "and you know I can't go back."

Lucas sighed. "That's such bullshit. Look, I do appreciate everything you and Kane have done for me since you found me in Yellowknife—but it's time for you to return to The Oracle. You have unfinished business there."

Aiden scowled. "Why would I return to a place where they can decide to lock me up at any moment?"

Lucas returned an even darker expression, the scar on his cheek stretching with his displeasure. "Damn it! Alec would never fucking do that—and Kane would never fucking let him!"

"I thought you were working on your cursing."

Lucas stopped and stared back at him with genuine pause. "I have been."

A smirk came to Aiden's lips; he knew his friend's response was completely sincere. The main context of Lucas's language had been cursing for practically his entire life. So much so that he didn't even realize when he *was* cursing. He'd set a goal to cut back on it, since the women he was attracted to didn't seem to find his colorful language as inoffensive as he did. "Keep working on that," Aiden suggested and then turned away until he soon felt Lucas's hand on his shoulder.

"You need to go back and face what's happening to you. The people who can help you and really care about you are there, and they will support you. I can't help you while I'm fucking bouncing between universes, and you can't keep running like this."

Aiden turned to his friend. "Aren't you doing *exactly* the same thing by not telling Alec you're alive? Not facing it?"

"I'm going to tell him! I have a plan to tell him—once I can find a way to keep myself on this goddamn side. *You* on the other hand have no plan, other than general avoidance of what's happening to you. And don't keep trying to pretend with me that nothing's happening. I can see the changes. *Fuck*, you use so much energy just to try and hide the fact that your strength, speed, and senses have grown tenfold. Wasn't that the whole point of wanting the transfusions in the first place? So why try to hide it?"

Clenching his hands at his side, Aiden tried to ease his building tension. "Because my anger, my frustration—my lust—have also grown tenfold," Aiden replied quietly. "I can't deny anymore what I'm becoming—at least in part—or maybe *mostly.*"

"Vampire," Lucas replied simply.

Aiden turned away to stare back out at the dark landscape. "I fear it . . . I fear what I am becoming. Perhaps I would be better off in that other world of yours."

"No, you wouldn't. Vampires are in the realm of Gods there. They are revered. And people are blind to what the Night-walkers are capable of."

"You mean they would be blind to me."

"*Fuck, no!* I never said you would be a Nightwalker. You know that *if* this transition does happen to you it's completely within your power to be a good vampire."

"A good vampire? . . . What does that even mean? Who do I trust?"

"You trust the same men who have fought by your side from the beginning—me, Alec, and Kane. You're still one of us. That doesn't change because you made one bad choice. *Hell!* Kane's probably made three since he rolled out of bed this morning."

Both men smiled at that, and Aiden had to admit it felt good to smile.

"You also need to go back for Lily Abbott." Aiden blinked with surprise but said nothing as Lucas continued. "I can tell that you care for her much more than you will ever say aloud. You ask me too many questions about her life on the other side with Kane. What she likes . . . if she's happy."

Aiden instantly lost his smile. "I was asking about Kane, not her," he defended. "I wanted to know if my friend was happy."

Lucas's snort of laughter was surprisingly loud. "Right. You're asking because you're concerned Kane is not happy being shacked up with two sizzling-hot women in an alternate universe. Come on! This is *Kane* we're talking about here. The man's in paradise in any situation involving two women." He put his hands up apologetically, "No disrespect meant to Lily."

Aiden couldn't stop an irritated growl from rising from deep in his chest. He couldn't stand to think about Lily living with his best friend (even if it was in an alternate universe) any more than he could stand seeing Kane making out with her in this one. Kane had already apologized to him for the phone closet episode while they were in Yellowknife, so Aiden didn't know why the thought of it still bothered him. Maybe it was because for a moment there, after they had left The Oracle and before Kane had met Skye Matthews, the woman he had just married, it looked as though things might repeat themselves in this universe.

"Doesn't it bother you that Kane's not with Skye in that world? That he's not with the woman he's supposed to be with?"

Lucas shrugged. "Who's to say he's supposed to be with Skye? Who's to say which way is right or wrong? You have to understand the rules are different there. From what I have seen so far, it's not necessarily bad . . . just not the same as here. All that matters is what's important to you in this world."

"I suppose you're right."

"Of course, I'm right," Lucas replied with an inappropriate amount of fierceness to his voice. "It's a different world. Take me for instance. My doppelganger on that side has fucking decided to chase after that ball-breaker, Sienna Scott, like some lovesick puppy. Tell me how that happened?"

"*Sienna Scott?*" Aiden repeated, raising his brow. "She is a ball-breaker . . . Sorry, man."

"Yeah, and let me tell you, the whole situation is completely terrifying. That woman is leading me around by my dick. It's like I've—or, rather, he—has completely lost any other senses—like his mind! It's the scariest damn thing I've seen in either dimension."

Aiden laughed hard once from deep in his belly. "You know, she's stationed at The Oracle right now." Aiden waggled his brows at his friend. "You could go back, tell Alec you're alive . . . ask her out on a date."

Lucas scowled at him—hard! "*Are you kidding me?* That woman's idea of a date is to rip the head off of a few Lycans and roast them over a campfire together. The sex is probably even worse. I bet she ties him—I mean *me*—up and has me whipped!"

"I'd agree—both literally and figuratively." Aiden's smile widened.

"I'm glad you're finding this so amusing, *oh, whipped one!*"

Aiden's amusement died off quickly. "I'm not whipped! I barely even know the woman."

"Who? Lemon?"

Aiden shot an angry glare right back at him. "Her name is *not* Lemon! It's *Lily*. I don't know why the hell Kane keeps calling her that."

"Well, at least we've clarified that you know her name."

Aiden tightened his hands into fists. "There can never be anything between Lily and me. There can never be anything between *any* woman and me."

"You don't know what will happen," Lucas reminded him. "The other Guardians were good men who didn't realize what was happening to them. You do! You have a lot more information to help you control the situation. And you are doing an amazing job of handling the side effects. Give yourself some credit. Go back to The Oracle. Deal with what's happening. Alec and Kane will help you—I promise. But it's not going to help you to run away from it. Or from her."

"This isn't about—" Aiden cut himself off. He raised his hands and placed them on either side of his head, responding to a feeling that he was being overcome by several strong emotions all at once—anger, stress and pain.

Strangely enough, despite his pain, the confusion cleared for a split second and he became acutely aware of what was causing all this: *someone was trying to send him a message!* And immediately he got his answer.

"What is it?" Lucas asked him, recognizing Aiden's obvious distress.

Aiden, feeling as if all the blood was draining from his head, said, "It's Lily . . . she's in trouble!"

CHAPTER FOUR

Lily was standing in the middle of a large medical lab that looked as if a giant hauling truck had blasted straight through it. Glass was shattered everywhere. Huge metal doors were stripped from their hinges. Steel cabinets were tossed about, and whatever had been in them before was now scattered, spilled or spread all over the floor. As she surveyed the damage she wondered how in the world she was going to explain all this mess. There *was* no logical explanation for it! She wasn't even sure herself how things had gotten so out of hand, but she had to start explaining fast because Dr. Li was staring at Zane with the closest thing she had ever seen to fury in his eyes.

Two guards were detaining the Guardian in their firm Dhampir grasps, a good distance away from her, at Dr. Li's instruction. Then, as if things couldn't get any worse, Elder Alec Lambert and Kane came charging down the corridor at a half-run and were brought to an abrupt halt when they practically collided with the giant mess. Lily had not seen Kane since he had returned to The Oracle, but the look on his face just then was pure concern as he stared at her and then, more pointedly, at Zane.

"What the hell happened?" Alec demanded, his eyes wide with astonishment.

"I didn't hurt her!" Zane declared for at least the fifth time since he'd been locked in the guards' hold. "Just ask her!"

Everyone suddenly turned to Lily in unison. She carefully squeezed her hands at her sides to calm her mounting anxiety over this situation. *What happened to her plan of remaining unnoticed? To blend in?* Damn, this was so *not* the meaning of low profile! She couldn't have any more attention heaped on her at the moment if she was standing in front of these men naked.

"The guards patrolling the grounds heard a commotion and came down here to investigate," Dr. Li began when Lily didn't offer any answer right away. "They found Zane attacking Miss Abbott here in the labs. After alerting me, I sent for you right away. I've been trying to get Miss Abbott here to tell me what happened, but so far she has refused to say anything."

Alec Lambert, a strong, charismatic presence even in the most heightened situations, approached her in his finest, tailored trousers and collared shirt, his concerned expression very clear. "Miss Abbott, are you injured? I don't see any visible cuts or scratches . . ."

Lily shook her head. "I'm fine," she replied calmly, though she did not exactly feel calm.

"She's not fine," Dr. Li complained. "She's appeared dizzy since we arrived."

"I'm over the dizziness . . .," she defended quickly, knowing this whole messy situation would get much worse if they were made aware how truly dizzy she still felt.

Alec nodded once. "I'm glad to hear that, but Lily . . ." (and it caught her off-guard that he used her first name—he hadn't done that even once in the entire time she'd been at The Oracle—just Miss Abbott) . . . "I need to know exactly what happened here tonight. I think you realize, being directly involved with Zane's treatment, that this is a very serious situation. I don't want to jump to the wrong conclusion here."

Lily inhaled a steady breath. "As I said, Elder Lambert, I am fine. Zane and I were equally at fault for this and I accept full responsibility as someone who's fortunate enough to work in this state-of-the-art facility. I can clean up this mess and will accept whatever consequences you deem appropriate."

Alec watched her carefully for a long moment as the entire room seemed to go silent. "You're saying that Zane did not attack you—but that *you* are just as responsible for the destruction of this lab."

Lily nodded quickly, not even following up the gesture with a confirming "yes."

"Miss Abbott," he began carefully, pausing after reverting to her formal name. " . . . This lab looks like it was bombed. And when Dr. Li—an expert in Dhampir physiology—tells me that you might sway right off your feet at any moment, I tend to believe him. So forgive me if I'm skeptical of the '*I'm fine*' and '*we're equally at fault*' explanation for this."

Lily did feel like she was about to sway off her feet. Zane had confronted her before she'd had a chance to recover from her latest episode. It had taken every ounce of strength she had left in her to fight Zane as she had, but you certainly couldn't tell that from the massive destruction of the lab.

"Lily . . .?" Kane voiced softly with concern. "Did you know Zane was coming down here tonight after hours?"

Lily hesitated, looking at everyone in the room except for Zane and then shook her head in clear answer.

Elder Lambert frowned. "When you first realized he was here, did he display any signs of aggression or sexual aggression towards you?"

Lily suddenly found it harder to breathe. She tried to compensate by taking deeper breaths, but she needed more air. Still, she calmed her mind and tried to figure how best to answer questions she really couldn't afford to have people asking her right now. "No, he didn't. We simply had a disagreement regarding the effectiveness of some of the physical exercises I suggested he use as a coping mechanism to deal with his increasing stress. He didn't believe they would help him. And when I assured him they would, he challenged me to show him. Before I thought better, we were sparring back and forth and doing full contact drills."

"*What?*" Dr. Li said with full frustration. "Full contact drills in this lab? How could you be so irresponsible, Miss Abbott? What if there is an emergency tonight and the people here need these supplies and facilities that are now destroyed?"

Lily swallowed hard. "You're right. I'm so sorry. I wasn't thinking. I will clean all this up."

Elder Lambert, however, did not look as convinced. "You want us to believe that *you* were executing fighting drills with Zane— one of the transfused Guardians who you yourself are helping Dr. Li monitor for signs of aggression toward women—in the middle of a lab . . . and things got carried away? This is what you say happened?"

Lily wished this whole moment would go away because the story she was trying to sell sounded ridiculous, even to her own ears. But right now she had little choice. "Yes," she answered confidently. Zane, meanwhile, was stone silent, as if he knew the best thing for him to do right now was to not utter a single word in his own defense.

She was doing a fine enough job for him.

Alec turned to the guards holding Zane. "Take Zane back to his room and wait there until you receive further instructions from me. Kane, Dr. Li, I will meet both of you in my office to discuss this further. But right now I want everyone cleared out of every one of these labs."

Kane nodded stiffly and then gave Lily a long, meaningful glance, as if he were trying to ascertain if she had been lying when she said she was uninjured, before turning to leave with the guards. *So not under the radar!*

Once everyone had left, leaving only herself and Alec, he focused his attention solely on her, so she felt compelled to break the silence. "Sir, I can have this all cleaned up—"

"I don't understand why you're lying, Miss Abbott," Alec said to her as if she hadn't started, "but I assure you, whatever you tell me now will stay in my confidence. No one else is here—and I am listening. If Zane threatened you in some way to keep you silent then I need to know."

Lily wished it were only that easy, but the fact of the matter was, it wasn't. "He did not threaten me. I am responsible for what happened here tonight."

Alec's expression narrowed into a hard frown, "I want you to be clear on what this means. I cannot hold him if you say none of this was his doing. And I cannot help him if I don't know what signs he's exhibiting from the transfusions. He will be released and free to do his regular routine. Are you sure that is what you want?"

Lily hesitated for just a moment and then nodded.

"Very well," he replied. "If you tell me your dizziness is gone and that you have no other side effects from this little . . . *scuffle* . . . I expect you to clean this mess up before you retire straight to your room for the evening. I will have guards posted outside the lab until you're finished. Perhaps the work will help you remember *more clearly* what happened here tonight." She nodded again—quickly—just grateful he wasn't making her clean the lab for a month.

Hours later, nearly at dawn, Lily emerged from the now set-to-right medical lab (except for the glass she could not replace) by way of the above-ground chapel. Feeling the cold, winter air on her cheeks, she made her way back towards The Oracle through the snow, hating how much time the jaunt had given her to replay the entire evening's events. This incident with Zane had heaped a whole bunch of undue attention on her, scrutiny that she could ill afford. She was taking a big enough risk, as it was, by continuing to stay at The Oracle. Why did she feel so compelled to help Zane when he so obviously didn't want her help? He'd made it very clear he was going to cause her problems if she stayed. The Oracle wasn't her home, and perhaps it was time for her to leave.

"Lily . . ." Her thoughts were interrupted by the sound of her name carrying on the cool night air just as she was about to enter through The Oracle lobby doors. She glanced up to see someone of extraordinary height standing in the shadows at the side of the building. As she walked closer, the man's face became visible in the moonlight reflected off the heavy snow all around them, a familiar face that was currently displaying a very concerned frown.

"Aiden?"

Just like that, after three long months, Aiden Rowan was back in Lily Abbott's life. For a long moment she stared at him blankly, not quite sure what to say. Then she felt her spine straighten as memories of the final harsh words he'd spoken to her that last day only a few yards from the very spot where they were standing now came flooding back. *"You are the last person here who can help me".*

"Are you hurt?" he asked, causing her to blink up at him. That certainly wasn't what she had expected him to say. Especially because he stared at her with no emotion readable on his face, as if he had no memory of a single day that had passed since the last time they had seen each other.

"What're you doing here, Aiden? After all this time . . .?" She continued to stand there in a state of confused malaise. Aiden simply nodded once, indicating that she should follow him into the trees, and then he turned toward the path that would lead them away from the building. Following Aiden now would certainly not fall under Elder Lambert's strict orders to return straight to her room after she finished cleaning the lab. And to go off alone with the only *other* transfused Guardian, merely hours after her altercation with Zane, would not win her any points with Alec or Dr. Li. But Lily found herself following him. She couldn't help herself. Transfused or not, she was not afraid of Aiden Rowan. She never had been. "Where are we going?" she asked him as her feet sank into the snow with each step.

Aiden turned to her and reached for her hand in what felt like an oddly familiar gesture. The backs of her fingers inadvertently brushed over the watch peeking from the cuffs of his dark knit shirt, a watch she had never seen him without. The classic Cartier Tank, with its weathered band and simple rectangular dial, was so far from the overblown gold, stainless and sparkly watches that men in the human world wore nowadays that it always caught her eye—just for its elegant simplicity.

As he closed his hand firmly over hers, she couldn't help but feel the quiet confidence that exuded from this man. She was quite sure that Aiden was unlike any other man she'd ever known. He was sparing and intelligent with his words, but also purposeful, as if he never wanted to reveal more than what was required. Lily was beginning to realize that's how he controlled people and situations around him. By making others always aware of his silent presence in a noisy room, encouraging them listen more attentively when he did speak.

"You're taking me back to the labs, aren't you?" she asked as he continued to lead her deeper into the trees and she suddenly realized where they were headed. When Aiden still didn't answer, she jerked him to an abrupt stop that brought him around to face her. "Why?"

"I want you to show me what happened there tonight."

"*What? Why . . .?* How do you even know something happened? You've been gone for three months. And now, suddenly tonight, you magically appear out of nowhere and expect me to answer your questions?"

Aiden stared at her with one of those, "*You know I'm not going to answer that,*" sort of looks, but, "*Yes, I do*". It ticked her off, which only made her asks more questions. "Why are you back here? And why do you even care if something happened? You made it quite clear when you left that I was the last person you wanted to see—"

"That's not what I said," he corrected her. "I said you are the last person here who can help me. I meant those words . . . but I wish I could take them back."

"If you meant them, then what does it matter about taking them back?"

"Because I didn't like hurting you."

Lily pulled her hand away from his. The contact suddenly felt too familiar in that moment. The way he stood there in black, fitted jeans, heavy boots, and a long knit shirt was *too familiar*. Seeing Aiden again pulled Lily back to the same thought she had the very first time she saw him. He was that neighborhood boy, the quiet one you never bothered to know but always wished you had. The one you most regretted later in life because you imagined he had grown into a quiet, strong, sexy man. And it pissed her off why her mind would go there, which she expressed in the form of . . ., "That's such a bullshit answer!"

"You're angry?" he asked with some surprise.

"Yeah, I'm angry. You just . . . left!" Lily hated that she gave him such a raw and honest answer. "I mean, you just gave up! On all of us who were trying to help you."

Aiden's expression tightened and he raised his shoulders, as if this conversation were physically uncomfortable for him. *Typical man. They never want to have the hard conversation,* Lily thought. She responded by bringing herself so close to him that she could practically feel his muscles tense at the contact with his shirt. "Lily, listen," he began.

"No! I'm tired of you pushing away everyone who is trying to help you," she began, feeling empowered to finally be able to say the things she wished she'd had sense enough to say to him that last day he left. "You are so stubborn! It's time you listened for once."

She was pretty sure she heard a rumble in his throat just then, possibly a growl, but she didn't care. "I never asked for help," he countered, still calmly, despite the growl.

"That's the problem. You don't ask for anyone's help. And you probably won't say thank you, either, when we beat this thing. But I'm helping you anyway. Why, I have no idea."

"Just tell me what happened tonight in the labs," he said, shifting the conversation back to where he wanted. "Tell me and then I'll—"

"You'll what?" she interrupted. "Leave? Can you not think of anything more original than leaving every time something gets difficult?"

"I'm doing this to protect you. You've no business being in those exam rooms."

"I have every business," she began awkwardly, realizing she must be worked up because her words weren't even making much sense. "It's my job! And I'm good at it. So why are you trying to have me fired?"

Aiden seemed to pull himself visibly tighter. "Can't you see Dr. Li is using you? He's looking for signs that Zane or I will start responding violently to a beautiful woman, as the other Guardians did."

Beautiful? Despite her current frustration with him, the idea that he found her beautiful made Lily wanted to smile. Men in the past had found her beautiful, but for some reason it meant more coming from Aiden. "I know," she replied to him.

At that declaration you could have blown Aiden—a ginormous six-and-a-half-foot man—over with a feather. "What do you mean, *you know*?"

"I mean, I understood what I was getting into when I accepted the position on Dr. Li's staff."

"What the hell?" he demanded. "Why would you do that?"

"Because I believe in you, Aiden—and in Zane, too. I believe you both can get through this."

Aiden looked truly and utterly perplexed by that statement. "You don't even know me."

"Perhaps not. But I do think I understand you."

Aiden rubbed his hands along his neck as if he was trying to process everything, but she could see he was struggling with it. If she had learned anything about Aiden in the short time she'd been working with him, it was that when he struggled with something he immediately tried to take back control. "Tomorrow you're going to tell Dr. Li that you want nothing more to do with these tests. I don't care what else you do in that lab to assist him—but you need to stay away from me, and you need to stay away from Zane. Is that clear?"

Lily snorted in a rather unladylike expression of response. "Ha! In your dreams, mister. You're the patient here—remember? This is my job and I don't take orders from you. And why do you presume to know *anything* happened with Zane? You weren't there."

"I don't know," he said with frustration. "That's why I've been asking! I'm trying to find out if he's showing signs. Did he hurt you tonight?"

Finally hearing concern within the deep tone of Aiden's voice, Lily was struck by his words. She reached her hands up and flattened her palms against his chest. He stiffened at the contact but made no move to push her hands away as his warm brown eyes stared directly into hers. After a moment, she could find the barely-there heartbeat inside his chest and heard his breaths pushing harder through his nostrils. Aiden Rowan had an almost instant physical reaction to her, and it surprised her to realize how much she liked that. "Lily, stop," he whispered roughly. "You don't understand how dangerous this is."

"He didn't hurt me, and there is still hope for both of you. Do you hear me? As long as there is hope. I will not ask Dr. Li to remove me from your case. So you better start dealing with that."

"Why are you not afraid of me?" he growled.

"I've never once been afraid of you. Never . . ."

Aiden clamped his hands over her wrists and physically removed them from his chest as if to show her how strong he could be. "You should be afraid."

"Why? Because you're changing?"

Aiden appeared so frustrated it seemed he might turn and leave any second. Lily had to do something quickly or she might never get the chance to get this close to him again—to actually break through to him. "You can trust me, Aiden. I'm here because I want to help you. So I'll ask you again. How did you know what happened tonight? How did you know to come back to The Oracle?"

Aiden clenched his fists at his sides. She suspected the stress of holding everything inside was nearly strangling him. She knew she was pushing him way past the point he was comfortable with. The remarkable restraint he'd honed to perfection over his life was beginning to slip as he visibly tensed in what was left of the moonlight. Lily decided that was exactly what she needed to do if she was going to succeed in helping him.

Push him.

"I saw the guards escorting Zane to his room," he growled. "Now tell me what happened!"

"That doesn't explain how you connected it to me."

"What the hell does it matter!" he burst out angrily.

"It matters because, if my suspicions are correct, you've built a connection with Zane through the blood transfusions. It makes sense. You and Zane shared the same vampire blood when you were transfused."

"Are you here to help me—or are you fact-finding for Dr. Li?"

She blinked back hard, understanding why he might think that but it still bothered her. "I wouldn't do that to you. You can trust me."

Aiden growled into the night, and this was not any type of human male growl. This was animalistic, angry, from deep within his chest. "I can't trust anyone!" he burst out. "Least of all, myself!" Aiden then surprised her by grabbing her hard at her shoulders and hauling her right up to him. "You think I can't hurt you? You're wrong! Both Zane and I can hurt you. Stop using yourself as fucking bait and tell Dr. Li you refuse to continue being part of these *damn* tests! Because I don't want you there! Understand!"

He pushed her away roughly but she managed to remain steady on her feet. "Aiden!" she called after him as he turned and marched with incredibly long strides back towards The Oracle. He refused to stop. Leaving her standing among the trees under the moonlight, alone . . . again."

CHAPTER FIVE

The sun had barely come up the next day when Aiden heard a familiar—*and ridiculously annoying*—rap at his door. The repetitive hammering wasn't just a beat or two against the wood but more like a whole chorus of knocks designed to drive someone who had only had about thirty minutes of sleep absolutely mad. And he knew of only one person who would be that obnoxious on his first day back at The Oracle. "Go away, Kane!"

"Well, asshole, it's really nice to hear your voice, too," he responded from the other side of the door, his voice dripping with characteristic sarcasm. "Now get your ass out of bed and let me in."

Aiden rolled over on the bed with an irritated groan, then rose smoothly to his feet. Not surprisingly, he didn't feel overtired, even on such minimal sleep. 'Maybe minimal sleep was becoming the norm rather than the exception,' he thought. But still, he wasn't quite sure he was ready to face his blissfully married friend this early in the morning. Lazily lumbering toward the door, he finally opened it with just a bit of reluctance at what might await him on the other side, and with good reason. "Buenos Dias!" Kane shouted as he burst into the room. "Isn't it a splendid day? The sun's up and the birds are chirping—"

"Oh, for God's sake, just say you got laid last night from that beautiful new wife of yours and let me go back to bed in peace."

"Till I almost wasn't able to stand this morning," Kane proudly declared. "Marriage is great when it's with the right woman. I don't know why it took me so long to find her."

Aiden just stared at his friend. He couldn't believe this was the same man who, in the entire time he had known him, found no useful purpose for marriage or commitment—not until three months ago. "Perhaps that's because your wife can't be seen most of the time."

"True. That did make her a little more challenging." Skye Matthews (whose surname Kane decided to take on for himself since he had none of his own) was in the realm of the Gods, but she lived in human form. She was only able to be seen by the people whose lives she was directly affecting at that time. Kane, however, as her true love and soul mate, was able to see her all of the time. "Lambert's still insisting that's she a blow-up doll until he actually sees her. I would tell him to piss-off and point out that he needs a good lay, but it appears our '*Oh, Elder One*' has already found someone to share his silk sheets with." Kane wagged his dark brows at his friend with a knowing smirk. "And she's a redhead. The man's done for."

Aiden stared back at him dully. "*This* is why you're bothering me just after frickin' sun-up . . . to give me status on Alec's sex life?"

"Hey, this is good news for both of us, buddy. You have to admit he's been more than a little grumpy since Brahm Hill." Kane then paused, as if considering something, and Aiden could tell immediately that his friend was not just there to deliver good morning wishes. "Alec knows you're back."

Aiden reached for the shirt that was hanging over his chair and put it on over his head, pulling it down quickly over his long torso. "Yeah, well not for long. It was a mistake to come back here in the first place."

Kane snorted. "Not going to fly, hombre."

"What's with the Spanish? I go away for a few months, come back, and you're hyperbolizing in a whole new language."

Kane wagged his brows a second time. "Honeymoon in Spain."

Aiden sighed and rolled his eyes. "All right, continue."

"After what happened in the labs last night with Lily, Alec wants you to see Dr. Li first thing this morning, then check in with him."

"What *did* happen?"

"Your guess is as good as mine. None of us bought the story Lily told last night—that she and Zane were going through exercises that got out of hand. That lab was torn to pieces."

Aiden clenched his fists tightly at his side. He wanted to kill Zane for surprising Lily like that, and for fighting with her, regardless of whether or not he knew she could handle herself. But he needed to keep his emotions in check when it came to Lily. "Seeing Dr. Li and Alec wasn't exactly on my to-do-list today."

"Well, if seeing Zane *is*—you can forget that," Kane informed him. "Despite telling all of us last night that he would have to let Zane walk, Alec's decided to keep him in his room, under constant guard, for the next three days. So whatever plan you may have had to talk to him will have to wait." Aiden growled a curse under his breath and turned to glare out the window. He needed to see Zane now! "Have you seen Lily? Did she tell you what happened?"

Aiden nodded and then answered, "And no."

"Look, I know the thought of Zane fighting her is driving you crazy—on like several levels. But it doesn't necessarily mean he's crossed that point. And Lily is a Dhampir. You know she can protect herself."

"Yes, but why lie about what happened?"

Kane rubbed his hand along his jawbone as he pensively considered that question. "It's possible Zane is threatening her in some way. That's what Alec believes. But she obviously more than held her own against him."

"I don't want to hear she held her own! *Fuck*, it just doesn't make any sense why she would fight him like that in the first place. I need to see Zane now! Not in three days."

"No—you need to do as you're told and see Dr. Li before you ruffle any of Alec's feathers. *I* may be able to get away with defying the Elder One, but he would eat you alive with all of your '*yes sir*' respectful crap."

"He's an Elder, Kane! That's kind of the point."

"Whatever. But after what happened last night, it's going to be more important than ever for you to keep a low profile. At least until we figure out what the hell's going on. This incident has a lot of implications built into it."

Aiden returned a very serious expression. "If he *has* crossed that line, then that more than likely means I'll follow."

"Hey," Kane replied. "We don't know that's what's going on here. So let's not jump to any conclusions. You're my friend and I'm here to help. And you know Alec has to do all this procedure stuff, but he's going to do whatever he can."

Aiden returned a brittle smile as he remembered that Lucas had told him Kane and Alec would stand by him. It felt reassuring to know his friend was right. "Thanks, asshole."

"Back at ya, buddy."

***

Later that morning, a satisfactory smile crossed Aiden's face as he made his way to his usual exam room, the one just down from Dr. Li's office. Lily was nowhere to be found in the labs, and he couldn't be happier about that fact. *For once*, in the four willfully-stubborn months she had been at The Oracle, Lily finally appeared to have listened to him and stayed away after her incident with Zane.

Relaxed inside his exam room, Aiden went into standard operating procedure, removing all his clothes, head to toe, except for his black boxer briefs. He leaned back against the exam room table, crossing his arms in front of him while waiting patiently for Dr. Li. He couldn't help but smile at the irony that there had come a day when he was glad Lily Abbott was not quietly sitting there in the corner, taking notes regarding his responses to Dr. Li's tests. In the past, he had wanted to come to his exams simply because she *would* be there. He liked when she pretended not to notice him while he undressed. But he would catch those eyes, that were sometimes more gold and sometimes more green, slyly glance up at him, following his movements. He loved that.

But his good mood was destined not to last.

"Good morning." The contented smile died on Aiden's lips the moment the door swung open and Lily walked in uttering those two words. She was wearing her usual oversized lab coat and carrying her tablet, her hair once again arranged in a sloppy bun that canted dangerously toward her right shoulder. *This*, he immediately decided, irritated him. Why did the woman insist on wearing her hair in a plain bun if she didn't even know how to fix it properly? It drove him mad! If you're a woman who wears buns, shouldn't you know how to fix them to keep them in place?

"What're you doing here?" he replied, a definitely contentious tone in his voice.

She ignored his question and smiled at him. No, actually, it wasn't a smile but rather a small smirk that appeared on her lips, as if she had been expecting that question. "Beautiful day outside, isn't it? We must have gotten another foot of snow this morning. I'll have to go for a run later."

Aiden couldn't decide if he was angry or stunned. "Lily, answer me. What are you doing here? We discussed this."

"You mean last night?"

"Uh, yeah!"

"I don't remember much discussion," she answered while tapping something into her tablet, "just you barking out some demand for me to not show up to do my job this morning, as if you had some say in the matter." She then patted her hand on the exam table cushion several times to let him know she expected him to have a seat.

Aiden blinked, feeling his body wrench instantly tighter with every pat of her hand on that damn cushion! There was no way to hide the rock-hard erection that was beginning to form as he stood there in nothing but his underwear, so he wasn't even going to try. While he'd been away from The Oracle he had been able to control his reaction to Lily Abbott by *not* seeing her . . . and by thinking of distasteful things such as cold, raw flanks of meat or by trying to link lemons, the scent along with lavender he found most appealing about her skin, with common household cleaning products such as Lysol or Borax. Kane had actually suggested that one, but Aiden never really found it very effective. *And it certainly wasn't working now!* Lily could probably scrub his entire body with lemon Borax and he wouldn't give a shit.

"Have you hit your head? It definitely was a discussion."

"Nope. It wasn't."

Lily crossed in front of him and set her slim tablet down on the exam table. She looked up at him, her eyes more gold than green today, and barely any makeup on her youthful skin. Aiden couldn't believe that the only thought plaguing his brain, even when he was this upset with her, was that of kissing her fiercely while dragging his fingers through that loose bun and drawing every strand of honeyed hair down around her shoulders. It was like a visceral reaction in his blood. A need he couldn't control or temper.

"We had an understanding."

"Oh, stick your understanding, Aiden. You disappear for three months, then show up here last night to dictate how things are going to be. *And what?* You just expect me to agree . . .?"

"When the hell did you become so unreasonably stubborn?" was all Aiden could think to ask as his breaths began to come faster and shallower the closer she came to him.

"I think that would be the moment you declared that I was the last woman here who could help you. It was a stupid thing to say, and I intend to prove just how wrong you are and how much *I can* help you."

***

Lily had to admit she found it amusing how this six-and-a-half-foot man just stood there in his underwear, blinking at her. He appeared to be trying to catch up to the moment but seemed completely befuddled as to how to do so. But she had to give him props. The man could rock a pair of black boxer-briefs like nobody's business. It was all that height he had on him. Long and lean, especially around the middle, he had the sexiest waist and hips she'd ever seen on a man. It was completely unprofessional of her to give a second thought to such details or to relish the full erection hiding beneath his briefs. But how could she *not* notice this man? He was just such a . . . *man.*

"Lily, this is not the least bit funny."

She smiled at him wickedly. "Actually, it might be a little funny."

"You were attacked last night! Does that not register with you?"

She arched one of her brows high at him to question that statement. "I told you that I am fine."

"You should be resting," he continued to argue.

"I don't need any rest." To offer him proof she opened her lab coat and pulled it down till it was dangling from her forearms, exposing a good deal of skin under her sleeveless shirt. "Look, not a single scratch," she pointed out. "Even Dr. Li couldn't argue that I am perfectly fine."

"You're a Dhampir. Just because you're not showing any marks this morning doesn't prove that you were not injured last night."

"Well, I can't prove to you that something *didn't* happen. So let's focus on the task at hand, shall we?"

Aiden straightened up from the table and crossed his arms determinedly, showing he had no intention of cooperating with her today.

"Do I have to call Dr. Li?"

"I told you last night, I don't want you administering my tests. In fact, I don't want to see you at all."

Refusing to be deterred by his demands, Lily decided to ease the tension by blatantly glancing down at his erection, which was showing no signs of easing, then smiling back up at him. "I think Benjamin, there, is glad to see me this morning."

Perhaps that was not the best idea. Aiden appeared speech-less for a moment. "Did you just call my dick Benjamin?"

"Well, I assume you have some sort of manly name for it. Most men do."

Aiden scowled at her. "If I did it certainly wouldn't be a pompous, uptight name like *Benjamin*."

"Very well . . . how about Benji? It's very British and sexy," she continued to tease him.

"Benji's a dog's name! What the hell is wrong with you this morning?" he demanded. "I seriously think you hit your head last night!"

Perhaps Aiden was right. She knew she didn't hit her head, but she did feel a bit off this morning, and she certainly was not acting professionally. She had no idea if it was because of the previous night's events with Zane, or perhaps the fact that Aiden had returned to The Oracle out of the blue.

"You're right. I'm sorry. I promised you last night that you could trust me and that I was here to help you . . . and I meant it. So let's get started."

"No," he replied flatly.

Lily rolled her eyes. "My, you're stubborn. Has anyone ever told you that?"

Aiden straightened to his full height, and she noticed his breaths beginning to come out fast and shallow again as he asked her, "Does Dr. Li know you're here with me?"

"What do you think?" she questioned back, because she could hardly afford to tell him the truth—that Dr. Li had no idea she was in here with him.

"I think that after last night I'd find it hard to believe he would approve of you being anywhere near me or Zane."

Lily stared at him with concern. Though he spoke clearly, he appeared to be struggling with his breathing. "You're breathing too hard, Aiden. You need to remember that the vampire blood in your system acts as a catalyst; pushing you towards more primal responses, such as anger and aggression. It wants to push at you until it drives you to feed your blood by consuming more blood."

"I can handle it."

"Yes, you can. But you need to recognize the signs and focus on clearing your mind. Focus on slowing your breaths." Lily moved close to him, placing her hands on each of his arms and leading him back to the exam table. "Think of your breathing as an extension of your control. When you have clear breath, clear focus, you can stay in the moment and not let those base desires control you. You must stay in control."

Unfortunately, Lily's words seemed to have the opposite effect from the one she'd intended. Aiden's breathing constricted to nothing more than a rough rasp, and his eyes swirled with blue—

vampire blue. "Stay back," he said quietly, almost as if he suddenly could barely speak.

Lily reached for his hand and squeezed. "I can't do that. Please, trust me on this. I know what I'm talking about. You *can* control this. Just look at me and focus on your breathing."

Aiden dropped his eyes to hers as his chest ballooned in and out. She could see an entire range of emotions swirling there in his eyes, from pain to anger to confusion in only moments. Rarely did Aiden show so much. He did as she asked, however, and kept himself focused on her. "That's it. You have control. Say it to yourself. I have control."

Aiden shook his head and pulled his now brilliant blue eyes from her. Lily reached for his wrist to monitor his pulse and felt the Tank watch he always wore. It was the first time she realized that he left it on even during his exams. She rubbed her fingers over the band, hoping this was a way she could calm him down. "Will you tell me about this someday?"

Aiden continued to breathe hard as he spoke but she could see hints of the amber-brown returning to his eyes like little flecks of melted gold in a sea of blue. "It's an old man's watch. There's nothing to tell."

"You always wear this watch, never taking it off. Even in here. Things we keep that close are important to us."

When her gaze returned to his, she swore Aiden's irises changed to blue fire. His head tilted lower, and before she knew what was happening he'd wrapped his hands securely around her upper arms and hauled her off of her feet. Lily became suddenly aware of every part of Aiden's fit body, his broad shoulders, his ample chest, and the woodsy scent that carried on his skin as he hauled her upward on his chest until her lips were right there, above his. She could hear the uneven pace of his breathing, feel the coolness radiating from him on her lips. She felt sure he was about to kiss her. But he held back. Lily found her breath halted in the same moment, and she was startled to realize how much she *wanted* him to kiss her.

He fought it. This man, whom so many others considered dangerous, showed more restraint and control than any other man she had ever met in her life, including her father. She wanted—just once—for him to break that control. "What game are you playing?" he asked her, his breath blowing like a cool breeze upon her lips.

"No game," she replied, allowing her full weight to relax against his body and feeling his erection press against her leg. "I just want to help you." Two small bulges formed behind his upper lips. Lily knew if he opened his mouth to her she would see the emergence of two fangs, relatively long in size. A confirmation, along with his blue eyes, that he was already far along in the turning process.

"No!" he shouted, shoving her back from him the same moment the door to the exam room opened again. Dr. Li entered, just as Lily found herself back on her feet, practically across the small room from Aiden. She was grateful to see that by the time he had turned around, Aiden's eyes had returned to their normal color. His breathing was still hard, but the bumps behind his lips had also disappeared. It was important that Dr. Li did not see the same signs she had seen only seconds ago.

"Miss Abbott, what are you doing here?" Dr. Li asked. "I thought we agreed that you were to work on reports in your office today."

"I knew it!" Aiden shouted before Lily could answer. "I don't want her doing my test!"

"Aiden, has Miss Abbott—?"

"Just get her out of here!"

"It's all right," Dr. Li responded to Aiden, and then much more firmly to her, said, "Miss Abbott, may I speak with you, outside."

Lily had really screwed up this time, pushing Aiden too fast. And now, she thought, she may have lost her chance to really help him. For good.

CHAPTER SIX

"I should've known you'd be stupid enough to show up here," Aiden said with contained anger to Zane as he came to stand alongside him near the rocky north shoreline of The Oracle's large-bodied lake.

Aiden had shown more restraint during the past three days than he thought himself capable of, since his thoughts had been volleying back and forth between feelings of betrayal and anger over what had happened with Lily in the lab. She was the one woman Zane knew Aiden would kill him for touching because he could no longer hide from Zane his growing desire for her. Lily had been right the other night. At some point, Zane and Aiden had become connected by the vampire blood they shared from the transfusions. So the real question was, had that same blood driven Zane to become violent and unreasonable?

"Of course," Zane replied, displaying a healthy amount of arrogance. "I had to see if the rumors were true . . . that after three months The Oracle's prized Guardian decided to return and grace us all with his presence."

Taking a step toward him, Aiden warned, "You aren't going to find it so nice when my fist breaks your jaw."

Zane just laughed off the threat dismissively. "Back a few days and already threatening to break something? Perhaps your time away didn't help so much with your own anger management."

"Why'd you do it?" Aiden demanded, crowding his big body into him. "Why did you attack her . . .?"

Zane's extraordinarily thick, black brows flattened into tight slits over his deep blue eyes, eyes the color of clear sapphires—a color so light in contrast to his dark brows that it always made him appear dangerous. "Attack her? Trust me, I know better than anyone that Lily can take care of herself. I went there to talk to her."

"In the labs, near midnight? Bullshit!" Aiden's hands then clenched at his side as he became fully prepared to hit the man soundly. "Alec has had you under guard for three days, so he obviously doesn't buy your bullshit either."

Zane snorted loudly. "You know as well as I do The Brethren has been wanting an excuse to lock us up ever since the truth came out about Reese's super-soldier experiments. That's why you hightailed it out of here when you had the chance."

"I left because I was sent on assignment," Aiden shot back.

"Yeah, well, Kane managed to bag his future wife, honeymoon and find his way back from '*assignment*' two months ago. Why didn't you?"

Zane's brashness didn't surprise Aiden, but he still really wanted to hit the man for his remark. What did surprise him was that somehow Zane had gotten considerably more combative since Aiden had last seen him. "Just answer the damn question! Why did you go after Lily in that lab?"

"I'm going to say this exactly once more. I went there to talk with her. Nothing more. Believe me or don't believe me—I don't give a damn! Things just got out of control."

Aiden smashed his fist into Zane's face without warning. He couldn't stop himself. The man deserved a swift fist to the jaw for how he was evading the questions. Why were he and Lily both evading his questions about what happened that night?

"Ouch! Damn it!" Zane growled as he recovered and turned back to face Aiden, his hand showing blood. "You nearly broke my nose."

"Those '*things*' that got out of control," Aiden growled, "are signs of aggression—aggression towards an innocent woman. You know damn well that may be a sign you are going into the next phase. And still you stand there and act with me as if it were nothing!"

"You better hope it's nothing . . . because if it's something, and if it's happening to me, then it *will* happen to you."

Aiden sucked in a quiet breath. Zane's words struck him hard. He was almost certainly right, and that scared Aiden more than anything. If Zane was showing signs of aggression toward a beautiful woman like Lily, it would be only a matter of time before he showed the same signs, too. Hell, he'd felt out of control the last time he saw her three days ago in the exam room. He'd be damned if he would allow himself to hurt Lily. He'd leave The Oracle again in a heartbeat to stop that from happening. "I've been able to handle it."

"You feel in control? And why's that, you suppose . . .?" Zane challenged him. "*Oh, that's right,* because you left! You haven't been stuck in the middle of all this shit—answering their damn questions! Taking their damn tests! Do you know what it's been like for me here? To have every person look at you as if they're prepared for you to become unhinged at any moment?"

No, he didn't. Aiden had been able to get away, at least for a little while.

After the transfusions, neither man had known a moment's peace for fear of what it would mean if they started showing the signs. And even though Aiden had not had to face that fear directly for the past three months, he could feel it now that he was back— *pressure.* The pressure he placed on himself to control the darker side that was growing inside of him. It had been a gift to get away, even for a little while, so he wouldn't be reminded every day what he was facing. Being away *had* helped him. But doing so meant leaving Zane behind to face all the questions alone. And despite how angry Aiden felt toward him in this moment for going after Lily, he had to acknowledge that leaving hadn't been fair to Zane. "You're right. I *don't* know what's it's been like for you. But that still didn't give you the right to go after Lily. She's done nothing—"

"*She's* the *only* thing that got you back here!"

Aiden blinked hard.

"Admit it! You didn't even consider coming back to this place until you thought her life was threatened." Zane pushed away from Aiden's grip, the sleek lines of his powerful body outlined against the fading light in a most strange way, appearing to frame him as though he were larger than he actually was." Zane slapped his open palm back against Aiden's chest. He repeated the slap a couple of more times while staring right at him. "I feel the struggle inside of you every day. I feel it! Just as I feel it in me—the struggle to stay human. The struggle you have with *her*. She's the reason you stayed away . . . but she's also the reason you didn't hesitate to come back."

"You used her to get me back here?" Aiden's anger broke through again. He launched himself at Zane a second time, grabbing two fistfuls of his jacket as he hauled the man right to him. His friend had pushed him too far, and now the roles were reversed. *He* was the dangerous one. "I don't care what you think you can feel. If you touch her again—if you use her like that again—I swear, you'll wish the transfusions finished you sooner," Aiden said, his voice becoming raspy from the internal tension— and fear for Lily—he was feeling. "Are you threatening her? Is that why she's protecting you?"

Zane shoved back from Aiden, a furious scowl marking his expression. "It would be easier for you if I was, wouldn't it? That would be the simple answer. I'm the bad guy, and you don't have to really look at her—really see who she is."

"The person I'm looking at is someone I don't recognize!" Aiden blasted back at him, now fully furious. "The man I knew— the *friend I* knew—wouldn't have fought a woman inside a lab until it looked like it was hit by a bomb." Frustrated, Aiden shoved his hand back into Zane's shoulder so hard that he stumbled back several steps and for a moment, it looked as if the Guardian might have trouble staying on his feet. "Now *you* listen to *me*, because I'm only going to say this once. I left here so she would be protected from me—*from us*—from what we're becoming. So you can swear to me all you want, but it doesn't mean a damn thing. From this day forward, if you touch her, you will answer to me for it."

Zane stared at him coldly. "You should be careful who you swear you allegiance to, brother. Don't be blinded by her just because she's a pretty face and says she can help us."

"We're not brothers," Aiden replied, jabbing a finger into the Guardian's chest. "And I know she can't help us. *No one* can help us. We are damned!"

"Yes, we are," Zane returned, noticeably more calmly, "and she, more than anyone, knows we are."

"Then why's she protecting you with Alec?" Aiden challenged. "She knows that one word from her and they would lock you up and throw away the key."

Zane's laugh came out sounding something like a deep-throated cackle. "Come on, man. You're smarter than that. It's never been about protecting me. It's about protecting herself . . . and *you*."

Aiden tried to process what Zane was implying, but in the same moment his head snapped around in an intuitive response to an overwhelming sense of danger that had just straightened the hairs on the back of his neck. Zane showed the same defensive behavior as they both turned to stare across the snowcapped landscape behind them. The overcast daylight was transitioning into darkness as the sun began to set behind the mountains, and both men could now feel the new and negative energy that was intruding on their confrontation. It was a dark energy, just waiting for the opportunity to be set free, to roam the night and take hold of it as they wanted, as they were driven to do.

"Nightwalkers!" They both said it at exactly the same moment. "You sense them?"

"Not just sense them," Aiden replied as he nodded towards a ledge in the mountains behind them. Zane followed his eyes and there, in the shadow of the mountain, stood a line of at least a dozen vampires. They appeared calm and organized, but ready to strike as soon as the final traces of daylight became masked behind the mountain. The evil group appeared uniformly fixated on Aiden and Zane, which was typical for a creatures who were often 'each to his own' when it came to their thirst and survival.

Aiden immediately pulled out his communication link, his lone connection back to The Oracle. "Matthias . . .?"

"Go ahead," was the immediate reply at the other end.

"This is Rowan. Merrick and I are at the north end of the lake, and we've got some serious supernatural company. I'd say we have about three minutes before they're on us."

"We've already spotted them," Matthias replied. "Hard to miss those numbers when they're so close. I've a tracking group coming from the south, on its way toward your position. Head towards them. Copy?"

"What. The. Fuck?" Zane said before Aiden could answer. Aiden dropped the arm that held the communications link and stared up at a different, higher rock ledge as even more Nightwalkers came into sight. There now seemed to be at least two dozen vampires, both male and female, and whom would have no trouble finishing off the two of them. Aiden cursed himself for having let them sneak up like this. "We're going to need more than a fucking tracking party," Zane growled under his breath.

"Copy?" Matthias called again across the voice link.

"No good," Aiden replied. "We're staring at two dozen of 'em now. No way to outrun them."

As if Aiden's words were the explosion of a starter's pistol, all traces of daylight suddenly disappeared, just as several dark shapes dropped from the enormous ledge, seeming almost to slow and float the closer they came to the flatter ground below. If any humans had been nearby and had seen their shadowed descent through the thickening darkness, they would swear that humans could somehow fly, because that was how gracefully the Nightwalkers landed on their feet.

Before Aiden and Zane could even begin to come up with a plan to handle the onslaught, the ghostly, white figures rushed over the great distance between them in a matter of seconds, until they were suddenly there, and Aiden found himself confronting a male Nightwalker. With no time to react, he punched his arms out and shoved the Nightwalker back at least twenty feet, realizing, just as he did the night of Brahm Hill, how much strength he had gained from the blood transfusions . . . which had been the whole point of volunteering for them in the first place.

Increased strength was the one thing Reese Lambert had not lied to him about. The former Elder had promised the Guardians that they would be able to battle hand-to-hand and strength for strength against a Nightwalker, and that much was certainly true. The fraction of a second Aiden had gained afforded him the opportunity to prepare for his attacker's return and to glance over to see that Zane was holding his own against the vampire attacking him. But neither one of them was going to last long while this outnumbered. Not only was his nightstalking buddy back on his feet and charging at him, but several more of the bloodthirsty creatures were nearly on top of them.

Luckily, Brethren reinforcements had already started to arrive, quickly moving into place to challenge the other Nightwalkers.

"Over there!" Aiden shouted as one grabbed him from behind, his cold breath on Aiden's skin and fangs ready to drive into his throat. Aiden managed to avert the vampire's grasp and swing low, effectively pushing him into another of the Nightwalkers he was also defending himself against. He then rolled out from between his attackers and leapt back to his feet, feeling for a brief moment that they had a chance to survive. A chance . . . but that chance evaporated much faster than it had arrived. Another Nightwalker had overtaken him from behind, just as even more Nightwalkers came at them across the landscape, moving at inhuman speed.

The collective vampire coven held their prey motionless in their clutches as they made way for a tall, slender female with platinum blond hair that hung all the way down to her hips. She was dressed in thigh-high, stiletto-heeled boots and a super-short, tight, black skirt that likened her to the modern day Joan Jett of vampires.

As she presented herself directly before Aiden and Zane, Aiden recognized her immediately and knew he'd heard the stories about this one, Caelestis (Celeste, to the modern world), a dangerous Nightwalker presence he had been informed about even before Brahm Hill. She was a six-century-old vampire who appeared to be not yet into her forties. And, if the rumors were true, she enjoyed killing more than just about any other vampire in existence.

"Well, now, doesn't this feel familiar . . . ," she began, "Brethren Guardians about to become lunch? How exciting. It's like settling for common rats on a platter. I'm almost bored with the prospect."

"Fuck you!" called out one of the Brethren Hunters, Jeremy, who was beside Zane and still fighting to get free from his capturer.

A particular gleam seemed to enter Celeste's eyes at the Hunter curse, as though she was thrilled that one of them had taken her bait so easily. She moved effortlessly towards him, her heels refusing to sink into the snow. "So brave . . . Is that how The Brethren teaches you to speak to a woman? A woman who is a superior fighter to you in every way?" She was warning him, as well as inferring that they were chosen today because of their association with The Brethren.

Jeremy smiled right back at her. "When I see a superior fighter . . . or a woman . . . I'll let you know."

Her smile thinned. "Let him go," she instructed the Nightwalker holding him. The second Jeremy was released from the vampire's grasp, he immediately drew a silver-bladed dagger from his belt. This dagger was like an extra hand to Jeremy, one he wielded with dangerous efficiency. But as he lifted his eyes to face his challenger directly, he was met by her luminously hypnotic eyes, lit up demonically like brighter-than-lavender-colored fire. Both Aiden and Zane quickly averted their gazes enough to avoid being hypnotized but not too far to catch what happened next in their peripheral vision.

Jeremy went still, instantly mesmerized by the lavender color. Celeste took a step forward, reached her hands up, and snapped his head around with the ease of turning a bottle cap, breaking his neck instantly and completely. Watching his head loll backward and his body slump in death, she then proceeded to face each of the Brethren fighters who had come to aid them, forced them to look at her, and did the exact same thing to each one until all six of them were down and dead. Aiden could only stand there and watch, an agonized grimace erupting on his face as each man fell lifeless at her feet, wondering when his turn would come.

"God, you're all so predictable," she said, as though thoroughly bored.

"Hey, that was lunch," one of the Nightwalkers complained.

Celeste snarled at him. "I told you, rats would be better." But the vampire disregarded her and dropped to his knees, immediately beginning to suck all the blood left in his prey. The other male nightwalkers behaved similarly, all of them clustered around the fallen men's bodies. But the females of the group, who were dressed as provocatively as their leader, gathered behind Celeste as she finally approached Zane. "You can let them go," Celeste said to the vampire warriors holding him and Aiden. "I think they understand what'll happen if they try anything."

Even though released from the vampires' strong hold, neither Aiden nor Zane moved a muscle. It was as though they, too, had been hypnotized; they simply could not budge.

"They were there that night," a female said from behind Celeste. She was a stunningly beautiful brunette woman, small in stature, but acted as if she had no fear of any of them, despite her size.

"Brahm Hill . . .? Yes, they were, Sherra." Celeste smiled as if amused and then spoke directly to Zane. "And that fact is the only reason you two are still alive."

"What do you want, Caelestis?" Zane growled at her, using her formal name, his disgust and hatred for the woman who had personally killed their brothers made clear by his tone of voice. "We assumed you'd gotten the hint when The Brethren kicked your ass that night that it was in your *surviving* best interest to leave this area?"

Aiden could detect the harshness in Zane's voice. His friend was having a hard time keeping his anger under control.

Celeste's sly smile morphed into some kind of perverse interest as she stared both men up and down like some sort of prized stallions. When Zane could no longer resist the urge to keep his eyes averted, that ice cold blue gaze of his met hers fully. Celeste's smiled widened, as if to say, '*do you know how dangerous the game is that you're playing*', but her eyes were not lit up, as they had been with the other men before she killed them. She was not using her gift on him, at least, not for the moment. "I guess you assumed wrong," she replied. "I have some unfinished business with your Elder. So if you'd be so kind as to not piss me off today, I will try to leave you two alive so you can deliver the message."

Zane's glare back towards Celeste was now dangerous, even flat-out bold. He had to know she could put him into a defenseless trance before he could even blink. Aiden had no idea what the hell kind of game Zane thought he was playing with her, but it was a stupid one. Then Zane said, "Why would our Elder give a *damn* about a message from you? He would liken it to your description of drinking from rats . . . *boring*."

Without warning, Celeste slammed her hand forward and seized Zane's balls in her grasp. Then she squeezed, pitching him forward as he uttered a harsh grunt and tried to breathe through his surprise . . . and *major* discomfort. "What did I just say about not pissing me off?" she hissed through her fangs, but then her lips morphed back into a smile. "I should just kill you. But you've got something, Zane . . . something dark and reckless inside you. I smell it in your blood. You're Hybrid." She then tightened her grip around his balls further and Aiden swore Zane's face was turning blue. "You know, I only need one of you to deliver the message. Perhaps you would serve better as my new mate. Tell me, does this giant cock of yours have as much bravado as your tongue?"

Zane just continued to breathe hard through his teeth.

"What's the message?" Aiden growled. "We'll give it to him." He was angry at Celeste, but even more pissed at Zane for goading the equivalent of a supernatural super-bitch. Though, he did find it curious that Celeste could not sense that he and Zane were not just hybrid but would fully turn on their own. Perhaps there was hope for them after all . . . if they could live through this day, that is.

Celeste turned her head slowly toward Aiden, never relinquishing her punishing hold on Zane's man-parts. "Of course, you will." Zane then grimaced fully as she brought her lips to his ear. "Listen carefully. Your Elder left Brahm Hill that night with something that belongs to me . . . and I want it back."

"Go to hell," Zane forced out between his teeth just before he managed to grab her wrist, squeeze until she eased her hold on his balls, and then shove her back from him, displaying an amount of strength that was impossible for a human—and impossible for Celeste not to notice.

"Zane, is it?" she asked, and Aiden instantly took it as a bad sign she knew his name. "Remember my message."

The all-female coven and the other males with them, now done with their feeding on the bodies, surprisingly retreated and disappeared into the darkness.

"I won't be so charitable with your lives when I return." Celeste said, then followed the others, disappearing into the night as quickly as she had emerged from it.

Aiden didn't waste a second, snapping his head around to Zane. "What the hell did you think you were doing? Have you lost your damn *mind*? You know Celeste could have killed you as easily as spit on you!"

A bitter smile edged over Zane's lips. He still looked as if he were trying to recover from her unceremonious hold on his privates. "Just trusting my new instincts."

"Yeah? Well, those instincts are going to get you killed."

"Probably," Zane replied dully. "Probably."

CHAPTER SEVEN

"Miss Abbott, may I have a word in private?"

Lily had been hearing those words *a lot* the past few days. She was nothing but polite to Dr. Li in return, determined not to make waves after the events of the week. But today he barely raised his head from his tablet when he approached her, only nodding towards his office for her to follow him.

"Is anything wrong?" Lily asked as she closed the door behind her and took a seat in front of his desk.

"Wrong? No," he replied, taking a seat in his own chair. "But I do believe we should further discuss the incident the other day in the exam room."

"There was no incident, Dr. Li. I was merely preparing Aiden for the standard tests—as I've done many times before at your request."

Dr. Li nodded his head. "Yes, . . . but I believe you exhibited poor judgment in doing so after I had expressed to you that I thought it best you stay in your office that morning."

Lily straighten in her chair, sensing she may not like the direction this conversation was headed. "I was doing my job. I am here to help Aiden and Zane. Nothing that has happened this week changes that."

"I disagree. What happened with Zane in the labs changes things a great deal."

Lily inhaled slowly. She had not expected such a response from the doctor, and she feared what it could mean for her involvement with Aiden and Zane's treatment going forward.

"I will admit that your behavioral evaluations have proven of great use to me with regard to their treatment. We have been better able to identify personal stress markers versus blood chemistry indicators. But you and I both know that there are other reasons for you being in those rooms. You've been a marker for us to track their developing aggression towards women. And both of these men are now showing significant signs that the blood in their systems is taking over. That puts you in much more danger."

"You've been up front with me from the beginning about why you wanted me in there."

Dr. Li relaxed back in his chair. "It simply made logical sense. We could evaluate changes in their behavior in a controlled environment by using a woman they had frequent contact with. And, for a while, I believed both men were showing few or no signs of aggression, which was very encouraging. But now we've had these two incidents."

"There was no incident with Aiden," Lily defended again, but Dr. Li continued as if he had not heard her.

"They're smart men. They know why I've been having you administering their tests. Their demanding that you be removed from their case is simply a sign that they recognize the path they're headed down—and the behaviors that will help us identify it."

"That is not true—"

"I'll stop you right there, Miss Abbott," he interjected, frowning and raising one hand in a cautionary gesture. "I can see that you've grown to care for both men on some level. Quite frankly, it's the only explanation for your defending their actions as fiercely as you have."

"I didn't say—"

"I'm not finished," he interrupted, the sharpness in his voice seeming to increase. "To be honest, both incidents have called into question the wisdom of allowing you to remain on this team and to work with the transfused hybrids."

"You mean Aiden and Zane, don't you?" Lily challenged him, and when Dr. Li only arched his brow, reflecting his curiosity, she felt compelled to push the matter. "Outside of those exam rooms you barely ever refer to them by name. They're not"—she made quote marks in the air with her fingers *'the transfused hybrids'*. Their names are Aiden and Zane. And they're good men who have been loyal to The Brethren in every way—through this entire process. And yet, because of something that was done to them by this organization over the course of the last year, they've been treated like lab rats instead of like men with basic human rights."

"Miss Abbott,—"

"I'm not finished!" she replied sharply, unable to suppress her temper, which was quickly destroying her emotional control. More gently she continued, "The support system they have known has eroded around them. And in my professional opinion—which is why I *am* part of this team—it's affecting their trust in just about every aspect of their lives. They are trying, as best they can, to deal with what's happening to them, but we are not giving them any answers."

"Miss Abbott," Dr. Li repeated, speaking slowly and carefully now, "perhaps it's time for you to consider that you've grown too close to this situation. Elder Lambert requested that I add you to this team because he believed your background and credentials would provide a much-needed voice when it came to the humanity of their treatment and testing. Which, I will say, I don't agree with. They would have been tested humanely either way. I would have made sure of that."

"Forgive me, doctor, but are you really trying to help *them*—or just trying to protect everyone else from a possible incident while they're under your care?"

"You go too far, Miss Abbott!"

"Why? Because I'm giving you my opinion on the matter? I was brought in here to observe, to teach them mechanisms for coping with the stresses they are dealing with. We are failing to really help these men, because they believe if they show even a single sign of anger or aggression, they will be locked away like caged animals. Surely you must see that?'

"I am aware. And yes, we would have a duty to report to Elder Lambert if or when these men start showing signs of sexual aggression. But you seem to be letting your empathy for their situation get in the way of recognizing what is most certainly happening to them. The fact of the matter is, blame or no blame to this organization, these men are becoming vampires and, as a result, they are extremely dangerous."

"What's happening to them is a direct result of one Elder's abuse of power. And now they are being questioned and judged and tested by the same organization that did this to them. It's not right."

"I agree, Miss Abbott. These men have been done a great injustice. And I have had many sleepless nights trying to figure out a way to rectify that. But, ultimately, this comes down to the medical realities—what is medically possible, at this point, to save them. Right now I have no medical solution. No matter how hard they fight, this will be a battle Aiden and Zane will ultimately lose in the end, just like the other transfused Guardians before them. We may have had some success in slowing the process, but the Nightwalker blood working in their veins has no weaknesses and is changing them almost daily now. It's only a matter of time before their human side is lost completely."

"You're saying there's no hope?"

"I'm afraid that's exactly the case. As rapidly as things seem to be progressing, both men will experience severe blood-thirst and anger within weeks, to the point where it will consume them. And I have no way to stop it. If you are to remain on my team, you're going to have to start accepting that."

Lily could only blink several times, unable to believe what she was hearing. "If you're so sure this is the only future for them, then why the charade? Why the tests? Why let Aiden start to feel like a member of the team again and—only months ago—send him on a mission for The Brethren? You're deceiving him into believing he can fight this, while in the meantime you're really making preparations for . . . for what? Are you going to lock him away—cage him up? What exactly is the plan?"

"There is no plan. Elder Lambert . . . Alec . . . does not yet know of my findings. You see, Miss Abbott, despite my extensive knowledge of Dhampirs, and being a Dhampir myself, part of me is still human and thus can also make mistakes. This supernatural world, by its very nature, defies logic and rules. Until the incident with Zane in the labs, I thought there was a chance I could save them. Elder Lambert is *counting* on me to save them. But I cannot ignore the medical realities in front of me. In the end, *none* of the methods I could use to counteract their vampire blood will matter. I'll not be able to stop the process."

"I can't believe this," Lily responded weakly, taking in a huge breath to steady herself. She then focused on Dr. Li's eyes and said, "You're giving up."

He ignored Lily's accusation. "I brought you in here today because I was hoping that you and I would agree on this point to some extent, so we'd be able to present our findings to Elder Lambert together. We can then decide on the next best course of action."

"I can't do that. I still have hope," she replied as calmly as she could, given the circumstances. Inside, she was a wreck, worried what all this would mean for Aiden. "I think it's a mistake to go to Elder Lambert with this until we've exhausted every option. We have to fight for them! If for no other reason than so they don't stop fighting for themselves. And so they don't have to fight alone!"

"Miss Abbott, you seem to be speaking not as their behavioral psychologist, but from a place very personal to you."

Lily gave the doctor a long, meaningful look before finally saying, "The distance between the human and the supernatural worlds is not so wide," she began, her voice more quiet and controlled now. "Perhaps it's time to consider that the solution we need may not be a medical one."

"You seem to be suggesting that you have another possible answer?"

"Perhaps. Give me a chance to put some things together."

"Tell me now," he urged. "We're wasting precious time here, time we don't have."

"Just give me forty-eight hours. There's some danger to what I want to propose. I need to make sure I have definite answers for both you and Elder Lambert when you ask me questions."

"Very well, Miss Abbott. But be quick. At this point, you may conceivably be Aiden and Zane's best hope."

Knowing she had a lot to do to pull her plan together, Lily immediately made her way back to The Oracle. As she passed through the lobby doors, intent on going upstairs, she suddenly felt a dizziness that threatened to knock her right off her feet. Her head started to pound and her pulse raced. Her eyes began blurring the scene in front of her. "No! Not now," she whispered to herself. "This can't happen now!"

Frantically, she searched the lobby for a place to hide. Her only chance was to make it to one of the rarely used banquet rooms on the same floor, and hope that no one would see her. Barely able to move herself forward in anything resembling a straight line, Lily headed down the long hallway towards the first available function room. *Thank God, no one was in there!*

She ran inside and spotted the door that would lead her into the storage room, where all of the extra chairs and tables were stacked. The pressure in her head was now so severe that she could barely see whatever was right in front of her. She slammed the storage room door behind her and leaned against the wall as she slid to the floor. Covering her eyes with her hands, she prayed that no one had seen her come in.

CHAPTER EIGHT

"That's it? That's all she said?" Alec questioned, frustrated, as he paced the room in deep contemplation. Alec hated losing any men, so hearing that they had lost six in one day was upsetting him to say the least. "Aaahhhh . . . Why is Caelestis still here? If I'd suspected that she'd be stupid enough to stay in the area, I'd have sent a tracking team after her weeks ago."

"We should've taken her out at Brahm Hill," Zane complained under his breath as he stood beside Aiden. Alec turned to them both. "You don't just *take out* someone like Caelestis. There's a reason she's lived six centuries. The woman kills because she's bored."

Aiden, who had been silent up to this point while Zane explained what had happened earlier that morning (obviously skipping over the part where she literally had him by the balls), finally asked, "Do you know what she's looking for? She implied you would and is very determined to get it back, whatever it is."

Alec sighed as he crossed his arms and leaned back against his desk. "She has to be referring to the red diamond dagger that Reese used to kill Lucas."

Aiden went quiet with guilt, knowing he and Kane were the only people who knew Lucas was still very much alive and currently in possession of said dagger. The dagger was the only thing keeping Lucas tethered to this world instead of being pulled to an alternate dimension. He had already crossed over several times since having been stabbed by it, so giving it to Celeste was not exactly an option for them at this point.

"Caelestis had been working with Reese when he went searching for the dagger. She may have some information on its origins and power. And, trust me; if that dagger's secrets benefit her in some way, then she's interested. It would also explain why she's still here."

"Where's the dagger now?" Zane asked.

Alec sighed grimly. "I don't know. We carried the dagger out that night with Lucas's body. The next morning we discovered both were missing."

"Missing . . .?" Zane replied with surprise. An item as important as the dagger didn't simply disappear from The Brethren and they all knew it. Aiden felt compelled to say something, suspecting Alec had lost countless nights of sleep believing they had lost Lucas's body and the dagger on the return to The Oracle, but a knock on Alec's office door stopped him. Alec's head guard, Sampson, entered the room and waited for Alec to approach him at the door, then handed him a piece of paper that Alec seemed to look over carefully.

"Thank you, Sampson. See that's it's done, and keep me informed."

Aiden caught a glimpse of a very pretty redhead standing just outside Alec's office door. When her eyes made contact with Alec's, she wordlessly drew him into the hallway where he reached for her hand and kissed her cheek just before the door closed, locking the couple away from his view, but not from his hybrid hearing. "I'm sorry to interrupt your meeting," she began in a gentle voice. "But it was getting late. I was starting to worry. Dinner's set up and waiting for you in your suite."

"You'll join me tonight, won't you?" Alec asked, in a voice that Aiden could feel the smile behind the question.

"Of course . . . if you would like me to."

"I'll be there all the sooner if you say yes . . . and I have a surprise for you," he replied.

"A surprise . . .? I love surprises."

"I know. And the best part is, I don't think you can even break this surprise."

Aiden had no idea what that meant. There was obviously a private joke between the two of them as the woman's responding laugh filled the hall. "Are you sure about that . . .?"

Aiden heard another kiss. "Yes . . . Now I promise I won't be much longer. I will meet you there shortly."

Aiden then heard several more kisses and some deeper breathing on the other side of the door. He and Zane exchanged knowing glances at one another. It appeared that Kane was right. Alec had found himself a rather fetching distraction from the daily stress he bore as Elder.

A few seconds later he returned to the office, appearing only slightly disheveled but with a bit more color to his lips and a barely perceptible smile at the corners of his mouth. He continued with their conversation as if they had never been interrupted. "We don't have the dagger, but Caelestis doesn't know that. We can use that to our advantage. Give me some time to come up with a plan. Until then, we'll get a tracking party out searching for her. She has to be holed up in those mountains somewhere."

"I'd like to be part of the tracking party," Zane replied, but Alec rejected the notion almost immediately, which didn't make Zane happy.

"I don't like how she's focused in on you and Aiden. She left you two alive today. There's a reason for it."

"She's just playing games," Zane replied.

"Yes, and she's fucking dangerous when she's playing games. She could have just as easily gotten her message across with both of you coming back here in body bags along with the others, but she didn't. Somehow you both fit into her plans. Until we know what those are, you two are remaining on Oracle grounds."

"We can handle ourselves against her," Zane came back, angrily. "We're well trained and stronger than ever. If you would just trust us—"

"This isn't about trust," Alec responded firmly. "I know you want to see her pay for the men we lost today, just as much as I do. But now that we know she's up to something, this is about being smart."

Zane did not look convinced. "You treat her as if she's the most powerful Nightwalker to ever walk the earth. She's just a cocky female vampire. No more."

Alec's gaze narrowed perceptibly on Zane, as if he were trying to assess something in his own mind. "Most powerful ever . . .

probably not. But the fact that you do not respect what she *is* capable of after what you witnessed today tells me you're not prepared to confront her again."

"He respects what she's capable of. We both do," Aiden replied in his friend's defense, believing somewhere deep down that, for Zane, this was about more than respecting his enemy. Celeste had humiliated him today, literally controlling him by the balls. Aiden knew that could not be sitting well with Zane. More than likely it was the reason for his short temper with Alec now . . . not that it was any kind of a good idea.

"Good to hear . . . because you're both lucky to be alive right now," Alec scowled at Zane.

"Is this is about *her* . . . or about making sure we never stray too far from a cage?" Zane challenged back.

Alec's scowl should have warned Zane that he'd said enough, but if Zane was one thing it was stubborn. His face becoming tight with anger as Alec continued, "Do you believe your recent behavior has earned you the right to question me like this? Because I don't. Lily Abbott is clearly protecting you with that story about what happened down in those labs." Alec then walked right up to Zane. "If you want me to fight for you—to grant you the honor of serving alongside your brothers for this cause outside this facility—then you need to respect me enough to stop lying."

"I did not lie!"

Alec then surprised Aiden by turning directly to him. "What do you believe happened that night, Aiden?"

Aiden stared blankly back at the Elder. "I don't see how my opinion is relevant."

"Humor me."

After a long pause, Aiden finally replied, "Zane promised me he didn't hurt her."

"If you had seen the state of those labs that night, I think you would challenge that notion more. And if you didn't challenge it, then I would ban you both from seeing her until I got to the truth."

Aiden shot Zane a meaningful glance and felt his whole body tighten involuntarily from the impact of Alec's words. Zane promised he had not hurt Lily, but hearing Alec's definitive doubt as to what really happened that night caused every muscle in his body to react within seconds. And it surprised him that he had such a visceral reaction to something implied, like not being allowed to see Lily freely. Freedom was the one thing he missed most since the transfusions. No one had given a damn if Aiden had visited a woman's room before the transfusions began, because they knew he was not the type of man ever to force himself on anyone, especially a woman. He would cut his own arm off before he would ever hurt a female. Now things were different. He was being watched carefully by everyone. But because Lily was, in a way, his doctor, he still had freedom to see her. What would he do if that were taken away, too?

Sampson once again knocked and entered the room. Aiden was barely paying attention to the fact that the guard had passed Alec a second note instead of speaking with him directly, which both he and Zane would have heard. Alec's guards were well trained to be aware of the hybrids' extra-sensory gifts at all times. He nodded to Sampson once more before the guard left the room.

Alec then returned to their previous conversation with a rough sigh of frustration. "You are both going to have to start figuring out whether you trust me enough to help you. Zane, you are excused."

Zane jerked his head back, obviously surprised that he was being dismissed without Aiden. But he held his tongue and respectfully nodded to Alec before leaving.

Aiden stood there, confused, in the strung-out silence that followed, watching Alec as he crossed the room to the large bay window that overlooked the spectacular lake and acres of the grounds. His mood had slowly shifted to something more reflective, quieter. "I have someone in my life now," he offered, as he shoved his hands deep into his pockets and stared out across The Oracle grounds. "Someone who is, to me, irreplaceable. And the feeling is so powerful, it seems nearly impossible to remember a time when she was not a part of my life. It's fascinating how our perception of time can change like that."

Struck silent for a moment as to how he should respond to such a personal admission, Aiden just stared at the Elder for a long while. Alec was not someone who normally shared private matters. He separated his duties as Elder from his personal life, especially since the night he had lost his best friend Lucas. "You are a lucky man, sir."

Alec let out a long, slow breath as he smiled back into the window. "I *am* lucky . . . and I also now recognize the signs of a man who is on the same path."

"Signs . . .?" Aiden was only growing more confused by their conversation. "I'm not sure I understand."

Alec turned from the window. "Then let me be clearer. I believe that you, more than anyone here, want to know the truth about what happened down in those labs with Lily. And despite what you stood here and professed only minutes ago, I think you *do* question whether Zane's telling you the whole truth. Yet you stood by him loyally. I understand that kind of loyalty. You two have survived something in the past year that no one else can fully understand."

"He promised me," Aiden answered with clear feeling. "He may be a lot of things, but I don't believe Zane would lie to me about hurting her."

Alec nodded. "I also promised you once that I would find a way to help you both. And, despite questioning what happened that night in the labs, that is a promise I fully intend to keep. I know, given what's happened over the past year, that you both probably feel you can trust only each other . . . but I believe in you, Aiden. You *can* trust me. And I'm about to extend you some of that trust."

Aiden frowned at Alec in confusion, wondering where in the world The Elder was going with this conversation.

"Sampson has been keeping me informed of a situation that unfolded about an hour ago. Lily Abbott was found unconscious inside one of the first floor banquet rooms."

"What?" Aiden felt as if he had just been sucker-punched in the gut, but he tried to show as minimal response to this news as possible. Any sign that he was agitated or stressed over Lily would

invite a lot of questions instead of getting answers to the half-dozen questions that had immediately shot into his mind. The first of which being . . . *why the hell was Lily unconscious?*

"I've had her brought up here to my private library, where Dr. Li is examining her right now. She is conscious and evidently insisting she's fine. But you and I both know that Dhampirs don't just show up unconscious on the floor."

"May I see her, sir?" Aiden asked with more emotion in his voice than he had intended.

Alec nodded. "Follow me."

Aiden couldn't remember a walk down that hallway ever taking so long. Each stride felt like he was moving in place while his mind tried conjured up two or three logical explanations as to why Lily would be found unconscious on the floor. But he didn't like anything his brain came up with. Had someone knocked her out? Was she ill? Kane had mentioned that Lily felt dizzy after her altercation with Zane. *Why* had he not pushed her on the subject when he saw her that first night?

Alec entered the Elder's Library, which had been recently renovated, ahead of him. Like the rest of The Oracle the Library was a Bavarian inspired mix of wood coffered ceilings and cushy seats in luxurious, earthy toned velvets arranged before a roaring fire that felt like a warm retreat from the often harsh Canadian winters. But Aiden could care less about all of that. He had to work at not shoving Alec aside as soon as they passed through the door. He just needed to see that Lily was all right, but his wish was hampered by the dimness of the room. There was no light aside from a small fire and a couple of candles burning on a table behind the sofa. Lily was standing in front of the fire with one hand on her hip while the other waved animatedly as she argued with Sampson, a man three times her size.

She certainly appeared all right as she barked at Sampson, "Don't touch me! I've said I'm fine! But it's too damn hot in here. "I don't—" Lily quickly jerked her head around as she realized there were now others joining them in the large room. The room was quite large, but it was still a huge concern that it would take her, a Dhampir, so long to sense that others had entered the Library. Her senses were normally much more attuned, which told him they had been severely compromised when she passed out.

And that meant she was *not fine*.

In that moment, Aiden's thoughts went to a strange place. He had known since the first time he laid eyes on Lily Abbott the night of Brahm Hill she had the ability to make him desire her in a way he was not sure he had ever felt with another woman. But it caught him completely off-guard to realize how much it upset him that something might be wrong with her. Even as she stood there challenging Sampson, showing no fear of the big guard, there was something different about her. It was subtle . . . but there. Like she didn't quite have the strength to back up all the female bravado she was currently displaying.

"Why are all the lights off in here?" Alec asked, which Aiden appreciated because that was only one of about a dozen questions swirling around in his head.

Sampson immediately came to polite attention as he faced his Elder. "The light was bothering her eyes, sir," he responded as he glanced back at Lily, who seemed none too pleased that the guard had just announced this fact to everyone.

"What . . .?" Aiden questioned aloud, and it was then he decided that he needed to get to the bottom of whatever was going on. He pushed around Alec and came toward her with purposeful strides, flicking off the gas switch to the fireplace, which made the room even darker. "Better?" he asked her.

He was about to ask more questions but was immediately struck by the intoxicating scent of lemons mixed with lavender. He braced himself in the darkness for the effect her scent always had on him. In the past, when Aiden had been close to Lily like this and his emotions were rolling, it had been a constant battle with his body not to drag her to him and kiss her senseless until she was flat on her back. His powerful desire for this woman was what drove him away from The Oracle the first time and would, no doubt, drive him away from her again. But Zane was right. That same desire would *always* bring him back if she needed him.

"Better," she finally replied as she looked up at him. The moonlight caught her face, making her appear even more youthful. Her eyes once again glistened with more gold than green, but Aiden could still see her stress.

"Where is Dr. Li?" Alec asked.

"I'm here," the doctor replied as he entered behind them through the Library door.

"Have you examined, Miss Abbott?"

"Yes, and aside from possibly a little fatigue, I can find nothing wrong with her. I was about to draw some blood for testing in the lab to make sure I'm not missing something."

"Elder Lambert, Dr. Li, thank you for your concern but truly, I am fine," Lily said much more calmly. "I can come down first thing in the morning to give you a blood sample if you feel it is really necessary, but right now I would like a moment to speak with Aiden alone?"

"That is not a good idea," Dr. Li replied carefully.

"I'm all right with it, Doctor," Alec said, surprising everyone in the room when he simply turned to Lily and answered, "I'm retiring for the evening, but one of Sampson's guards will be right outside that door should you need anything. And in exchange, Miss Abbott,"—which Aiden understood meant in exchange for his granting Lily's request for time alone with him—"I prefer that you stay here tonight. There is a guestroom through those doors. And yes, I would like you to report to Dr. Li in the morning for a blood test." Alec then turned to Aiden. "Keep things brief so she can get some rests. Understood?"

"Yes," Aiden answered, knowing that the question was directed primarily at him. Alec, Dr. Li, and Sampson all began to leave the room, but Aiden called Alec back from the Library doors. "Sir . . .?"

Alec turned to him.

"Thank you . . . ," Aiden said, quietly, and both men understood he was thanking Alec for the trust the Elder was showing him right then, allowing him to stay with Lily unguarded. It was a trust he had rarely been shown since the transfusions had begun, and it meant the world to him. The Elder simply nodded in reply and left the room, closing the doors behind him.

Aiden returned his attention to Lily, taking her hand and squeezing it. "What happened tonight? Dhampirs are not found unconscious on the floor. And light does not bother their eyes."

She squeezed his hand in return and stared up at him with a reassuring gaze. "You heard Dr. Li. He can find nothing wrong with me. I was just tired. I could challenge you right here and now and I'd not miss a step. I promise."

Aiden scowled at her. "You seem to be challenging people a lot lately. Why is that?"

She showed him a smile and teased, "A girl has to show off her skills somehow."

But Aiden did not seem to be amused. He led her over to the sofa, where he sat her down and bent on his haunches in front of her, never letting go of her hand. "Is that what happened with Zane that night in the labs? You were showing off your skills?"

Lily's smile softened as she slowly lay back on the deep, leather sofa, never taking her eyes off of him and encouraging him to join her by patting her hand on the seat. "I don't want to talk about Zane right now."

Aiden stared at her, understanding what Lily wanted. For them to become physically closer. All he'd wanted since the first day he'd met Lily was to be physically closer. To know what it would feel like to have her body against his as he relished her scent. And he'd spent every day since that first one making sure that *didn't* happen because he didn't know if he would be able to control himself once he touched her.

That barrier was broken the night he returned to The Oracle and touched her, and again when he held her in his arms in the exam room. *Control* was something he questioned whether he would ever get back if he was around Lily Abbott. He kicked off his heavy boots and stretched himself out alongside her on the sofa, pulling her body slightly beneath his before reaching out to hold her hand. His thumb began to run small circles inside her palm. He kissed her gently on the cheek and then on the forehead. She smiled up at him, and, for the first time in his life, Aiden felt as if he was exactly where he was supposed to be. With the woman who felt perfect beneath him. "You've got to give me something here, Lily. I need to know why these spells of dizziness keep happening."

She squeezed her fingers over his circling thumb, drawing his eyes to hers. "All I can do is assure you that I'm OK."

Aiden recognized the words were meant to placate him. "*Why? Why is that all you can do?* You said you want to help me—well, that goes both ways. If something is wrong, then I want to help you. I came back here to make sure you were all right."

"And you're also planning on leaving again, aren't you?"

Aiden dropped his head without an answer, and he could feel the low growl begin to form deep in his throat as his hand reached lower to curve his palm around her dress at her hip. He caressed the soft fabric over her skin, which seemed to make her draw her own breaths more deeply. He had wanted so much to be close to her like this, and he didn't want to give her the answer he knew would ruin this moment between them. Aiden then surprised himself, tilting his head above Lily to kiss her on the lips. At first he kissed her slowly, then more passionately as she allowed it. The taste of her lips was divine, causing his breath to grow rougher before he pushed his tongue inside her mouth, needing to explore her more thoroughly.

Lily responded to his kiss with all the eagerness and excitement that he'd always imagined she would give. There was no hesitation in her response. There was no hesitation in her body as she arched into his kiss. This is how it felt when two people wanted the other equally. He recognized it. He was in no way forcing himself on her, and that only made him want this woman more. But the moment couldn't last, as she pulled away and lifted her eyes back to him and asked, "*Are* you leaving again?"

"If I leave it's because I want to protect you," he said, hoping that his answer would be gentler than a definite yes.

"Protect me? From who? You?"

"Yes," he answered, emphatically. "Can you feel, right now, how much I want you? This is dangerous. Us being close like this, is dangerous." Breathing just above her lips, he kissed her again, pressing his body hard against hers so she could feel his excitement, feel his cock, hard and pulsing against her inner thigh. Perhaps then she would be able to understand how dangerous this was becoming for both of them. But she responded, unafraid, and *God*, she felt soft beneath him. She felt perfect.

Lily stroked the side of his face as their lips remained close, their rough breaths tangling with each other. "Can you feel that I want you, too? You must feel it. This want is always there. But you have to let me in," she replied in a whispered breath. "You can't just keep pushing me away every time things get difficult and at the same time demand that I tell you what you want to know, as if it's your right."

Aiden pulled back, carefully. In his mind, he *did* have a right. It was completely logical to him he would want to protect her when he posed such a threat to her. But then he felt his heart beat stronger when she looked at him fully in the moonlight. For a moment, he believed she had control of what was left of his human heartbeats. In a strange way, she was absolutely familiar to him, as if he had known her much longer than a few months. And yet the truth was, they barely knew each other at all.

"Let me in," she pleaded with him again.

"How?"

"How about by starting at the beginning."

He kissed her more, still breathing quite deeply, his body more and more comfortable being intertwined with hers like this. "OK, we'll start at the beginning . . .," he replied—more to himself than to her. "The first night we met . . . The first time I opened my eyes and saw you, you knew my name. How?"

Lily blinked up at him, seeming surprised that was where he wanted to start. But the closer he got to her, the more Aiden believed that she had, for some reason, found him, and he wanted to know why. "I heard someone that night call you by name."

That made sense. Kane had been trying to find Aiden in the middle of all the chaos. "Why were you there? At Brahm Hill, I mean?" With that question he shifted his hips slightly, trying to appease his growing excitement as he curled one of her legs around his hip, making sure he was keeping her intimately locked with him, keeping the tension high between them.

She gasped in response to feeling him move against her. "Why do you get to ask all the questions?"

"Because I'm trying to seduce you," he said in a gravelly voice even as he smiled. "I don't really want you to be able to think."

She touched her hand to his bristled cheek, and he swore the tenderness he felt from that light contact made his body even harder. "It's working."

He laughed gently at that.

"I'd been searching for The Oracle that night. I'd been searching for this place ever since the night I lost my family in a battle between Lycans and Nightwalkers. I had heard stories that this was a place where I would be welcomed and accepted."

Aiden closed his eyes and kissed her temple, inhaling the scent of her hair. "I'm sorry you lost your family like that."

"That's the world we live in—a world of loss," she replied softly, and pure emotion pulled over his heart.

"Yes, it is."

Lily then reached her hand to touch the tank watch around his wrist. "Is this a reminder of someone you lost?"

He nodded. "The watch belonged to my older brother, Keegan."

"Another loss . . ." she began. I'm sorry. How did he die?"

"He didn't die," Aiden sighed. "He was turned by a Nightwalker. I managed to get away. Well, actually, he helped me escape. He sacrificed himself to save me." There was a long, unnatural pause in their conversation before he continued. "This watch was the only thing left to remember him by. It represents the night my human eyes were opened to the supernatural world. I could never go back to my human life, or return to the family I knew."

"Is that why you did it?" she asked him. "The transfusions, I mean?"

Aiden hesitated to answer for a moment. He had been asked many times why he'd volunteered for the transfusions, and he always gave them the truth, just never the real answer, until now. "I wanted, needed, to become physically stronger . . . so I could find Keegan. I know he's not the same . . . He's not my brother anymore. But he *is* out there somewhere, and I need to see him again for myself."

"Vampires became your enemy because they stole your brother from you," she pointed out. "I can understand that. But why would you would volunteer for something that would change you into the very thing you hate?"

"Saying yes to the transfusions—becoming able to match their strength—is the only way I can infiltrate the Nightwalker's world to find him. It's the only way I can fight my enemy. I don't expect you to understand."

"I'm not judging you, Aiden. We all have our reasons for why we are here fighting for The Brethren. I needed to find a place where I felt like I belonged . . . a place where I could fit in."

Aiden stared at her so intensely just then, it was as though he was truly seeing her for the first time. "Have you found a home here?"

"I hope so."

'*Aw, shit*', he thought. He liked that answer, and she felt so good. Talking to her like this felt good. And surprised him, all at the same time. He hadn't opened up to anyone about the loss of his brother. That made him feel close to Lily, because she understood parts of him now that no one else did, except for maybe Kane. Aiden pressed his body harder against hers. He began rolling his hips and knew he was in trouble here. He felt hot all over, combustible even. She just did that to him. His fingers strummed over her cheek as their heavy breathing exchanged hung in the air between them. "Lily, I need you. Please, I have to have you. But . . ."

"Yes," she replied breathily. "We can do this. You are in control, Aiden," she reassured him breathily. "You don't have to be afraid. You won't hurt me."

Aiden felt his breathing becoming constricted; it was impossible to achieve a full and fully controlled breath. "I have control," he repeated quietly to himself, but he didn't believe his own thoughts. His body felt as if it was on fire! Lily shifted beneath him. Being this close to her was exquisite torture. He loved being pressed to her body, loved feeling her this close, but it was taking every ounce of energy inside him not to let his dark desires completely fill his mind. He *wanted* her. And he wanted her bare— no condom, nothing between them. It was completely caveman and animalistic, and he had no explanation for it. He'd never had sex without a condom, even the few times he'd been with a woman since the transfusions. But with Lily he felt a primal mandate to mate and spill himself inside her until he was spent. And then he was pretty sure he would want to do it again.

***

Lily's stomach fluttered as Aiden continued to excite her in a way she had not felt in a very long time. She reached her hand under his shirt and began caressing the firm muscles and dark dusting of hair that ran along his abdomen. He raised his hips from her and began pulling at her dress. His breathing was becoming faster and his cheeks looked flushed, even in the moonlight. That made her smile. The color meant there was still a part of Aiden that was human. Not that it mattered to Lily whether Aiden was human, hybrid, or vampire. What mattered was how he made her feel when she was close to him like this. She hadn't expected it. She knew there was something about Aiden Rowan that had pulled her to him from the beginning. That quiet, protective way about him, or the deep sound of his voice when he spoke. Something that she hadn't been fully prepared for, but somehow always wanted.

"Lily . . .," he said her name in a breathy whisper in response to her stroking touch. "This is not a good idea." When she still didn't stop, his head pulled back on his shoulders and he groaned as her fingers teased him just at the edge of his jeans. When he opened his eyes again to look at her, she watched as they swirled with a harvest gold. Then swirled again with a brilliant blue.

"Lily . . .," he said again, this time with warning in his voice. She opened his jeans and slid her hand lower, caressing him, causing his entire expression to tighten. He was always working hard to stay in control, to fight what he wanted. It's the only way he knew how to live since the transfusions. "You're not afraid of me, are you?" he asked her with breath and surprise.

"Never," she replied, kissing him quickly. "Never." He dropped his head so he could take her kiss even more deeply. As soon as he made contact he pulled himself to her, while Lily's whole body seemed to come alive under his embrace. The sensation was devastatingly sharp. Her tongue was insistent, pushing against his, and she could tell he liked that. Lily had never been afraid to show what she wanted or what excited her. And right now *he* excited her.

"Lily, are you sure?" he asked her, wanting his intentions to her to be absolutely clear.

"Yes," she replied, allowing herself to relax beneath his kiss in response, letting him take complete control, something the vampire blood circulating inside him would demand. His long body pushed her deeper into the sofa cushions, but she could tell he was trying to be gentle, even though she preferred for him to use his new strength. His taste was intoxicating, like apples and something spicy—like brandy—and the more deeply she kissed him the tighter she could feel his muscles pull. His fingers began to dig into her flesh, and he pulled her to him until there was not one inch of her curved shape that was not molded against his body.

A growling sound escaped his throat as his hand reached behind her, pulling her head back. 'This is not a good idea' he repeated quietly to himself, but he still couldn't stop plunging his tongue deeper into her mouth. He was searching, exploring, seemingly with the intent to know every detail of her taste from these kisses. She had enjoyed when Kane had kissed her in the closet that day. He had made her feel warm inside, something that had been missing from her life for a long time. But when Aiden kissed her, he made her feel *hot*, off balance and dizzy; her thoughts could spin out of control inside her head just from the pure perfection of it.

"*Fuck*, Lily, you taste so sweet," he said from a place that sounded gutturally-deep inside him. She felt his kisses and his tongue move lower along the column of her throat just before she felt a sharp prick at the base of her neck. Lily gasped as she felt fangs—*his fangs*—sink into her throat just then. The sensation was painful, powerful and thrilling all at the same time. Her body tried to arch to him, but he held her still. She could feel the blood being sucked from her neck while the weight of his big body settled more fully against her. Her own body seemed to charge like an electric current. The sensation was amazing! Her hands reached up and squeezed his arms with a desperate gasp the moment she felt his long, sharp teeth sink in even deeper into her throat.

"Aiden . . . ," she gasped a second time. Hearing his name suddenly seemed to snap him out of whatever daze he had been in. His head pulled up, removing the clenching hold he had on her throat. He stared back at her as if he just realized what had happened, and she could see that realization scared the shit out him! "Aiden it's all right," she said as calmly as she could to try and reassure him. "I'm all right. I liked—"

Without warning, Aiden shoved himself from the sofa and came to his feet, his still swirling eyes of gold and blue wider than she had ever seen them as his hands clenched into solid fists. "It's not all right! I just drank from you! What the hell is wrong with me?"

Lily stared back at him, unsure if she should utter even the slightest word. She knew that Aiden already had the answer to that question, but he didn't want to say it out loud. He had believed he could beat the transfusions, believed he could have a different result from what happened to all of the other Guardians, and in one moment those beliefs had been destroyed. "Fuck, Lily, I'm sorry . . ."

Aiden turned from her and rushed from the Library into the hallway, where the guard was waiting, just as Alec had promised. Lily jumped up from the sofa and raced to the door as Aiden pushed past the guard, who looked as if he were considering stopping him. "He's OK," Lily assured the guard.

"Are you all right, Miss Abbott?" the guard asked. "Do you need me to get Dr. Li?"

"No, I'm fine," she answered, keeping her neck turned away from him. But as Lily stood there and watched Aiden race away from her yet again, she wasn't really sure that was true.

CHAPTER NINE

Two days later, Aiden found himself standing on the banks of the same large glacial lake where Celeste had confronted him and Zane . . . and he couldn't believe he was still a free man. Surely, someone was about to come shackle his wrists and ankles in chains and toss him into a cage that would forever seal away his freedom. But, inexplicably, no one had. By now someone would have to know what he'd done to Lily in the Library. Drinking from her throat like a common, bloodthirsty vampire. An act that he knew he should have already confessed to Alec. But he was still having a hard time processing in his own mind and heart what he'd done.

Until that night in the library, he couldn't let himself acknowledge his more frequent thoughts about blood, or the clear evidence of his growing fangs. What had started out as an amazing connection to an amazing woman had changed very quickly to something he wanted to wipe from his memory forever, but that was futile. To forget her was impossible. She had freely given her touch, her kisses, and her body to his every demand that night. The memory of that kind of trust humbled and excited him, even now. But that good was outweighed by visions of him sucking from her throat, a memory that had haunted him for the past two nights as he lay wide awake in bed. The mere fact that his body hadn't needed an ounce of sleep in the last two days was the first telltale sign he was changing. Fast.

Every instinct inside him wanted to find Lily to make sure she was all right and to apologize again for his actions . . . but he feared what he might find. He couldn't know how far along he was in his transition, how lethal his bite was to another Dhampir. It was completely irresponsible of him to drink from Lily like that, but he hadn't been able to stop himself. The inability to control his desires was the very trait that had doomed the previous transfused Guardians before him.

"Thought I'd find you here," came Zane's familiar voice behind him. "You do remember that Alec will have our asses if he catches us outside Oracle lands?"

"I remember," Aiden acknowledged, then he turned to back to quietly admiring the incredible scenic view. "And yet, here you are."

"Are you surprised? You know I don't give a shit about Brethren goals anymore. They've proven time and time again that they'll always put themselves first—even if they are wrong."

"You still blame them."

"And you still don't?"

Aiden gave him a smile that faded almost instantly. "Yeah, well, today it's not about blame. I'm just finding it easier to breathe outside of sacred ground."

Zane snorted at that. "Shit, it's been like that for me for weeks now." Aiden simply stared back at him, understanding what his friend was confessing. Being unable to remain on sacred ground would signal a turning point from which there would be no coming back. "It's too late for me. You know that, right?"

Aiden simply nodded.

Zane purposefully walked forward until he stood right beside Aiden, staring out at the same magnificent view. "You are the only person I will admit that to. You're the only person who won't condemn me for it."

"I'm hardly in a position to be condemning you. Like you said, you're a reflection of what's to come for me."

"Then you also know it's time for us to leave this place. We have a better chance of surviving out there if we stick together?"

"I'm not sure it's going to matter in the end."

An odd expression flashed onto Zane's face. "What the hell is that supposed to mean?"

Aiden quickly shook his head, as if to dismiss the idea. "Nothing, really. A friend just told me that he believes The Brethren is losing this supernatural war, and we don't see it yet."

"Did you not just hear me? I don't care about this war anymore. I don't care about The Brethren. I care about finding a way to survive this. And you should be thinking about that way, too."

"And what of the people we keep hurting? The ones trying to help us? Do you care about them?"

"You're the only person I give a damn about in this place anymore. Why do you think I'm here? It's time for us to leave The Oracle . . . and you know it. We need to decide the rules we want to live by and stop letting others decide them for us. If we stay here The Brethren will just lock us away in a cell somewhere and throw away the key."

Aiden was quiet for a long moment, remembering that he had told Lily he would leave her again if it meant protecting her from him. Those words seemed even more real than ever after the other night. "You're right. It's time to go."

Zane blinked at that. "Since when have you ever agreed with me that easily?"

"I don't really have much of a choice, do I? We are the only ones who can understand what the other is going through."

"It's not like that for me. Your friendship means something."

Aiden then turned and showed Zane his disapproving scowl. "If my friendship meant so much to you, you wouldn't have betrayed me by going after Lily."

Zane sighed and rubbed his hand tiredly over his forehead. "Not this again . . . OK, look, I get it. Going to see Lily that night was a bad idea."

"It doesn't matter anymore," Aiden replied dismissively, causing Zane to stare back at him, completely confused.

"If it doesn't matter, then why keep bringing it up?"

"We must accept that we're capable of things that we wouldn't have been even just a few weeks ago."—or as Aiden was thinking at the moment, just a couple of nights ago—"So you're right. It's time for us to leave."

"It's the best thing for everybody—including The Brethren."

Aiden believed he was doing the right thing, but there was an odd pressure in his chest when he thought about leaving Lily again. What would it feel like to know he would never see her again? Never feel her reaching for his hand as she had done several times since he'd been back at The Oracle? Never kiss her again after having the first taste of her lips? He supposed he was about to find out, because after what had happened in the Library there could be no denying that his leaving would be the best thing for her.

"There's no reason for us to show allegiance to The Brethren. They're responsible for this."

"Tell me, Zane . . . Why did you volunteer for the tests? Were you doing your duty? Or was there another reason? A reason that served no one's interest but your own?"

Zane scowled back at him.

"I just want to make sure we're clear on this point," Aiden continued, "before we proceed with anointing you to sainthood."

"I had my reasons," Zane growled back. "We all had them."

"We said yes. We chose this. The Brethren didn't force us to do anything. I'm leaving here because I made a mistake and I need to accept the consequences and protect the people I care about. If there is an ounce of humanity left in you, you will do it for the same reason . . . not because it's a way of saying 'fuck you' to The Brethren."

They both fell silent for a long while, as if neither of them knew what to say next. These two men were tied to each other by circumstance and by blood they shared from the transfusions. But would they rely on each other—hell, would they even be friends—if it weren't for those transfusions?

"Where should we go?" Zane asked, quietly, seeming to concede to Aiden's point. Aiden turned to gaze out at the lake again. He would miss this place, miss this beautiful land. He hated the idea of leaving here. No . . . he hated *most* the idea of leaving Lily. He just wanted to touch her one more time, to hold her close to him like he had in the Library. To smell her hair and touch her soft skin. But he had to leave. He would not risk her life again as he so carelessly had the other night. "I don't know," he replied grimly. "I don't care."

Zane kept a neutral expression. "I'll meet you back at this spot at midnight. Be ready to go."

Aiden nodded but said nothing else as he continued to stare across the lake. He heard Zane leave, and he wasn't sure how long he stood there before he sensed someone new behind him. "What're you doing here?" has asked without turning his head.

"Call it intuition," Lucas replied. "Lately, I seem to have it in spades."

Aiden cast him a bored glance over his shoulder. Lucas stood there, dressed in a fitted dark grey leather tunic, like some sort of modern-day avenger, a crossbow hanging from his back on a custom harness he had fashioned himself. He wasn't nearly as tall as Aiden, but he certainly wasn't someone to trifle with. Lucas was a damn skilled fighter. Aiden noticed he had a new trick. "Is that why I can't sense you now until you're practically on top of me?" he asked as he returned his attention to the lake

"How the fuck do I know? Nothing about this stupid dagger or how it changed me makes any sense," he replied, pinging his nail against the ornamental gold handle of the knife that was solidly nestled into the scabbard at his hip. "But I overheard your plans with Zane and I know one thing . . ."

Curious, Aiden finally turned to face his friend. "What's that?"

"You shouldn't leave The Oracle."

Aiden laughed quietly with no humor. "Look, Lucas, I know you have this endless faith in Alec, but good intentions or not, even he has someone to answer to."

"Alec has dominion over any decisions regarding the wellbeing of the people within that facility. The other Elders will not interfere unless there is a strong reason to."

"The reason the other Elders will interfere is because Zane and I are too much an unknown, a reminder of the mistake they made." Aiden then waved a dismissive hand at Lucas. "Besides, who are you to lecture me on this when you're doing the same thing by not telling Alec your alive?"

Lucas took a deep breath before responding. "The difference is, I'm trying to get whole again so I can come back here—so I can fight by Alec's side. I'm trying to get back. You're running away. And you've been running since you left here the first time."

Aiden gave his friend a stormy look. "Don't give me the lecture about how I have to face things. You don't know what I'm capable of or what I've done."

"Fuck, you're right. I don't know—because you don't let people inside that loud head of yours. But you have to live with your decision to leave here this time. You may not have the option to come back next time Lily needs you."

Aiden understood Lucas's full meaning. If Aiden turned, he wouldn't be able to cross back onto sacred ground. He hated the idea of leaving Lily permanently, but what choice did he have? Leaving was the only way to truly protect her from what he was becoming, and soon the choice would be out of his hands completely. As fast as he was changing, he would soon no longer be able to remain on sacred ground. "I'll be able to live with the decision as long as I know she's safe . . . safe from me . . . and safe from Zane. Why do you think I'm bringing him with me?"

After taking in another deep breath, Lucas answered, "If that's your decision, then I'll go with you. You need someone watching your back besides Zane."

Aiden gave Lucas a grim but grateful smile. "Thanks . . . but that's not—"

His next words were cut off by Lucas's hand gesture and the swift jerking of his head back towards the direction of The Oracle.

"What is it?" Aiden asked.

"Come on!" Lucas bellowed as he began to race back towards the property.

Aiden fell into fast step right behind him. "What's the matter?"

Lucas didn't answer and kept pushing forward at a breakneck pace until they had reached the property line several minutes later, where they remained out of sight behind a cluster of trees near the mountainside. Lucas glanced up toward the roof of the main building. Both men then watched, transfixed, as two women ran along the very steep edge of the Oracle rooftop. Aiden recognized one of them immediately as the woman who had been outside of

Alec's office the other night, Poppy Honeywell. She appeared completely distraught as she followed behind the other very recognizable Dhampir, Maya Brunetti, who was currently balancing a stiff figure in her arms while racing to the other edge of the roof.

"What the hell's going on?" Aiden asked. "They look like they're trying to escape from something—or somebody."

Poppy stopped and quickly turned to stare straight in their direction. It was as if she sensed they were there, even though they were standing, hidden and outside sacred ground. That would be impressive, considering that it is difficult, at best, for a Dhampir to sense much of anything while on sacred ground. "I don't know," Lucas finally replied after Poppy continued forward towards the edge of the roof, apparently at Maya's insistence. "Something's wrong with Alec, though."

"Alec . . .?" Aiden asked with concern. "That's who Maya is carrying? Our Elder? The guards will be on top of them in seconds."

Lucas turned to him. "I thought you were leaving tonight. That would make him not your Elder anymore. Or your concern."

"Now is not the time to be a jackass. Of course we have to help Alec if he's in trouble."

Lucas nodded in agreement. "I'll follow the women and try to figure out what's happening. But I don't have a good feeling about this. Maya would never take Alec away from Oracle lands—or his guards—unless . . ."

"Unless she had to," Aiden replied quietly.

"Shit!"

"Just go," Aiden encouraged him. "I'll find out what's happening inside."

Lucas nodded at him before racing off in the direction the women were moving, which he needed to do in a hurry because it appeared to him that they were headed toward the parked caravan of SUVs.

Holy shit, something was really wrong. Lucas was right. Maya would never risk taking Alec off sacred ground unless she had to.

Aiden needed to get back to The Oracle as soon as possible and see what he could find out.

***

Lily had been searching for Aiden for two days. The man was doing an unbelievably good job of avoiding her since that night in the Library, especially considering that there weren't all that many places for a person to hide at The Oracle. She hadn't sensed him in his room or on the grounds, and it was starting to scare her that he may have left sacred ground. He had been so upset when she had last seen him. She knew that nothing she could have said or done would've gotten him to see reason in that moment, but she hoped, after he had a chance to calm down, he would realize that he had not hurt her.

She hadn't considered the possibility that he would disappear altogether!

That's what brought her out to the snowy edges of The Oracle's property line, near the Northeast base of the mountains. This remote corner of the property would be a good place for someone to get away from others if he didn't want to be found, especially near the line of sacred ground. That line, the separation between sacred and natural ground, was an invisible wall that vampires and other evil supernatural creatures such as Lycans and Warlocks could not pass through. Lily understood the fact that the more Aiden changed towards being a Nightwalker, the more difficult it would become for him to stay on sacred ground. Her hope was that he merely had been trying to find a place where he could breathe more easily while he was so upset.

"Hello, Lillian," a female voice said, catching Lily completely off-guard because she hadn't sensed anyone was there with her. Instantly, her heart dropped. She knew that voice! And she especially knew that nickname—because she detested it. Not so much for the name as for the woman who used it. Lily turned and tried to show no reaction as she stared back at Celeste, who was standing no more than ten feet from her. "All this talk of hybrids losing their senses on sacred ground sounded like rubbish to me.

93

But I'm starting to think there is something to it," she began. "I swear, you look completely startled to see me."

"What are you doing here, Celeste?"

"You are surprised! Isn't that interesting . . . Because I'm not the least bit surprised to find you hiding here on sacred ground," Celeste continued in a sarcastic tone, stepping forward in her thin-heeled boots and super-short, super-tight skirt. The absurdity that any woman would be dressed in so little clothing on a day this damn cold was openly flaunting to the rest of the world that she was not human. "When you dropped off of my senses like that, I had a feeling you had somehow managed to hide on sacred ground. It's impressive . . . I'll give you that much."

Lily hands tightened into fists at her sides, an automatic response to seeing the Nightwalker she believed she had managed to get free of months ago. The night of Brahm Hill, the last time she'd seen Celeste, Lily hadn't exactly announced her intention to leave the coven. She assumed they would all believe she had been killed when she did not return and they could no longer sense her. Celeste was obviously too smart to fall for Lily's deception.

"I'm curious," Celeste continued, injecting a mild lift into her voice. "Why The Oracle, Lillian? Wouldn't have anything to do with that Brethren hybrid male whom I detected your scent on the other night, now, would it?"

Again, Lily tried to hide any reaction, even though a sinking feeling of dread spread deep inside at what Celeste was implying—or, rather, *who* she was implying about.

"Let's see, what was his name? The temperamental one—that was Zane. I do remember that. But I can't quite remember the name of the giant." She smiled to herself as if she was entertaining some delightful little thought. "Perhaps that's because he didn't offer it. Such a shame."

Lily felt frozen to the ground where she stood. She was talking about Aiden! How in the world did she know about him or Zane? And when had she been close enough to Aiden to smell any scent on him? Lily's mind started to rush. She would surely have remembered if Aiden had told her he'd encountered Celeste. This woman was the most dangerous Nightwalker Lily had ever known, and she had brought that danger right to Aiden's door—to The Brethren's door. "As usual, I have no idea what you're talking about," she replied blandly, hoping to throw Celeste of the trail.

"Don't be dull and stupid, you little chit." Celeste took several steps forward, her footsteps barely making a mark on the fresh snow as she came right up to the boundary line of sacred ground. Her eyes gleamed in the darkness as they brightened to an extraordinary lavender color. Luckily for Lily, sacred ground also seemed to be protecting her from Celeste's gift to entrance. That powerful gift was why Lily had been trapped with her coven for so long. "If you crossed this line right now I bet my life I would smell his scent on you again."

"You don't want to make that bet."

"Really? I think I do. Why don't you come over here and prove me wrong."

"I'm not in the mood to entertain your boredom. There are lots of reasons why my scent would be on these men, I've been training here with them for the past few months. You know what I think? I think you manufacture this stuff to keep yourself from feeling endlessly bored."

"Training? Do you take me for some kind of fool? This scent was deeper, under his skin, in his blood."

Lily was starting to become fairly alarmed. If Celeste detected Lily's scent on in Aiden's blood, then somehow there was a chemical marker or link that was forming between Aiden and herself that Lily had not picked up on. Perhaps Aiden's scent had been changing along with his transition. Her brain raced as she heard Celeste say, "His body's trying to mate with you, you dim wit. Good God, I should know! I've had enough men try to mate me!"

"Forced men to mate you, you mean," Lily replied through clenched teeth.

Celeste clicked her long nails against the invisible wall that separated them, and it was spooky to hear the sound echo against the base of the mountains in the night air. "I think this Brethren ground must be addling your brain, child. Because that's the *only* explanation for why you dare talk to me that way!"

"Careful," Lily smiled at her, "your age and temper are starting to show."

Celeste snarled wickedly, but in a flash her expression smoothed to a surprisingly convincing veil of calm. "You've been such a troublesome little bitch from the very beginning. Why I put up with you, I have no idea. Are you not grateful for everything I've given you? Why, I've practically been like a second mother to you."

Lily blinked hard in disbelief. "You *killed* my mother!"

Celeste sighed at that, which actually came across as another indicator of boredom. "Yes, yes, you just keep rehashing the same point. Blah, blah, blah. It's all very tiring. Why bother, Lillian? We both know, like the dutiful daughter you are, you'll cross over that line right now if you don't want to see anything happen to the hybrid."

"Why do you even care if I'm with you?" Lily challenged her. "Why are you still here?" Celeste harrumphed as if that were a dumb question, but it was one Lily genuinely wanted to know the answer to. Lily was not afraid to fight Celeste, but she recognized that the Nightwalker was much more powerful (a perk of living for six centuries).

"A vampire does not live as long as I have by being careless or stupid, Celeste continued. "You would do well to learn from me. I adapt. I take what I want, and I use others when it helps me triumph against my enemies. It's called survival." She then scratched those same exceedingly long nails against the invisible wall once more, and it might as well have been a chalkboard, the way it screeched on Lily's nerves. "The gift inside you is powerful. I knew it the day I found you—the first time I felt it inside of you. If I could steal it, I'd do so in a heartbeat and leave your worthless body for scavengers."

"Gee, and just when you were about to convince me you cared."

"I control you, Lillian . . . and I control your gift, just as if it were my own."

"You've never had control over me!"

The vampire laughed wickedly. "Wanna bet? I control you through the people who are connected to you. That's human nature 101. You try to mate that hybrid—I'll kill him. He cares about the temperamental one—I'll kill him, too." Celeste then tapped a finger against her bottom lip as if she were thinking, reconsidering something. "Or perhaps I'll just fuck that one."

Celeste then waved her hand for Lily to come to her. "Enough with this!" she barked, her voice rising in a threatening way. "It's time to go."

"I'm not leaving," Lily replied firmly.

"Then you give me no choice but to take pleasure in dismembering that hybrid of yours, limb by breakable limb. Better make sure he does not take one step off this ground."

Lily gritted her teeth. For all she knew, Aiden could be running around outside sacred ground right this second. So to think she could guarantee he would stay inside the perimeter of the sacred property did not seem likely. She was running out of options here. If she left The Oracle with Celeste tonight, the answers on how to help Aiden would leave with her. But if she stayed, it could end up costing Aiden his life. When given a choice between the two, the answer was clear. She took a step forward. "Will you swear to me that if I come with you now we will leave this place and never return?"

Celeste smiled, realizing she'd won.

"Swear it to me," Lily demanded again.

"Stop!" This voice, a male voice, came from behind her.

Lily swung around to see Zane, the absolute last person she thought would ever give a damn either way whether she stayed or left The Oracle, running straight for her. Before she knew what was happening, he was pulling her back from that critical line that marked the boundary of sacred ground, away from Celeste. "Get the fuck back!" Zane yelled, and at first, Lily thought he was yelling at Celeste, but then she realized he was actually yelling at her! "And you," he continued, pointing his finger at Celeste like a sharp dagger, "you're almost becoming predictable, hovering this way. I take it you haven't found your missing toy? Or, should I say toys. You seem like the kind of woman who has more than one."

Lily blinked back in utter astonishment. What the hell was Zane doing? With those few sentences, the odds of Zane living to a ripe old age were suddenly becoming longer and longer.

"I should have killed you when I had the chance, hybrid."

"That's *Mr. Hybrid* to you—when I'm standing on this side of the line."

"Zane, don't—"

"Oh, it's already too late for apologies," Celeste said, glaring at Lily, but, at the same time, there was a sly smile on her lips. "He's already sealed his fate, trust me." Celeste then moved her gaze directly to Zane, who matched her stare for stare, unafraid. "I can't decide if you're dangerous or just plain stupid."

"Well, I certainly wouldn't want to make things too taxing on that little old brain of yours. All that peroxide must make things tough as it is."

Lily decided that Zane surely had a death wish.

Celeste made a noise through her teeth, a noise that sort of resembled a hiss, but was much more evil sounding than that. "You asked if I've found what belongs to me. . . I have. And she's standing right next to you." Celeste stared boldly at Lily, and, for the briefest moment, Zane showed just a hint of surprise in his frosty blue eyes. "So unless you want me to rain the fires of Hell down on this place, you'll back the hell away and let her cross over here to me—as she wants to do."

Zane slid a quick 'what the hell' glance over to Lily. Then his entire mood seemed to lighten, his voice lifting and becoming gentler, more tuneful. "I don't care what you want, you six-century-old hag. You're not getting her—or anything you want from The Brethren. So just stick your fangs in that and suck on it!"

Celeste didn't just appear frozen in place by her shock; she appeared as if she were about to implode.

Lily instantly moved back into panic as she thought, 'No one— and I mean no one—has ever dared talk to Celeste with such blatant disrespect'.

"You're just lucky you're standing on that side," Celeste warned. "Because if you weren't, I'd cut off your balls here and now."

"Not even the best threat I've had today," Zane countered.

Celeste directed a stare of true hate at Lily. "Are you coming, or shall I just kill every last Guardian I come into contact with?"

"What did I just say?" Zane answered before Lily could, mimicking the tone and sarcasm Celeste had used with him earlier. "She's not going with you—so get out of here."

"Are you not a trained soldier? Why don't you come over to this side and try running your mouth off at me like that?"

A distasteful snarl curled Zane's upper lip, as if he'd just smelled something foul. "Not interested."

Celeste's eyes transformed into indignant, lavender-colored saucers as her hands balled into sharp fists. Lily felt the dryness in her throat as she watched Celeste give Zane the equivalent of a death stare. "You'll regret this! I promise you!" she warned, and then disappeared into the night as quickly as she had appeared.

Lily remained frozen in shock for a long moment.

Finally, Zane murmured, "Let's go," as he turned back towards The Oracle.

"Are you crazy?" Lily managed to shout at him. "You just pissed off the biggest night-walking super-bitch there is! Why?" she questioned. "I thought, of all people, that you would want me gone from here the most. So why not just let me leave with her?"

Zane simply continued walking away from her, making no effort at all to answer her question.

CHAPTER TEN

"What do you mean he's not available?"

Lily wasn't quite sure how she ended up in Alec Lambert's office listening to Zane Merrick rant on and on to Brethren Guide Gideon Janes as if he had some kind of authority. But she was. What was worse, though, was the fact Aiden had been in a heavy discussion with Gideon and Sampson when Zane burst off the elevator, dragging her behind him and charging right into the room, demanding to see Alec "immediately."

Alec was nowhere to be found.

"As I said, he's not available," Gideon replied in a cool, controlled tone, his remarkably dignified English accent seeming quite out of place, given the intense tension electrifying the room. "It should go without saying that Elder Lambert has many responsibilities to tend to. And just because you demand to see him right this moment does not mean he can do so."

"Are you kidding me?" Zane exploded. "I'm telling you, he's going to want to hear this. It's about Caelestis."

Lily and Aiden had been focused on each other since she had entered the room. He appeared fine, for which she was grateful, but he seemed to be focusing on how Zane was currently holding tightly to her left wrist. Aiden's jaw tightened and an instant stiffness straightened his shoulders. "Lily, come here," he said, reaching for her hand. When she reached back, she was struck by how confident his hold felt as he brought her to stand beside him. She also wondered if he had any idea how cold his skin felt.

Without another word, his communication occurring only by the intensity of the dagger-like gaze he directed at Zane (which seemed to be the way Aiden preferred to communicate when he was upset), Aiden made it clear to his friend that he was to stay back from her while he was in the midst of his mini-rant.

Zane got the message. "Hey, look, man . . .," he responded with a defensive hand extended toward Aiden, "before you get all pissed and grow a few more inches—hear me out. I just found Lily at the Northeast corner of the property, confronting Celeste. And yeesss, that's Celeste—as in 'that six-hundred-year-old, stiletto-wearing hag!'"

Aiden blinked hard as he heard the information, but Lily wasn't sure if it was because Celeste was involved or the incongruous fact Zane had just referred to a very dangerous vampire as a 'stiletto-wearing hag'. But it didn't take long to clear up any confusion. Aiden turned to her silently, those amber eyes of his seeming to ask everything all at once as he stared at her.

"Is that true?" Gideon interrupted, and it took Lily a moment to realize Aiden had not actually verbalized the question. "Did Caelestis confront you just now at the edge of the property?"

Lily swallowed hard. Had she completely forgotten the meaning of the term *'low profile'* since she'd been here at The Oracle? "Yes, it's true," she sighed. "But nothing happened. She just wanted to talk."

Aiden's eyes opened wide in response to that news, and his whole expression turned incredulous. Lily suddenly realized that this change in Aiden's expression was the most revealing she had ever seen on his face. "Talk about what?" he pressed, as if he thought the very idea was completely ridiculous. "Celeste doesn't talk—she kills!"

Just that fast, the rest of the room faded away and it was just Lily and Aiden, standing there having a private conversation. "She told me about the day she confronted you and Zane off the property. You never said anything to me about that." Lily instantly hated the fact that her voice sounded bitter. It wasn't actually bitterness she felt, it was some indefinable emotion arising out of both concern and deep fear for him, but he was already dealing with enough.

As she noted her feelings she also saw Aiden's expression flatten in what looked like regret. His voice became gentler as he answered, "It wasn't worth mentioning. She confronted us off the property two days ago, but we're fine. She just likes to play games."

Lily's senses went into 'warning' mode as he spoke, somehow knowing that she was not getting the full story. "Nothing Celeste does is a game," Lily frowned back. "She's manipulative and cruel, and—"

"How do you know?" Aiden interrupted, "Or, better yet, how does *she* know *you?*"

"Tell him," Zane interjected boldly, reminding her that she and Aiden were not alone in the room. But Lily suddenly found herself at a loss for words. Where would she begin? How much could she afford to tell them and still keep Aiden safe from Celeste's threat to kill him? In the time between confronting the vampire and being hauled back here by Zane, she hadn't had time to prepare for this. Zane, however, was no mood to be patient. "The *thing* Celeste wants back," he said, extending his arm toward her, "the thing we assumed was the dagger that killed Lucas . . . well, it wasn't. It's *her*. Celeste wants *Lily!*" Whirling around toward Gideon, he pointed an accusing finger at the guard and said, "Now don't you think Alec's going to find this more important than whatever else he's working on at this moment?"

Gideon's expression mirrored his agreement, but he still made no move to contact Elder Lambert. Instead, he questioned Zane's revelation, saying, "Why would Caelestis want Lily? It seems illogical that a Dhampir would hold much interest to her."

"I don't know. That's kind of the point," Zane replied. "I came in on the tail end of the conversation, which I'm guessing Lily's probably grateful for right about now. But it was clear to me that Celeste sees Lily as her property—property that we've stolen from her! And I doubt very much that the old hag is going to be very patient about getting her back. I bought us a little time in stopping Lily from leaving with her, but she'll be back. You can count on it. And we probably don't have much time."

Lily felt Aiden squeeze her hand to draw her attention back to him. "You were going to leave with her? "Why would you do that if you know what she's capable of? What's going on here?"

Lily fervently wished that she and Aiden were alone in the room. She wanted to tell him everything. She *would* tell him everything, if they weren't standing in a room full of other people. Lily focused on him again, and everyone else in the room fell away. "Remember when I told you my family was killed in a battle between vampires and Lycans?" Aiden nodded, his expression etched with concern. "Celeste was there. The Lycans killed my father and sister, but Celeste and her coven pushed the Lycans back and . . . I thought . . . just for a moment . . . that she might help us." Lily then shook her head, as if trying to shake out bad memories. "But Celeste slaughtered my mother—as if she hadn't even given her life a second thought. I was in total shock. None of it made any sense to me. Why bother saving us and then turn around and kill my mother?"

Lily was quiet for a long while, and the silence seemed to expand to fill the entire room. "She kept you alive?" Gideon finally asked.

Lily nodded. "She forced me to serve her and her coven. Before that night at Brahm Hill I'd been with them for seven hundred and twenty-four days. I know that because I've counted every single day since my family was slaughtered in front of me." Lily looked to Aiden, saying, "The night—when I met you—I saw the chance to escape her in all the chaos. So I took it!"

"Shit, Lily," a stunned Zane replied under his breath. "All this time you've been here—why have you not said anything?"

Lily turned to him. "I thought Celeste was in my past. I thought I had escaped her when I made it onto sacred ground. That she would no longer sense me. But I should've realized, she's more powerful than that. She won't give up. And she'll continue to slaughter the people I care about until I do return to her, just like she did my mother." Lily then turned back to Aiden, hoping he would see the truth of Celeste's threats against *him* without her having to say it. And, judging by his careful expression, he did. "I can't let that happen."

Aiden raised a hand gently to her face, the tips of his fingers and then his thumb stroking her cheek. She detected such compassion in his expression that it startled her. She no longer cared what anyone else believed; they would never convince her that Aiden Rowan could become a cold, blood-thirsty Nightwalker. Underneath all that towering height and quiet determination was just too much empathy and protectiveness. He still cared like a human. "She isn't going to take anything else from you. I promise you that," Aiden said in a quiet but determined tone. "But if we're going to stop her, we need to understand what she wants from you."

Lily shook her head, a heavy sigh rising from the very center of her being. "Something she has placed too great a value on. Nothing more . . ."

"Miss Abbott," Gideon began, as he cleaned his glasses on his shirt tails. "I have had the great misfortune of a few past dealings with Caelestis—and if I've learned one thing about her, it's that she only covets what is of use to her. For her to still risk being here means she covets *you*—or what *you* can do for her. She needs you in some way. My guess would be that it has something to do with your Dhampir gift."

"It's not a gift," Lily replied, steadfast, which caused a frown to crease Gideon's brow.

"All Dhampirs have gifts," he explained. "I am sure you're no exception to that."

Zane then evidently decided he needed to intercede. He took a long stride toward her. "Look, the time for games is over. I get that you're afraid of the old hag. Hell, most *men* are afraid of her—"

"I'm not afraid of Celeste," Lily replied calmly and clearly. "I just want a different life; I want to be free of her."

"OK," Zane allowed, "but you've been lying to us this whole time. How do we know—?"

"Zane!" Aiden interrupted, speaking through clenched teeth. "Back. Off."

"Come on, man," Zane countered. "Are you still going to refuse to see that she came to Brahm Hill that night—*came here*—for a reason? Do you really know—I mean *know*—deep-down-in-your-gut—that she's been completely honest with you, except for this one thing? We need to be prepared for anything here."

Aiden didn't say a word in response, and Lily feared what it might mean. Did he doubt her? Suddenly, she wished there were at least ten things she could take back or do over so that she could land again on this moment and have the outcome magically changed. That he would have no reason to question her truthfulness and he would have complete faith and trust in her. "I like it here," Lily defended, and stared directly at Aiden so he could see the sincerity in her words. "I want to stay. I wouldn't jeopardize that by betraying you."

"Matthias?" Gideon called to the guard, who appeared rather anxious during this whole exchange. "I know you have urgent matters to attend to, but will you please see that Aiden and Zane are escorted back downstairs first? I need a few minutes to speak with Miss Abbott alone."

Lily watched as Aiden immediately let go of her hand and turned on his heel without another word, his long back stiff as he strode toward the elevator. And the sight crushed her. He hadn't even asked to be allowed to stay while Gideon questioned her further, and that left her feeling strangely alone. She wished she could have known what Aiden had been thinking in that moment. Had she lost his trust by not revealing her connection to Celeste sooner? But until tonight, she hadn't even known that Celeste was still here, or that she had confronted Aiden and was threatening his life because of her.

She was a split second away from running after him in the hall and begging him to forsake his quiet nature and talk to her, but Gideon quickly reminded her they were not done speaking. He instead led her in the other direction, down the hall to Elder Lambert's private library. "Would you like something to drink?" he offered once they were inside.

She shook her head. "I'm fine."

Gideon poured some water for himself. "It would appear, Miss Abbott, that you have a few secrets," he began. "I actually understand the need for secrecy in this dangerous, supernatural world. But it would also appear that you've grown quite close with one of the transfused Guardians whom Elder Lambert is counting on you to help. And that, I'm afraid, requires complete disclosure. These men have been through enough. We will not see them betrayed again by one of our own."

"I would never betray them—either of them! And I'm doing everything I can to help them," Lily defended. "I would swear that to Elder Lambert himself if he were standing here."

Gideon appeared uncomfortable just then as he fidgeted with the small, wire-framed glasses resting on his nose. "Yes. Well, we have a few things we're juggling at the moment. But Zane is right. Alec will be very concerned about this news regarding Caelestis. Why she is still here. Her presence has been of great concern to him since he learned of it."

"I'm sorry—," she began, but Gideon put up his hand to stop her.

"First, let me say I'm sorry to hear about your family. That must have been a terrible way to lose them—all at once like that. I'm afraid the demons we fight in this world have no conscience. But I can tell you, Elder Lambert will do everything in his power to protect you from Caelestis."

"I'm not asking for his protection," Lily replied. "If Celeste and her coven won't leave, I'll go to her myself to protect those here from her vengeance."

Gideon paused, a slight frown showing in his expression. "From my experience, the answer to handling Caelestis is not in giving her what she wants but, rather, in offering her something of greater value in exchange."

"What would be of more value to her?"

Gideon smiled in a small, wistful sort of way. "I don't know yet. But Elder Lambert saw something special in you the day you came to The Oracle. He talked to me of it. That's why he assigned you to Dr. Li's team so quickly. He could see, even then, how much you wanted to help Aiden and Zane. Perhaps we should have questioned your motives more then—but they are good men who've not had many allies since the discovery of Reese and his tests."

"I *can* help them if you give me a chance. I swear it. And I can handle Celeste. I've done it for two years now."

Gideon's brows tugged together across his forehead. "There isn't much you seem to be afraid of, Miss Abbott. It is a rare trait for a Dhampir who has been previously enslaved."

"I was not enslaved," Lily said, with surprise in her tone.

"You don't consider being forced to stay with Celeste's coven against your will enslavement?"

Lily could tell she was frowning. "No. Enslavement implies she was controlling me. She forced me to stay with them, but she did not control me."

Suddenly, Matthias came barging into the Library without knocking and went directly to Gideon. He nodded once, and Gideon seemed to understand whatever he was trying to tell him. Lily feared that something was terribly wrong at The Oracle tonight, which was not good, since Matthias had just left here with Aiden and Zane.

"I'm afraid, Miss Abbott, I must keep this conversation brief. There is something I must attend to right away. I believe you when you say you want to help Aiden and Zane. But if Caelestis insists on having you back, that may be our biggest obstacle to helping them. I implore you to reconsider what may be motivating her. I believe you know much about that. Have an answer ready for Elder Lambert when he returns."

"Returns . . .?" Lily questioned.

Was anyone even aware that Elder Lambert had left?

CHAPTER ELEVEN

Lily made her way down the long corridor toward her room, trying to ease the knot in her stomach at remembering how Aiden had left the twelfth floor without saying a word. Having him discover her past with Celeste in front of everyone had clearly not been her intention, but that didn't make his silence sting any less.

As she processed her thoughts, a familiar sensation, a tickle on her skin, seemed to prod at her, and she immediately recognized the pleasant feeling. Raising her head, she smiled at the reason for the feeling—Aiden—waiting at her door. His long frame leaned against the wall, his hands casually shoved into his jean pockets. As she drew closer, he pushed himself away from the wall and stood directly in her path, presenting an expression that was neither angry nor judging, just focused on her. "You're here," she said as she came within arm's length of him.

"I needed to see you," he replied, using a tone that suggested a deep need within himself. "I needed to make sure that you're all right." His thoughts then seemed to drift for a moment. "When you walked off that elevator as if everything were normal . . . Lily, I don't understand how my bite did not hurt you the other night in the Library."

Lily suddenly understood what was troubling him, and she impulsively reached for his hand to ease his worry. "I tried to tell you I was fine that night. But you rushed out of there before I could." She began to stroke her other hand over the back of his. "And I'm sorry I didn't tell you about Celeste. I just thought I was free of her. I never considered that she would remain here in Alberta."

Not surprisingly, Aiden didn't say anything in response. He simply continued to watch her, as if he was waiting for what she might say next. She loved that about him. That they could be saying nothing at all to each other, but it never felt awkward.

"I wanted to move forward with my life and leave her in the past. Can you understand that?"

Just when it appeared that Aiden was about to say something, his attention shifted to a man who had just stepped off the elevator. He was simply returning to his room but had momentarily glanced in their direction. Aiden responded by straightening his shoulders, but he kept his hand confidently around Lily's. At first, the action seemed small, but then Lily realized that Aiden was responding to whether the man perhaps thought that Lily might be in danger because she was alone with one of the transfused Guardians. She hated that he even had to consider such things in his everyday life.

Once the man entered his room and they were again alone in the hallway, she squeezed Aiden's hand, this time pulling him forward as she opened her door. "Here, come inside," she said, but she felt a resistance, as if he had dug his feet into the carpet where he stood.

"That's not a good idea." Aiden said, then dipped his head and slowly moved in close to her. Soon she felt the door against her back and his breath puffed lightly against her cheek as he said, quietly, "You know how much I wanted you the other night?" he began, causing a shiver to run through her whole body from the memory of him tangled there with her on the library sofa, his body rigid and tight as he covered hers, his long cock pressing against her thigh.

She nodded. "Yes."

"I still want you."

Lily touched her hand to his face and whispered quietly back to him, "I still want you, too."

His whole body went rigid in response as his hand slid down her arm. "I don't know if I can control . . . this. You and me alone in your room . . . Do you understand?"

Lily could see he was being completely honest and open with her. He was laying all his cards on the table and admitting his fear that he might push her too far, like the other transfused Guardians when they'd become focused on one woman. The difference, however, between those women and Lily was that she wanted Aiden just as much as he wanted her. She cared for him more than she knew she had any right to, given that she still thought of herself as one of the treating professionals on Dr. Li's team. It had been so long since her heart and her body felt anything close to this kind of attraction. Every time Aiden touched her she would feel herself coming alive, and she wanted that feeling, the warmth of it. She wanted to grab on with both hands and never let go. "I trust you, Aiden. Now, will you trust me?" she asked as she pulled him forward into her room, never letting her eyes waver from his. "I know what I want."

This time he allowed it.

Once she closed the door behind her, Lily backed herself against a wall and pulled Aiden to her. He needed no convincing and quickly covered her mouth with his, kissing her hard the moment their lips made contact. She could feel all the passionate need he'd kept perfectly coiled up inside him as it rushed out in one sudden burst of breath. Then a low groan rose from deep in his throat as his long hands settled firmly around her hips. He allowed himself to sink even deeper into their kiss and, in no time at all, Lily felt as if she couldn't breathe. His tongue was insistent, possessing her mouth in a way that would leave no doubt as to the desire he felt for her.

Soon, Lily lost track of time as she felt her legs go weak and the world begin to spin out of control around her, in a good way. Aiden pulled her tight to him, as if to keep her grounded there with him, kissing her with an intensity that proved he was just as starved for her touch as she had been for his. And even as her mind told her what she was doing was wrong—that she was supposed to be assisting Dr. Li in helping Aiden, not full-on seducing him—she couldn't stop herself. The way Aiden made her blood warm in her veins every time he touched her stole away any thought of stopping him—stopping the big, strong hands that were caressing her body possessively, over and over again, as though he was trying to commit her every line and curve to memory.

"Aiden," she said breathily as she rose onto her toes, pulling at the ends of his shirt. "This feels good. Don't stop."

Aiden didn't stop. Lily suddenly felt herself hoisted off her feet and her back tightly pressed against the wall behind her. Aiden's big hands held her by her haunches, and her legs flailed in the air for a moment before she wrapped them around his hips to balance herself. The hard surface at her back, coupled with the hard man in front of her, felt perfect, making her want to rejoice! There was just no way she could feel cold or unresponsive in this man's arms. No way!

But then, without warning, Aiden backed away from her, dropping her back onto her feet as suddenly as he had lifted her up just seconds before. His breathing was audible as the air dragged in and out of his chest. Briefly, she could see the flash of his fangs as he turned his head from her. "We have to stop!" he said, returning his gaze, the intensely blue color once again swirling through his eyes. "I want you too much . . . I want to drink from you again! And *God*, I don't want to push you too far too fast."

Aiden knew that he needed to slow down or he would begin to submit to the dominant behavior his new vampire blood would demand. Lily understood the one thing Aiden needed more than anything else in is life, right now, was to feel he still had control of what was happening to him. She gently placed one of her hands on each side of his face and held him there, staring at him intently as the blue continued to swirl through his eyes, the vampire within him fighting to come out. "You're not pushing me," she replied firmly. "That's not what's happening here. I accept everything about you, Aiden. Everything. I'm here with you because I want to be."

His fingers dug into her clothing as his hands balled into tight fists. "I've never wanted a woman like this before. I want to own and possess every part of you. Right now it doesn't feel real. It feels—chemical." He was shaking his head back and forth as his eyes cleared up and he again resembled more the human man who was so familiar to her. "I'm not telling you this to hurt you. I just . .

. I want to be honest with you. This lust I feel may be a response to the transfusions."

There it was. *Lust.*

What Aiden was feeling for Lily might simply be *lust,* caused by a chemical reaction of his new vampire blood. She, of course, understood that possibility. She just hadn't stopped herself long enough to consider his motives, or her own. The truth was, they hadn't known each other very long. Lily wasn't sure what she was feeling right now. This attraction had been moving at a whirlwind pace since Aiden had returned to The Oracle. Was she OK with whatever was between them just being lust?

She lifted her chin again and confidently replied, "It's all right." Lily didn't want to take the time to evaluate seriously and rationally how she really felt in that moment. She just wanted to continue feeling good. Could she settle for being with Aiden for just one night? Yeah, she thought she could. He made her feel things, stomach tingling things that she hadn't felt in a long time. She couldn't see the harm in surrendering to that feeling just once. "I want you to stay."

Lily suddenly found herself swept back off her feet and carried across the room in his arms. Her hands wrapped around his neck for support as he stretched his fingers along her legs and carelessly flung her heels from her feet, one at a time. He tossed her backwards onto her messy bed and followed her down until his long body completely covered hers, slowly caressing her hip as he kissed her shoulder. His lips bantered back and forth between slow, thoughtful kisses and completely demanding, possessive ones, as though he was trying to make up his mind about which he preferred. So it surprised her when he suddenly stopped altogether. "Aiden . . .?" she questioned breathily. "Everything all right?"

He nodded without hesitation, breaking into the sexiest smile she had ever seen on him. "For the first time in a long time I feel . . . really good. I want you, Lily Abbott."

Lily smiled at him as she rolled beneath him onto her back, her palm once again coming to rest on his cheek. He tipped his head forward 'til their foreheads met. She felt his fingers wiggle through her hair, causing her messy bun to fall free of its pins and coming to rest on her shoulders, the little hairpins getting lost in the bed coverings as they came out. Aiden stared at her now as if he was staring at the most fascinating thing he'd ever seen. "You've no idea how long I've wanted to do that," he laughed.

Lily blinked up at him. She had never heard Aiden laugh before. He had a wonderful, deep laugh, the kind that rumbled through his entire chest with masculine ease. "You want me to wear my hair down?"

"No . . . not out there. I want to be the only one who sees you with it down around your shoulders like this," he said as his fingers combed through her hair. "It makes you look very soft and sexy." I want that only for me."

"Oh really," she teased him.

Lily had expected their playful banter to continue but she was surprised when a strained expression appeared to invade his face, which seemed completely at odds to their current mood. "I was going to leave again. Tonight . . ." A growl-like rumble sounded from his throat, and she could see whatever he was about to say was difficult for him. "I made plans to leave here with Zane—to walk away for good and never look back."

"But you didn't. You're here with me instead."

He nodded. "Whatever this is between us—real or chemical—I have to see it through. I can't leave. There just isn't a choice for me anymore. Do you understand what I'm saying?" Lily nodded, her breath strangely trapped in her lungs.

Fighting for control, Lily finally exhaled. "Good," she said. "Because it means you are open to giving us a chance to figure this out. I want that too. And if it turns out this isn't real, then that's OK."

***

Lily lay there, her back against the sheets, a soft smile on her lips, and her long, honeyed hair spread over her shoulders. Aiden couldn't remember another time when a woman appeared so beautiful to him. She wanted him; he could see that need in her eyes. She was sexy and strong. Her Dhampir strength was only one of a dozen things he found sexy about her. But he decided his most favorite thing about Lily Abbott was . . . her smile. She could light up a room with her smile. He kissed her and she smiled. He kissed her again and she smiled at him more. Then he just couldn't stop kissing her. He took her mouth, full and hard, until he felt the fire rise in his blood. She moaned against his lips, and to Aiden it was the most perfect sound.

"Damn, if this woman doesn't know how to push all my buttons!" he thought. Sometimes he felt as if she controlled his every reaction.

He meant what he had said. There was no way he could leave her again. He had to see this through, whatever this was between them. Even if, ultimately, his response turned out to be only a reaction to the changes happening within his blood. He had to be with this woman for whatever time they had together.

Aiden's body, now covering hers quite completely, pressed her deep into the sheets, their breathing both labored and excited. Her small hand worked with difficulty at his jeans until he finally helped her by raising his hips slightly, lifting some of his weight. She dragged down the zipper and slipped her hand inside, feeling his hard erection pulsing underneath. His whole body felt powerful as she cupped her hand around him, squeezed gently, then began to stroke the length of him, back and forth, back and forth. Ever so slowly, back and forth. His shoulders tightened as he braced himself above her. Aiden was so turned on by how masterfully she stoked his desire that he swore his body was about to go up in flames right there on the bed. "Aw, *God*, that feels good, beauty," he whispered to her, coming to him completely unbidden.

"You like this?" she asked him in a teasing voice.

"Yes!" he growl playfully back to her as it was now his turn to work at her jeans.

And for some reason, fate or karma chose that moment to cause him great difficulty in working to open a simple pair of women's jeans. He was so turned on, so anxious to sink himself inside this woman, that his fingers fumbled to release a button and unzip a zipper. He wished she had worn a skirt today. He wanted to see those great legs of hers peeking out from under a dress or skirt. During his exams she often wore a dress or skirt under her lab coat, and he had many fantasies of taking her, quick and hard, on the exam table. He imagined how their bodies would fit together. Hers, tall for a woman, soft and curvy in the right spots. His, hard, long and lean. How would being inside this woman feel?

Finally able to get her jeans open and tugged down well below her hips, Lily moaned as Aiden slid his hand under her lace panties and reached for the soft flesh between the apex of her thighs. Her flesh was wet for him and his fingers were probably a little cold, but she didn't seem to mind. She arched upward, gasping, and her head lolled back as his first two fingers entered her, his thumb circling over her clit. He wanted to stoke the same desire in her that she had in him. He was patient, and as she began to pant he changed the pace of his stroking to match her breathing, which was becoming very erratic. She reached up, curled an arm around his neck, and kissed him hard as he continued to stroke her expertly with his fingers and thumb. She moaned as she kissed, and he could feel the undercurrent of energy her body was building. It was fantastic! Aiden sensed she was close to exploding, and the visual in his brain of watching her orgasm in front of him was about to drive him insane. "Tell me you want this, beauty."

At first she didn't respond, just continued to moan in these sweet, little breaths. "I want this," she finally said. "I want you." In response, Aiden could feel himself changing, feel the surging of the blood in his veins, emit the deeper growl lurking in his throat, and he became aware of the pressure of his emerging fangs against his lips. This woman brought out the most dominant parts of him, and he knew there was no turning back now.

He had to have her.

Aiden pulled back his kisses as he realized that his fangs were now making it too dangerous to continue kissing her. He stared down at her as he methodically pumped his fingers inside her, stroking his thumb over her clit. He wanted to watch—no, *had* to watch—her reach for that very edge, the very second before she would go off . . . and he would hold her there for as long as he possibly could. Her moans grew more erratic, and he could tell she was nearly there, still responding to his every touch. Seeing it on her face made him feel like a king! Then she arched her back and started to gasp. Aiden pulled his fingers from her heat and she gasped a second time, but now in protest at being stopped just short. He quickly flipped her onto a pillow on her stomach, pulling that pert little derriere of hers up towards him. His hands, now getting back with the program, he deftly worked at pulling her jeans off her legs, hurled them to the floor, and followed almost immediately by her panties and shirt. He left her bra on, though, a bright, lemony-yellow confection full of lace that made his mouth water at how perfectly it curved her breasts upward.

Moments later, when he returned to her on the bed, he was naked as the day he was born, his body fully erect as he covered her, licking at her neck with his tongue, since his fangs were fully out and present. "Drink from me," she pleaded, lifting her head up as if to encourage him. "You won't hurt me, Aiden. Drink from me, please!"

"Awe, fuck, Lily . . ." he said, struggling to maintain control around this woman but needing no more encouragement than her plea. He pulled her head back and sank his fangs into her throat, drinking from her as fiercely as he had that first night in the Library. Her blood was the sweetest taste in the world to him. Intoxicating, drugging—electric! The red cocktail seemed to charge his blood and supercharge his body to a level he had never known before. She cried out beneath him, a cry of both pain and pleasure. So he continued to drink, one hand holding her head and neck still as the other slid down her body to spread her legs wide over the pillow, preparing to enter her from behind as soon as she came for him. He lifted his weight from her and slid three fingers inside her from behind, stroking her in an even rhythm. Her inner muscles responded almost im-mediately. She was perfect, her body soft and responding to him exactly as he had fantasized about all those times he watched her in the exam room, taking all those damn notes.

As he continued to drink from her, he exulted at the complete control he had of her body. She was responding to him even in her tiniest movements; how she lifted her rear end to rub against him, encouraging him. She was responding in her labored breathing, her soft cries. She was driving him mad! "Aiden . . . Aiden, I'm gonna . . .!"

She never finished that sentence. He felt her body tighten and explode like a firecracker around his fingers. He pulled his fangs from her tender throat and just let himself experience what it was like to hold her while she orgasmed. She was completely free in her surrender to the pleasure, and he believed she might just be the most beautiful thing he'd ever seen, though, he couldn't actually see her face because she remained turned away from him.

When her orgasm finally began to subside and she collapsed against the mattress, he leaned forward and touched his lips gently to her skin. Inch by inch he began to trail kisses along her back, very gently, so his fangs wouldn't harm her. He wanted her to feel how precious this moment was to him—how precious *she* was to him—and he wanted to give her even more pleasure. "You're gorgeous when you come, Lily," he whispered over her skin. "Beautiful . . . my beauty . . ."

He was expecting to hear one of those sated sighs or maybe a sweet endearment in return as he lined his body up behind her, stroked his cock a couple of times and prepared to enter inside her. But instead, the moment between them seemed to change in an instant. "*Oh, God,*" she said miserably into the sheets. Aiden could then feel Lily shaking beneath him. This wasn't the good *you-just-rocked-my-world* kind of shaking, either. This was a violent, jerking kind of shaking.

Aiden froze above her, even though he was harder than an iron pike and ready beyond belief to sink himself inside her. "You have to go!" she cried, suddenly rolling out from under him, pushing him away from her with incredible strength, and frantically launching her nearly naked body from the mattress onto the floor in what appeared to be a move to escape him. "Go!"

Aiden couldn't move. His brain couldn't come down from the lust fast enough to process what was happening. "Lily, what the hell? What's wrong?" he asked with a ragged breath that had nothing to do with any exertion on his part. She was just scaring the shit out of him!

Lily continued to crawl away, toward the Juliet balcony. Finally, Aiden's brain caught up with what was happening, and he jumped off the bed to go to her on the floor. But as soon as his hand touched her shoulder she jerked away from him, "No! Go! Go now!"

Aiden was stunned. He didn't understand what the hell was happening. She had been fine thirty seconds ago. "Lily . . . Did I hurt you?" he asked in nothing more than a whisper, and then he watched helplessly as she continued to shake against the floor, still wearing only the lacy bra he had left on her.

"Aiden, I need you to leave! Now!" she repeated and he understood if he didn't leave, there would be people busting through the door any second to drag him away because she was crying out so loudly. How the hell would he explain this? The situation would certainly look like a transfused hybrid attacking a woman in the midst of an episode of sexual aggression. Not what he believed it to be, two consenting adults enjoying being with one another. And that killed him!

Turning to dress quickly, Aiden forced himself to stop long enough to turn back to her one more time. She was bunched up in the corner with her back to him, her shoulders—*no, her entire body*—shaking as she obviously tried to hold her shoulders rigidly straight, but that effort seemed to be taking every ounce of energy she had. She was breathing incredibly hard. "I can't leave you like this," he said miserably. "I will get someone to help you—"

"*No! Oh, God, please* . . . I just need you to go. *Please!*" she begged, although her voice did not sound like her own anymore.

Aiden felt as if someone had just gutted him with a knife. The next thing he knew he was standing outside her locked door, staring back at it. This didn't feel right to him. Everything had been fine. She had been into the foreplay the entire way with him until her orgasm. Had he blacked out or something and just didn't realize it? Had he somehow hurt her?

People began milling about in the hallway, so Aiden decided that he needed to go somewhere else to sort this out or guards would be showing up ready to drag him out of here in chains. But if he had somehow hurt Lily . . . he would deserve it.

CHAPTER TWELVE

When Lily finally heard the door close behind Aiden, she continued to shake but let out a long moan of relief. She wasn't sure how much longer she could have held on before the complete violence of the shaking currently racking her body would have become impossible to contain!

Lily never wanted to hurt Aiden like that. She could hear in his voice that he had been drastically shocked and that he blamed himself for her current condition, which she knew had absolutely nothing to do with him. She hated herself for causing him to feel that way, even for a moment, but there had been no other choice. She couldn't afford to let him see her like this. This episode had caught her totally off guard. And just after she'd just experienced the best orgasm she'd had in recent memory . . . maybe even in her entire life! The way Aiden's hands felt as he touched her, the way he held her, controlled her body's responses, had been mind-blowing! Especially for a woman who had begun to believe she had become a cold fish. None of her responses had been manufactured or forced. They just sort of exploded out of her naturally, as if her body had been holding everything back, waiting to erupt in that one fantastic moment.

Unfortunately, a different kind of shaking, the upheaval that was responsible for ruining her bliss in that moment, was not over yet. She continued to fight, slapping her hand over her mouth to cover up the agonized sounds that were demanding to come out, while at the same time trying to take in enough air through her nostrils. Despite her efforts, Lily felt the changes happening inside her body. Her head was beginning to swim with images—layer upon layer of images that, when put together, formed a picture so clear in her mind that it became the only thing she could see in front of her.

Then, suddenly, the room around her became cold, freezing even, as she slowly crawled on her knees to her dresser. With her vision blocked by the image in her head, she blindly searched through drawers in an effort to find the one item she needed in that moment more than anything else. Pawing through drawer after drawer, she searched frantically, shoving clothes around in piles, growing more frustrated with herself until, finally, the shaking stopped on its own as her hand found, tucked into a back corner of the drawer, the thing she had been searching for. She grasped several small sticks fiercely between her fingers, as if her very life depended upon them.

***

Aiden continued to pace back and forth, etching a deep trail of footfalls into the lush carpet beneath his feet. *What the hell had just happened?* Lily had felt tender and beautiful in his arms, passionate against his lips, and she had responded with pure excitement to his bite. *No*, he hadn't seen her face as he drank her sweet blood with a need that threatened to topple him over at one point (he still didn't understand why her blood had such an effect on him), but he hadn't needed to *see* anything! He could *feel* the total surrender in her soft moans, her deeper breathing, the strong way she dug her fingers into his arms. She was definitely into their foreplay when he began stroking his fingers inside her. Her body had arched to the pleasure and molded itself to his. And the gasps and shrill cries as she finally orgasmed? She was fantastic!

So what the fuck had happened?

It was driving him crazy. He couldn't stand the thought that he might have hurt her. He believed *wholeheartedly* that she had been enjoying their passionate exchange. But was he wrong? Was this what it felt like in the minds of the other transfused Guardians when they tried to rape a woman? The first super-soldier, Guardian Jude Garrison, had tried to rape The Charmer, Olivia Greyson, while she was training at The Oracle. Had he been thinking that everything was fine, even while he was actually hurting her?

He came to a stop, pausing long enough to drag both his hands through his hair, almost as though he was trying to pull it all out by the roots. "No, no, no!" he said out loud. "Just think this through."

At moments like this, when Aiden questioned how the transfusions were affecting him the most, he would repeatedly tell himself that he needed to trust his instincts, and they were telling him that he was fully tuned in to Lily. Her pleasure *was* his pleasure. It had been that way for him from the very first moment he touched her in the Library. If he had been hurting her, he would have known it. And, more importantly, he knew he would have found a way to stop. Somehow, he would have stopped!

When she had shouted at him to go, he was so stunned he hadn't been able to think clearly. But now that he was away from the situation and able to think through every step, he knew *something* had been wrong with her . . . and, like a damn coward or fool (neither of which he was proud of), he had just left her there! He should've asked more questions—demanded, if he had to—so he could have helped her.

Aiden whirled around and strode toward the door, his mind made up. He was going back to Lily's room! But his momentum was broken when the cell phone in his pocket started buzzing. He was deciding that the call could wait when he pulled the phone from his jeans, an automatic response to its insistent buzzing. He recognized the number on the screen and knew he had to answer. "Hey, man, this is kind of a bad time"

"Well, it's about to get worse," Lucas replied. "Alec's been turned. I'm almost sure of it."

"*What?*" Aiden barked, pulling his hand back from the door handle.

"Yeah, I know!"

"When? How? Who . . .?"

"Look, all I fucking know is that I'm following Maya and Poppy Honeywell right now—yes, the same Poppy Honeywell who's shacked up with Kane and Lily in the other universe—driving at the speed of light over the border into Washington State."

"Why are you bringing that up?" Aiden asked, an angry tone revealing his displeasure about being reminded that Lily was with

Kane in the other universe . . . and also with Poppy, the same beautiful woman he'd seen latched on to Alec with such affection in the hall outside his office only a few days ago.

"I have to say this stuff out loud so I can remember which universe I'm talking about," Lucas explained, defensively. Then, reacting to Aiden's angry tone, he said, "Just be fucking grateful you're in this one." Aiden snorted at the irony, considering the mess he had just made in *this* universe. "Anyway," Lucas continued, "They made one stop, where I overheard them talking. Poppy told Maya that Alec had asked her to mate him, but when she bit him, to exchange their blood, something went wrong."

"Holy shit . . ."

"*Holy shit* is right! I was about to march up to Maya and chew her butt into next Sunday about what the fuck she thought she was doing when I suddenly remembered she thinks I'm *dead*. I decided that seeing a ghost right now was not going to help her current situation—especially because it turns out I'm not the only one following them."

"Who else is following them?"

"A whole shitload of motherfucking Lycans! They're coming out of the woodwork around here! I can't see the bastards yet, but I can hear them gathering. Everyone in a *goddamn* five-mile radius can hear them! It's the freakiest damn thing I've ever heard. Why the hell are they not keeping to their Dead Zone?"

Aiden felt his head pound as if he were being hit repeatedly by a hammer. There were too many things hitting him all at once! He took a deep breath. He needed to get back to Lily. But the fact that their leader was turning into a vampire and being taken away from The Oracle, the one place where they might have the technology and equipment to help him . . . well, that was definitely an emergency!

Maya knew this, though. And the reality was, if Alec was turning, he would have to be taken off sacred ground. There was nothing that could be done to stop the process. "OK, let's set the problem with the Lycans aside for a moment."

"Shit! That's easier said than done. *Your ass* is not out here in the middle of all of them!"

"I assume," Aiden continued as if Lucas had not interrupted him, "you're in no immediate threat from them, or you wouldn't be wasting your time on the phone with me."

"I'm in my fucking car, breaking every goddamn speed limit known to man so as to keep up with Maya. Who the fuck knew Maya could drive like Mario Andretti?"

"Is Alec still with them?"

"Yeah. I'm following right behind them. It looks like they're headed towards Seattle."

"Seattle?" Aiden questioned. "Maya's taking Alec back to Olivia Greyson?"

"More than likely back to Caleb and Jax," Lucas growled under his breath. "Being that they're Daywalkers, she must be hoping there's a way they can help him."

"That's actually not a bad plan," Aiden responded, seeing the possibilities. "The Daywalkers may not like Alec, but they won't hurt him. And they'll know how to protect him while he's transitioning."

"Fuck!" Aiden heard Lucas curse again under his breath. "This is not what Alec would want . . . to become a fucking vampire! He wanted to lead the fight against them—not become one of them!"

Aiden swallowed hard. He understood the feeling. "Just stay on their tail."

"Oh, I'm staying on their tail, all right! And when Maya realizes that I am still alive—*then* I'm going to chew her ass into next Sunday for doing something this dangerous and this stupid with our Brethren leader!"

"Yeah, well, I need to warn Gideon about what's happening. He's going to have to cover things here." Not surprisingly, Gideon had known right away when Alec went missing. That's what he and Aiden had been talking about when Zane had charged off the elevator, dragging Lily behind him. Aiden had just finished explaining to Gideon that he'd seen Alec leaving The Oracle with Maya and Poppy, leaving out the parts about Alec being unconscious and that Lucas was still alive and following. But now he was going to have to tell Gideon the whole story.

"So Gideon hasn't hit the panic button with the other Elders yet?"

"Gideon knows Alec's left The Oracle. Well . . . more like he thinks he's gone on his own accord. He's agreed to act like Alec's really busy in meetings until Alec or Maya checks in with him."

"Good thing you spoke to him, or Maya might have the entire Brethren on her tail, as well. Shit, could the woman cause a bigger ruckus?"

"You're going to have to get word to Maya that she has to call and tell Gideon something or she *will* have The Brethren forces headed for Seattle right behind her."

"*Aw fuck!* That means she's going to know I'm alive. That wasn't part of the plan. I don't want to involve her in this mess."

"She's an Empath, Lucas. Sooner or later, you won't be two headlights behind her, she'll feel you following her."

Lucas sighed something under his breath that sounded like, "You're probably right."

"Look, I've got to go."

"What has you so upset?"

"I didn't say any—"

"It's in your voice, man."

Aiden's thoughts were already back on Lily. He should never have left her, and he needed to be back with her to make sure she was all right. "I can't really get into it over the phone, but I'm worried something's wrong with Lily. I need to go to her."

"Then go. I've got this covered as long as you can stall Gideon for me. I swear, I think you've been half in love with that woman since the day you met her."

"I never said—"

"Dude, you never fucking say *anything*! That's half your problem."

"I don't have a problem!"

"You've got several of them—just like the rest of us. The only one who seems to have his shit together right now is Kane. And who the fuck ever saw that one coming? Later." Lucas finished before hanging up.

Aiden had been making his way back to the fifth floor, heading straight for Lily's room. When he got to her door he pounded on the hard surface and called out to her, but there was no answer. He could sense that she was still inside, and when the light scent of lemons and lavender hit his nose through the door he swore he was going to go crazy. She was really starting to scare the shit out of him! If she didn't open this door in a few seconds, he would break it down. He didn't care if they hauled him off in chains. "Lily!" he called again.

Not a sound, not a single movement.

That's it! He was really going to break down the damn door. Then he stopped for a moment to think rationally. He needed to get inside to check on her without causing a huge scene. He looked back and forth along the empty hall to the large casement window at each end. Granted, he was five-floors-above-the-ground-kind-of up, so he guessed now was as good a time as any to see how much of a vampire he was becoming . . . because he was going to need some strength and a lot of balance to do what he was about to try.

Aiden wasted no time. He hurried to the north end of the building, unlocked and opened the window, and crawled onto a very thin ledge outside, knowing he was kidding himself that the night would provide much cover for him, given that he was among a bunch of hybrids with superior vision and hearing. At least a dozen people would spot him if he crawled around to the west face of the building until he hit her room, which was located somewhere just shy of the middle. His best option was to '*pull a Maya*' and go up to the roof, then crawl down the face to her balcony without alerting anyone on the higher floors, especially the twelfth floor, because that would undoubtedly involve Alec's guards.

He was surprised at how easily he managed to climb himself to the roof, which was, he thought, also probably not a good sign for his slim hopes about keeping himself human. Once he was on the west face and directly above her room, he waited till he saw no one on the ground below, then dropped down from deck to deck, surprised at how quiet his landings were at each level, using the narrow decks as floor counters. When he reached Lily's deck, he surveyed the area again to make sure no one was watching him, then swung over the railing and went to the sliding doors. They were locked, but through a slivered opening in the drapes he could see Lily's slim form lying on the floor, her beautiful body clad only in the same lemon colored bra he had left in place when he undressed her. Had she even moved since he'd left her? Or had she passed out right there next to the balcony door? Man, he was an idiot for leaving without making sure she was all right.

There was a slight cracking sound as he exerted enough force to break the slider lock. Gently, he pulled her inert form away from the door as he entered the room, then knelt beside her, lifting her head a few inches and holding it gently in his hands. "Lily," he whispered, tapping her cheek just a bit with one hand, hoping to get a response.

No answer.

Lily was still breathing, but her respirations seemed incredibly labored, as if she were having a difficult time doing so. He feared that couldn't be good and knew he needed to act quickly. Realizing that he had already wasted a bunch of time in getting to her, he refused to waste any more dressing her completely. Instead, he grabbed the first cotton dress he could find and awkwardly slipped it over her head, covering her as best he could. Then he picked her up, intending to carry her down to Dr. Li's office, this time through the main building. He didn't care what anyone would think or whisper about him when they saw him carrying an unconscious woman. He just cared about getting Lily whatever help she needed so she could look at him again with those beautiful eyes of hers.

Aiden didn't have the patience for the elevator; he decided to take the stairs all the way down to the lobby and was amazed no one spotted him. Once he was outside, he raced as fast as he could with Lily in his arms toward the chapel and the below ground lab entry. When he got to the steel door leading into the labs he remembered it was the middle of the night and the work spaces would be empty of people and locked down for the evening. He would have to call back to The Oracle, let them know there was an emergency and have them come down to let him and Lily inside. Even with all of his newfound strength, he certainly wasn't going to be able to break through the giant steel door himself.

Reaching for his communications link to make the call, Aiden heard a light moan and felt Lily stir in his arms. In that moment it was the best sound he could have hoped to hear. He gently set her down on the floor right outside the steel door and cradled her head in one arm, stroking his other hand back and forth along her cheek. "Lily, can you hear me?"

Lily slowly opened her eyes, blinking frequently in her confusion, and raised her hand to her head as if she were in pain. That's when he noticed her hands. They were all different colors, like green and blue and gray, but at the same time they were swollen and raw, as though she had rubbed them to exhaustion for hours. "What happened?" she asked him, her expression lost as she looked around and realized where they were at. She then sat upright to a straight seated position, showing much more strength than Aiden would have guessed she had. "*Oh, God, Aiden!* You haven't called Dr. Li, have you?"

Aiden's brows pulled tight as he wrapped his arms around her protectively. "I was about to. You've had me scared to death, Lily." She tried to straighten up but Aiden held her tightly. "No, stay still," he ordered.

"I'm all right. Just promise me you won't tell Dr. Li about this."

Aiden's frown had turned to a full-fledged scowl. "No! No, I won't promise you that!"

Lily blinked up at him in surprise.

"I found you unconscious on the floor of your room. Again! Whatever is happening to you is happening so fast you didn't even take the time to put your clothes back on. And your hands are raw. I'm *worried* about you, Lily. Do you get that? And unless you start talking *right now*—unless you start trusting me to help you—then I *will* get Dr. Li."

Lily said nothing, and, in a sort of defeated response, merely dropped her head against his chest. She wasn't crying or shaking; she was just very quiet. He could see that she was still tired and physically recovering from whatever had happened to her in that room. He lifted her chin until she faced him again. "Give me the code to get us inside the labs," he said, in a calmer voice, before delivering a reassuring kiss to the top of her head. "Let's take it one step at a time, all right?"

She nodded against his chest, and within a minute they were inside the labs with the door closed behind them. Despite her weakened condition, Lily insisted on walking once they were inside the main lab corridor. Aiden didn't like it, but agreed and led her toward an exam room. He helped her get seated on the exam table and then began to look her over more closely for injury, starting with her hands. Lily tried to pull them back from him, but Aiden wouldn't allow it and started to rub them gently, transferring some of the color into his own hands. "I'm all right," she said softly.

"This is like the third time—that I know about—when you've been found unconscious. That's *not* all right, Lily. *What is going on?*" Lily remained silent, but Aiden could see she was not going to try and keep anything from him. She appeared to be figuring out the best way to explain things to him. He was glad to see that but he was still worried. Aiden stroked her cheek to draw her attention more directly to him. "Did I hurt you? When we . . . ?"

"No," she responded without hesitation, placing her hands on each at each side of his face. Her expression was very fragile and it seemed to him that she might be wanting to cry, but she didn't. "I loved being with you like that. When you touch me . . . I feel more alive than I have in a very long time. You have no idea what that means to me."

"Then what happened tonight? You scared the shit out of me, Lily."

"I'm sorry I scared you. I've just been afraid to tell you everything. I care about you, Aiden. I want to know—like you—if what this is between us is real. But I'm afraid once you know everything . . . that will be the end of it."

He kissed her, light and quick, on the lips, because he simply had to, and then he stared at her, his eyes fixed earnestly and directly on hers as he said, "I can't promise that once you share your secrets with me everything will be fine. But I do know that if we're afraid to talk to each other, tell each other everything, especially the hard stuff, then it isn't going to work. No matter how much we want it to."

Lily gazed back at him just as directly, her beautiful face radiant in that moment. She nodded slowly and said, "I have something to show you."

CHAPTER THIRTEEN

"Why are we here?" Aiden asked as he stood in front of the massive steel door that separated the labs from the recently constructed underground tunnel.

"What I need to show you is inside," Lily replied, turning away from him to enter a long code into the keypad. Aiden's brows furrowed. "Inside a tunnel? This thing has been sealed off since . . . since Reese's reign,"

Saying Reese's name out loud reminded Aiden of the poor choices he had made in his life over the past two years and of the very experiments that gave him the strength he'd desired more than anything but were now violently changing his life. "No one has the code to this door."

"Are you asking me how I do?"

He shrugged with an expression of, *'Well, . . . yeah'.*

"I stole it."

"You stole it," he repeated, blinking his disbelief at her answer just as Lily pushed open the massive door. The occupant sensor lights in the tunnel started to come on, one right after another, giving light to the dark hallway. Lily immediately pushed inside, with Aiden right in step behind her. "Why would you steal a code to a tunnel no one uses?"

"I had to," she replied. And soon Aiden could see they were walking towards something . . . something very large, something drawn on the tunnel wall. "I needed a place to hide these."

Aiden stopped well short of what could only be described as an enormous wall of one-dimensional life. Hand created images, painted in what looked like watercolors or chalk, covered every inch from floor to ceiling. Altogether, the images created a sort of storybook mural, extraordinary in how each scene appeared to morph into the next. The detail and vividness of color was quite unlike any painting he'd ever seen in his life. Or at least it was from a distance. As he came closer, the images became grainy, unreadable. Like giant sweeps of color, brushstrokes that blended into one another many times over. He realized he had to stand back from the wall to really see the story the image was telling. Aiden was simply stunned. "Did you do this? This is . . . incredible."

"Incredible . . . ?" she asked with a note of surprise in her response. "Look at them. Most of these images are of horrible, bloody events."

The fact that many of the images were depicting death had not escaped Aiden's notice. But somehow the violence did not take away from his appreciation of the skill it would require to create them. Or the fact that she had drawn them. The very scale of the images made them extraordinary.

"Lily, this rival's works of some of the greats, who often took years, even decades, to paint something of this size. And, to my knowledge, you have only been here a few months. So I think that deserves a moment of awe."

"You don't understand. These images are what I see in my head. They come to me and they take over, so strong, so painful. I can't think or see anything else until I get them out. Until I draw them."

Aiden stared back at her, a realization just coming to him. "What happened in your room . . .?"

"What happened in my room today had absolutely nothing to do with you . . . I wanted to be with you, Aiden. You have to know that."

"So the pain you were in happened because one of these images came to you?"

She nodded. "As suddenly as the last one I suffered, the night in the Library. There will be a drawing like these on one of the walls in my room. I can't tell you how many times I have had to scrape those walls clean."

Aiden felt truly astonished by what she was telling him. He had been so focused on finding her there on the floor in the dark that he hadn't even noticed if there was some sort of drawing on the wall. Only the chalk residue on her hands. "When I found you, you were unconscious . . . Just like when they found you in the banquet room."

Lily nodded. "Drawing these images takes a toll on my strength."

Aiden felt as if all Lily's strange and unexplained episodes over the past few weeks were suddenly becoming clear in a single moment. "That is why the light affected your eyes that night in the Library."

"Light always affects my eyes," she answered, rather strangely.

Aiden took several steps towards her, suddenly feeling the need to be close to her. "The night Zane confronted me here in the lab," she told him, "I had finished one of these drawings and he caught me coming out of this tunnel."

Aiden reached his hands to grip her arms gently, almost as if he were trying to support her weight. "Tell me the truth. Did he hurt you that night?"

"No," she answered sincerely. "Zane can't hurt me."

That answer didn't make sense to Aiden. Of course, Zane, a man twice her size who was gaining the strength of a Nightwalker every day, could hurt her. She might be a kick-ass Dhampir, but there was a limit. The human side of her ensured that. "Lily, this . . .," he began, looking back to the drawings on the wall, "this is a gift . . . , your Dhampir gift. Why didn't you just tell me what was happening to you tonight instead of throwing me out of your room? I was terrified I had hurt you."

An almost shameful expression spread over Lily's face as she shook her head. "I didn't want you . . . to see . . ."

"See what?"

When she didn't answer him he returned his focus to the drawings, hoping to find the answer to his question there. Several images were of events he did not recognize, but two he did. The image closest to him, the one she must have drawn most recently, had occurred only days ago. He remembered how surprisingly affected he had been when he heard that Sienna Scott, the woman Aiden had been teasing Lucas about in the other dimension, was reported to have been killed in England by a female warlock. Her heart had been savagely ripped from her chest. Aiden could see that savageness in Lily's drawing. It made him feel like he had been standing there, witnessing the brutality himself.

The second image re-created the exact moment Aiden and Kane had discovered a Lycan's body in Yellowknife a few months earlier. The Lycan had been ripped to shreds, and it was a grotesque sight. But there it was, right in front of him again, as if someone had taken a snapshot of the moment. "How did you know about this?" he asked, pointing to the Lycan. "The only person I spoke with about the details of what happened in Yellowknife was Alec."

Lily laughed, but there was no amusement to her voice. "I drew that about an hour after you and Kane left for Yellowknife."

Aiden stared back at her with bewilderment. "You're saying you drew this days before it happened? That's not—"

"Not possible," she finished for him. "I assure you it is. I drew all of these events before they happened. The day you left with Kane I knew Lucas was still alive and that Kane would cross paths with him in Yellowknife. I just didn't see that you would be with him."

"Why didn't you say anything?"

"I was trying to tell Kane when you found us that morning . . . in the closet." Aiden showed no reaction to the memory of finding Lily with Kane. Even though Aiden had no claim to Lily, the thought of her with his best friend still made him want to find Kane and punch him in the jaw. "Before he left with you," she continued, "Kane said he knew what I was trying to tell him. I thought he meant he already knew Lucas was alive. Of course, now I realize that wasn't what he meant at all." She sighed and pressed her hand onto her temple. "I'm sorry. I should've tried harder to warn you both. I was just so caught off guard at how angry you were with me that morning."

"Don't apologize. There were a lot of things I could've handled better that day."

She smiled easily, as if she understood. "It's just that . . . it's not easy telling people about what I see. I don't know what I'm risking. I don't know how I'm changing the future, changing the balance of things. And I don't understand how you can look at these images and see them as a gift? These images are of death."

Aiden reached for her hand and pulled her closer to the wall that displayed her work. "There is a reason *you* are seeing these images. As Gideon always says, Dhampirs are not given gifts they cannot handle."

She shook her head. "You don't know what you're saying."

It was another strange answer from her, he thought, as his eyes moved to another image farther down the tunnel. This one he recognized from the day he and Zane confronted Celeste. Celeste held Zane locked against her as Aiden stood there, watching. Only in Lily's image, Celeste had her fangs driven deep into Zane's throat, holding him there. "Wait a minute . . .," Aiden said. "This drawing is of the day Celeste and her coven confronted us in the forest. I thought you said you didn't know about that?"

A confused frown crossed over her faced as she stared again at the picture. "I didn't . . ."

"This isn't what happened, Lily."

"What do you mean?" she asked him.

"Celeste grabbed Zane like this—pulled him back against her. She even threatened to suck him dry right in front of us—but she didn't. She let him go. She never bit him."

Lily seemed truly stunned. "I guess that makes sense. Of course, Zane wasn't turned that day."

"Don't you see what this means? Not all of these images you see are actually happening the way you see them. You must be seeing what *could* happen. A version of the future. That doesn't necessarily mean it will happen."

"I suppose that's possible," she replied, obviously giving his remark considerable thought. "I don't witness most of these events."

"Gideon once said he sees time like a leaf in a storm. The leaf is constantly in motion, with so many converging forces pushing against it that it makes it nearly impossible to predict the path it will take next."

"But why do I see so many bad things?"

Aiden squeezed her hand as she so often did with him, to try and reassure her. "I don't know. But I don't think this is a gift you need to be afraid of. You're aren't causing these events. And unless you witness them you've no way of knowing if that's what actually happened."

"I've never thought of it that way." Lily looked away from him and down the long hall filled with drawing after drawing. She seemed to be giving even more considerable thought to what he was saying.

Aiden frowned. "You've been hiding this from everyone this whole time? I don't understand. If you would tell Gideon and Dr. Li, they could help you manage these episodes so we don't have to find you passed out on the floor, completely drained of energy." His frown pulled tighter. "It would help me. I can tell you that much."

Lily shook her head, then took a step back and turned away from him. "Aiden, you don't understand. You don't see . . . "

"You keep saying that. What . . .? What don't I see?"

She was silent for a long while, seeming barely to breathe in her sudden nervousness, and it was the first time Aiden had ever seen Lily Abbott nervous about anything. It was driving him crazy! He wanted to go to her, wrap his arms around her, and assure her that she could trust him because *he could see* something was wrong. "Talk to me," he finally said into the silence.

Lily turned around slowly, her eyes cast downward, toward the floor. "I'm sorry," she began. "I'm so sorry. Zane was right about me. I haven't been honest with you—with any of you."

She raised her head to face him, and there was no hiding the rush of Aiden's quick intake of breath. Lily was staring right at him, but the lines of her face had shifted. Her perfectly supple and gentle complexion was harder, her forehead more bulging above her brow. Her lips were parted by a long set of long fangs. And her eyes . . . a brilliant blue, the brightest blue only associated with . . .

No it couldn't be. It just couldn't be!

"Now you see . . .," she said. "Now you see me . . . I can't believe I convinced myself that somewhere deep down you already knew," she said with resignation before pulling her shoulders back as if to brace herself for what was coming next. "I discovered this gift shortly after the night Celeste killed my mother . . . The night she turned me."

Aiden stared unblinkingly into the face of the woman who, until that moment, he was pretty sure he was falling for on some level. Possibly something he could call love. And she was not a Dhampir.

She was a vampire.

CHAPTER FOURTEEN

Lily wanted this moment to go away. Now. She wanted it all to disappear in the time it took to blink her eyes. She was aware that Aiden had no idea how much courage it had taken for her to stand there in front of him, fully exposing her true vampire side, with no way to take the moment back.

Initially, he appeared so struck by shock that it threatened to topple him back from where he stood. Once he recovered from his initial reaction, though, he became very still, his expression unreadable . . . and, of course, he didn't say a word, which made her wonder whether she had just made one of the biggest mistakes of her life.

"Please say something," she said, finally injecting her voice into the silence. "Now is not the time to go quiet on me."

"You're a vampire." He began, shaking his head as if to assure himself it couldn't be true. "How is that possible?" he asked, his surprise and disbelief coming through in his voice. "How can you be standing here on sacred ground? That . . . that's not possible."

"Obviously, I'm proof that it is," she replied, taking a step toward him. But Aiden immediately re-established the distance between them by taking a step back. That single step, it seemed to Lily, was aimed right at her heart. She inhaled slowly, deeply, and tried again. "It is not easy for me to be on Oracle lands. I have trouble breathing sometimes. But slowly I've adapted."

"This doesn't make any sense. Adapted? How can you adapt? You're a vampire!"

"Aiden, I know this is a lot to process right now but you have to listen to me . . . I've never killed a human for food. I've never drunk from someone with the intention to kill or harm them. I've only fed from my sire so I can survive. I guess for what it's worth, that deprivation allows me to cross onto sacred ground."

"No—that's not right," Aiden insisted. "Once you're bitten, there's a darkness that takes over. It won't allow you onto consecrated ground."

That stung. By saying 'you', Aiden was already lumping Lily in with every vampire he'd ever come across, ever fought against in his life; and that wasn't fair. He knew her better than that. Lily was good, despite the fact she was a vampire. But she also accepted who and what she was.

"The darkness is there. I know it is. I feel it inside me every day. But until I make that first kill—take that first human life—the darkness is under control." Lily then reached up and touched her fingertips to her shape-shifted face. She felt all the lines that defined the dark side of herself, the side Aiden was seeing now. "I want that kill. I won't lie about it. After I woke from Celeste's attack, I thought I was dying. I was consumed by thoughts of drinking until my belly finally felt full. I still am."

"Why come to The Oracle, Lily? Why come to a place where everyone is trained to kill you?"

Lily turned back to the wall, more specifically, the images of the battle of Brahm Hill, appearing to recount parts of her own story inside them. "My plan was to escape with the Daywalkers that night. I had heard the stories of vampires who didn't feed on humans . . . even lived among them. I prayed the stories were true because it meant if I could find them, be accepted by them, I could live my vampire life in a way *I* could accept." She then turned back to Aiden, who was standing perfectly still. "But that night I saw you and my plans changed. I knew you were fighting for the Brethren and that you came from The Oracle. I saw an opportunity to . . ."

"To what . . .? Use me somehow?"

Lily looked away for a moment. A long, unnatural pause followed, until she finally managed to continue. "No. You misunderstand. What I mean is, I felt the struggle inside you. I knew that struggle. The struggle to stay on the side of good. Suddenly, all of the awfulness I had gone through with Celeste had a purpose. I could help someone else. And maybe, if I could help you and Zane, I wouldn't be alone anymore. So, instead, I came here. A place where Celeste could not sense me. I didn't even realize I was not supposed to be able to pass onto these grounds until I was already on them."

Aiden rubbed his hands over his face and released a deep breath, "A vampire just walks onto sacred ground . . .," he mumbled under his breath. "That's a new one. OK . . . What aren't you telling me? No one changes their life plan because they see someone on a battle field. Unless . . ." Aiden stared intently at the paintings on the wall in front of them for a long while, his thoughts going back to that night. Then he turned back to her. "You knew my name that night. Like you had met me before" He wrapped his knuckle on the image of the battle scene in front of him. "Maybe you had . . . In one of these drawings."

"It's true," she admitted without hesitation, which felt particularly unnerving to him. "I had seen you in one of my drawings before that night."

"What did you see?"

"I saw you on a table, receiving blood transfusions alongside six other men. But there was an odd look on your face, a sadness. Even then, you seemed to be questioning why you were there."

Aiden took a step back, then walked slowly around in a tight circle, from wall to wall of the tunnel, clearly struggling to process Lily's revelations. "You saw me in one of your drawings more than a year ago," he said quietly, more to himself than to her.

"I know this a shock," she replied gently. "I had seen you in my drawings but I had no idea who you were or how to find you until I saw you there that night at Brahm Hill."

"Drawings . . . ? Have there been more than one?"

Lily nodded slowly in reply.

Aiden responded by dragging a rough hand through his hair. "OK, Lily, we're going to have to start at the beginning here because I can't . . ."

He didn't finish that thought.

***

At least Lily could take comfort in the fact that Aiden was still referring to her by name. That had to count for something. She put her hands out in front of her in a complying gesture. "We'll start at the beginning. Maybe it would be best if you sat down over there," she said, pointing to the other side of the wide corridor. "I'll stay here."

Lily took a seat on the concrete floor and waited quietly for him to do the same. Characteristically, he didn't say a word; he just sat down with his back against the wall. His long legs were stretched out in front of him, making him appear closer to her than he really was. "Starting at the beginning means telling you about my father, Charles Abbott," she began. "He was a Professor of humanities, history and anthropology at UC Davis." Familiar images of the man Lily had loved and respected her whole life popped into her consciousness. The memories made her smile as she continued. "He was a brilliant man. Absolutely fascinated by history. He was considered a bit unorthodox by his peers, though, because he believed there are as many clues to the past in old, oral history stories or written texts as in the bones and artifacts unearthed from the ground."

Lily could see that Aiden was listening to her with deep interest, even though she had given him quite a shock by revealing her true self. That helped her relax a bit as she spoke. "There was a colleague of his, Thomas Moore, excavating near Wood Buffalo National Park. That area was of particular interest to my father. He'd read some old research text about the discovery of bone fragments on park lands, remains that seem to have come from a creature larger than a Wood Bison. There just wasn't enough in the fragment to make an accurate identification."

Aiden's expression grew more serious. "Wood Buffalo National Park," Aiden spoke. "Where the Lycan Dead Zone is?"

Lily nodded. "Professor Moore contacted my father saying that they had found something very strange. My father made the mistake of assuming Thomas was referring to bones they were excavating, but after meeting with him, father realized that Thomas was talking about something that they had seen . . . a creature. Something very large that moved very fast."

Lily closed her eyes and inhaled a deep breath. "I think my dad thought they were dealing with Bigfoot or something. When I spoke to him that day, just before he left to meet with the men again, he couldn't help but laugh at the notion. For all of my father's openness to text and lore, Bigfoot was no part of his belief system. But something happened to him that night. He saw something. And when he returned to California he was never the same."

"Did he ever tell you what it was he saw?"

Lily shook her head. "He began talking about things that just didn't make any sense. Especially for a man of science. He was suddenly telling stories of a world filled with vampires and demons from the darkest fiction. It was just too crazy. But a week after he returned, he quit his job at the university and spent weeks hauled up in his library, studying every ancient text he could get his hands on. My mother was sick with worry. There was no communicating with him. It was obvious to both of us that whatever trauma he experienced that night in Wood Buffalo National Park was deeply affecting him."

"I think you and I both know what he saw, Lily."

"A Lycan," she replied. "I know now, because I've seen this world with my own eyes many times over. But back then, I thought the man I had so loved and respected my entire life had gone insane. And he knew that. I will never forgive myself that he knew I saw him as deranged until he died."

Emotion swept through Lily then, a combination of sadness and fear that she rarely felt anymore, but she recovered more rational feelings before Aiden had a chance to respond. "He returned to the park without telling anyone he was leaving. The family rushed up there after him, hoping to bring him back, to get him some help. But . . ."

Aiden stared back at her, his whole expression suddenly responded to her tale with a horrible understanding, and he asked, "You saw a Lycan for the first time?"

She nodded silently. "I saw Celeste battling a Lycan. It was completely unexplainable, because the Lycan was the biggest biped creature I had ever seen. And here was this woman, in a short skirt and five-inch heels, battling him with a strength that seemed impossible. That night, we all became witnesses to something humans were never meant to see. And everyone—my family, Thomas, and his men—paid with their lives. I was the only survivor."

Lily knew she should at least be tearful over the loss of her family, but she wasn't. In fact, she had been unable to shed a single tear since becoming a vampire. That fact only served to remind her that she was less alive.

"Why do you think Celeste kept you alive?"

"I'm not sure. I think she was trying to find replacements for the women she lost battling the Lycan. She turned me that night. And sometimes I've wished I hadn't survived. I don't want to remember the things I saw—or what I felt."

"I saw the same thing," Aiden began, his voice dropping almost to a whisper. "On the night the vampires left with Keegan."

"We share the same pain," Lily said to him. "We have both lost family to this supernatural world. Just because I'm a vampire now does not mean I have forgotten."

"I suppose that's true."

Lily touched her fingers again to her face. Her human face had returned. But did it really matter anymore? Would Aiden be able to see only her vampire face?

"After Celeste turned me, I woke to a need for blood that was painful, consuming. It felt as if nothing would be able to satisfy the hunger. The one thing I focused on was something my father had said to me in our last conversation. He said, 'To save your soul you must never succumb to your greatest want.' At the time, I didn't understand what he meant. After I turned, then I realized he was warning me against not making that first human kill. I thought I would surely die if I ignored my thirst. And for days I thought I *was* dying . . . but resisting my thirst was the only way I could think to honor my father in death, the only way I could say I was sorry for not believing him."

She had been speaking these words without looking at Aiden, her eyes cast downward and her feelings turned inward. And when she finished speaking and looked up again, she saw the emotion in Aiden's eyes. She saw caring and understanding. The sight of it pulled at her heart in a way she had not felt since the night her human heart had gone still. "Lily, no human would have believed what he was telling you."

"Maybe not, but he *did* save me; I'm certain he *knew*. When I refused to drink on that very first night, Celeste threatened to kill me. She told me, flat out, that she had no use for a weak Nightwalker. But that was also the night when I had my first vision. I intentionally cut my hands against the cave rocks so I could draw what I was seeing, in my own blood. I couldn't stop myself. At first, Celeste thought I was insane. But then she realized I had drawn an image of an attack on her coven by the same Lycans. Because of my drawing, she was prepared for their attack that next night and was able to defeat them. Of course, then she decided there was a use for me, after all. So she kept me alive."

"A forced slave to do her bidding," Aiden responded, his anger rising and showing plainly on his face. "Sounds like Celeste. Did she feed you blood to keep you alive?"

"Her own blood, actually. After I'd gained enough strength, I began setting traps for small animals. I didn't want to become familiar with the feeling of predatory hunting, for fear I would become too comfortable with it. So I set traps. The animals died quickly and painlessly, but I always felt hungry, never satisfied. When I came to The Oracle, I was able to drink the blood supplied here for Dhampirs. And, oh, it tasted so good. I could actually feel myself getting stronger the more I drank."

Aiden pressed his fingertips into his temples. "How did none of us realize . . . I mean, Dr. Li . . . He's a Dhampir himself! How did you manage to fool us all for months?"

Lily bristled at the term 'fool'. It made her sound deceptive, which she rather supposed was at least partly true. She just didn't like to think of herself that way. "It's not about fooling anyone. You just aren't looking for it. You accept what you've been told—that vampires cannot cross onto to sacred ground."

"What about your skin?" Aiden asked. "Your skin should feel cold."

In the blink of an eye, Lily placed herself right in front of Aiden, crossing the corridor between them in an instant. She stared directly, and deeply, into his brown eyes, asking him, without words, to understand, even a little bit, as she reached for his hand. She squeezed, wondering if he would pull away . . . but he didn't. He just continued to sit there, calmly. "My skin *is* cold. You are the only one I have let touch me since I have been here— aside from a few initial tests that I had to work my way around."

Aiden surprised her by reaching his other hand up to stroke her bare arm. "You don't feel cold to me."

She nodded. "You don't realize how cold your own skin has become."

A humorless smile crossed his lips. "Am I becoming a Nightwalker?"

Lily shook her head as she settled herself more comfortably astride his stretched legs. Aiden didn't seem to object, even resting his hand against her low back. "You're becoming a vampire. There's a difference—a very critical difference." She pressed her hand to his cheek, feeling the rough stubble under her palm. "You and Zane still have a choice. To never take that first human life. Just as I never did. And you have the supplies and facilities here at The Oracle to do that less painfully."

"You're suggesting that Zane and I fully transition here? That's impossible."

"It's not impossible. I'm proof that it's not impossible." Lily leaned forward and touched her forehead to his. Their noses were nearly touching as she stared into those warm brown eyes, squeezed his hand in a gesture of encouragement. "You can do this. But we have to have a plan, and it has to start with you and

Zane accepting what's happening to you. Not being afraid of it. Because you don't have to be afraid."

Aiden sighed in resignation, breaking eye contact with her and dropping his gaze downward. "To do that would mean exposing to yourself to Alec, Dr. Li . . . to everyone, who you are."

"Then that's what we'll do."

"You have no idea what The Brethren will do when they find out they have a vampire living on *their* sacred ground. That's the one thing we were assured was not possible."

"I can handle it. Think about what this could mean for you—both of you! If this transition works, you'd be free to choose to stay here at The Oracle—your home—or to leave and search for Keegan, if that's what you wish. The point is, it's your choice . . . not one that someone has taken away from you."

Aiden reached up to thread his fingers through Lily's hair. There were times he just had this incredible gentleness about him, in spite of the fact he was a lethally trained Brethren hybrid transitioning to an even more dangerous vampire. His expression was quiet, intensely sincere, as he struggled to say, "You represent everything in this world I have been fighting . . .," his last word spoken with roughness, but Lily could somehow hear in his tone all the other words he left unsaid. How *she*, as a vampire, represented where he had invested all of his anger and hate since he had joined The Brethren nine years ago. Since he had lost his brother, Keegan. That all of his training and experiences, which led him to this moment, told him *she* should now be his enemy.

"You don't need to fight me," she said softly. "I'm a vampire, but I'm not your enemy."

Aiden simply drew his right hand down to rest below her collarbone, almost as if he were searching for the heartbeat she had not detected for some time. "You are what I am becoming. And God help me, I still want you, Lily Abbott . . . I *need* you. This changes nothing for me."

Lily was speechless. This man of few words had just somehow managed to make it impossible for another word to be spoken between them. She wasn't sure anyone had done that to her in her entire life!

She wondered if Aiden was experiencing the pull between them in that moment as strongly as she was. But he answered that thought by adjusting his position beneath her, bringing her close. So close, Lily suddenly became aware of the unsteadiness of her breath as his fingers pulled down the loose strap of the sundress he had hurriedly thrown on her earlier. The fabric fell easily over her shoulder and down her arm, exposing her creamy white breast to his view. His thumb began to caress her nipple in small circles, causing the nub to enlarge and harden. Her blood responded, racing inside her veins, causing Lily's face to revert to her vampire side.

"You are beautiful," Aiden said, in a dark, husky voice as continued to watch her, then without warning, dropped his head to take her breast into his mouth.

Lily gasped and arched her back quite naturally, allowing his tongue to massage and abrade her nipple until sparks began to fire like little electric shocks throughout her entire body. "More . . .," she pleaded. "Just a little more."

Aiden secured his hold around her, a smile coming to his lips that she could literally feel the pull of on the very most sensitive part of her nipple. "I've wanted you since that first night and saw you at Brahm Hill," he said before continuing his task.

Lily pressed her palms to the wall behind him, pushing her breast deeper into his mouth, even as she debated the wisdom of allowing the five-alarm-fire that was happening between them to continue. "It's natural you would feel that way," she swallowed with barely any breath. "Transfused soldiers—" this time her breath halted altogether when he lightly bit her nipple "—show a tendency to fixate all their energy on a single woman. Since I am around you most, it's logical that you would focus on me."

Aiden then pulled her in for a long kiss. When she tried to pull back so her fangs wouldn't cut into his lips, he brought her right back. His kisses forced her mouth to open wider, allowing his tongue to explore thoroughly. She felt his hands tugging hard at her dress. "I'm definitely fixated," he smiled into their kiss, displaying the confidence of a man who knew exactly what he wanted, and was unafraid of the danger their coupling might present to himself.

"Aiden, we should slow down." She was gasping for breath at this point. "This is dangerous for you—when I am changed like this."

He pulled back and stared at her, his breathing as heavy as hers. "You want to slow down?" he asked her. When she didn't answer right away, debating in her own head the answer, he smiled and added, "All right."

Lily wasn't quite sure what to expect next. He tugged and pulled at the loosely-fitted dress tangled around her legs. When her thighs were revealed beneath it, he started to caress and massage them with his strong hands. Lily inhaled the sensuality of the moment, breathing hard into his ear. This man knew how to touch her to drive her higher, and it surprised her how she could smell her own scent of citrus and lavender mixed with her natural womanly scent on his skin. As if somehow she was already a part of him.

"We can go slow, beauty. But this *is* happening this time." His confidence, his transitioning dominance, was on full display, and seeing it only made Lily want him more. He nipped at her ear before dragging his teeth along her neck. As he reached her main arterial vein, she wondered if he would drink from her again. It surprised her how much she wanted him to drink from her! "Tell me now if we should take this back to your room," he whispered to her.

Lily almost didn't hear the question she was so tuned to how he was making her feel. "No . . . here," she replied. "I can breathe easier here."

Without hesitation Aiden slid his hands to the juncture of her thighs, his fingers playfully searching her soft, wet flesh for that most sensitive spot, her clit. He brushed and teased, pretending he had lost it and then he would return. But, ooohh, did it feel good when he returned! For the first time in a very long time, Lily felt *warm.* Not just warm—*hot*! It was such a remarkable sensation, to remember human warmth. Hearing her approving moans, his fingers circled her clit faster. Lily's blood was surging furiously. The pleasure was overwhelming. *"More!"* she gasped as her hips came forward and her hands squeezed his shoulders with all the strength in them.

"Yes, more. Ask me for more, beauty," he whispered in her ear. "I want you to breathe easy. I want you to feel everything I'm about to do to you."

CHAPTER FIFTEEN

Aiden meant those words. He wanted Lily to feel every bit of pleasure he could give her. The why of it was simply a mystery to him. Was he being led by his hybrid lust? His new hybrid blood chemistry? Or was the answer more elemental, more basic. Vampire drawn to vampire. Was he latching on to the female his mind and body was selecting as a mating partner?

Right now he didn't care. He just knew he needed her.

His fingers continued to stroke and caress Lily's soft flesh. Her increasingly visceral moans delighted him. "How do you do this to me?" she asked him. "How do you make me feel so much when I've felt nothing for so long?"

"Come here," he said as he curled his arm low around her back and lifted her up to settle against his chest. Inserting his free hand between them, he clumsily sought the front panel of his jeans, considering his awkwardness justified as he realized the difficulty of balancing a woman while trying to unbutton his jeans in a haze of lust. That was just too much to ask of one man in that one moment!

Lily tilted her head back, inhaling a large breath as her fangs unsheathed further, reaching an impressive length. "Aiden . . ." She said his name as she dropped her chin to face him. Her eyes were the most brilliant blue color he'd ever seen . . . even for a vampire.

Finally, he'd gotten his miserable jeans open and had reached his hand inside, around his straining shaft. Stroking himself several times, he was now becoming the one inhaling labored breaths. Positioning Lily right above him, his other hand held his fully erect shaft beneath her, he slowly eased her down on him, controlling how she took him in. This time he made sure to notice that she was still with him in every moment of pleasure, and she was. She inhaled one big rush of breath, then exhaled a long, sighing moan. It was the most beautiful sound he had ever heard, like a combination of desperate need and complete satisfaction, all at once.

"Feels good?" he asked, his hold on her leveraging her weight at her hips as he continued to draw her down on him in slow increments.

Lily didn't answer but flattened her palms against the wall behind him and nodded quickly. Yeah, she definitely seemed to be enjoying the feel of him inside her.

Moments later, he felt the head of his cock pressing against her cervix. That wasn't surprising, since everything about him was very long, but he wanted to make certain he wasn't going to hurt her. Gently, his hands shifted, and he lifted her slight weight upward, drawing her down again. He repeated the motion several times, and each time her inner walls adjusted around him more easily, more readily.

Then she began to roll her hips on her own. At first slowly, then she increased her pace. Aiden released his controlling hands, allowing her to move freely as she liked. They maintained their lock on each other's eyes as her movements began to take him to another level of pleasure entirely. A place where the only sound he could hear was his own breath inside his ears. He growled under those breaths and dropped his head back against the wall, letting her move however the hell she wanted. Her body felt fantastic! Her inner muscles encompassing every inch of his rock-hard flesh, tightening and pulling at him until he thought he might lose the ability to breathe altogether.

"Yes, beauty," he whispered, needing this woman unlike any other lover he could remember in his life. ". . . Just like that."

Lily kept whispering his name, as if the very word was something solid for her to hold on to while the rest of the world threatened to fall away.

"That's it . . . Let it come," he whispered. "Lily . . . my beautiful Lily."

Oh, damn, she was tightening around him. She was moving fast now, and he could feel how close she was to shattering. Moments later, she did exactly that, crying out loudly, and holding back nothing! Aiden could see on her face, in those beautiful eyes, that she knew she deserved this pleasure. He loved that! He wanted her to have every moment of it, every cry, every sighing breath. And when her wail rent the air at the same moment she exploded around him, the sound was like the sweetest music he had ever heard. She pulled at him with curled fingers, her gasps coming hard, at erratic intervals, as her inner muscles repeatedly tempted him to give in to his own explosion. But Aiden held steady and continued to rock into her orgasm so she could experience every last moment of pleasure he could give her. "Aiden!" she cried out one last time and then fell limp against his shoulder.

They sat there, curled up like that, for several moments. He was still hard inside her, and an amazing sensation was still welling inside him, even though he desperately wanted to finish. Lily stared up at him, her face showing him the soft, sated beauty that made his gut clench with pride. "You didn't . . .?" she began, her expression questioning.

"Don't you worry, beauty," he said, kissing her sweetly on her lips. "We're getting there." He leaned forward, balancing her on his lap while somehow removing the jacket from his shoulders, one arm at a time. When he was free, he spread the coat out over the steel floor behind her and gently laid her back onto it. His body rose over hers as he curled her legs around him.

Lily was breathing in deep, full breaths beneath him, as if she were trying to take in as much air as possible. He hoped they were breaths of anticipation but he sensed it was something else. "Are you all right?" he asked, brushing his hand along her smooth cheek.

Her skin was dewy, her gaze certain as she nodded her head. "I like being with you like this . . . I need it. I just lose my breath here sometimes."

Aiden smiled, taking the time to remove her dress completely so he could just take in the whole amazing body underneath. "It's amazing to me that you have adapted to sacred ground as well as you have," he said while taking note of her buttery soft skin and breasts that were just the right size for his hands. Her hips had a little curve to them that molded perfectly to his palm. She seemed even to be taunting him a bit as he removed the dress, arching her back and breasts to tempt him further. He loved that she was not embarrassed by her body. Nothing was worse than when a woman tried to hide herself.

When the last bit of clothing came off, he situated himself above her, threading his fingers through her hair as he supported her head, entwining his body with hers from head to toe. He slid his other hand down her buttery skin, all the way to her lower thigh and curled her leg upward around his hip. With one hard thrust he entered her, and the remembered feeling were as if he'd died and gone to heaven. He pulled back and thrust forward again. Lily gasped hard as Aiden claimed every inch her body had to give him. This woman felt perfect. Her nails dug into his back as her legs tightened around him. He plunged into her several more times. The pleasure he fought to hold back at each thrust telling him he was on the precipice of a major orgasm. He wanted to be close to her, inside her like this, overwhelmed by the sensations like this . . . he wanted everything she had to give him! "Do you trust me?" he asked her, his hand supporting her head now arching her neck upward.

Lily nodded quickly. "Yes," she answered.

Aiden smiled and pulled her forward, his breath hard against her skin. He drove his fangs into her neck, holding her tight as he drank from her throat.

***

Lily reveled in the shuddering sensations that were sparking her from head to toe. Aiden stilled his body as he drank from her throat. She wanted to protest the delay to climaxing again but there was a whole new series of sensations for her to absorb. Her inner muscles still trembled around his cock from the first massive orgasm she had experienced earlier. Her skin felt warm and finely misted with her own sweat as blood rushed through her veins and Aiden drank arduously from her throat. Every feeling made her want to freeze this moment in time, because she was feeling something! Something wonderful! She had feared that long-gone were the days of powerful, passionate intimacy with someone she really cared about. Times when sex was about more than just a primal need. "Yes," she moaned, a broad smile coming to her lips while luxuriating in the feeling of her fingers threading through his soft, chestnut hair and knowing that this sense of wonder could still be hers.

Aiden pulled his long fangs from her throat, his eyes swirling, now almost entirely in blue. He looked up to the ceiling of the tunnel and then closed his eyes. His large hand clutched around her thigh and he thrust forward several times, penetrating her deeply. "Fuck," he said, breathlessly, before settling into a more controlled, more even rhythm. He lowered his chin, bringing his neck to her lips. "Drink from me," he said.

Lily squeezed his arms as he continued to drive her body higher. Her hands slid down his sweat-misted back and beneath his loose clothing, sliding his jeans and boxers farther down his buttocks before squeezing firmly over the two muscled rounds of flesh. With each thrust, she felt imprinted by him, owned. Lily had imagined being with Aiden sexually many times. Right now he was exceeding any and all of her fantasies, but that didn't mean she could have everything she desired. This tiny, negative thought began to dull her perceptions.

"We can't . . .," but that was as far as she got. She then moaned louder as Aiden's thrusts suddenly became stronger. His strength was impressive and left little doubt in her mind that he was well on his way to becoming a powerful vampire. The jacket she was lying on slid back and forth along the floor beneath her, but the rhythmic rocking of their movements, and his interlocking hold on her, ensured she would not go far. The sex between them was simply the best feeling her vampire life could offer. Never would she know what it would be like to carry a child. Celeste stole that right from her the night she turned her. She would never age, never know human disease or sickness. But she could know great intimacy with Aiden, to feel him erupt inside her without worry. And that was enough, she decided, reconciling herself to her fate.

Soon Lily could feel her inner muscles tighten again, and her hips rose. She clutched Aiden's shoulders and barely kept breathing. What breath she did have evolved into a passionate cry as she climaxed around him a second time. Aiden's orgasm arrived just at the height of hers, and she enjoyed watching him take his pleasure. His joy was radiant on his face and audible in his groans. He seemed to sink into the moment, relaxing so all his weight collapsed on her for a few seconds, making her feeling of oneness complete. The whole experience was so gratifying for Lily that she nearly forgot where they were.

Her happy fortune changed, however, when Aiden pulled himself from her body almost immediately upon finishing. He was perfectly polite in how he created the distance, putting on a careful smile and reaching for her dress to hand to her, a wordless request to put it back on. No loving talk between them? No body contact? The chill she felt after he left her in such an intimate moment threatened to rival the day he'd left her standing in the lobby of The Oracle as he walked out.

Aiden sat up and rubbed his cheeks. While in most situations he maintained a very quiet look about him, showing the world a very neutral facial expression, right now the look appeared rather confused, perhaps even frustrated. She ignored the dress he offered, instead pulling his coat around her, unsure why the mood had changed so quickly. Finally, he asked, "Why won't you drink from me?"

Lily blinked and rose to sit beside him, still bewildered.

"You let me drink from you, but you wouldn't drink from me."

"Aiden, you must know it's too dangerous. We've no idea what my bite might do to you before you're fully transitioned. There's no precedent for this. I won't risk hurting you like that."

"Even if it's what I want?"

"And what if my bite turns you within hours? Are you prepared for that consequence?" Aiden turned his head away from her. It was pretty clear to Lily that he was not at all prepared for that. Lily rubbed her hand along his arm, letting his jacket fall back to the floor. She already felt completely comfortable with him in her nudity. "Until you've fully turned, there is always hope we can stop this. I want you to have that hope."

Aiden turned back to her, capturing her lips in a passionate, steal-all-the-breath from her lungs, kiss, then clumsily spread the jacket once more on the floor behind her. He guided her down gently, never letting go of their kiss until she was lying flat beneath him. "I accept this change—who I am becoming. I want this strength. I want to be with you like this. And I *want* you to drink from me."

Lily lifted her palm to one of his cheeks, her heart-space as open and sincere as the day she was human. "We can be together like this. That doesn't require you to make a life-altering decision today. You forget, I know what that's like to have your human life stripped from you in an instant. I will never experience things such as hunger for real food, or a consistent need for sleep. I'll never give birth to my own child. Celeste stole all of that from me. I won't do the same to you."

"Lily, I don't—"

Aiden stopped and they both turned their attention toward the lab entry of the corridor. They had been so preoccupied with their lovemaking and discussion that neither of them had paid attention to the fact that others had entered the lab and were now headed straight for them.

In fact, they were practically on top of them!

The next seconds were a mad scramble for clothes as the door at the other end opened and Dr. Li stepped inside, accompanied by several guards. He walked towards them with purposeful strides, his eyes going straight to the detailed drawings on the wall. "What is this? How did you two get in here? You know this area is off limits." Dr. Li then scanned Lily more closely and saw the blood droplets left on her neck from where Aiden had drank from her. The bite itself was already healed, but Dr. Li knew how to recognize a vampire bite. "Aiden, you'll need to come with us," he added, and nodded to the guards. "Right now."

"No, Dr. Li," Lily responded, stepping between Aiden and the guards. "This isn't what you think."

"Don't interfere, here Miss Abbott. It's obvious that Aiden's transitioning much faster than I anticipated. He needs to be examined and monitored until we figure out the next steps—for both his safety and your own."

Lily had no idea what had gotten into her, but she had grown tired of Aiden being examined like a lab rat. He had complied with almost everything they asked of him . . . and still they took away all of his choices. "No!" she shouted back at them as a way to halt the guards. "You're not taking him. Just give us a chance to explain."

The guards ignored Lily and proceeded to go for Aiden.

"Lily, it's all right. I'll go with them," Aiden said, but she could see by the stern look on his face as they grabbed hold of him that he was not happy about it.

Lily decided she was done playing nice. Aiden had played by their rules, submitted to every test, and where had it gotten him? The minute Dr. Li decided there was no way to stop his transition, Aiden became something that had to be locked away and separated from everyone else. She wouldn't let that happen. "I said no!" she shouted, a moment before her face shifted in front of all of them.

No longer was it the face of a Dhampir with fangs; this was the full shift of a vampire, and it caught all of them totally by surprise as she pushed the guards back from Aiden.

"What the . . .?" Dr. Li blinked with utter astonishment, and in just that moment, one of the guards raised his crossbow and fired a direct shot at her.

Lily hadn't considered that these men she had worked alongside might ever turn on her so fast. The arrow slammed into her chest and went straight into to her heart. The pain of the silver tip piercing through her skin froze her instantly. Her skin began to burn, and she suddenly had severe trouble breathing. Her normal reaction as a vampire would be to yank out the offending weapon, but she couldn't do that because silver lodged into a vampire's heart rendered the creature immediately frozen. She fell back from the force of the weapon and would have crashed onto the floor, stiff as a board, had it not been for Aiden catching her.

"Back off!" he yelled, swinging her around so his back was shielding her in case one of the guards might try to shoot another arrow. "She wouldn't have hurt you!"

"Stand down," Dr. Li ordered, and the guards heeded his order immediately, even though they were just as stunned by what they were seeing as was the doctor himself.

Dr. Li approached Lily. "How is this possible?"

"She would have explained if you'd given her a chance."

"Set her down, Aiden. If you don't want to see her hurt any further, then surrender to the guards. You know it's your only choice here."

Aiden snarled at the doctor, and for a moment it looked as if he was prepared to fight all of them, but he did as the doctor commanded. He gently set Lily down on the steel floor and rose to his feet, and the guards immediately grabbed him.

With Aiden restrained, Dr. Li used the opportunity to crouch over Lily to make a quick examination. She could see and feel everything that was happening, even underneath the fiery pain burning through her, but she could not speak or move. It was damn frustrating!

"At least remove the goddamn arrow so she can breathe," Aiden snapped at the doctor as he fought once more against the guards restraining him.

"Not just yet," Dr. Li replied. He then reached out to touch Lily's cold skin.

That made Aiden furious. "Do not touch her! I'll kill you if you touch her again!"

Dr. Li looked back at Aiden with rather minimal surprise, and then he turned back to Lily. There seemed to be some flash of recognition in the doctor's eyes before one of the guards said to Aiden, "Calm down, man. We don't want to hurt you."

Aiden then felt a needle being jabbed into his arm. It had to be jabbed because the closer Aiden came to being a vampire, the tougher his skin and everything about him was becoming. "Fuck!"

he said as he felt his limbs becoming limp beneath him. They gave him something that would knock him out in a matter of seconds. He pointed a sharp finger at the doctor and said, "Don't touch her again! You touch or hurt her and you'll answer to me."

Lily watched Aiden collapse to his knees under the drug they had injected in him. She wanted desperately to reach out to him, but she was stick straight like a damn Popsicle, paralyzed by the silver arrow in her chest.

One of the guards held onto Aiden to keep him from falling completely. "What would you like us to do with him, doctor?"

"I'm not sure," he replied, a perplexed look on his expression. "We seem to have a bigger problem on our hands here, gentlemen. It appears Aiden has identified his mate. And she is a vampire on sacred ground."

CHAPTER SIXTEEN

Lily jerked in response to the white hot pain reignited and suddenly blooming inside her chest after one of the guards had ripped out the silver-tipped arrow lodged through her heart. She gasped and sputtered, trying to get her breath back, then rolled onto her side atop the enormous ottoman she had been placed on.

"I had the guards bring you up to Elder Lambert's private Library by stretcher," Gideon told her.

Lily glanced back to see Gideon and Dr. Li standing across the room with several additional guards. "You won't need the guards," she told them. "I've been among you for several months now. If I wanted to hurt anyone, I would have done so long ago."

"Yes," Gideon agreed. "A rather astonishing fact. And one of many points which obviously need to be discussed. Unfortunately, Elder Lambert is detained for the moment."

"He needs to be here for this," Dr. Li interjected, his voice sharp with criticism. "A vampire discovered living among us on sacred ground affects the safety of every person here."

In response Gideon proceeded to clean his glasses on the tail of his shirt. "Of course he would, but I'm afraid it's quite impossible at the moment. He has asked that I take his place and report to him later."

"That doesn't make any—"

"Where's Aiden?" Lily interrupted the doctor. She sat up to a seated position on the ottoman while covering the bloody wound in her chest with her hand. The guards stood ready to respond, but Gideon motioned to one of them to bring over a warm water basin and a towel from a nearby table.

"You may use this to clean your wound," he said. "And Aiden is fine. Dr. Li has already examined him and given him something to calm him down. He's under guard in a room down the hall."

Lily directed a small snort of laughter at Dr. Li. "Aiden hasn't been taking the medication you've given him . . . not for weeks. I doubt he's going to start now."

Dr. Li's lips thinned. "He was given an injection, not pills."

"Regardless," Gideon continued, "Aiden has made it very clear that we are not to touch you, Miss Abbott. And considering all of the shocking revelations we've had today, I think it's a good idea to listen to him on this one."

"Under guard, but not locked up?" Lily questioned. It was very important to her, aside from the fact Aiden was okay, that he was not locked up.

The two men exchanged a quick glance that seemed to say there had already been much discussion on the subject. "I feel confident in speaking for Elder Lambert here. It has never been his intention to have either Aiden or Zane locked up," Gideon replied, while Dr. Li remained quiet beside him. "They are a part of this community. We want to help them. Especially after they've been so wronged by Reese and his tests."

Hope filled Lily's chest for the first time in a long while. "If that's true, then let me help you." She finished cleaning the blood from her wound as best she could and rose slowly to her feet so the guards didn't sense a threat to Gideon or the doctor. "What's happening to them doesn't have to be something bad. We can still save them. I am proof of that."

Gideon took a few steps forward, cutting the distance between them in half. "Proof of what, exactly? I'm not sure why a vampire would choose to take refuge among the very people trained to kill her . . . or how it's possible that you can. Even the Daywalkers we have met have not been able to pass onto our lands. It is an understatement to say that the very fact you are here is quite remarkable."

"I have never taken a life. That is how I am here among you."

Gideon took another step forward, his hand motioning for the guards to stay back. "How have your fed your thirst?"

"Initially, I fed from my sire, Celeste, to survive. Then I began to trap small animals."

Gideon nodded, appearing to slowly take in Lily's admissions. "Now it makes sense why your sire is here. The question is, why does she want you back so badly? Even a vampire from her coven has not merited this kind of effort from her in the past."

"She needs my gift. If there was a way for her to steal it from me, I'm sure she wouldn't hesitate to kill me."

"Your gift?" Gideon questioned.

"The drawings," Dr. Li answered.

"Ah, yes, the drawings . . . remarkable, they are . . ."

"Yes, Gideon," Dr. Li began, "I think we're getting the idea that you find this all remarkable. I, on the other hand, find it disturbing how something like this could be possible and we've remained so completely unaware of it."

"On the contrary," Gideon countered. "I think I was made aware of it . . . I just missed the signs."

Gideon turned back to Lily. "The woman being held captive that night at Brahm Hill, Olivia Greyson-Wolfe, had the gift to be able to see inside a vampire's consciousness. She had discussed with me previously a theory she had about the darkness inside a vampire. She was positive that there are levels to the darkness. If that were true, it would stand to reason that those who have remained purest to their original human form—in other words, not to have killed humans for food—would have the greatest freedom. At the time, I didn't take the theory seriously because I had never witnessed anything that would lead me to question that such a thing might be possible. We know vampires are led solely by their thirst. But the Daywalkers—and now you, Miss Abbott—are physical proof that her theory is correct. That is . . . well, remarkable."

"I don't know about all of that . . . but I survived it. And it's why I came here to The Oracle. I knew, because of what I had gone through, that I could help Aiden and Zane."

"You sensed on that night of Brahm Hill that they were changing?" Dr. Li questioned.

"I sensed it in Aiden because I'd been given a hint to look for it," she replied.

"How?"

"I believe she is talking about the drawings again," Gideon said. "That is your gift that Celeste wants so badly."

Lily nodded. "The drawings have given her warning of oncoming threats and saved her ass on more than one occasion."

"You're implying you see these images of the future? That would, indeed, be a tremendous gift."

Lily sighed. "How can something be a gift when I only see bad things?"

"You must be careful how you interpret 'bad things'," Gideon replied. "These events are important, just by virtue of the fact that you're allowed to see them. That also could mean you have an opportunity to affect the outcome . . . though any specific outcome is never guaranteed."

"All that's important right now is that I believe can help Aiden and Zane. They can make this transition and remain on sacred ground as long as they never make that first kill."

"I can't believe this . . ." Dr. Li replied. "You can't seriously be suggesting that these men transition on sacred ground among a smorgasbord of people to feast upon. Not to mention the transition here would kill them!"

"That's exactly what I am suggesting. I'll admit it will not be easy. It's difficult at best when all you can think about after being turned is your thirst. Trust me, I know. But they can survive it, and The Oracle has the blood supplies and the treatment facilities needed for them to make a safe transition. Safe for them and safe for all the people here."

Dr. Li blew out a rough breath at the notion he considered nonsense, but Lily did not let that deter her.

"We know Aiden's and Zane's transition is different from other vampires. Theirs is not a turning that's a shock to the system in twenty-four hours, like normal turning's are. What's happening to them had been happening slowly over the last year. Their turning is more controlled. We can use that to our advantage."

Gideon drew his glasses from his nose and began to clean them again on his shirt-tail. After seeing him do this several times, Lily couldn't decide if the glasses were really dirty or if this was how the man thought his way through stressful situations. "Isn't Aiden already compromised? Dr. Li mentioned seeing the bite marks on your neck in the tunnel."

"That's different . . .," Lily began, then paused, not quite sure if she should finish. "He wasn't biting me with the intention to harm or kill."

"No, he was drinking from the woman he has identified as his future mate," Dr. Li replied. "Aiden's reaction to you being struck by the arrow in that tunnel wasn't merely a man trying to protect a woman, it was a vampire trying to protect his mate at all cost. Because, as he sees it, your wellbeing is now directly tied to his."

Lily remembered Dr. Li having said that Aiden was trying to mate her when she was on the floor in the tunnel. She hadn't had a lot of time to process the information, but she thought back to her time there with Aiden, before they had been discovered. When he was inside her, she felt, on some level, as if she was supposed to be with him. Despite what she had told Aiden about the dangers, she had wanted desperately to drink from him. She wanted to bring him closer to her by connecting them with blood. But, in the end, she couldn't do that to him. They hadn't known each other long. What if they were both wrong? What if all they were feeling was simple lust? That also was common in the vampire world. After all, it wasn't as if she's had any experience with this kind of thing before. She had been with men when she was human but not since she was turned. She had found that eliminating sex made it easier to control her thirst.

Unfortunately, the side effect now was that she wanted to taste Aiden's blood almost desperately . . . and she wanted to have sex with him again.

"Has Aiden mated you, Miss Abbott?" Gideon asked into her desirous thoughts.

Lily knew Gideon was asking specifically about if they had exchanged blood. That was the only way for vampires to mate, and once the action was complete there was no turning back. They had not exchanged blood, but she felt resentful of the question. She lifted her chin, straightening her back. "Quite frankly, that's none of your business."

"Actually, it is, when it comes to the effectiveness of treating Aiden," Dr. Li replied. "If he believes your are his mate and feels threatened that someone is blocking that from happening—a characteristic inherent in all male vampires once their mate has been selected—he will fight to the death to defend you. And that will only expedite his transition."

"That's a very logical assumption," Gideon replied.

Lily compressed her lips, hating that she couldn't keep whatever this was between her and Aiden separate from his transition. But she knew, deep down, that was impossible. From Gideon's and Dr. Li's perspectives, the other ten Guardians, who had already succumbed to the effects of the transfusions, targeted women before they exhibited signs of extreme aggression. So far, Aiden and Zane had not shown those signs to the same degree, but their absence didn't mean that his focus on her was not of significant concern to them. "We're not mated," she answered both men. "And we won't be, at least not for now. I want to focus on how to make this transition happen as smoothly as possible for him."

Dr. Li came forward. "So what's your plan?"

Lily was pleased to hear that Dr. Li was at least open to hearing her plan. "The plan is to set up a portion of the labs to allow them to transition fully, here, on sacred ground. They're going to need a lot of blood—fresh blood—but also be allowed to stay someplace safe, where they can feel unthreatened. They'll need access to lands off the property to adjust to their new abilities and for us to be able to measure how far along they are. If we do this right, they can continue to have a life here. I'm asking you to give them that chance."

"We can't have these men running around off the property," Dr. Li pointed out angrily. "It would be completely irresponsible of us with regard to the safety of everyone else out there."

Lily returned a fierce expression. "So how, exactly, did you plan on taking care of the situation once you decided their transition could not be reversed?"

"I can assure you," Gideon began, obviously in all sincerity, "Elder Lambert never would've allowed any harm to come to those men, if that's what you're asking. Never."

"Then that means they would've been turned out to fend for themselves. The risk to my plan is no greater than that, and I would argue that its merits for success are much higher."

Both men were quiet for a long while, their thoughts seeming to be mired in deep concentration. "If this is the answer," Dr. Li began, "then why has it taken so long for you to come forward? Why the charade of working with me and my staff?"

"I needed information on how far along they were in the process. And I needed to get familiar with this facility to know the best way to treat them safely. As I said, this is not a typical turning. We don't know how long this is going to take."

"I don't know about this, Gideon," Dr. Li said. "Both men are exhibiting signs of Alpha behavior. This is a huge risk. There will come a point where they are stronger and more powerful than anyone here."

"I'm a vampire," Lily replied. "I can stay with them. And I can provide them with fresh blood to drink to supplement non-fresh blood."

Gideon turned to her. "Fresh blood? As in drinking from you . . . like a sire? You know as well as we do that if Aiden's trying to mate you, he will never allow Zane to touch you, even if it's to help him with his transition."

Lily sighed, recognizing instantly that Gideon had a very good point she had not considered. When Lily had thought of this plan, it had never occurred to her that she would fall so hard for Aiden. And now that she had, and Aiden seem to care just as much for her, it did put a big hole in her plans. "Let me talk to him. I know he cares for Zane. He's very loyal to him because of what they've both had to go through with these transfusions."

"I think we should consider the option of feeding Zane bagged blood—" Gideon began, but Lily was shaking her head.

"They're both going to need fresh vampire blood to get through this. And especially Zane, since he doesn't appear to be trying to mate right now. Drinking for a new vampire is about more than the blood. It's about the security of the action. They're learning to do what's natural to the creature they are becoming. Drinking from the throat is nourishing to them, comforting. As strange as it sounds, it's true. After a victim has been turned, it's very common for the sire to offer their blood for some time. It was that way for me with Celeste. As much as I despised her, I needed her blood to keep me alive, especially because I refused to kill humans in order to drink."

"I find it hard to believe that's a common action for Caelestis," Gideon said. "Every act of violence in her history suggests a significant detachment from the consequences of those actions. But what you're suggesting would be in complete contrast to that."

"Trust me. I was there. She offered it . . ."

Gideon's face reflected the depth of his thinking. First he had a perplexed look on his face, but then he brightened and said, "Perhaps, in trying to keep you alive because you refused to drink, she formed a bond with you she does not have with the others in her coven? It might explain why she's still wants you with her."

"The only bond Celeste has is with her own ego. I merely provide her access to a gift that'll warn her of who might be coming at her next."

"I'm not so sure about that. You're talking about building a bond with a sire. As acting sire to Aiden and Zane, you would be building that bond with both men. We must all carefully consider that if it's possible for a six–hundred-year-old vampire like Caelestis to feel more connected to you, then it may also hold true with them—including Zane. Are you sure you're prepared for that?"

"Yes," Lily responded without hesitation, though she wondered if she should consider it the question a bit more thoroughly.

Dr. Li straightened his glasses on his nose, an action that reflected the doctor's unease. "What she's proposing is dangerous, Gideon—dangerous for them, for her, for the people here. I don't know if I can be a party to this."

"What do you propose as the alternative?" Gideon asked him. "You yourself told me, not an hour ago, that they are too far along in the process and that you have no way to stop the transition. So are we to just throw them out and let them fend for themselves? I think you know, we owe them more than that. Elder Lambert certainly knows that."

Dr. Li sighed heavily. "I have no other solution."

"Then I suggest you get your people working on changing out some of lab offices into comfortable rooms for them to stay in while they're transitioning. But I agree with you, we must keep tight control of this situation."

Lily was about to further question the "tight control" when Gideon turned to her. "I'm sorry, but we're going to have to implement strict security procedures. That's the only way any of us can feel good about agreeing to this. We still have an obligation to protect the people here at The Oracle."

"If you'll excuse me, I need to get some things prepared," Dr. Li said, moving toward the door.

After Dr. Li had left, Gideon excused the guards so he could speak with Lily alone. "There is still the matter of what's to be done about you, Miss Abbott. You may not have come here with the intention of harming anyone, but that doesn't mean we can just ignore the possibility. You're a vampire. And you're proof that the one thing we all felt certain of—that vampires cannot cross onto sacred ground—is not true."

"Nearly everyone here has the capacity to harm someone else. They are super-human. But they don't, because they want to be here. They respect the life and the purpose created here. I am no different from them. I want this to be my home, too."

"And what of Caelestis . . .?"

"I believe Celeste will move on."

"I don't agree. If she has remained here all this time, she has a purpose for doing so. You seem to be that purpose."

"Let's get Aiden and Zane through their transition. We don't have a lot of time to prepare. Then we'll deal with Celeste together."

"I can agree to that. For now, I would like you to stay in your room, under guard supervision, until arrangements can be made for all of you in the labs."

"Can I see Aiden? I want to make sure he's all right."

Gideon considered her request for a long moment, then responded, "I'll have the guards take you to see him once we have some temporary living quarters set up in the labs."

Lily frowned, realizing that answer meant she would not see Aiden tonight. She was surprised at how much that affected her, how much she craved to see him. But she still had a job to do, and she needed to show both Gideon and Dr. Li that she took this plan of hers to help Aiden and Zane seriously.

"When you do see Aiden, you'll need to be careful. Whether he's loyal to Zane or not, I'm afraid he'll not take well to your plan to transition them both."

"My relationship with Aiden is separate from this—"

"Aiden will never see it that way. He is now a vampire who has chosen his mate. Until that task is complete he will focus on little else."

Lily rubbed her hands tiredly over her face. "Unless he wants to doom Zane to a life on the dark side; then he will have no choice."

"You might be surprised that is exactly what he *will* choose."

CHAPTER SEVENTEEN

Before dawn on the following morning, the guards escorted Lily to what would be her temporary home. Along with Aiden and Zane, she would be in a cordoned off area inside the labs, an area they now referred to as the North sector. The space included three offices that had been quickly converted into habitable living quarters, common restroom with one shower to share, and a former glass lab that was now an open meeting space with some soft seating. This rec-room-type of environment provided a place to roam so they did not have to spend all of their time in their sleeping quarters.

"This will be your room," the guard said to Lily as he opened the steel door. "Hopefully it will be to your satisfaction. Gideon instructed us if there was anything you needed, we were to ensure that you had it." Lily glanced around the comfortable-looking room and was pleased with what she saw. The bed was full-sized instead of a single and was fitted with some basic linens and blankets. A small sofa had been placed along the opposite wall, along with a small desk and a book case, filled with books that had been brought down from her upstairs quarters. On the table beside her bed she noticed a wash basin, toiletry items, towels, and even a pitcher of water.

"This should work fine," Lily acknowledged. "Are Aiden and Zane's rooms similar?"

The guard nodded. "The walls in these offices have been reinforced with steel panels and doors." Lily noted that the panels appeared to be identical to the ones that lined the underground tunnel. "You'll have privacy in your rooms, but there are cameras recording in the common space at all times."

"Concrete bearing walls, steel panels and doors—and cameras. I guess we aren't going anywhere," she teased.

"No, ma'am," he replied, "At least . . . not that we won't know about or be able to track." He then walked through the common space to another steel door at one end of the room. "Gideon has authorized access to the tunnel and outside lands through here." He pointed to a secured access panel on the front of it. "The code changes every four hours, so you will need to get the current one from the staff. The tunnel is also being monitored with cameras and voice equipment as you come and go. Is there anything else I can answer for you?"

"Where are Aiden and Zane?"

"In their rooms. The doors will be released as soon as we leave this section."

Lily blinked back at the guard. "Is that really necessary?"

"We've been instructed to adhere to strict protocols when coming a going through this area."

"By whom?"

"Dr. Li."

Lily glanced up at one of the cameras with a look that said she was well aware that the doctor was probably watching them at this very moment. "Of course. You have your orders to follow."

"Well, then, if that is all, we will be on our way." He motioned the rest of the guards to follow him toward the door leading back into the rest of the laboratory facilities.

Lily turned and focused her attention on the other two doors that led away from the common room. One shared a wall with her room, and the other was on the opposite side of the common space. She walked to the room alongside her own, knowing that it was Aiden's room; she sensed that he was in there.

She turned back to one of the cameras. "Open the doors," she instructed, but she was surprised when she heard only the click of the lock on the door in front of her. Knocking lightly, she called his name, "Aiden?"

When he didn't answer, she turned the handle and pushed the door open enough for her to see into his room. Aiden was standing there quietly, watching her as she entered, closed the door, and rushed to him. He reached out his arms to greet her and pulled her in close, surrounding Lily with his strength. She raised her head to stare up directly into his concerned expression as he threaded his free hand through her loose bun, unraveling several pins in an instant before he lowered his head and kissed her lips, gently at first, then with more passion. Lily felt the response in her stomach and instantly re-lived and re-felt the memory of having him inside her, pleasing her body with all of his quiet strength. He brushed her lips one final time before he whispered in her ear, "Are you all right?"

Lily nodded with a smile. "I was about to ask you the same thing."

He drew a finger down the front of her shirt, releasing several buttons from their holes as his finger moved across her skin and revealed the place where the arrow had gone into her heart. "Are you all right?" he asked again, with even greater resonance and concern in his voice. "Did they touch you—*hurt you?*

She stared up at him, realizing what was causing all of his concern and remembering what Dr. Li had said, *'you're wellbeing is now directly tied to his'*. "They did not touch me and I'm all healed. You don't need to worry."

"Can I see that for myself?"

Lily tipped her head back. He pulled the shirt open wider, thoroughly examining the area before releasing the shirt completely from her shoulders, exposing her bare breasts to him. A sexy smile crossed his lips. "You're not wearing a bra."

"No, I'm not," she smiled, watching him continue to stare. "You don't have to ogle them," she laughed.

"Yes I do," he replied, playfully sliding his fingers down to caress the soft mound of one breast. He was very gentle as he lowered his head and kissed her already engorged nipple. His lips on her skin and that tongue swirling around in all sorts of delicious ways was all it took to make her whole body shudder. "You do seem better," he said, and she could feel the smile pull across his lips as he continued to adore her nipple. "But if I never see you shot through the heart again, it will be too soon. You scared the shit out of me."

"You know I am only paralyzed by an arrow to the heart, not killed."

He gazed down at her, his expression agonizingly sincere. "It's one thing to know that when you're fighting faceless Nightwalkers. But it's another matter entirely when you're watching it happen to someone you . . ." He didn't continue his thought, just finishing with, "You looked so still and lifeless . . . I hated it." His hand slid farther into her shirt and massaged her entire breast as he resumed kissing her mouth, taking playful little nibbles with his teeth. She moaned beneath his kiss and didn't feel any particular rush to stop him. But she needed to.

"Aiden, this feels really nice, but . . . we should talk about why we're here."

Aiden withdrew his kiss slowly, tipping his head until their foreheads met. "I suppose I should thank you for convincing Gideon and Dr. Li to let us transition here."

"So they've explained that much to you?"

Aiden didn't answer. Instead, he led her toward his bed, which he had pushed to the corner of the room. It was a double, like hers, but his super tall frame made it a sure thing that his feet would hang over the end of it as he slept. He sat on the bed and pulled her down beside him, kissing her several times before guiding her to lie flat against the mattress. Lily became aware of every physical aspect of the moment. His body was totally overwhelming as he lay down beside her. Long, lean legs. A broad, firm chest and strong arms that were so good at making a woman feel safe when she was wrapped inside them. This was the kind of man any woman would dream of kissing. Oh, there were stop-you-in-your-tracks gorgeous men, like Kane. Sexy, take-charge leaders like Alec. Dangerous bad boys, like Zane. But Aiden was the strong, quiet man who didn't have to say a single word to hold your attention. The intelligence and intensity that were such an inviting draw to the man inside were all there in his eyes. Right now, those eyes said he wanted her!

His kisses became more urgent, his hands more insistent as they continued to draw her shirt fully open to the hem. "Uh-hum!" she said, clearing her throat. "This is not talking."

"Let's talk later," he replied. "Right now, I'd like to concentrate on seducing you."

"Seducing me, huh."

"Damn right."

Lily was definitely feeling a little breathy at the moment, but she knew she had to talk to him, and couldn't wait. The success of her whole plan rested on Aiden's cooperation. "Aiden," she insisted, pushing back gently, but remaining in his embrace on the bed. "We need to talk before . . . that part."

He groaned and dropped his head back against the mattress. "Whatever you want to talk about, the answer is, yes."

"I don't think that will be the case once you know what it is we need to discuss."

Aiden rolled onto his side, his hand caressing her back, and kissed the tip of her nose. "Try me, beauty," he responded gently. "I can be a very agreeable man when it's accompanied with the promise of sex with you."

"Of that I have no doubt," she teased before her expression turned more serious. "Did Dr. Li explain to you and Zane why you've been brought here—what our plan is? Well . . . I guess it's my plan . . ."

Aiden nodded. "As you can imagine, Zane's not happy about it."

"Why? This will help him in the end."

"We're still locked up."

Lily felt the hard pull of her frown. "You can't look at it that way. You have to realize what it can bring you in the future."

Aiden sighed. "Yes, but it means accepting that there's no stopping our transition. Over the past year we've gotten used to the headaches, the sleeplessness—the bouts of anger . . ."

"I think I understand what you're saying. Getting used to something tricks you into believing you can beat it."

Lily saw in his expression that she was right on target. "Well said," he whispered, staring thoughtfully at her as his hand stroked her arm. "How have you gone all of this time without

174

feeding on a human?" he asked, not really as a question, but more as a statement of admiration.

"It doesn't bother you, then, that I'm a vampire?"

He shook his head, his hand moving from her arm to her cheek. "Like I said, you are what I am becoming. We are the same. You give me hope that I'm not destined to become some horrible monster."

"You could never be a monster. Not to me." Lily reached for his hand, playing with his long fingers as she thought about the tremendous struggle ahead for both him and for Zane. "But this won't be easy."

"No, it won't," he replied quietly, his steady voice and serious expression conveying a full understanding of what he was about to take on. "But I'm grateful . . . because this is a choice I didn't have, even two days ago."

Lily stared at him for a long while. Despite all of her good intentions to help both Aiden and Zane, she still wondered whether she had accomplished anything yet. The hard part was still very much ahead of them. "I need to talk to you about . . . about Zane, actually."

"All right," he answered.

"I'm sure you're aware he's been having a very difficult time with his transition."

Aiden nodded. "I know he hasn't been the easiest guy to get along with recently. But he will come around. Just give him time."

"That's not exactly what I meant . . .," Lily began, forming her thoughts and words carefully. "I know why he's having a harder time. It's because he hasn't been drinking fresh blood—only the preserved blood provided to the Dhampirs. That goes against the nature of what he's becoming. By denying that nature, his transition becomes increasingly difficult for him. And, in turn, that affects our chances for success."

"So what do we do?"

"He's going to need fresh blood if we're going to make his transition work. And a lot of it since his body is already in a state of feeling deprived."

Aiden frowned. "How is that different from me?"

Lily softly touched a fingertip to his bottom lip. "Because you have been getting fresh blood from a vampire. From me. And it's been helping you, whether you realized it or not."

His eyes blinked, slowly, as if the thought had occurred to him just in that moment. "How do you expect Zane to . . .?" Lily watched Aiden as his words trailed off. She followed his eyes as his mind seemed to slowly piece together what Lily was trying to tell him. "Oh, no . . . hell, no!"

"He needs vampire blood, Aiden. I am a vampire."

"No!" he said more defiantly. "Not yours! Not my . . .!" Aiden was off the bed and standing tall above Lily before she could blink. "I forbid it!".

"You forbid it?"

Lily was surprised by the ferociousness of his reaction. Even though Gideon and Dr. Li had adamantly warned her that he would react this way. Aiden may be quiet most of the time, she thought, but when he fights something, he's all voice! Aiden's burgeoning primal side, the side that said he'd laid claim to Lily, was not about to accept this. She realized she'd have to tread carefully. "Listen, I understand why you're upset—"

"You understand why I might be upset?" he repeated back to her. "Why it might bother me that the woman I care for refuses to drink my blood, but now, all of a sudden, is volunteering to let everyone join the party in drinking hers?"

***

Aiden was angry. No, he was suddenly furious! How could Lily expect him to accept sharing her blood with Zane? Yes, the man was his friend, his Brethren brother; and they had shared an ordeal the past year that no one else would be able to understand. But Aiden knew, deep down, Lily belonged to him. He'd laid claim to her with his kisses. With his body! He laid claim to her every time *he* drank from her. Drinking blood from Lily was not about nourishment to him. It was about the connection he felt growing stronger every time he was with her. Did she not feel that same connection because she refused to drink from him? That bothered him endlessly. When they were together, he felt like a king. Like he was in exactly the right place, with the right woman. "I can't allow this! I cannot allow him to touch you!"

"Aiden, be reasonable," Lily protested. "Zane has to receive blood. There's no other way for him to receive that blood safely."

"There has to be another way! Because *this way* is not safe for *you*! I know what we are capable of. I feel what I'm capable of every time I drink from you. I want more. I want more from you. And you keep refusing me!" Aiden's hand suddenly curled into a fist before he whirled around, swinging his back to her and pounding that tightly clenched fist against the steel wall behind him. The dent his blow imprinted in the metal was a reflection of how fast his burgeoning vampire blood was taking over. But his bloodied fist also revealed that he was still capable of feeling human pain.

"Aiden, stop!" Lily shouted as she came to her feet off the bed and reached for his hand, covering the knuckles that still had the capacity to bleed. "Please stop," she repeated with a quieter voice, raising her eyes to meet his. "This has nothing to do with wanting to drink from you. I want that! You have to know I want that. This is about understanding the consequences of that decision. If we exchange blood, I believe we will form a connection—a powerful connection. I felt the pull of it when we were together in the tunnel and again when you drank from me."

"You do feel it, then?"

"Of course, I feel it." She opened his hand, which was already swollen and reddened by his bloodied knuckles, and moved his palm till it was placed over her chest. He slid his hand just enough to cup her breast, caressing the soft mound. She sighed breathily in response, and he could feel how her whole body registered its pleasure at this simple touch. "I feel it now, when you touch me. "But I can't allow myself to feel this yet."

Aiden shook his head and pulled her close, asking in a dark, husky voice, "Why not?"

Lily dropped her head to rest against his very solid chest, her palms open and caressing him along his ribcage. "Because you would have soul claim to me. And I would never want another man to touch me."

Aiden slowly dropped to his knees in front of her, his hands drawing the collars of her shirt down her back with him until the fabric was free of her arms and hung loosely at her waist, leaving her standing there, beautifully naked from the waist up. His tongue began circling around her navel, kissing and teasing her skin, sparking intense delight as he continued to hear her sighs of approval above him. "Do you want another man to touch you?"

Lily shook her head and quietly replied, "No. Never. But I also don't want either of us to have to live with the guilt of knowing we could've done more to help Zane."

"I can't let you do this," Aiden breathed heavily through the fabric of her skirt as his hands slid up her legs to the shapely thighs underneath and pulled at the strings of her thong, drawing the material down her legs. He could feel his body growing impatient for this woman. His need for her was almost overwhelming as his cock turned to granite inside his jeans. "Lily, whether or not you want to admit it to yourself, I've already laid my claim. Tell yourself whatever you want. That it can be held off. That it's for the right reasons—it doesn't matter. You're already mine."

Aiden worried his commanding tone, his absolute words, and the fact he was staring at Lily so intently might scare her, but she returned his stare, her breaths beginning to come out a little deeper. Then her hands pulled at his shirt and she tried to reach for the front panel of his jeans but he was too far beneath her while he was there on his knees.

Suddenly, Aiden sprung to his feet, carrying her with him to the bed, where he laid her out flat and came down over her body. His hands pushed up her skirt then curled her legs around his waist and he shoved his jeans down his hips, freeing his cock and lining up his body with hers. "You are mine," he repeated, showing no hesitation before pushing inside her. Instantly he felt lost, in a good way, hearing his beautiful Lily gasp beneath him the same moment he groaned loudly and pushed himself all the way forward. "Do you feel this?"

Lily, at a loss for words simply nodded her head quickly, gathering several more breaths. For a moment their intertwined connection felt like they were one person. Her arms curl around him as he held the outside of one of her legs and he began to thrust inside her, balancing himself on one elbow, watching her accept the pleasure he was giving her with no reluctance, no hesitation. He loved how her face showed exquisite passion and unashamed desire as her hips moved in conjunction with his. Her pleasure was turning him on even more!

For the next hour, (or it might have been two) there were no words between them. Aiden promised himself he would not stop until he orgasmed some *sense* into the woman. Until she came several times beneath him and begged him never to leave the comfort of her body. He could hear when her breathing quickened, delighted at her nails clawing into his shoulders while tingles of excitement would snake lower and lower along his spine. He waited patiently for what was building in his body, a feeling he couldn't say he'd ever quite felt before. An orgasm that could possibly top the previous one. He thrust harder, his frustration that she could dare expect him to share her with anyone, in any way, expressing itself in his powerful motions. He knew she was talking only of sharing her blood with Zane, but to him that was on the same level as sharing her body with another man. It cut him deeply.

Harder and harder, faster and faster, he waited to hear her cry out her pleasure and then he would start all over again. "You're mine," he would say to her each time.

"Aiden," she gasped out along with one final orgasm.

"Fuck!" Aiden ground out, his mind spinning with pleasure as he came inside Lily again, shocked that he had anything left.

"Oh God, you're amazing," she breathed, throwing back her head, exposing her neck to him, and Aiden did not need to be asked twice. He dropped his head, his fangs deploying instantly . . .

easier every time, it seemed to him. He punched them into her throat. She gasped and curled tightly around him, moaning louder the longer he drank.

When Aiden was finally finished, he pulled in his fangs and rolled over onto his back beside her. His body and thirst felt completely sated, exhausted, but his heart and mind felt as if he was in a war—a war he couldn't win.

After a few quiet minutes, Lily curled her body towards him, her hand stroking up and down his chest. "You're insane if you don't think I feel what's happening between us. But I still need to do this. Despite how angry or frustrated you may be with me right now, I've watched you be nothing but a loyal friend to Zane—when no one else would be. I refuse to believe you would now condemn him to a life of darkness because you and I can't find a way to work this out. Not when we can prevent it. Not when we know he's fighting for his choices as much as you are."

Aiden lay there, silent for a long while, all the thoughts in his head virtually overwhelming him. "He's my brother," he finally said. "We've survived together. But this is different. You know this is different."

"I do. And ultimately this decision is yours. I can't go to Zane if I know you don't support it. Just make sure that whatever you decide, it's a decision you can live with."

"That's not fair," he said under his breath as he turned his head away.

"No, it's not. Nothing about this has been fair for either of you. But we have time. Let me stay with you and we will figure this out. I promise we'll figure it out."

He then rolled his body over hers, kissing her lips suddenly, as if he were a man thrown a life raft. She held on to him as tightly as she could. "Yes, stay with me, beauty," he said. "Stay."

CHAPTER EIGHTEEN

Lily was lying in a strangely contorted position, with Aiden's bed sheets wrapped around every part of her, and yet she couldn't remember ever feeling so comfortable.

She had lounged all day with Aiden, in a sort of erotic luxury. Her body tingled, shivered even, stimulated so much, and in so many unusual places, that she couldn't stop smiling. The best part was that these tingles and shivers reminded her what it was like to feel human.

She hadn't believed it would be possible to feel much of anything once Celeste had stolen her human life. She had long since recognized that within days of that awful night she had become cold and unfeeling, far removed from the happy, loving woman she had been in her mortal life. The fear of losing those parts of herself she most recognized was what drove her to deny her own blood thirst for so long. And at times that state of denial could be a miserable existence.

But Aiden changed that. With him she felt so many things; calmness, peace and even warmth. Feeling again made it possible for the world to not be so closed off from her.

"It's not like you to be so quiet," Aiden spoke out in a deep, raspy voice as he continued to kiss his way along her stomach.

"I'm too sated to talk," she replied. "Besides, it's hardly fair if I'm being compared to you—a man who says little most of the time."

His answering smile was sexy as it beamed out from below his dark hair, which was all disheveled and framing his face, making him appear quite young. "I don't seem to be quiet with you. In fact, I would say I can be rather vociferous."

Lily laughed, another one of those very human sensations she had been missing. "I don't mean during sex."

"I didn't mean during sex, either. Although . . . that, too." She nipped at his shoulder as he slid back up her body, encouraging him to continue his lustful pursuits. Aiden growled in response, his eyes shining out at her like ambered gold as he quickly pinned her wrists above her head on the small bed. "You like to bite, don't you?"

Lily snapped her sharp teeth together with conviction, just inches from his mouth.

Aiden laughed. "I tell ya . . . if there was ever a sexier vampire in this world, I've not seen her."

There went those little tingles again. The man could make her tingle not only with his touch and kisses, but with his words. "I like this more talkative side."

He stared up at her with a cocky smile. "You want me to talk more?"

Lily's corresponding smile faded ever-so-slightly. "I want you to let me in. When you talk with someone, you're letting them in."

Surprised by that answer, Aiden let go of her wrists, rolled to his side, and encouraged her body to curl up in his embrace. "There are many ways to let a person in," he responded, now quietly serious. "Every time I kiss you—come inside you—I let you into me."

"Here . . . ," she said, curling her hand behind his neck to draw him down to her throat. Immediately she heard his breath quicken. His excitement was electric, something she could tangibly feel, almost smell, in the air around them. She then stretched her long, slender neck out to tempt him to the fullest to drink from her, and Aiden couldn't resist. His fangs sank into her throat with a fervor that would be hard for any man to match, at least with her. She gasped and, quite naturally, her body pressed against his, her back arching into his bite, which only molded her breasts more closely to the contours of his chest. Yes, there was pain when he drank from her like this, but there was also incredible pleasure. It felt as though he was connected to her in a very special way—an elemental way. Her body hummed with excitement, and she moaned as she felt the blood being drawn quickly from her veins.

Aiden Rowan would be a powerful vampire someday. She could already feel that.

She whispered her gratitude, wishing she could give him every drop of blood she had in her because she knew that giving her blood freely was the key to making his transition easier. Her fingers stroked their way up his arms and shoulders, ensuring that he was relaxed when he drank from her. Unfortunately for her, it was turning her on sexually again. If someone had told her only a couple of weeks earlier that she would become a sex-addled vampire from a man simply drinking her blood, she would have laughed at them.

When Aiden finally withdrew his fangs from her throat, she stared up into his eyes, which once again swirled with their most beautiful blue. "Kisses, sex . . . drinking from me are all ways to let someone in. But there's a difference between physical contact like that . . .," she paused and drew her hand down his arm until she brushed over the old tank watch at his wrist, "and truly letting someone into your life."

***

Lily pulled the tank watch from Aiden's wrist and dangled it over her own hand. She seemed to be appraising the old timepiece, as if she were trying to see a secret hidden within it.

Aiden wondered if this woman had any idea how beautiful she was. He wasn't trying to hold back from her. In fact, he was pretty sure he'd give her just about anything she asked for.

"There's such a simple, classic elegance to this watch," she said to him. "It fits you, you know?"

Aiden kissed her forehead while he watched her continue to play with the watch in her hand. She turned the band inside out and saw there was an inscription on the back of the case: *Omnes una manet nox.* "Latin?"

He nodded and pulled her in close. "My great grandfather loved Latin—spoke it fluently. My father once told me that his grandfather often referred to Latin as the 'knowing' language. That if you looked deep enough, it was the key to unlocking life's greatest mysteries. I'm not really sure I believed that . . . but the thought always stuck with me."

"What does the inscription mean?"

Aiden gave her a small smile. "Omnes una manet nox. It means 'the same night awaits us all'."

"The same night awaits us all," she repeated. "That's beautiful . . . and a bit ominous."

"My father gave this watch to Keegan when he was a boy. I remember feeling jealous that he'd gotten it instead of me because he was the eldest son. But in time I came to realize it really meant something to my brother. I never saw this watch off his wrist . . . until the night he was attacked."

"He left without it?"

Aiden nodded with a rueful smile. "Sometimes I wonder if he left it for me. It was part of him—part of my memory of him. Felt right that I keep it."

Lily brushed her finger over the dial. "This phrase is strangely fitting for this world, isn't it? Do you think that somehow your great-grandfather already knew about the supernatural world? I mean, is it possible?"

"Funny, I've asked myself the same question . . . I don't know." Lily squeezed both his arms, her eyes full of an unspoken understanding, which tugged at Aiden's heart. "The irony is not lost on me, though . . . That a vampire life I would once go to any length to fight against now feels like something I was destined for the whole time."

"Maybe we were both destined for this life?" Lily said, pensively, as she slipped the watch onto her own wrist, holding it there with her free hand to keep the dial where she could see it.

He kissed her. "Maybe . . .," he said and then touched the dial. "You know, I haven't taken this watch off since the day I lost Keegan."

"You miss him, don't you?"

He nodded in silent reply, the emotion readable on his face as he slipped the watch off her wrist and slid it back onto his own.

"When you finish your transition," Lily remarked, "you'll have been given the strength and gifts you need to be able to find Keegan."

He nodded. "He's the reason I volunteered for Reese's tests in the first place. I need to know what happened to him—good or bad. It's the only way I can truly put that night behind me."

Lily tucked her head into the comfortable space where his neck and shoulder met. "Thank you . . .," she replied quietly. "Thank you for sharing this with me."

Aiden hugged her tightly and rolled her onto her back. Once he was directly above her, he kissed her deeply. Soon she was softening beneath his kisses. "I need you again," he said. "I want you more every time . . ." She nodded and inhaled deeply as his hands cupped her nice, round flanks to secure her to him as tightly as he could. He then eased himself inside her, slowly—possessing her completely, until her eyes shut closed with a smile on her lips. Her body was becoming more accustomed to taking him, he thought. It was one more thing that reinforced the growing belief inside him that this woman was meant for him.

Aiden thrust himself inside her warm, snug flesh fully, loving the sound of her pleading gasps as he began to rock into her, picking up his pace. He was not gentle with her. Lily didn't want him to be gentle. She wanted to feel his strength, and he was happy to oblige. Lily Abbott was one of the strongest women Aiden had ever known, and she liked her pleasure. Her fingers clawed and dug into his skin as her inner tension built toward an orgasmic peak. "Do you still want to talk?" he asked her between thrusts.

She shook her head, opening her eyes, making sure to keep contact with his eyes. "No," she whispered, the word barely more than a breath. He rocked her hard, and he could see in her face that she was lost in a blissful, hazy fog of pleasure. Right now he didn't give a damn about vampires, about transitions; he only wanted to continue to feel lost inside this woman's lush body. For just a few minutes, the outside world didn't exist. Their problems didn't exist. Neither his transition nor her secrets, secrets forced upon her so as to keep herself safe. All that existed in this moment was pleasure and the inevitability that they would both cry out under one whopper of a release.

"Aiden!" she gasped, and it felt like her body was crushing his cock in a chokehold inside her!

"Damn!" he groaned several times as she fell away from the world in a blissful release.

After her release, he held her head in his hands, continuing to thrust, more slowly and gently for the moment. "Look at me, beauty," he said, feeling the wonderfully simple sensation of perspiration break over his skin. She blinked her sparkling green eyes once, twice, then opened them wide as he reached the peak of his desire and lunged forward so deep inside her that he feared he would never be able to pull himself back out. Then he came so hard he lost his breath, but he never once moved his gaze from her. He held it steady. He wanted her there with him completely in that moment.

As he finished and she continued to shake beneath him, he said, "You should know, whether I drink from you or come inside you, there is no difference to me. I am leaving my mark either way. You are mine . . . here," he said holding his hand over his heart. Do you understand?"

Lily nodded, and there wasn't any part of her that contradicted what he was saying. That was good, he thought, because he realized that he sounded a bit like a caveman just then, but this territorial, possessive instinct for her ran through his blood more strongly than just about anything else ever had before.

Aiden wasn't sure how long they stayed curled up together, just staring at each other in the silence. He was acutely aware that this was, hands down, his most favorite moment with her so far (aside from the fantastic orgasm parts). That feeling of being completely connected in a silence that went beyond words. The quiet made him certain that there was nothing more important than just appreciating what he had right now.

Then she had to ruin the moment for him. "Aiden, it's time. I need to know if you're OK with this plan."

He dropped his arm behind her and squeezed a handful of the bed coverings in his fist. Nothing seemed to rip him open with a raw wound faster than the thought of her going to Zane and letting him drink from her. "Lily . . .," he began, "I don't want you to do this. I can't let you do this!"

"Then I won't go." Lily touched his arm gently. "I just wanted you to be sure."

"Sure of what?" he asked her. "Sure that I don't want him touching you? 'Cause I'm damn sure of that!"

"Aiden, I don't know if we can save him if he doesn't get fresh blood. Right now I don't have another solution. And I want to be really clear about that—because I know he is your friend."

"There must be another way. There has to be! I can't be responsible for the same thing happening to Zane that happened to Keegan." Then it hit him. That was what Lily had meant when she said she wanted him to be sure. Aiden was already having a hard time living with what happened to Keegan, knowing that he was out there, somewhere, living a dark life because he chose to save his younger brother. Could he really allow that to happen to Zane, as well?

Lily remained silent, knowing this was a decision he had to struggle through and live with on his own. She had been right to push him on it.

Aiden sat up and swung his feet off the bed, lowering his head into his hands in misery. He was angry that he didn't even need time to consider his answer once he'd asked himself the real question: *could I live with it?*

"Go," he said, even though the word contradicted every new, dominant instinct inside him. He reached back for her hand and squeezed it. "Go."

CHAPTER NINETEEN

Lily approached Zane's door with much more reluctance than she had anticipated. She knew from the beginning what she'd volunteered to do. After all, it was her idea. She understood her blood was crucial to helping Zane, but until she had to leave the comfort of Aiden's caring embrace, his warm bed, she hadn't let herself really considered how difficult this was going to be.

Lily knocked on the door but there was no answer inside.

As she stood there, she glanced back toward Aiden's door at the opposite end of the space. The separation between the two men had been very intentional. Dr. Li warned Lily beforehand that creating a physical separation between her and Zane would be important. Aiden needed to feel secure in his right to continue his pursuit of her as his future mate, reinforcing the primal vampire instincts that were developing inside him. Zane would be seen as a threat to that goal, and Lily needed to be mindful of that at all times.

"Unlock his door," Lily said up to the camera above her.

She waited until she heard several steel bolted locks slide free of their housing, unlocking Zane's door while simultaneously locking Aiden's. She knocked a second time. After a few quiet seconds she heard a low, warning growl on the other side of the door.

"Zane, its Lily." she announced as she slowly pushed the door open and blinked at what she saw. Zane's room was completely tossed. His bed frame was flipped upside down, with blankets and pillows thrown about, and several empty bags of blood were scattered all over the floor. Dressed in only sweats and his feet bare, he had his back to her and his palms pressed against the wall, the sweat of exertion showing along his toned body.

Lily was cautious in her approach. Zane was smart, but there was always something dangerous lurking behind his handsome good looks. Even though Aiden was a much taller, larger, more muscular man, he could never convey the anger or the cold indifference that a single glance from Zane could. "Get out," he warned her.

Lily ignored his warning and closed the door behind her.

"Are you deaf? I said get out!"

Lily calmly held her ground. Zane might not be as tall as Aiden, but he was still considerably taller than she was, and not exactly in the best mood at the moment. "I'm not leaving, Zane. You need fresh blood in order to make this transition easier. My understanding is that Dr. Li has explained—"

"Was this your fucked-up plan?" he asked as he finally turned around to face her. His cool, piercing blue eyes glared at her like accusatory darts. She hadn't seen Zane look this dangerous since the night he confronted her in the labs. "Was it your idea to lock us away in here? I bet when you approached The Brethren they nearly jumped for joy at their good fortune. Here was a chance to finally lock up and seal away forever its mistake under the guise of helping us. And they don't even have to take credit for coming up with the idea!"

"That's not true! This is going to help you. We've worked hard—"

"Bullshit!" he barked. "You've worked hard to save him," he said, pointing his finger towards Aiden's room. "You don't give a damn about me. And I never asked for your help. I never asked for any of this!"

The man had obviously been holding back a bottle full of emotions: anger, stress, physical thirst. Lily wasn't sure she wanted to be the one stupid enough to uncork them, but she decided she might have to in order to get through to him.

She took a step towards him. "We're doing this to save both of you. And from what I can see, you need the help. More specifically, you need my help. Your anger and aggression is caused by a lack of fresh blood. You're transitioning faster than Aiden, and if we don't do something now to slow the process down, this is going to be a lot more difficult for you. But it's your choice."

"*Choice?* Are you shitting me? I have no choice! And I'm not taking one fucking drop of blood from you. He would kill me for touching you."

"If you are referring to Aiden, I assure you he knows I'm here and why."

"Oh, so the fucking like rabbits I've been hearing all day means nothing to him," Zane threw back at her. "I'm not stupid! He's trying to mate you. And if I touch you he would kill me without thinking twice about it. Our friendship would mean nothing to him."

"You're wrong," Lily defended. "He cares a great deal about you. He has to care to even allow me to come here like this. You know that!"

"So what? Now you care?"

"Actually, at times like this, it escapes me why I do care. You can be one incredibly bitter and selfish man if you want to know the truth."

Lily then breathed in deeply and blew it out slowly to compose herself. She was allowing this argument to get the better of her, and it was helping no one. "I'm sorry. That was not appropriate for me to say. Zane, we have to figure this out. You need to feed. If you don't, you won't be able to control your thirst much longer."

"You're just loving this, aren't you? Putting me at odds against him? He's the only damn friend I have left in this place. And if I touch you to end—even temporarily—this fucking thirst, I will lose him."

Lily blinked back. That was the first time she had ever truly felt the extent Zane cared for Aiden, and it was a relief because until that moment Lily had wondered if Zane really gave a damn about anyone but himself. "No, you won't. Not if we do this right," she assured him. "Aiden doesn't want you to suffer like this."

"I don't need to hear this from you!"

"You obviously need to hear it from somebody!" she jabbed right back. "You know what lies ahead if you do nothing. Your thirst will become a fire in your throat that will drive you to the most convenient warm body to put it out. That would put every person here at The Oracle in danger. Is that what you want?"

"Uhh, no, I'll just feed on tiny little animals like you did. That should work, right? Rats for lunch? Yum." His strikingly attractive face suddenly became very ugly. "You think I trust you in any way? You can't even get being a vampire right! What did you tell Aiden . . .? You're the virginal vampire who has never taken her first kill."

"I told him the truth!"

Zane roared out before grabbing a desk chair and smashing it into splinters against the steel wall. "No, you didn't! You're incapable of not lying! Did you tell him the truth about what really happened that night?"

Lily was confused by the question. She wasn't even clear which night he was referring to. But she certainly wasn't going to let him continue to have the upper hand with her. "You mean the night I kicked your ass down here?"

Zane lunged toward her and got right in her face. "I've never trusted you, Lily Abbott—if that's even your real name. I've watched you betray your own kind. So why should we trust you not to betray us. He may not see the real you yet—but I do!"

Zane's blue eyes swirled with darkness until they were almost black. His face went incredibly pale. Lily could see he was beginning to shake, and she knew that the symptoms he was experiencing were all the direct effect of lack of blood, but there was no time to respond.

The events that followed seemed to happen in the same moment. Zane snatched his arm around Lily's waist and lifted her off her feet and slammed her against the wall, causing all the air to rush from her lungs. Then he wedged her between his body and the cold plate of steel. She had a millisecond of time to turn her head to the left, the side opposite from where Aiden always drank from her, before Zane's long fangs punctured into her throat. She gasped and her whole body jerked as she tried to brace herself from the pain and coldness of it.

Lily didn't fight him. She knew Zane had fallen to a dark place and that he needed her help, but it wasn't supposed to feel this way. She wasn't exactly sure how she thought it was supposed to feel, but it wasn't this way!

Zane sucked her blood with a force that almost instantly made her feel woozy. She should have considered the fact that she had lost a good deal of blood feeding Aiden. And now it was possible she was losing too much blood too fast. Her fighting instincts were taking over. She tried to push Zane away, but he fought her. Any fear on Zane's part that he might lose the blood he needed so badly would only cause him to fight harder to take it. The only advantage Lily had right now was being a vampire and understanding the psychology behind his feeding. She needed to relax and let Zane drink, try to get him to calm down so he could learn how to stop on his own, just as Aiden had. But Lily only continued to feel dizzier as he sucked her throat ravenously. He was taking too much.

She no longer had a choice.

Lily reached a hand behind his head and yanked him back, tearing his fangs from her throat and causing an excessive amount of blood to spill down the front of her. "Stop!" she yelled.

His eyes were wild as she shoved him back against the opposite wall. He stumbled over his tossed bed, and the impact seemed to shock him back into reality. He stared at her for a long moment and then, leaning back against the wall, slid slowly to the floor. He sat there with his head down, refusing to look at her. When he finally did raise his eyes, he was observing her with his human eyes, and, for the first time since she had met Zane, Lily saw a surprising vulnerability there—a softness she recognized but would wager that few besides Aiden believed he even possessed. "You're in over your head," he said, his agony showing in his expression, in his eyes.

Lily wasn't sure what she would have expected him to say in that moment, but those words hadn't been it. Without another word, unable to respond, she turned and left the room, trying to hide the bloody fang marks on her throat from the outside camera. Quickly, she moved close to the wall right under the rotating camera, though she knew there would eventually be another one that would catch her, she at least thought she could buy herself a few seconds to collect herself.

She slid down to her knees against the wall, holding both hands over her mouth. She wasn't even sure what it was she was trying to keep held inside. She knew she would be fine, that everything had just happened so fast it had surprised her. That was all. She just needed . . .

Lily didn't know what she needed. Her mind was a blank. She had lost too much blood and couldn't think straight.

Several silent minutes later, she finally recovered control of her dizziness enough to stand up. Aiden would need to see her to be assured she was all right, so she needed to get her act together, or her whole plan would unravel on the very first day. She headed down the hall to her room, making sure to keep her back to the cameras as much as possible. The first thing she needed to do was to get cleaned up before she saw Aiden. Her neck was already healing, and she felt pretty confident that by the time she went to see him all traces of the damage would be gone.

About thirty minutes later, when Lily finally emerged from her room in fresh clothes, she went directly to Aiden's door but she didn't knock. She placed her palms flat upon the metal, almost as though she was searching for his heartbeat on the other side. Within seconds, she heard the bolt locks on the door snap open, and she was grateful that she didn't have to speak to the monitoring guard at that moment. She couldn't have done it. "Aiden . . .?" she finally called, softly, almost desperately wanting permission before she entered. But there was no response from him. Her sensitive hearing could detect his heavy breathing. "Aiden . . .?" she called again, and then opened the door herself and stepped inside.

Aiden was crouched on his knees beside his bed, his long, muscled back to her, his arms and shoulders flexing as he covered his face, which was hidden from her view in his hands. He appeared very stiff, as though it were painful for him to move. Something was very wrong. That was when Lily suddenly remembered that Aiden and Zane were connected by blood. The indicators of it had been happening for months. Aiden as much as admitted it to her the night he returned to The Oracle. And if she was right, he would have been feeling what was happening between her and Zane, through Zane!

Lily brought her hand up to her mouth in horror, realizing Aiden was oddly positioned on his knees trying to control his rage. Quietly, she moved across the room and dropped to her knees, pressing her cheek against his back as her hands went to his shoulders. "I'm sorry. I didn't remember your connection to Zane."

Aiden said nothing in reply, or even acknowledged she had entered the room. But she could feel the rage inside him vibrating against her cheek. Lily knew she should say something to comfort him, but she just didn't know what. She was still trying to sort her own feelings out for herself. It never occurred to her that she would feel so mixed up after letting Zane drink from her. Almost violated, in a way, and it seemed crazy. The whole thing was her idea! Drinking was a natural condition of being a vampire. So why did she feel this way?

Aiden finally lifted his head, dropped his hands, and surprised her by turning and pulling her into his arms. He lifted her onto his bed and lay down beside her. Her arms, which had encompassed him in response to his, refused to release any part of him as she pulled herself as close as she could. She buried her head in his chest and felt his hand stroking her hair. His fingers then moved lower and touched the nearly-healed tear in her throat, and she heard him make a strange sound beside her, a groan, very deep and guttural. "Look at me," he finally said, but she couldn't. She could only pull herself more tightly against him. What was wrong with her? She was acting like a weak human . . . and she didn't like it. She was a vampire—who absolutely had the power to snap a human's neck in half. "Please."

Lily turned her head to face him, only to find misery in his eyes. How could she have been so careless as to forget than he had a connection to Zane? "I'm all right."

"No. No, you're not," he said, but didn't press the matter any further, letting his arms stay wrapped securely around her. They remained interlocked in silence for a long while before she eventually escaped her tension by falling asleep in his arms.

CHAPTER TWENTY

The next morning, Lily woke to find herself alone in Aiden's bed. And, to her surprise, sitting across from her was Dr. Li. He pushed his glasses up onto the bridge of his nose and nodded to several bags of blood that were sitting on the bedside table. "You need to drink all of those," he instructed. "You lost too much blood yesterday and you've slept for nearly five hours."

Lily sat up. Five hours! That was almost unheard of for a vampire.

"Exactly," he answered, as though reading her thoughts. "Perhaps we need to re-evaluate this plan of yours."

"Where's Aiden?"

Dr. Li paused for a moment, as if considering how best to answer that question. "He seems to agree with me that your plan needs some tweaking. He asked my permission this morning to speak with Zane alone, outside of the facility."

"What? And you just let them go?" Lily leapt to her feet. She was caught off guard by the slight bobble in her normally powerful legs as she did it.

Dr. Li pressed a firm hand on her shoulder and forced her to sit right back down. "You may be a vampire, Miss Abbott, but right now you're a vampire who's weak from too much blood loss. Now sit and drink."

"I'm fine," she defended. "Dr. Li, we cannot let them talk alone. That's not a good idea. I've not had a chance to explain to Aiden what happened."

"May I . . .?" he asked her, reaching to pull back the collar of her shirt. He appeared to ignore entirely what she had just said. Lily nodded and he proceeded to examine the area, placing two fingers on the exact location where Zane had bitten her. "I saw the damage to your neck on the camera footage." The wound was now fully healed, of course, but it was obvious to Lily that Dr. Li was still concerned. "This plan of yours has placed you in the middle of two transitioning alpha males, one of whom has every intention of mating you."

"Dr. Li, I—"

He cut off her next words by raising his hand. "Let me finish. I'm impressed with the changes I see in Aiden. He's exerting much more control over his change than I have seen from any of the previous transfused hybrids. I believe that control is coming from the blood he's been receiving from you. If that's true, you are correct to assume that this may be the only way to save Zane."

"It *is* the only way to save him," Lily answered confidently.

"Yes, but for Aiden, that does not change what happened last night."

Lily stared at the doctor, unsure of exactly what he was getting at.

"I've been a doctor for the supernatural realm a long time. And despite all the science and the research on how to treat these spectacularly powerful beings, sometimes it simply comes down to understanding the nature of people. In this case, two very prideful men. This is between them now. You need to stay here and let them work it out . . . or your plan to save them will fail before it even gets started."

"But the plan will work of they just give it a chance."

"I can only tell you what I saw on Aiden's face when he left here this morning . . . a storm. I assure you, Miss Abbott, there is absolutely something more important to him right now than a smooth transition."

***

Zane's head snapped back on his shoulders from the force of Aiden's fist against his jaw. The punch was a powerful blow that also sent him staggering back on his feet. But Aiden had to give Zane some credit. He recovered quickly, merely taking time to spit out the blood before turning back to face Aiden square again. "I suppose I deserved that," he said in a calm voice, but wagging a pointed finger in warning. "But you only get one."

"You deserve a hell of a lot more after hurting her like that," Aiden replied angrily, realizing that this confrontation with his friend had been coming for a while. "I trusted you with her. Against my better judgment, I agreed to this crazy plan! And what do you do?" Aiden lunged forward and grabbed fistfuls of Zane's jacket in both hands, furiously hauling him forward once again. "You slammed her against a steel wall and tore into her throat as if she was just any low-life Nightwalker feeding your greedy thirst, you son-of-a-bitch!"

"That wasn't me!" Zane defended hotly. "You know that wasn't me. It's this damn thirst. It's painful!"

Aiden's gaze narrowed. "Does that make it easier for you? Blaming it on your thirst? So, what? I hit you a few times and everything's fine? Is that how you see this playing out? You better start rethinking that plan and coming up with a better answer than that."

Zane's expression turned suddenly cautious, revealing that he wasn't sure exactly what he was being baited into. "I said you only get one free hit, brother. How this goes from here is up to you."

Aiden shoved Zane several steps back. "You don't get off that easy. I want you to have to think about this! Be reminded of how much you hurt people. You want to know why I'm your only friend? It's because you don't give a damn for anyone but yourself."

Zane only smiled in response. "You might be surprised what I give a damn about." The dangerous gleam that always seemed to be present in Zane's eyes faded, and by the time he had drawn one deep breath and exhaled it through his mouth, it was replaced with a surprisingly contrite expression as he rubbed at his sore jaw. "For what it's worth, I'm sorry. I knew my blood thirst was out of control and I asked her to leave. She didn't."

"You're not helping yourself here!"

"I'm trying to say that I wish I had a fucking choice! I didn't want to hurt Lily. But ever since The Brethren realized these transfusions had gone bad on them, we've had all of our choices taken away from us. Do this! Report here! Take your pills . . . Now it's—'transition here in a locked up room and drink her blood. It's the only way you'll transition smoothly, they say. Well, it's all shit! Nothing about this is smooth or easy. And I have no choice in any of it. I'm tired of people taking my choices away from me!"

"And what would you choose, Zane? Do you just want to say 'fuck it' and give up?"

Zane shook his head. "I want another choice than to drink from your woman! Look, I admit I don't have control over this right now. When she came into my room and I smelled her blood, I wanted it like I've never wanted anything in my life. Can you understand that?"

Aiden scowled, but at the same time, he realized it was an acknowledgement that he did understand.

"It was like I didn't see her," Zane continued. "I saw a way to feed this fuckin' awful thirst. And, for about five minutes after she left, the fire in my throat went away. Now I want more."

Aiden gave Zane a stern look of warning. Zane would be lucky if Aiden let him back in the complex with her, let alone available to feed his thirst again.

"I want to fight this, but I want another choice . . . one where you don't end up hating me."

Aiden turned his back to face the still lake as dawn began to crack over the mountains. Rubbing his hands over his face, he knew Zane was being completely honest with him because Aiden had experienced the exact same feelings of resentment about not having a choice. "I get it," Aiden began. "But that doesn't change what happened last night. You hurt her! And Lily probably believes this morning that she can keep doing this—but she can't. I can't let her."

"Yeah, I kinda figured that much."

Aiden exhaled a heavy sigh and ran a frustrated hand through his hair. "But no matter how angry I am at you right now, I have to acknowledge I've had an easier route in all of this. I leave for months, escaping the judgment of others—and Dr. Li's tests. I've gotten close to the one woman who can make both of our transitions easier. And now, when you need her blood the most,

I'm going to stand here and refuse to let her do it? Yeah, it sucks, but I'm still doing it."

Zane rolled his eyes and snorted. "You should've refused when she suggested this stupid-assed plan."

"Then why didn't you refuse?"

"For the same fucking reason you didn't—we have no other choice! Our choices were taken away from us the day we agreed to those damn tests. We just didn't realize it."

"All right, then, let us start making some choices now—together. And if Gideon and Dr. Li don't agree with them, we'll be on our own."

"I like the sound of that," Zane said, finally sounding somewhat more relaxed and open.

"But first you need to accept that whatever my future is, it's going to involve Lily. And right now we've got a big problem in that I don't trust you with her. And it's not just because of last night. This divide started between us when you refused to tell me the truth about what happened the night you confronted her in the labs."

"Then ask her—"

"I'm asking you!" Aiden interrupted boldly. "You're the one who went down there to confront her. You knew I cared about her. That it would upset me. And still you did it. Why?"

"Fuck!" Zane cursed under his breath, rubbing his hand quickly over his buzz-cut hair. "I told you the truth. I didn't go down there to hurt her. I just . . . needed answers."

"Answers about what?!" Aiden demanded.

"About that night—Brahm Hill. I saw something . . . I saw Lily . . ."

"*And . . . ?*"

"And you were busy being unconscious."

Aiden snorted in response. "Unconsciousness tends to happen when you get whacked from behind by a Lycan while fighting a vampire," Aiden answered, dredging up one of the few things he could about that night.

"It wasn't the Lycan who whacked you. It was Lily."

Aiden blinked hard, but remained quiet and calm in his surprise. "That's impossible. I remember fighting the female vampire when I heard the Lycan coming up behind me."

"That's right," Zane agreed. You had the vampire bested when the Lycan charged at you through the trees. I saw what was happening, but I knew I wasn't going to be able to get to you in time. That's when Lily appeared out of nowhere! She reached you at the last, split second, crashing into you and throwing both of you out of the path of the Lycan. You hit your head on a rock and was out."

"I don't understand . . . Why—"

"Why didn't she tell you this . . .?" Zane questioned for him. "That's one of the many answers I was looking for the night I confronted her in the labs. It wasn't clear to me if she was trying to save you from the Lycan or kill you. Then she suddenly shows up here at The Oracle days later."

"Why would you think she was trying to kill me?

"I saw her face shift that night—a full shift—if you know what I mean. Just for a brief second; just long enough for me to question if I'd really seen it, because she also appeared completely . . . startled."

"Startled . . .?"

"Yeah, startled. Like she recognized the female vampire you were fighting but she wasn't expecting her to be there? The next thing I knew, you were unconscious, twenty feet away, and Lily was putting a sword through the Lycan's middle, taking him to the ground while barely breaking a sweat. Do you know many Dhampirs that can do that?"

Aiden gave him a brittle smile. "You suspected from the very beginning that Lily was a vampire."

"Yes."

"Then why didn't you say anything?"

"That's a question I've been asking myself for months. But when she showed up here on sacred ground, I started to question what I thought I had seen that night. If she were a vampire it shouldn't be possible, right? So I confronted her in the lab."

"And what did she tell you?"

"Absolutely nothing."

Aiden just gave Zane a look of 'and you're surprised' with a shrug of his shoulders in response.

"I don't know," Zane continued. "I challenged her. I wanted her to feel cornered. I wanted to see what she would show me if she was pushed."

Aiden rubbed his hand over his neck, struggling with what Zane was confessing, but in a strange way he could understand his friend's desire to know the truth. Until a few days ago, as far as they knew, it shouldn't have been possible for Lily, a vampire, to be among them on sacred ground. The fact it was possible changed everyone's perceptions and beliefs about the capabilities of their supposed enemy.

"I admit I handled it badly, and that things got out of hand. But I was telling the truth. I didn't hurt her. I couldn't have hurt her. She kicked my ass all around that lab! And once the guards showed up I decided it was best to just keep my mouth shut . . . because no one was going to believe me."

"You should have told me," Aiden scolded him.

"Told you what . . . exactly? That the woman you were already half in love with was a vampire walking on sacred ground? There are enough people around here who think I'm crazy."

"And I have never been one of them. So that answer doesn't fly."

Zane sighed. "You were angry with me when you returned, angrier than I thought you'd be. I didn't know if I could trust you anymore. You'd been gone a while . . . a lot had happened."

Aiden was quiet. For the first time in a long while, he finally understood Zane. And he suspected he knew what had happened with Lily and the female vampire that night at Brahm Hill, especially knowing what her gift was. But he needed to hear Lily tell him herself.

Aiden walked over to his friend slowly. "You let this come between us."

"I did. And I'm sorry for that most of all, but I can't change what happened yesterday. So what do we do now?"

Aiden placed his hands on his hips as he faced the man he still felt loyal to, despite all that had happened between them. "Lily's plan is still our best shot at a decent life, but I refuse to see her as weak as I saw her last night. Ever."

"Understood," Zane replied. "I won't touch her—no matter how badly I want the blood. You have my word on that."

"Thank you but it's not all on you. I drank from her several times yesterday. She was already weak from feeding me."

"So what's the solution?"

Aiden was quiet for a long while, considering his *very few* options. "Dr. Li can draw Lily's blood for both of us to drink fresh from bags—or as fresh as we can get without hurting her."

Zane blinked at him. "Are you saying what I think you're saying?"

Aiden nodded. "I will take her blood in the same way you do— until we both beat this thing. It may be a more painful way to transition, but we can do this together—and, more importantly, we won't hurt her. OK?"

Zane offered his hand and smiled; a genuine smile that, for once, lacked that dangerous glint. The two men shook on their verbal agreement. "Well, all right. That sounds like a plan."

"It's not the best plan . . . But at least it's a choice."

***

What was taking them so long?

Lily was tired of pacing a hole through the floor while waiting for Aiden and Zane to return—alive. And Dr. Li seemed tired of watching her pace. "Miss Abbott, it would probably be good for you to sit down and relax for a bit."

"I feel fine," she defended. "Completely back to normal. Which just proves I can do this if—"

Before Lily could finish her thought, both she and the doctor turned their head toward the entrance from the tunnel as the steel door opened and Aiden, with his shoulders back, emphasizing his full height, came through the door. "No, you can't," he said, contradicting her sentence for her.

Lily blinked as she looked past Aiden's shoulder and saw Zane following behind him, looking relatively unscathed except for the shiner in his right cheek. "You're alive?"

"Do I look dead?" Zane grumbled.

"Not exactly," she replied, displaying less enthusiasm than what was probably appropriate. A barely-there smile cracked Aiden's lips as he came to stand behind Lily, placing his hands over her shoulders. She liked how Aiden was showing affection towards her in front of the others. It surprised her, actually, since he'd grown so accustomed to hiding his feelings about nearly everything.

"I assume you've come to some sort of understanding," Dr. Li said, stating the obvious.

"Yes," Aiden replied. "We're sticking with Lily's plan, but going forward, we will be receiving our blood from Lily after you've drawn it from her, doctor."

Lily's mouth dropped open as she turned in Aiden's arms to face him. "But that's not the same . . . Drinking from the throat is natural to who you are becoming."

"Maybe to who we are becoming—but it's not who we are now. We still have the choice to control it," Aiden said in response, smiling down at her unexpectedly, caressing her cheekbone with his thumb. "You look as though you feel better."

"I do. I feel fine. I can do this—"

Aiden put two fingers over her lips to silence her. "The point is—I can't let you do this. And I can't let Zane face this alone. So this is the solution we have both found acceptable."

Lily reached for his hands and squeezed them. "Aiden, this will be much more difficult for both of you."

"You survived it," he replied. "And you didn't have a team of doctors, these first class facilities, or people who cared about you to support you the whole way. We're going to be fine." Lily couldn't help but smile as she tipped her head to his chest.

"You've been gone for a while," Dr. Li began, pointedly appraising Zane with his gaze. "I think we'd better prepare some blood soon. Your eyes are swirling with black."

Zane dropped his eyes. "Right," he half growled. "I guess I need to get used to this."

"Should I join you, doctor?" Lily asked.

He shook his head. "Let's see if we can control his thirst with our stored blood. I would like you to have a little more recovery time before we draw again."

Lily was disappointed, because she felt fine. She just wanted to help. Aiden took her hand and pulled her over toward the seating area in the common space, sitting her down beside him on the sofa. "Is everything all right?"

Lily nodded. "You had me worried this morning."

"Why?"

"I thought you were going to kill Zane."

Aiden smiled, although there was no happy light in his eyes. Lily placed her open palms on his forehead and cheeks. "You're cold. I think I need to be the one asking you if you're everything's all right. Are your headaches worse?"

Aiden lowered his head and kissed her on the neck. "I am a little thirsty."

Lily nuzzled in closer, arching her neck slightly. "Then take—"

He shook his head before she could finish. "I must keep my promise to Zane."

"I don't want you to be in pain."

Aiden held her face in his hands, his expression incredibly sincere as, he said, "No matter how much blood you give me, there is going to come a point where I'm just going to have to get through it. And I can't allow what happened with Zane yesterday to happen again."

"I'm sorry," she replied quietly. "I didn't remember that you were connected."

"I'm not sorry. Today was a long time coming. And it was time Zane and I started taking responsibility for the decisions that directly affect us."

Lily pulled him closer to her, and she could tell he held her a little stiffly now. He was indeed, in pain. "Well, then, if you won't take the blood from me, you need to get some soon from Dr. Li."

He kissed her softly on her brow. "I will. But there's something I need to talk with you about first. The night of Brahm Hill."

Lily looked up at him. "Zane told you what happened that night?"

"He told me what he saw. Why it led him to confront you that night in the labs. I wish you would have told me."

Lily nodded, at first not offering him any more explanation. She realized where this conversation was going, knew it had been coming for a while.

"I was battling against a female vampire that night," Aiden began.

"Her name was Arial," Lily continued for him. "She was the newest member of the coven. Celeste had turned her about a year before. I had tried to teach her my way, show her how she could feed her thirst without taking human lives." Lily was surprised at herself when an odd sounding laugh escaped her throat. "The whole thing seems silly now . . . trying to convince a vampire to go against her nature. I guess I was hoping to not feel so alone in the coven, that there could be someone else like me, someone who did not kill humans. But Celeste wouldn't allow it."

Aiden remained silent and let Lily continue to speak, though he squeezed his arms around her to remind her he was there.

"At first, Celeste didn't stop me. Perhaps she was just amusing me . . . But, after a while, she began to torment Arial, separated her from me, and starved her until her thirst was at a breaking point. By the night of Brahm Hill, Arial had grown strong off her human kills and there was no turning back. She was a Nightwalker. And, if given the chance, she would have killed you without thinking twice about it."

"Were you trying to save her that night?" Aiden asked her.

Lily blinked up at him with surprise. "I was trying to save you. An image had come to me about a week before that night—of you. You were lying on the ground, slain by your own sword. And I just kept staring at the awful image I had drawn."

Aiden lifted his head in utter surprise. And why wouldn't he? Lily had just told him she had seen his death!

"Your death felt so wrong—and your face had become so familiar to me because I had drawn you before." She then sighed heavily and tipped her head to his shoulder. "I was tired of having all of these bad images—of having such a cursed gift. That night, when I realized my image was from that battle, I knew I finally had a chance to change what I saw. I searched for you, but by the time I found you the circumstances of my drawing were happening in real time, and there was almost no time to react. I pushed you out of the Lycan's path, and for a moment I was so happy I had been able to change what I had seen. But soon I realized there was a consequence for my decision."

Lily closed her eyes, remembering the sequence of events that night ever so clearly. The image of watching Arial being torn to shreds by the Lycan still haunted her. "What I hadn't seen in my drawing was that you'd been slain by Arial, my own coven sister. By taking you out of the Lycan's path, I had put Arial directly into it. Changing your future also changed hers."

"Hey," Aiden began softly, tipping her chin back up to face him. "You're not responsible."

"Of course I am," she answered. "Who else would be?"

Aiden frowned to show that her answer didn't make sense to him. "Every time we step onto a battlefield, we know there's a risk. That's just a fact of this world. It could have as easily been my day to die as Arial's, and which one was supposed to happen, we'll never know."

"Don't say that. I've never regretted my choice to save you. Never."

Aiden kissed her softly on the lips. "I'm thankful you made the choice you did. It seems I may owe my life to you. But perhaps you're focusing too much on the whole of your image rather than the parts. If you consider that any one part may be what you're really meant to see, that changes the purpose of the vision."

"I'm not sure I understand."

"Well . . . Maybe the point of the image of Brahm Hill was not who you were seeing but where you were seeing. Trying to change what you saw led you along the path to finding The Oracle—a place where you could be free of Celeste. Where you have a home, people who care about you. Seeing that vision got you on the path to a better life."

"I've never thought of it that way, but you're right."

He kissed her tenderly again, and the sensation made her stomach move. Then the rest of the world fell away. There was no testing, no labs, no locked doors. Just the two of them, talking in a quiet place. "I wish you wouldn't see your visions as a bad thing. You can't let them make you fearful of your gift. And that's what you have—a gift."

"You really believe that, don't you?"

He nodded. "I think Gideon might be able to teach you how to read your images better. He's very good at relating supernatural gifts to how they apply to this world. Since you came from the human world, like me, you may still be interpreting what you see from that point of view. That may not be the right way to look at things."

Lily cupped his face in her small hands, feeling the rough, masculine stubble on his skin. "I'm really glad I saved your life, Aiden Rowan."

He smiled. "Me, too."

CHAPTER TWENTY-ONE

"I love you." The words quite surprised Lily as she lay comfortably against Aiden's side with her head on his shoulder and one arm draped over his chest. She hadn't planned on saying them aloud, but as she watched him sleep they just sort of popped out.

She couldn't remember another time in her life, human or vampire, when she'd been this happy. The feeling was remarkable considering what she was, a vampire. A cold, lifeless creature who was supposed to feel next to nothing except basic, primal need. Aiden made her feel as though a part of her was still human, still desirable, her heart still capable of love.

Aiden did not wake. She wondered if her proclamation was cowardly, having been uttered while he was sleeping. "I do love you," she said again, brushing her fingers along his bare chest and stomach. Aiden had a slim, beautiful body, with sculpted lines and light patches of hair that formed a fascinating path all the way down to his groin. She wished they could stay here like this, in the silence of the dark room and with no interference from the outside world. Lily was finding herself growing rather fond of being alone with this quiet man.

A mischievous smile crossed her lips as she allowed her fingers to slide lower on his stomach. She felt his muscles twitch in response. Her eyes lifted to him, hoping she was about to successfully draw him out of sleep so that he might ravish her again. But when his body jerked more forcefully a second time, she stopped moving her hand, suddenly becoming aware that something else was going on. Aiden's head started to roll back and forth and his skin seemed to become instantly feverish under her palm. "Aiden, are you all right?"

His entire body seemed to seize up in reply, jarring him violently out of a sound sleep and into a consciousness that, by the stricken expression on his face, seemed to rival the fires of hell. "Easy," she said, trying to hold him still on the bed. "Tell me what's happening." For a moment it appeared that everything had returned to normal. But then, without warning, his arm swung up and he shoved her back against the wall. Lily was stunned. It was not clear to her that Aiden even knew where he was or what he was doing.

Aiden came awake and rolled off the edge of the bed, crashing to his knees on the floor. The muscles in his arms and legs were rigid, frighteningly flexed, as he crawled from the bed across the small room. He growled loudly, fighting just to take each breath, then reached up to grasp one of the packages of blood that Lily had left on a side table before he fell asleep. He punctured the bag with his now prominent fangs and proceeded to drink as though he had never had a drink in his life.

"Aiden!" Lily said, leaping from the bed in the blink of an eye.

Aiden shot his hand out in warning. "Stay back!" he snapped, then drove his fangs into a second bag of blood and sucked the contents of that bag dry within seconds. He was still breathing hard and blood dripped from his fangs and lips.

"Let me help you," Lily said calmly.

"Goddammit, stay back!" his shredded voice scratched against his throat. "I don't want to hurt you."

"Listen to me. You can't hurt me. So let me help you."

Aiden turned away from her and, still on his knees, slammed both his hands against the wall. The metal buckled under the blows and imprints formed in the steel. He cried out in agony and frustration, a terrible, painful sound that Lily hoped she would never hear again because there was so much suffering in it. "Fuck, it burns," he said miserably, reaching for yet another bag and sucking its contents down even faster than the previous two.

"I know . . . I'm sorry," Lily replied, and she did know. That feeling of your throat burning so hot you feared there would not be enough blood in the whole world to quench the fire was all too familiar.

Reaching for his shoulders in a gesture of empathy Lily held on to him firmly, but again he tried to shove her back. She was prepared for him this time, however, and held herself steady. "You need fresh blood, Aiden." The blood in the bags he had just drunk was collected from her only a few hours ago. But Lily suspected, given the agonized state Aiden was in, nothing would satisfy his thirst except blood straight from her veins. "Let me give you what you need."

"No!" he growled.

Lily's grip on his upper arms tightened. "You can't ask me to sit here and watch you suffer like this. Not when I can help you." Aiden's powerful arms and shoulders swung back into her with unbelievable quickness and force. She was slammed all the way back to the wall on the opposite side of the room and she fought to recover and defend herself against what might come next.

Aiden's stunned gaze swung around to meet hers. His eyes swirled with gleaming blue, so much so that it threatened to drown out any of his natural color for good, but she could see he was shocked by what had just happened. "Lily . . . I didn't mean . . ." He tried to reach for her, then immediately pulled his hand back and turned away from her as another wave of fire hit his throat, causing him to growl out an agonized groan from deep within himself. The sound made her chest squeeze. His thirst wouldn't relent, even for the few seconds it would take to allow him to come to her.

Lily sprang into action, closing the distance between them and curling one arm around his chest from behind, pinning his much larger arms to his sides. Aiden was incredibly strong, and growing stronger by the day, but Lily knew which one of them was the vampire. She had the strength to hold him still, though she had to exert every ounce of energy in her to do it. He was shaking badly, and Lily would give anything to make the pain stop before it took too large a toll on his body . . . and she did.

Lily pulled his head back and slashed her free wrist against her own fangs. Aiden was breathing hard as she moved her wrist to his lips and let the blood flow freely from the wound she had just created. He licked the blood from his lips and opened his mouth wider for more. After about thirty seconds, her wrist started to heal, so she had to slash it open again and begin the process over.

Aiden didn't refuse her offering, In fact, he tried to reach for her arm to pull it to his mouth, but she managed to keep his arms pinned enough. Eventually, she could detect a change as his breathing began to slow, and she felt his shaking starting to ease.

When her wound healed for the fourth time, Aiden dropped his head. "No more," he said in a deep, deep voice. Lily wrapped both her arms around him and kissed his neck before resting her cheek there. Aiden was quiet and still, but she could tell he was far from all right. The next minute passed slowly, with both of them in a sort of suspended state.

"Leave me," he finally said.

Lily held her breath and closed her eyes, hoping she had not heard him right, but she knew she had. He was sending her away. "Aiden, don't do this—"

"Leave, Lily! Go to your room," he ordered, reaching his hands up to pull her arms out of their grip around his chest.

Lily grabbed his shoulders and spun him around to face her. Given his size, he couldn't help but fall into her awkwardly, but she didn't care. Her hands went to his cheeks and forced him to look straight into her eyes. "Listen to me," she began. "You didn't hurt me. And I know you would never want to. You're suffering through something that no one should ever have to suffer. And I'm not going to let you go through it alone."

His gaze set firmly on hers. "I can't do this with you here."

"I don't accept that."

"Then accept that I need to keep my promise to Zane. That means you can't be slicing your wrists open every time things get bad."

"Why are you so loyal to him?" Lily spouted in frustration. "You sacrifice more for him than he would ever return to you. Why?"

"Because he has no one else," Aiden answered. "You just said yourself that no one should have to go through this alone."

"So instead . . . you'd rather shut me out?" Her hand reached for him and she stroked the side of his face. "I am here and I want to help. Just let me in."

Lily waited patiently for him to reply. She was pleased that it did seem he was considering what she had just said. But when she noted his shaking beginning again, she tried to reach to embrace him more fully. But he turned away, placing his back to her as he continued to shake. With another craving for blood happening practically on top of the last one, she knew the rough part of his transition had arrived and he wasn't going to let her help him with it.

"Go!" he said again, and the painful pressure on her heart was complete. She knew it was time to surrender. She could talk to him until she was blue in the face and he still would not let her help him.

Lily grabbed two more bags of blood from the table and took them over to him, dropping them at his feet. "Drink these," she ordered him. "I'll see that you get some more."

Aiden's shaking grew fiercer. "Lily, go now!"

Lily quietly covered her nakedness, throwing on her shirt and jeans. "As you wish," she replied to him with a surprising lack of emotion. Reminding herself that the cool, distant comfort she was all too familiar with in her life as a vampire was never that far away.

CHAPTER TWENTY-TWO

For the next week, Aiden felt as though his own body had turned against him. There was no relief from his unending thirst. And despite his best efforts to spare Lily from the pain and ugliness of his slow transition, he couldn't, not even by half.

Some days were so bad that he was unable to focus enough to communicate what he needed to Lily or to anyone. The irony of the situation was feeling the increased strength growing throughout his body with each passing day, but to get that strength he had to watch Lily give her 'fresh' blood until he feared she would drop to the floor from either exhaustion or blood loss. She had simply refused to let Aiden go through his transition alone. And how had he thanked her? By slamming her against a wall in an angry bout with his own thirst. Whether the act had been intentional or not mattered little to Aiden. He hated himself for it. And he feared it was a reflection of the person he was becoming. A cold, emotionless, killing machine.

He and Zane had not been able to go outside their retro-fitted section of the labs in a week. Hell, Aiden hadn't been outside his room! The violence of their transitions had made it impossible for either of them to be out where they might encounter other people. Only now was Aiden starting to feel some control over his thirst, and he could be proud of how he fought to get to this point. Aside from the first night, when he had let Lily give him her blood direct from her wrist, he had kept his promise to Zane and only accepted her blood as Zane did, from bags.

As a result, the bond between the two men became closer than ever, but he'd created a divide between him and Lily. He could feel it, and he had only himself to blame. Though she never left his side during the entire week, she was guarded around him. Very professional, like a doctor would be, and he hated it. He missed her closeness, and at times he missed her most when she was standing right next to him, because he could feel her pulling away, as though she were trying to protect herself. Could he really blame her? Of course not; he'd practically thrown her out of his room that first, awful night. Lily didn't understand that his reaction had nothing to do with how much he cared for her and everything to do with his wanting to protect her from the violence and the ugliness of the transition he was going through. Now that he was starting to feel a bit more under control, he was bound and determined to erase some of the distance he had created.

Aiden stood outside Lily's door thinking about all the things he wanted to say to her, but his words seemed to be failing him. "Come in, Aiden," he heard from the other side, before he'd even knocked.

When he opened the door every thought of what he'd wanted to say vanished from his mind completely. She was beautiful standing there in a simple, white shirt, a short, dark skirt and gray leggings that it stunned him. For once, her honey-colored hair was not pulled up in a sloppy bun but was spreading prettily over her shoulders, and it made him want to gnaw on something, preferably her. What an idiot he had been to even give her a reason to distance herself from him! All he wanted was to be close to her.

Lily was staring back at him, confused. "Did you come here to actually say something?" she finally asked him. "Are you feeling all right?"

Aiden nodded at first and then, as if he'd suddenly changed his mind, began shaking his head. "No, it's not all right. I'm not all right."

A sharp crease appeared across Lily's brow as she continued to stare at him. Aiden took a step toward her, quietly reaching for her hand. Lily pulled her hand away at the last moment and removed her watch, dropping it on the end table beside her bed. The action was a clear indication that she was trying to maintain her distance.

When she turned around to face him again, he reached for her hand a second time. This time, he didn't allow her to pull it away and squeezed his hand gently around hers. "It's not all right . . . ," he said again with a quiet voice. "I've made a mess of things between us, haven't I?"

Lily answered with something Aiden was all too familiar with—silence, not even attempting to contradict his question that sounded more like a statement.

"That wasn't my intention," he continued. "I knew this transition was going to be rough, but . . . slamming you into the wall like that? That's not who I want to be. Can't you see I'm trying to protect you?"

Lily snapped her hand away. "I wish you would stop trying to protect me," she said with plenty of frustration in her voice. "Have you forgotten that I'm a vampire? I could kick your ass three ways to Sunday and not break a sweat." She then suddenly turned her back to him and looked to be inhaling an unusually deep breath, one that lifted her shoulders. "Telling yourself that I need to be protected from this justifies in your own head your reasons for pulling away. And that's not OK with me."

Now it was Aiden's turn to be surprised. He truly did not realize how much his distance throughout the past week had hurt her. "You're wrong. It's not possible for me to pull away from you. Not anymore."

Lily turned back to him with the same frustrated look. "How can you say that? I wanted to stay that night! I wanted to help you. You were the one who demanded I leave."

"No . . . I begged you to close a door between us. There is a difference," Aiden replied and there was an audible pause in Lily's breath. "I begged you to leave so I wouldn't hurt you and still you were in my every thought from the second you walked out that door. I could hear your voice challenging me to fight harder. That night, when I was weakest, I wished you were there beside me so I could hold on to you. That's when I knew the truth."

"What truth?" she asked him.

"That we will be mated. Of that I have no doubt," he said confidently.

"Not at the rate you're going," she replied bluntly. "I don't want to be mated to a man who pushes me away the moment something gets difficult. I want a man who fights with me. All you've done since that day in the Oracle lobby is push me away and I'm tired of it!"

Lily's declaration caught him off-guard, because he feared he'd screwed things up with her this time to a point where they couldn't be fixed, but he didn't let his fear stop him from finishing what he wanted to say. "I know I screwed up here . . . but I'm fighting now. You bring out all of the very best parts of me, Lily Abbott, and I have missed you these past seven days."

As she listened to his words Lily's expression started to crumble. She dropped her head as though she didn't want him to see her face. Suddenly she wasn't looking quite so tough. "I wanted to be there with you," she replied in a soft voice, nearly a whisper.

Aiden approached her slowly, wrapping his arms around her to pull her to him, which she allowed. He stared at her for the longest time before dropping his lips to her ear and saying in a quiet voice, "I'm sorry."

She shoved him back, but there was almost something playful in how she reprimanded him. "You better be."

He smiled and regained the ground he had lost. "I want you with me. I want us to fuck like rabbits, and I want you beside me every night when I sleep." Before she could answer, Aiden pulled Lily in for a kiss, his palm holding her tenderly as his fingers weaved themselves into her flowing hair. Lily did not try to stop him as he explored her lips, enjoying them, tasting them, almost as if he had no intention of ever letting her go. When he pulled back, his hold on her cheek remained as he stared directly into her eyes. "I love you, Lily Abbott. I think I've loved you for some time. Give me a chance to show you. Drink from me tonight," he whispered. "Mate with me—right now. Be mine and I swear I will never again give you another reason to doubt that."

Lily tipped her head and laid it on his shoulder, and she sighed heavily. "It's not that easy, Aiden. I wish it were, but it's not. Even if I wanted to drink from you—which I do—you're not fully transitioned."

"Fuck! Does it matter?" he replied in frustration. "I'm going through this damn change either way. And the last week has been .

. ." Aiden fell silent. He knew if he said what he was really thinking—that the last week had nearly killed him, that there were times he really didn't know if he had the strength to make it—she would worry. "I'd rather get this whole thing over quickly so I can move on with my life."

Lily wrapped her arms around his middle, squeezing him tight. "I know this has been hard for you. Harder than what you've been telling me. But you need to remind yourself what you've accomplished. You're still here on sacred ground, and you're talking to me right now like the Aiden I've known since I met you. You're not some uncontrolled monster set on killing humans and thinking of nothing but filling your blood thirst. What we're fighting for is working! If I turned you now—interrupting that process . . . we can't possibly know what the repercussions of that decision could be."

"I can handle the repercussions if it means that you would finally be mine—just mine."

"I am yours," she assured him with a smile as she slid her hand down to his thigh and caressed the cock that was rapidly stiffening beneath his jeans. "Just yours," she reaffirmed. Aiden sucked in a quick breath in response and stared at her unblinkingly. The amber color in his eyes seemed to positively smoke and his breathing quickened with her touch.

"Say that again," he murmured to her.

Lily lifted onto her toes to be able to stretch upward and kiss him on the mouth while her hand continued to stroke and excite him, causing his whole body to tense up with the pleasure as he held her. "I. Am. Yours."

Aiden abandoned her lips and slid his hands down over her clothes as he fell to his knees in front of her. Slowly he watched her, un-tucking her blouse from her skirt and pulling several of the buttons from their holes. Her eyes radiated her desire for him as she stared back, and he could feel his body becoming rock-hard.

He released the button at the back of her skirt. The fabrics of her top and shirt loosened and billowed around her middle. Aiden pushed them aside with his large hands as his breath puffed across her skin just below her navel, followed by kisses along her stomach. Lily inhaled deeply above him. He glanced up to see her head roll back on her shoulders in response to his lips. He loved seeing and hearing how easily she was responding to him. His hands tugged at the leggings under her skirt, drawing the fabric down on her thighs, then her calves, until they reached her ankles. Removing them completely took a while because Aiden kept getting distracted by her scent. By how her skin tasted. How her shape curved inward at her stomach and outward at her hips. There were all sorts of things to be fascinated by with this woman!

"That feels so good," she said, breathily, and he needed no more encouragement to take things to the next level. He walked her backward until the wall was at her back. His hand curled on her thigh to draw her leg over his shoulder. "Oh, my," she sighed as he pushed her skirt up with his hands, then pushed her intimate folds apart with his fingers, his short, breathy exhales suddenly hitting her clitoris. The scent of her drove him wild, causing his fangs emerge.

He stared up at Lily, hoping he knew the answer to his next question. "Do you want me to stop?" he asked, in a suddenly deep voice that even he himself didn't recognize. She shook her head quickly in response, which made him smile. His tongue snaked out between his fangs to slowly lick over her clit. At each of her responding gasps, which did nothing but encourage him further, he circled and teased the small, sensitive bump. Aiden knew he must be careful of his growing fangs, Fangs he wasn't entirely used to yet, but there was no way he wanted to—or could—stop. He slid his hands to her low back to hold her steady as he continued to pleasure her. Above him, she was moaning, pure music to his ears. Pulling his head back quickly, he hoisted her other leg around his neck, lifting her completely onto his shoulders but leaving her back supported by the wall. There were several more audible gasps as she clasped her hands around his head to steady herself, and he let his tongue continue to drive her to new heights.

Aiden was able to find a good rhythm, rocking her just a bit on his shoulders as he worked and never once clipped her with his sharp fangs. "Just yours," she repeated aloud, reminding him where their conversation had started. He quickened his tongue, focusing it tightly on her clit until her hands gripped and pulled at his hair. Her back tried to arch off the wall before she cried out loudly for several seconds and her whole body went limp in an instant.

Damn. Was it possible for this woman to have Aiden any more excited? As he watched her continue to absorb her release he didn't think so. It had been a week since he'd been inside her body, and as far as he was concerned, that was seven days too many. Frantically, he began tugging at his jeans. A button here, a zipper there, it seemed to take forever for his hand to find his own cock. Once he did, he gripped around the base tight, teasing himself a little while he stared at Lily. Her eyes were on fire again, and he worried he was going to lose the capacity to hold off his own release behind the impenetrable fog of lust ratcheting higher with each passing second. She was not helping matters. Lily started unbuttoning the few buttons that were left on her shirt, pulling the fabric over both of her shoulders and exposing a very sexy pale lemon-colored bra, a lacy confection created for the sole purpose of stunning a man's mind at how beautiful the female body could be. He drew his head back for a moment so he could admire what was his, what he believed in his soul was his. She released the front clasp and pulled her bra free from her breasts, touching her nipple to tantalize him and then sliding both her hands fully around the perfect mounds.

"Are you trying to make me insane?" he blinked.

"Yes . . . ," she sighed in response, a contented and breathy little sigh. "Is it working?"

"Are you kidding me?" he replied, dropping her legs from his shoulders to slide her down on the wall till he could reach one of her breasts with his tongue. "You're going to have me coming on this wall!"

She gasped, arched her back, pressing her breasts against his tongue to increase the pressure of the caress. "Aiden!" she cried, squeezing at his shoulders, her breathy sounds continuing to warm his skin, warm his blood. He reveled in her pleasure, sampled every taste, because he planned to memorize her body with his tongue, teeth and fangs, hoping she would receive pleasure in a little bit of pain.

Lily began digging her nails into his back. With her strength, her nails should have hurt, but he could feel no pain, only the pleasure from knowing he was driving her responses to such extremes. "You're anxious today, beauty," he breathed as he moved from one breast to the other, loving the sound of her gasp once again as he did so.

"I have missed you," she replied with a note of sadness in her voice.

Aiden managed both their weight against the wall. "I'm sorry," he repeated, bringing her lips close to his. "I'm sorry that I hurt you."

"I love you, Aiden," she said to him, her words coming out with difficulty. "Whether your man or vampire or something in between. I just really love you."

What more encouragement did a man need than that? The woman he just professed to loving, loved him back. Aiden curled her legs around his waist just before he straightened on his knees, thrust forward, and sank himself inside her. A hard groan escaped his lips as her inner muscles clamped snugly around him. The same three words repeated over and over in his mind, "I love you, I love you, I love you." The thought then became the lightest sound on his breath, their very whisper a heavy contrast with the weight of the words, which he would much have preferred to scream out at the top of his lungs. But he wanted her and only her to hear them over and over, and to know just how he meant them.

Her honeyed hair bounced around her neck and shoulders as he rocked into her body. Never had fucking against a wall been so hot! It was sexy as hell to see her all disheveled, her shirt and bra puddled around her waist, while he thrust deep inside her body. Her gaze came back at him unashamed, her face now having fully shifted into its vampire form in her excitement. He wasn't sure how it was possible for her to be more beautiful. The confidence she displayed as she faced him struck him deep, making him harder than iron for her. Really seeing her like this, so open and intimate with him, made him realized that Lily's hiding the fact she was a vampire had nothing to do with her ever being ashamed of who or what she was. She had accepted her life, even if it was by no choice of her own.

His spine tightened, tingles rolling up every inch along his back. Oh, his body was tight! Lily's heavy breathing was now echoing his own as her knife-like fangs hovered just above his lips. He wanted to kiss her again, desperately turned on by the idea of feeling the pain of her bite on his tongue, but he could see in her eyes that she was not about to let that happen. Other pleasures would have to suffice. He easily balanced her weight and raised her higher on the wall. "Fuck! You have no idea how much I want you to drink from me," he growled. "Look at me," he commanded. Let me watch you."

"Aiden . . . ," she exhorted, her voice now a throaty gasp. He could feel how tight she was around him. How, in this position, her inner muscles had to stretch to accept him. She moaned, then arched back as he lunged forward again, refusing to stop now that he could tell they were both so close. She just kept whispering his name like a prayer, his lips only fractions of an inch from hers, and it was the damn hottest thing he'd ever heard or felt.

God, he was lost! To feel her this way, to be lost inside her, was like coming home after the worst storm. The warmth and familiarity of it was home to him.

He squeezed his hand around her soft thigh. Their bodies seemed to entwine and move together, as if they were one thought. Yes, he thought, I'm in the right place at the right time and with the right woman!

Here began to feel the gigantic release that was snaking up the back of his spine. Lily's fingers dug into his back and she began to claw at his skin as his thrusts pushed her to the very edge. Her head fell back and her eyes widened, giving away her intention to cum for him a second time.

Then she did.

She was beautiful.

He could see the lost glaze in those pretty vampire blue eyes of hers, the choked scream that lay just beneath her breath. Lily blinked hard, her hips locked, and he knew there was nothing that could stop his beauty from experiencing the pleasure he vowed only he could give her. "Aiden!" she screamed her fingers clawing, her inner muscles tightening until he couldn't hold back any longer, his own shuddered release threatening to either destroy him or send him shooting to the stars. As he came, the feeling of releasing inside her was primal, exactly true to the very nature of what he was becoming. He could feel the power of it, as if his body demanded that he continue to lay claim to this woman, spill his seed inside her until their mating could be completed. Until then, he would challenge to the death any man who would try to interfere with his connection to her.

All these thoughts in his head seemed to roar out of him as his body jolted forward and he came inside her again. She had somehow mastered his body, bringing forth an orgasm the likes of which he had never felt before. The power, the utter satisfaction after he was finished, dropped him on top of her without any regard for how heavy he might be. Lily simply laughed and used her strength to prop her arms underneath him, reminding him to lift his weight.

"I find it interesting," she began in a breathy voice, "that for such a quiet man you're definitely not a quiet lover. That really turns me on."

His head popped up, his hair curlier than usual around his face as he continued to breathe hard. "Does it?" he replied with a cocky smile, then hooked her leg over his shoulder and place several slow, light kisses along her inner thigh. "Would you like to hear more?"

"Yes . . . ," she sighed. "Yes."

CHAPTER TWENTY-THREE

Aiden wasn't sure how long he had been asleep when he awoke to the sound of clashing and banging about the room. The sounds were metallic, screechy, and some even made his ears ring with their scratchiness. He sat up on the bed, where he remembered having fallen asleep very comfortably with Lily snuggled at his side. Now he found her scrounging the floor, dressed only in his tee shirt. Lily's right hand pressed watercolor chalk over the steel wall, while the other searched frantically the small end table beside the bed for more pieces. Even with all the obvious clues right there in front of him, it took Aiden a moment to realize what was happening.

Then he saw her eyes.

Lily's green-sometimes-gold irises were completely gone, vanished under a sea of bright, bright blue. No other part of her displayed normal vampire features. There were no fangs, no shifted facial form or skin, and she appeared blind to everything around her.

"Lily?" he spoke to her worriedly, and certainly loud enough for her to hear him over the scraping of the chalk, but she didn't answer him, she just continued to search for more chalk. Finally her hand dragged several more pieces out from under the end table. Aiden dropped to his knees on the floor beside her, naked from their lovemaking. He wrapped his arms around her, quietly repeating her name into her ear, hoping that the gentle sound of his voice would somehow break her out of her trance. But it didn't. She threw her shoulders back against his chest, forcing him back against the bed. It shocked him. There wasn't even an ounce of hesitation in her movements. She leapt to her feet and her hands began dragging the chalk against the wall with such force the small pieces scraped horribly against the steel, the same sound that had originally awakened Aiden. She now had her back to him and he could see the rippling muscles in her arms and shoulders driving her exertion as she began to draw the outline of an image at an ever more frantic pace.

"Lily? . . . Lily?" Aiden tried several more times to bring her out of her trance for fear she would work herself into exhaustion, but nothing he tried seemed to work. He felt helpless as he stood back, following with his eyes the image she was creating along her bedroom wall. As she worked there appeared a drawing of a man's face. Then he recognized it as his face! She quickly filled in the details of his hair, nose, mouth, and lastly his eyes. The drawing had the clarity of a photograph. The rest of the image surrounding him began taking shape, and Aiden stood where he was, transfixed. Lily's chalk continued to scrape until she was down to her knuckles and there was nothing left of the pieces she was working with. Then she would reach down for yet another few. Her fingers were already red and raw, even bleeding in places. "Lily, stop! You're bleeding!" he warned . . . but she would not stop.

Soon he recognized the scene she was creating. He sat transfixed on the edge of the bed, absolutely speechless as he watched her continue. Dark blue, maroon, and many different tones of reds and oranges covered her hands and powdered over his gray tee shirt as she continued to draw faster and faster. The image was from Brahm Hill. The night, in the middle of a supernatural war, depicting the moment when Lily had brought him to consciousness after he'd blacked out. The expression on her face was caring and concerned as she held him, exactly how he'd remembered her that night. But why was she drawing this scene? Something from the past and not the future? Why was this scene so important that her mind couldn't let it go?

The supernatural war of that night was coming into focus with startlingly clarity. It was almost as if he could step into the image right now and be transported back to the single moment when every violent feeling, every horrid scent and every clashing sound would hit him just as squarely as it had then, when he had come to. Vampires, Dhampirs, Lycans, witches, warlocks, shape-shifters and humans clashing in a titanic battle that would change many lives.

But why did this moment keep coming back?

Aiden had been so mesmerized by what he was witnessing that he almost didn't react quickly enough when Lily stopped drawing as suddenly as she had begun. Her strained and worn fingers dropped every piece of chalk at once. She then fell backward, limp as a rag, headed towards a loud smack with the floor, and Aiden just barely caught her in his arms. Somehow, she felt paper thin and utterly small as he scooped her up in his arms. She was completely unconscious and scaring the hell out of him. He cursed himself for not having a better idea of how to help her.

Placing her gently onto the bed, he brushed the hair back from her eyes. "Lily?" he called. "Lily!"

Still no answer.

He debated whether or not to contact Dr. Li to come and help her, but he remembered what Lily had said about her episodes, that she would fall unconscious, devoid of all strength for a little while, but that she would always recover. Apparently, this was how her gift worked. He just hated himself at that moment for feeling so damned useless having to wait for her to come back to consciousness.

Aiden lay down beside her and covered them both with a blanket, then took her into his arms to make sure she wouldn't slip away from him this time. He spread several light kisses over her forehead and closed his eyes, praying she would wake soon. But his eyes wouldn't stay closed. He just had to look again at the incredible image on the wall. There must be a reason her gift had compelled her to recapture that night at Brahm Hill. She was meant to see something. As he studied the rendering she had created, his frustration increased; he just couldn't figure out what that something was.

Hours passed and Aiden really started to worry. Lily remained unconscious, and Aiden increasingly regretted that he had not called Dr. Li sooner.

He re-dressed both Lily and himself when a knock on the door came. It was Dr. Li who went straight to the bed to check on Lily's breathing and vitals, glancing only briefly at the drawing. "How long has she been like this?"

"A few hours," Aiden replied, raking his hand through his hair. "I should've come to you sooner but she said these spells always wear off. I didn't think . . ."

Dr. Li stared back at Aiden with what appeared to be empathy. "She'll be all right," he reassured him. "I don't see anything unusual in her breathing or vitals. More than likely, this is just a case of her recovery time being affected by the blood draws."

Aiden felt his temper starting to flair. "We can't keep doing this to her."

"I can assure you," Dr. Li began, "that as a Dhampir myself, we are not given gifts we cannot handle."

"It was never intended for her to handle both her gift and being a sire to two men turning into vampires!" Aiden replied hotly. "It has to stop!"

"Then it will stop," Zane reaffirmed, quietly, from behind him. Aiden hadn't realized that Zane had entered the room. He was barefooted and unshaven, wearing only a tee shirt and jeans looking about as shitty as Aiden felt.

"You look like hell," Aiden said.

"Not a great night."

Aiden turned back to Lily, then said, "She can't give you any blood right now."

"I'm not a complete asshole, you know." Zane took a step towards him. "I won't ask for her blood again, in any capacity. She's your mate now." Aiden stared back at Zane, knowing that he and Lily still had not yet exchanged blood. So what Zane was saying, while one hundred percent true in Aiden's mind, was not, in fact, the case. Zane then nodded to Lily. "I can smell it on both of you. Your scents have changed. They're starting to match."

Dr. Li turned his head to Lily and inhaled slowly, as if he were just realizing the same thing. "That's not possible," Aiden replied. "She has not taken blood from me yet."

"He's right," Dr. Li confirmed. "Their scents won't match completely until they exchange blood and a mating occurs."

"Well, try telling that to the supernatural world. It seems to have other plans," Zane replied with a half-smile before turning to Aiden. "And you shouldn't have to sit by and watch her grow weaker. If she were my mate I wouldn't stand for it, either."

"You both need to think about this carefully," Dr. Li cautioned them. "You're not through your transitions yet. There's a chance things may get worse before they get better. But you are both making tremendous progress, and you're still able to remain on sacred ground. Miss Abbott was right about that. We have much to thank her for in providing a solution that can go a long way to helping others in the future, as well."

"Right now I don't give a damn about helping others. I care about helping her!" Aiden snapped.

"I agree," Zane nodded. "We'll find another way."

Aiden looked at the man he considered a true friend for what he had sacrificed for him and Lily in the past weeks, and nodded in agreement.

"Did she draw this?" Zane asked, staring at the image that was really the elephant in the room.

"She did," Aiden replied, feeling the tightness in his own voice as he remembered the superhuman energy it took for her to complete it. Suddenly, Aiden realized that Zane was in Lily's drawing, as well. He was standing over the body of the Lycan who had attacked Aiden. Zane's sword was dripping blood over the lifeless creature, just as Aiden remembered first seeing when he regained consciousness. The chaos of the giant battle happening around them was drawn in perfect detail, viewed from a distance.

"This is incredible," Zane said. "It feels like we're standing back there."

"It's her gift," Aiden replied. "But something's not right."

"How so?" Dr. Li questioned.

"This image is from the past. Lily told me she only draws images of the future. I'm trying to figure out why her gift would focus her on a night that has already happened?"

"That is curious," Dr. Li replied. "Perhaps bringing forth an image from the past in such detail might also explain the additional stresses on her physical strength."

"Perhaps you might ask me," Lily said from the bed behind the men. She brought her hand to her head as if to steady herself, and Aiden felt as though his stomach had lurched into his throat because he was so relieved to see her awake.

He pushed passed Dr. Li and fell to his knees beside the bed. "Are you all right?"

Lily looked past him to the giant wall mural, and her eyes showed her confusion. "Brahm Hill . . ."

Aiden turned to the other two men and nodded towards the door. "I need everyone out. Now."

"Aiden?" Lily questioned, undoubtedly surprised by his growing worry. "I am fine."

Aiden leaned down and kissed her gently, feeling the intensity of Dr. Li's stare coming from behind him. The doctor was watching to see how far Aiden would let his rising frustration go, but Aiden felt he had a right to be upset. As Zane had put it, Lily was his future mate; that meant it was his responsibility to take care of her, not the other way around.

"Very well," Dr. Li responded. "I'll check back on you in a little while," he said to Lily.

"I'm fine, doctor . . . really."

"I wasn't offering you an option, Miss Abbott," the doctor added before leaving the room.

Zane stepped forward and clapped his hand on Aiden's shoulder. At first Aiden kept his gaze fixed on Lily, but he eventually turned to face his friend. "You once made a promise to me," Zane said, "that we would do this together. Now I'm making one to you. We won't use her blood anymore. We're stronger. We can do this."

"Thank you," Aiden replied.

After Zane left the room and shut the door behind him, Aiden crawled onto the bed beside Lily and curled his arms around her, pulling her against him. His breath came out as a sigh of relief as he held her. "I didn't mean to scare you," she said.

"I know."

"What happened? I don't remember much . . . except that I had fallen asleep next to you.

Aiden pulled her bruised and swollen, chalk covered fingers into his hand, covering them. "I woke to find you searching the drawers of the table and pulling out all colors of chalk. It scared the hell out of me. You've been out for several hours." Lily nestled her head into his chest as if to rest it in a strong place. "Do you feel weaker than usual after one of these episodes?" he asked, stroking his hand along the back of her arm.

"Whatever weakness I feel is already going away," she answered, almost dismissively, and then nodded towards the wall. "The drawing is showing the moment you came to."

"Yes—but more importantly, it's a night from the past. Do you have any idea why you would draw that now?"

Lily shook her head. "I've never drawn something from the past—at least, not that I'm aware of."

Aiden kissed her again, hoping his kiss would reassure her that he wouldn't rests until they had the answer. "Then there is significance to it. We just have to figure out what it is."

"Aiden, you have enough to worry about. We need to focus on completing your transition. Dr. Li is right. You and Zane still need my blood to finish safely. Whatever this drawing means, can wait."

He glanced to the drawing then back to her. "I'm not so sure it can."

CHAPTER TWENTY-FOUR

"You two need to stop clowning around and take this seriously," Lily frowned at both Aiden and Zane after Zane smashed yet another giant boulder against the ground—for fun! The rock shattered into dozens of pieces on the icy tundra, creating enough noise to scare off any small animal that might have been in a half-mile radius. "Someday your lives could depend on the skills I'm teaching you right now."

Zane snorted back. "I hardly think chasing fucking rabbits qualifies as life-saving."

Lily frowned harder. She supposed that learning to track and kill small game did seem silly to men who were soon to be powerful vampires, but it was important. What really concerned her was that Aiden and Zane seemed to be acting more like kids out in a new winter's snow! This was the first time any of them had been allowed outside the labs in weeks, and Lily had to admit the fresh air felt like freedom. The men's transition had continued to be difficult, but they seemed to feed off each other's determination not to let this hard work beat them. Eventually, they gained more control over the frequency of their drinking, though not necessarily how much they drank. So Dr. Li agreed that it was time to allow the three of them to go off grounds during the night to begin a bit of training.

The men just weren't taking it all that seriously.

"I often depend on these small animals for blood," she said. You never know when you'll be trapped by the sun and have to survive on a 'not-so-planned' blood supply. Now, focus and track your prey in the dark using the animal's body heat."

"First of all," Zane began, dropping a smaller rock from his hand. "I'm a man. Men don't eat fucking rabbits. If we need prey it will be something worthy—like a bull elk."

"That is the dumbest thing I've ever heard. What are you, a caveman or something? When you need blood you don't care about the worthiness of the animal."

"A man does," Zane replied, leaving Lily speechless, staring back at him with her mouth ajar, unable to respond knowing what she was about to say would further belittle his manhood.

Aiden simply smiled and walked over to kiss Lily on her forehead, as if to offer his support in a quiet way. Lily didn't find that particularly helpful just then, even if it was endearing. His eyes sparked a bit more in the moonlight and his hand lingered on her hip, which made her stomach flutter excitedly. So she forgave Aiden for not helping her more with his friend, who had been a constant challenge over the past few weeks but who, strangely enough, for the past few days was becoming more tolerable. Finally, she was able to say, "You can't be serious!"

"Like I said . . .," Zane replied while patting off the bolder dust from his hands, "it's a man thing. You really wouldn't understand."

"Well, listen, *man* . . . You need to learn to kill quickly, without triggering the animal's 'fight or flight' response. You have to control the amount of adrenalin your body is taking in. Adrenalin is now like a drug to you. Everything you do should be focused on controlling and regulating your thirst. The more control you have, the more freedom you'll have in this life. That's more difficult to do when you're trying to take down a bull elk with a six-foot rack, don't you think?"

Zane stared back at her with a casual expression. "No."

"Lord, help me," Lily sighed. "OK, let's try something else." She looked to Aiden. Though it was by no means unusual for him to be standing there quietly, large amounts of blue continued to swirl in his eyes. He was thirsty. He had really exerted himself that night. Unlike Zane, Aiden was focused (aside from the fun in the snow part), working hard to master and improve his new skills. It worried Lily, sometimes, how hard he pushed himself. "We don't have much time before we'll need to get you both back. It'll be dawn soon and you'll need to drink."

Aiden turned to gaze out over the steep, wintery canyon below them, a bit of a wistful expression on his face. He had made no secret of the fact that he liked being out in the cold, gray weather despite the freezing temperatures, which were hardly affecting them now. He breathed easier. He spoke even less. Lily decided that silence was often a sign that Aiden was most happy—when he said nothing, it meant he was at peace inside and taking it all in. If she were to be mated to this man, she had to respect that boundary within him. She shouldn't try to force him to talk when he didn't want to. Quietness was just his way.

Lily walked over to Aiden and reached for his hand. She searched through the darkness of the canyon with her night vision, locating the rock ledges below them that worked their way down the mountain, like a giant ladder. In a relatively short time, they had climbed about 2,000 feet up one of the many mountains that were close by The Oracle. Lily was concerned about getting both men back without their having to expend much more energy, knowing that the effort would take a toll on their control. They had been doing a remarkable job of sticking to the bagged blood, not asking for any of hers. She was fine with that insofar as Zane was concerned, but she missed sharing her blood with Aiden. She missed the connection she felt to him in doing so. "Since we need to head back anyway, why don't we have some fun?"

Aiden lifted his brow curiously and turned his attention to the path down the mountainside, then back to the steep drop beneath them. Zane came over to stand next to him, displaying a characteristically testosterone-laden smile. "Nice," he replied.

"Now hold on there, thrill-boy," Lily warned him. "I'm not talking about taking one giant leap. But you are nearly transitioned—stronger. And, instinctively, you should be able to control your descent."

"We can control gravity?" Aiden asked her. "It certainly appears that way from watching vampires we've fought in the past."

"Not exactly control . . . More like there is some 'give'."

"I'm not sure I understand."

"Well, if a human were to jump from here—say, down to that first ledge, about thirty feet—he wouldn't be able to control the speed and force of the decent. Its simple physics: force equals mass times acceleration. They would fall, uncontrolled, and crash, most likely breaking every bone in their spine."

"That would suck," Zane offered.

Lily couldn't help smiling at his easy nonchalance. Few people got to see Zane's humor, but now that he was a little less guarded around her, she did. "Vampires, because of their strength, can handle the forces against their body as they fall, allowing them to keep their feet always beneath them. That is part of it. Slowing down the speed at which you fall takes a little more practice. But, in time, you'll get the hang of it. Then scaling all of these mountains will be a cakewalk."

The men looked at each other as if trying to decide if she knew what she was talking about.

"So who wants to go first?" she asked.

"I will," Aiden replied.

"Very well," Lily smiled. "Let's start with jumping down to that first ledge. I'll jump first to show you how it's done. This will be a little tricky because it's still pretty dark and icy out here. Just remember to focus your energy on keeping your feet directly underneath you, and use your senses to track where you're at on the mountain, OK? Your stronger body will be able to handle the harder landing—at least until you can learn more control."

Lily pushed off the edge of the cliff without any fear. She knew what her body was capable of and how to land properly on icy terrain. She just hoped she was a good teacher. What had surprised her was that when she landed she turned back to see Aiden landing practically on her heels. Her eyes widened with surprise as he landed smoothly and wrapped his arm around her waist to pull her in for a kiss. "I just wanted some time alone with you," he whispered before covering her lips again with his, this time not letting go.

Lily smiled into his kisses and then fell into them for a long while.

"You know, I can still hear you down there," Zane yelled over the edge, reminding them that they were not alone.

Lily pulled herself from Aiden's arms and gave him a quick wink. "Be right back." She dipped low on her knees and lunged back upward towards the edge of the cliff, where Zane was still standing. "See, nothing to it. You ready to try—"

Zane didn't even wait for her to finish her sentence before he jumped. She glanced over the edge and watched him land, not quite as gracefully as Aiden had (although her memory might be a little foggy from that kiss), but still was very good for a first try. "Not bad," she teased just before the hairs on the back of her neck stood on end and she swung around to face the frozen terrain behind her.

"My turn," a familiar voice echoed off the icy rock walls around them as two swirling masses of fury came at her—one straight at her! Before Lily even had time to react, a massive force smashed against her chest and blew her off her feet, right over the edge of the steep canyon. Forget what she had just said to Aiden and Zane about controlling your descent. Lily had just been hit so hard that she was spiraling backwards, way out of control, with Celeste's angry, lavender gaze burning right into her.

"Lily!" she heard Aiden shout, already from somewhere above her. She knew she was falling at a rate faster than her mind could keep up with. Years of practice was the only thing that helped her manage to get her feet back underneath her seconds before she crashed hard against some rocks, and then she was flipped over one more time before plunging downward again. Luckily, she was facing downward by now, so she could finally see the ground coming at her. When she landed for good this time, it was, somehow, on her feet, but her relief only lasted for a split second before Celeste hit her a second time and drove her hard against the ground on her stomach. She felt all the breath leave her at once, and she certainly was not immune to the pain she still felt from spiraling into that rock ledge about thirty feet ago. Her mind was trying to process what to do next as she pushed immediately to her feet.

"Oh, that felt good," Celeste hissed back at Lily, standing there, in the freezing weather conditions, in platform heels and a short skirt that covered about as much of her legs as a hair band. "I have wanted to knock you on your traitorous ass since Brahm Hill."

Their coven sister, Sherra, a stunning brunette who had been fiercely loyal to Celeste for over a century, was now standing by her side. "We've been looking for you, Lily," she said. "I didn't want to believe that you would leave your coven sisters like that."

"Yes . . .," Celeste agreed. "It's about time you learned a little loyalty to your coven and a whole lot more respect for me, your sire."

Lily just smiled at Celeste. "Not going to happen."

***

"Lily!" Aiden's heart jumped into his throat when he saw Lily blasted off the edge of the cliff, flailing backward in a steep drop. His eyes followed her as she crashed against a rock ledge that momentarily broke her fall, bounced once, and then continued to freefall down into the canyon below. Before his mind could even process what had just happened, his stronger, faster body responded. He leapt into the air, using the rock ledges as a ladder down to the ground. He didn't care that he hadn't had a lot of time to practice. He would figure it out. "Zane!"

"Right behind you!" his friend responded, propelling himself down to the next ledge right on Aiden's heels.

Celeste and another female were already confronting Lily at the ground level. Aiden was just grateful to see Lily still standing after that brutal fall, but she popped right back up to her feet. One thing was for sure, when he reached them he was going to kick Celeste's stiletto-heeled ass across this mountain. He was much stronger than the first time she confronted him. The only problem was he could feel the hunger for blood burning in the back of his throat. He had gone too long without drinking, and now it was costing him some physical strength and the mental ability to maintain control over his anger, which Celeste was currently fueling, in spades.

"Shit!" Aiden hissed, nearly missing the next ledge. But he didn't miss a beat as he landed hard on one foot and stretched his body outward towards the next ledge.

Lily looked up to meet Aiden's gaze. There was a momentary flash in her eyes that said she had a plan. He had no idea what it was, but he knew that Lily was smart. She would let him know somehow what he needed to do to help her. "Try to keep up," he heard her say to Celeste, then both women turned to blast off in the other direction.

Once the men hit the ground they continued on right behind Lily and Celeste. Aiden became frustrated when he lost sight of them in the trees, but his ever-increasing vampire-hearing could detect the barely audible sounds of them racing through the forest ahead.

"She's leading them back towards The Oracle. Smart girl," Zane said, sounding as if he were trying to reassure Aiden.

"I don't like it," Aiden replied as they continued to speed through the forest in the direction that the women had taken when they had disappeared from view. "Celeste will know exactly where Lily's leading her. If she's being led, it's because she wants to be led."

"You give that overly-peroxided bitch too much credit."

"And you don't give her enough," Aiden growled, feeling his temper rise even more. He needed to be careful. He had to keep control of his current thirst and anger so he could think one step ahead and fight like a lion when they caught up to the women. "She's dangerous."

"So I keep hearing. What's the plan?"

"The plan is, Celeste is mine!" Aiden replied before he summoned a new power to speed himself up. Every day, he was getting stronger and faster, and right now he was never more grateful for it.

"I'll handle the leggy brunette," Zane informed him.

Soon they hit a ridge, where Aiden caught sight of Lily again. Watching her run over the frozen ground was amazing. Her feet seemed light as air and she appeared to be barely exerting herself.

She raced along with the grace of an angel with wings. Then he lost her again when she disappeared down an embankment. Aiden drew on his ever-increasing senses to listen to what was happening ahead. "I've got her," Celeste declared.

"Faster!" Aiden barked at Zane.

When they reached the edge of a clearing just shy of Oracle lands and sacred ground, they caught site of the three women again. A new threat of sunrise breaking over the mountaintop added to the urgency of the situation. There were no clouds this morning, which would make things dangerous for Lily, and for them, as well, now that they were nearly transitioned. Celeste bounded forward and tackled Lily to the ground, instantly punching her fangs into Lily's throat from behind. Soon a long trail of blood rolled along Lily's shoulder and arm. She was able to fight her way back to her feet and even returned a hard elbow to Celeste's stomach, but not before a lot of damage was done by Celeste's fangs as they ripped from Lily's neck.

"There's no escape for you today," Celeste said in a growl of frustration.

Lily turned to face her pursuer. "Funny, I was about to say the same thing to you." And the two women began an exchange of walloping blows.

Zane had already veered off to challenge the leggy brunette when Aiden threw himself into the middle of the fight between Lily and Celeste. He'd had enough of watching Lily defend herself alone against one of the most dangerous Nightwalkers in existence. They were stronger as a team.

Aiden charged at Celeste, hitting her dead-center with a force that drove her to the ground about twenty feet away from Lily. Celeste didn't stay down, however. She somehow managed to do a fancy mid-air twirl that more resembled flying than a battle move, then she came right back at him, kneeing him hard in the thigh, just missing his groin, for which he was eternally grateful. If she had succeeded in hitting him square in the nuts by one of those heals, he probably would have been incapacitated for a good, long while. Aiden tried to turn back toward her, but she managed to get an arm around his neck. She yanked him back to her and laughed. "You are nearly one of us. I smell the change in your blood. It matches Lily's scent," Celeste said to him. "Aw, are you two trying to mate? That's very sweet, but I'm afraid Lily's coming with me today. So no mating for you . . ."

"Fuck off," Aiden snarled, feeling the sharpness of his fangs as he grabbed her arm and pulled her forward over his shoulder until she crashed against the ground beneath him. He was feeling rather victorious when he went in for the kill but Celeste rolled to her back, her eyes firing up like brilliant flares of purple.

"Don't look at her eyes!" Lily shouted to him, just as she was rammed to the ground from behind by Sherra, who had momentarily gotten away from Zane. But Lily's warning had come too late. Celeste locked her hypnotic gaze on him and Aiden suddenly couldn't move a muscle.

Celeste looked to Lily with a devious smile and said, "What did I warn you I would do?" right before she snapped Aiden's left arm at his shoulder, dislocating the ball from the socket, then breaking his humerus in two. White-hot pain tore up Aiden's arm and he could do nothing to respond as he lay there frozen against the ground. "You still feel pain, don't you, Aiden?" Celeste asked in his ear just before she snapped his other shoulder. Aiden held in the most painful cry of his life as his arms hung limply at his sides. The small part of him that was still human had just experienced the pain of having both shoulders dislocated and his left arm broken.

"No!" Lily cried, fighting to get free of Sherra while watching Celeste wrap her hand around Aiden's throat, her fangs hovering just above the major artery there.

Aiden then heard a woman cry out behind him and prayed that Lily was all right. He couldn't move his damn head to see her!

"Sorry for breaking those strong shoulders of yours, but I don't need you fighting me on this." Celeste opened her mouth wide, about to sink her fangs deep into his throat, when he felt the weight of her suddenly removed from him, as well as her freezing glare. He swung his head around to see that Lily had somehow managed to escape Sherra and had essentially saved him from a nasty bite. Lily then fought Celeste with a strength he had never seen in her before. But he could not let her continue to fight on her own.

The pain in his shoulders was overpowering and his arms hung limply at his sides, but he couldn't focus on that. Instead, he focused on a plan to get some function back into his right arm, the one Celeste only dislocated, so he could help Lily. Locating a small rock ridge along the icy ground, he fell to his knees and used the hard edge of the outcropping as leverage to try and jam his right shoulder back into place. More pain raced up his entire arm and neck. He swallowed the pain and prepared to do the same to the other shoulder. Celeste's strange cry stopped him short of accomplishing that, however. He turned to see that Lily was on top of her. Her fangs snapped into Celeste's throat as Lily pinned Celeste down with her body and, with her other hand, pulled the vampire's chin back.

"Lily!" Aiden called out to her, though his voice hardly sounded like his own. He knew he hadn't gotten his arm completely back into place because it still didn't feel all that functional, and the other was useless to him.

Celeste roared out before finally pulling Lily off her. Lily immediately turned to find Aiden. When she saw him she ran to him, quickly scanned the damage in his shoulders when she reached him. "Are you all right?" he asked her, and Lily blinked up at him with surprise.

"Get him out of here!" Zane shouted to Lily, referring to Aiden while still fighting a very resilient Sherra.

Aiden didn't have time to respond before Lily was sweeping his large frame up into her small arms. He swallowed back more pain when his shoulder pressed against her body. Counting to three, he tried to refocus his mind so he could think. He then glanced over Lily's shoulder to see that Zane had managed to free himself from Sherra and was heading right toward them. Celeste had other ideas, though. With blood rolling from the wound Lily had inflicted on her neck, she lunged for Zane and wrapped him up in her grasp. "Wait, Lily!' Aiden cried, "She's got Zane! We need to go back. I can still fight! Just help me get my shoulder back into place."

Lily dropped to her knees and set him down just shy of sacred ground. They exchanged a meaningful look before she wedged his right shoulder between her palms. "This is going to hurt a little."

"Just do it," he told her.

Lily lifted her hands to his shoulder to snap it between her hands, but instead of feeling the pain he expected to feel, he felt her hands disappear. Then Aiden was suddenly rolled onto his other side, and his other bad shoulder. He raised his head to see Sherra had just smashed against Lily, throwing her several yards away from him.

Lily was battling Sherra and Zane was losing his advantage in the battle with Celeste. "This has been a long time coming," she said to Zane right before she snapped her long fangs into his neck. Zane was a confident fighter, almost arrogant about his skills. But the shock on his face the moment he realized Celeste had bested him was a surreal sight for Aiden.

"Zane!" Aiden blinked back, realizing this moment was the exact image Lily had drawn in the tunnel at the laboratories—the one of Celeste attacking Zane. What he believed was Lily's apparent representation of a similar past event was, in fact, spot on. It just hadn't happened yet!

Aiden tried to rise to his feet, but Sherra had escaped Lily and was on him again. She pinned him to the ground by his two injured shoulders and was coming at him with her own lethal fangs. At the last second, Lily wrapped her arm around Sherra's shoulders and yanked her roughly away from Aiden, so hard it didn't quite seem real. Lily held the woman down and drove her fangs into her throat, drinking from her until Sherra stopped fighting. She then shoved Sherra to the ground, while Aiden managed to come to his feet. The pain in his arms, combined with the thirst in his throat, had him feeling useless, and his anger was building fast. He looked around, trying to locate Zane, and he watched his friend's body fall limply to the ground from Celeste's arms.

Everything was happening too fast! Aiden needed the world to slow down. It was as though he was moving slower than everything else that was going on around him.

Celeste smoothly came back to her feet. She smiled as if she didn't have a care in the world. The front of her clothing said otherwise; it was stained with both Zane's and Lily's blood as she looked to the horizon line. The sun would appear any second now.

"It's over, Celeste," Lily warned her. "It's time to go back to your cave before the sun cracks over that horizon line." Lily returned to Aiden and lifted him more carefully into her arms. He choked back the pain in his shoulders and the burning in his throat that charred all the way to his stomach as he stared back at a motionless Zane. "I'm sorry," Lily quietly whispered to him. "There's nothing more we can do for him."

Celeste laughed at Lily. "You don't realize what's happened, do you? That is funny. Always missing what's right in front of you."

"What's in front of you Celeste, is the sun . . . and it's about to come up and char your six-century-old ass!"

Celeste laughed harder, but Lily ignored her. She carried Aiden forward, refusing to turn her head back to acknowledge her sire's laughter. He couldn't blame her for that. Until Lily was safely on sacred ground he didn't want her to look back to see her sire's cruel, taunting expression. But Aiden suddenly found himself propelled forward and planted on his butt on the ground. He looked see Brethren guards heading towards them, but Lily was no longer there with him. "Lily . . .?" he said and turned to see her, several steps back from him, a lost expression on her face that seemed to indicate she was in as much pain as he was. He didn't understand what was happening.

Lily rose to her feet and took three steps towards him, then raised her palm, pressing it flatly against the invisible wall that would no longer let her pass. That wall of safety that they all took for granted every day had suddenly become a barrier between him and the woman he loved. "Lily, what's happening?"

Her head tipped down and she closed her eyes, as if to shut away an unbearable amount of pain. Aiden had no words, was barely able to take a breath. Lily opened her eyes and turned her head to find Sherra back on the ground where she had left her. The vampire was dead and Lily had taken her life. Whether it was with the intention of saving Aiden or not, it was a life. Her blood thirst had taken over, and now she had sacrificed any chance to return to sacred ground with him.

"Well look at that," Celeste chortled, detectable glee in her voice. "Tsk, tsk, tsk . . . you're one of us now, sweetheart. So you can stop pretending to be someone more worthy. You're not! And that sun is about to prove it to you."

"No . . .," Lily replied quietly, more to herself than anyone else.

Celeste picked up Zane's body in her arms, not even giving a second glance to Sherra's lifeless body, a woman who had fought by her side for a century, proving her innate cruelty. "It's your choice," she added, lifting her arms and offering Zane's body like some kind of present to her. "Are you going to let me finish him?"

With that threat still hanging in the air, Celeste turned and disappeared with Zane into the shaded cover of the trees, toward the mountains.

Moments later, the sun lifted over the mountain. Lily turned to Aiden, who couldn't seem to shake off his own shock. He blindly rose to his feet and started to walk toward her with his arms ridiculously hanging at his sides. She threw up both hands, her palms flat against the invisible wall. "No, you must stay here. You must finish alone what we started together." Her eyes showed so much human emotion it would have been impossible for anyone to tell she was a vampire. "You're strong, Aiden. You can do this. I know you can."

"Not without you," he added fiercely. "I'm not doing this with you!"

"I can't stay . . ."

"Don't! Don't you leave me, damnit! Don't leave! We'll find a way."

She shook her head at him as the sun's rays burned into her back. The sound and smell of flesh burning hit him like a bomb. He was losing her, and there was not a damn thing he could do to stop it. Lily flinched away from the unfamiliar burning pain. She was not disintegrating into ashes, like Sherra's body behind her, but the fire on her skin had to be tremendous. It was written all over her expression.

"I love you," she said in an anguished voice. "And I promise, I'll do whatever I can to save him."

Zane. He registered she was talking about Zane.

Lily then disappeared right before his eyes.

"Don't leave," he said as the Brethren fighters reached him. "Don't leave!"

But Lily never heard his final plea.

She was gone.

CHAPTER TWENTY-FIVE

"Well, look who's decided to return," Celeste said with a particularly amused glint in her eye as Lily entered the dark, stank, high-mountain cave where she had followed Celeste. "Really, I'm touched," Celeste continued. "Had I'd known you'd be showing up this soon, I would have rolled out the red carpet or something."

"I'm not staying," Lily informed her calmly, knowing exactly what she needed to do: find Zane, hope that Celeste had not completely drained him of all his blood, and get them both out of there alive. Not easy tasks when you don't have a plan and time is not on your side. It might already be too late for Zane and she hated the thought because she really needed a purpose after suddenly finding herself torn away from the man she envisioned spending her life with. Saving the friend Aiden cared for was that purpose.

"You're so fucking tiresome sometimes. 'I'm not staying,'" Celeste mocked. "I want to live my own life," she mocked further still. "Your life was decided the day I turned you. And you're here because I want you here. I control you. This fantasy you have about living a pure vampire life with tall-n-hunky-back-there is nothing more than a human girl's fantasy. Grow up!"

Celeste's shrill words and an equally shrill howl of wind echoed along the icy rock walls. Both sounds grated on Lily's ears, reminding her of the dark, empty life she believed she had escaped when she came to The Oracle. And now, she could see she was going to have to fight the coven leader again for her freedom. "I'm here for Zane. That's all. Then I'm going to walk out of here and never return."

Her sire laughed wickedly. "Doubtful . . . but I'm encouraged by your pluck. You've always had this sort of overblown sense of self. It's admirable, really, if we could just channel that energy into something more useful . . ."

"You think *I* have an overblown sense of self?"

Celeste came forward slowly, her long, platinum hair swaying on her hips as her dangerous eyes illuminated the cave with their lavender brilliance. "You've a smart mouth, Lillian . . . I've killed for less, you know. Luckily, I'm in a very amenable mood today. So, maybe I'll let you have the young vampire. After all, he means nothing to me."

Lily peered into a dark corner of the cave and saw Zane's inert body lying on the floor. She sensed he was still alive, but if she had any hope of getting him out alive she knew the smart play was to continue distracting Celeste, giving herself time to assess their best possible chance for escape. "He means something to you, or you wouldn't have kept him alive this long and brought him here."

"Yes, well," Celeste sighed, as she tapped her finger to her chin, "I suppose that's true. He certainly does have a few assets. He's hung, for one. How could I not be entertained, even intrigued by the prospect?"

"Any man can entertain you," Lily replied with disdain. "Why Zane?"

Celeste smiled back wickedly. "Because he means something to you."

Lily blinked at this assertion. Zane had done nothing but frustrate her since she met him, and Aiden's loyalty was an even bigger puzzle. The two men appeared to be in stark contrast to one another. Where Aiden was calm, disciplined and purposeful Zane was a loose cannon, a defiant survivor. He pushed and challenged, always questioning what he was being told. Told by The Brethren with regard to the transfusions. Told by the men who fought alongside him. And he pushed Aiden to do the same. In fact, Lily now wondered if Zane's defiance was something Aiden needed during the past year in order to survive the transfusions.

"I haven't quite figured out this weird triangle thing you've got going on with him and the tall, brooding one—but I will. Dare the thought that dull-little-Lily has a three-way going."

"You can't possibly be this bored," Lily came back at her. "To care about my love life? At least with the old you—and, believe me, in your case I'm using that term loosely—"

Celeste interrupted with an ugly snarl. "—it was entertaining to see you throw yourself at every Alpha that walked by and then watch them run for the hills."

"Aw Lillian, is that the best you've got?"

Lily cringed at Celeste continuing to calling her Lillian. That was the endearment her mother used with Lily in the years before she died. It was unacceptable that Celeste, as her sire, would feel entitled to do the same.

"I mean, seriously . . . what have I ever done to incite such hatred from you? Did I not generously bestow upon you the gift of immortality? Have I not guided and cared for you like most would a daughter? You should be grateful."

"Grateful?" Lily choked. "You killed my mother and doomed me to a life of blood and dark caves. And now you've . . ." Lily stopped herself. She had already said too much and was letting Celeste get the best of her.

"I've what . . .?" Celeste challenged her. "Finish that thought, Lillian. Destroyed your happiness with the brooder whose shoulders I bent into a pretzel today? Trust me, I did you a favor! He was holding you back by keeping you tied to The Oracle . . ."

Lily held her tongue but ground her teeth together so hard she worried they would break under the pressure.

". . . or perhaps all this tantrum you're displaying is for him," she said, motioning to Zane in the corner. "The newest member of our coven."

"You said you didn't care; that he meant nothing—"

Celeste vaulted at Lily with the speed and force of a lightning strike. Lily's side seemed to collapse in an instant as she tried to catch her breath before Celeste jammed her against the cave wall. "I lied! Neither of you are leaving this cave!"

Lily shoved Celeste back to the other side of the cave with an equally walloping blow and a gamely smile. "Wanna bet?" The two willful women proceeded to engage in a battle of strength. The scene inside the cave suddenly became one of two battle-tested fighters vying for the upper hand, smashing each other against rock with the gentleness of a pair of hammers.

Returning to her feet after Celeste's last blow, Lily circled the Nightwalker carefully. "What need do you have for a male vampire in your all-female coven?"

"Hmmm, sad, isn't it . . .?" Celeste hummed. ". . . That you can't think of a use for him. Threesome . . . what was I thinking? You haven't the desire, knowledge, or skills to keep even one man interested."

Lily swung around, sweeping her arm at her sire's legs to drop her on her back. But Celeste was too quick, leaping into the air to avoid the tactic. Lily prided herself on being an adept fighter despite the short time she had been a vampire. But Celeste had centuries of experience, and that was not easy to best. "By skills do you mean forcing them to mate you?"

"Exactly . . .," Celeste snorted as she came back at Lily, practically smashing her into the wall just above Zane's head. The older vampire braced Lily there with a stiff forearm to her throat and with Zane right there at her feet. "Men are no better than animals. They think with their cocks. I am merely giving them what they want, and I've heard no complaints."

Lily roared out, driving Celeste back from Zane. "How are you this arrogant? Or this delusional? They're too busy running to complain. You're so-called last mate took off within a month of being mated to you."

"Caleb Wolfe," Celeste grit through her teeth, "had issues. I don't waste time on mates with issues."

"He mated another woman. That's more than an issue—"

"Ooohhh!" Celeste replied angrily, throwing an arm into Lily's side that brought her to her knees. Celeste then caught the young vampire's chin in her hand and forced Lily to look at her. "What we need to discuss, Lillian, is your lack of respect for your sire and loyalty to your coven! You tried to kill me today—after you've already killed two of your own sisters without my consent."

Lily was about to respond when Zane suddenly made an agonized sound from the corner that drew her attention momentarily away from Celeste.

"Hey! I'm talking to you!" Celeste snapped, shaking Lily's chin in her hand, causing her to make the mistake of looking directly into her attacker's lavender eyes, which instantly livened into purple fire. Lily immediately went numb and couldn't move so much as a finger as she tried to find Zane there on the floor. She knew better than to look directly into Celeste's powerful eyes. Her gift to entrance was what made her so dangerous. What had she been thinking?

But that was just it. She hadn't been thinking. Her only concern had been trying to save Zane so she could keep her promise to Aiden. Now her carelessness had probably cost both of them.

Celeste pushed Lily against the wall with one hand and reached the other hand into a nearby crack in the rock wall's surface. A second later Lily felt a white-hot blast of pain tear through the muscles of her upper left arm. Then the right arm. She didn't need to see what was happening to realize she had just been staked through both of her limbs by thick, iron rods. Lily was a vampire, but that did not mean she couldn't feel pain. Vampires could just withstand more of it and recover more quickly. But right now, being staked to the cold, rock wall was painful!

"Do I have your attention?" Celeste asked in her ear. "Now watch and learn how a queen re-builds her coven when an ungrateful vamp like yourself kills its members every five *damn* minutes!"

Two more rods went through each palm of Lily's hand. The pain was excruciating!

"Punish me if you must!" she cried out through her own agonized breathing "But let Zane go. You don't need him anymore!"

Two more stakes stabbed through her thighs, tightly staking all her limbs to the wall.

"You still don't get it, do you? This isn't about him. It's about you! Watching him suffer is painful for you. That gives me pleasure."

"That's all that matters to you anymore, isn't it? Causing pain to others because you can't feel anything!"

Celeste simply smiled in response. "Oh, I assure you, I feel plenty." She motioned over to Zane. "Watching this cocky Guardian reduced to nothing more than a useless, miserable pile gives me great pleasure. And knowing that drives you insane gives me even more."

Lily had no response. How did you reason with a Nightwalker who clearly had no desire to be reasoned with?

"You can't win here," she continued. "I was born for this life. I own it! I am a god walking among the weak—simply because it amuses me to see them fail. And I'm offering you—*you*—the chance to learn from me. To walk by my side. Together, with your gift to see all who oppose us and mine to entrance, we would be absolutely unstoppable. You can't possibly be foolish enough to refuse that."

Celeste was truly insane if she thought Lily would ever agree to such a partnership. She tried to move her arms and free herself from the punishing iron that had her pinned, but the rods were intentionally hooked at the exposed end to prevent escape. She was trapped and bleeding all over the floor.

The Nightwalker turned her attention deeper into the cave. "Make sure she does not interrupt me." Lily then became aware that her blood was driving her former coven sisters from the shadows within the cave. They were next to her, breathing hard through their nostrils and taking in her blood scent while Celeste stalked over toward Zane, who was now writhing in pain on the floor. Lily wondered how much pain he was in to have his slow transition forced in to a near-death-sudden-one.

"Zane, get out of here!" Lily cried the moment she felt one of her sisters lick at the blood rolling down her arm. Then she flinched back as another sank sharp fangs into her thigh and feverishly began to drink from her. Having her own coven sisters drink from her body against her will was a violation that sickened her to no end. She raised her head and tried to focus on the cavern ceiling above her, blocking out as much pain as she could. More fangs punctured the flesh of her midsection, and then the other thigh.

"Aw, Zane . . .," Lily heard Celeste say through all the madness. "The beautiful man with the large cock and those dangerous blue eyes. You do have potential."

Lily could hear the life-giving air sawing in and out of his chest as he growled back at Celeste, in obvious misery as the result of his blood thirst.

"You need blood, don't you? In fact, your body craves it so much you believe you might burn to death from your thirst. But I can take all that pain away. I can give you what you need. You just have to accept my offering."

"No, Zane! Don't do it," Lily cried out again, trying to block out her own misery. "Refuse her! I can give you the blood."

"Lillian, keep this up and I will let them suck you dry. You're hardly in a position to offer your own blood."

Zane sat up, his face coming out of the shadows. His once searing blue eyes were now coal black as he sniffed around Celeste's neck. She was straddled intimately over his legs, leaning in to tempt him to her fullest ability, pressing her breasts to his chest. She stopped her seduction of Zane only long enough to glance over at Lily. "That's enough, girls," she ordered. "I don't want her dead, just in a more reasonable frame of mind."

For a moment, a couple of the women did not stop at Celeste's command. "Perhaps I'm not making myself clear! The sister who causes her death will ensure her own. Is that clear enough, you little bloodsucking tarts?"

Lily felt the fangs release immediately from her throat, legs, and arms. She felt so weak at that moment that she doubted if she could save a fly, let alone Zane.

"Do you accept my offering?" Celeste repeated to Zane.

Zane responded by grabbing on to Celeste and savagely punching his fangs into her throat. The force was so severe that Celeste jolted in his arms, but hissed a smile of satisfaction. "Smart man," she purred. "I'll take that as a yes."

CHAPTER TWENTY-SIX

Aiden was sitting at the edge of Lily's bed, steadily focused on the wall that was covered in the detailed image from the night he first saw her at Brahm Hill. A week had passed since she had left, leaving him completely numb. She had to leave, despite all his pleas to her that last day. He knew that. And for five days, he had experienced the worst bouts of thirst, the worst bouts of anger, and the worst bouts of loneliness he had ever experienced since this whole process had begun. There were points at which he wondered if he would even survive the whole damn thing. Then, two days ago, he awoke and all of his pain was gone.

Aiden was now a vampire.

Just like that, Aiden's transition was complete and, miraculously, he was still standing on sacred ground. The strength he felt inside both his muscles and his mind were incredible, feelings of utter invincibility, but his thirst was just as powerful. Yet he knew that in time he would learn to control the thirst. He would truly own his life, his fate. He would be free to go in search of Keegan, the brother he had lost all those years ago. Playing with the watch on his wrist, he asked himself, "Isn't this what he had wanted, all along?"

"You've been staring at that wall for two days," boomed a welcome voice from the open doorway. Kane was standing there with an uncharacteristically serious look on his face. He had come to Aiden's aid when they had to reset both of his shoulders and arms so they would heal correctly. And he continued to check in on his friend as much as Dr. Li would allow during the worst moments of the past week. "Dr. Li is touting you as a miracle," Kane continued. "A vampire on sacred ground, one who has control of his thirst. You're free, my friend. It's pretty remarkable, if you think about it."

"Remarkable . . .," Aiden conceded hesitantly, ". . . but not really important, is it?"

Kane crossed his arms and leaned against the door frame. "I think it's damn important to the victims Dr. Li will be able to save, thanks to the success of this program."

"You know that's not what I mean."

"I know," Kane replied, and then he nodded toward the wall. "It's an amazing drawing, isn't it?"

Aiden was quiet for a long while before responding, "Drawn by an amazing woman."

"Definitely an amazing woman." Kane turned to Aiden to see his surprise. "You know, that day—when you caught me with her in that closet—I saw something flash in your eyes. Something I had never seen before."

"Kane, I don't want—"

"No, just listen," he said, walking into the room and taking a seat alongside his friend on the bed, who continued to stare at the drawing on the wall. "At the time, I thought I recognized it for some serious, kick-ass jealousy. But now I think it was something much more. You knew then . . . somehow you knew, didn't you? What Lily would mean to your life. And still you left with me that day for Yellowknife."

Aiden blinked, finally tearing his gaze away from the drawing. He swore he'd felt at least a dozen times over the past week the same emptiness, the same pain he felt that day as he walked out the door of The Oracle on her. "When she confronted me in the lobby and I inhaled her scent, I knew then—she was my mate," he confessed.

Kane stared at him with surprise. "Then why leave?"

"Because it scared the shit out of me," he replied with wide eyes. "Accepting I could identify my mate like a vampire also meant accepting that I would not be able to stop the process. I still had hope. But when I was near her that morning . . . I could feel the truth as simply as an undeniable fact. And, irrationally, I blamed her for it."

"You blamed her for your change progressing faster?"

Aiden nodded his head quickly, as if he were ashamed but also relieved to be admitting the truth. "God, I wanted her! You don't understand how much I wanted her. And I was insane with jealously when I saw you touching her. But I thought if I left—left her—I could stop . . . something . . . anything."

"A stupid plan, for sure," Kane replied dryly.

Aiden snapped his head around. "What do you mean stupid? Leaving her was the hardest damn thing I have ever done! And in case you missed it, when the situation was reversed a week ago, she had no problem leaving me. I begged her to stay. Begged her! I told her we would find a way, and she still left."

"She left because that's what was best for you seven days ago. You weren't in a position to focus on anything other than healing and completing your transition. She knew that. What I don't understand is why your ass is still here when you could have left two days ago to find her."

"You're an asshole," Aiden replied with much less humor or sarcasm than when he usually called Kane an asshole.

"This has been established," Kane replied easily. "But if we were talking about Skye, I wouldn't have let five fucking minutes pass before I went after her. I didn't, even after she drugged me to get away from me. So what the hell is stopping you?"

Aiden shoved away from the bed, turning his back on Kane and raking his hand roughly through his hair. "You don't think I want to find her? That's all I've thought about for two days of staring at this damn picture!"

"Then why?"

"I don't know how to find her, Kane! We're not connected. She refused to let me drink from her."

Kane came to his feet to challenge him. "Horseshit! You two are connected."

"We're not! I can't feel her. Believe me, I have tried. And fuck, I can't stand thinking about what she might be going through right now."

"So, what, then? You plan to stare at this fucking wall until the answer magically comes to you?"

"Yes!" he shot back angrily. "The answer has got to be here—somewhere in this drawing. There is a reason this image keeps coming back to her. I just have to figure out what it is."

The room was silent for a long moment before Kane finally said, "All right . . . then tell me what you know. Let's figure this out together. Because I gotta be honest with you, here—you've got your full brood on right now and it's damn depressing."

"You pick now to be an even bigger asshole?"

Kane clapped his hand on Aiden's shoulder. "It could be worse . . . I could be standing here completely naked dispensing this heartfelt advice!"

Aiden scowled at his friend. Kane was referring to one of his frequent shifts. As a shifter, his nearly constant state of undress was something Aiden had gotten used to a while ago, but that didn't mean he needed to be reminded of it. "Just tell me what you know?"

Aiden rubbed his hands tiredly over his face. "That's just it. I don't know. Every detail here is spot on to what I remember about that night at Brahm Hill."

"Maybe that's the point," Kane suggested. "You and Lily are supposed to see something in this drawing you couldn't see that night."

"Why me and Lily? It's Lily's gift that created this image."

"Because you two are at the center of the image. This whole drawing is like a storyboard. Everything is happening around you. Look, here . . . this is the moment I was consoling Maya after Phin disappeared into the trees." Kane then pointed to another corner of the drawing that was farther away. "Alec went here to help Olivia. Neither of you would've been able to see these events, given your vantage point on the ground."

Aiden took a step forward. "You're right. I didn't see any of that. You're saying I need to focus on what I couldn't see that night."

"Exactly."

Aiden began running through the events he remembered, narrating the story aloud. "Lily had just saved me from the fatal Lycan attack. She was telling me everything would be all right."

"Yes . . . she is focused on you, just as everyone else is focused on who they are either helping or battling with."

"Except for Zane, here," Aiden pointed out. "He's standing alone over the dead Lycan. I remember seeing this."

"Ok, so what couldn't you see?"

"I remember most of this . . .," Aiden replied but then his words began to trail off. "Wait a minute . . . I didn't see this," he said as he focused on the upper left hand corner of the drawing. "Look who's watching Zane." Kane didn't see it either until Aiden drew a line with his finger, indicating a field of view from Zane to a leggy platinum blond fighting, her eyes lit up in lavender fire. "It's hard to tell with her eyes lit up like that—but it definitely looks like she is focused on Zane."

"Celeste . . .?" Kane asked. "That doesn't make any sense. Why would—?"

"Oh, fuck," Aiden replied miserably as again he rubbed his hands over his face and began to pace. "The other drawing in the tunnel . . ." Kane was staring at Aiden with a look that said, 'I need more explanation, please'. "Lily had drawn another image of Celeste attacking and biting Zane. What if both images were trying to tell us something? We've assumed Celeste has been hanging around because she wanted Lily, but what if getting Lily back was merely a bonus to what she really was after?"

"Dude, that's not a good thought. The only reason that trampy excuse for a Nightwalker would fixate on any man is because—"

"—Is because she's selected a new mate!" Aiden exclaimed. "Shit, I've missed it this whole time. That's why she left Zane alive that first day she confronted us in the forest. But why not kill me? And why not just take Zane?"

"Because, like you said, she still wanted Lily. She must have recognized Lily's scent on you and knew you were the key to luring Lily off sacred ground. She was waiting for the perfect opportunity to nab them both."

"Fuck!" Aiden growled. "And we walked right into it."

"If Lily went after Zane, there's a good chance Celeste has them both."

"If she does, they could be anywhere by now!"

Kane was nodding his head in agreement when another voice entered their conversation. "Actually, this could be good news," Gideon chimed in from behind them. Aiden and Kane turned to see the Brethren Guide and Dr. Li. standing at the door. "Sorry, we were both coming to check on how you were doing when we overheard your conversation."

Kane held up his hands, palms out, in a sign of resignation. "OK, Gideon . . . I realize you've probably already extrapolated some genius theory as to what may be going on within the confines of the supernatural universe—but we're in sort of a time crunch. We've got a beautiful woman to save for my buddy here, and Zane's definitely going to need some serious saving if that bitch intends to mate him. No man deserves that fate."

"I agree," Gideon replied. "What I meant was, this could be good news on two levels. One, if it's Celeste's intention to mate him, that means she did not kill him and her bite began completing his transition."

"How in the world is that good news?" Kane replied sourly. "I swear, sometimes you inhale too much print glue when you do all this reading."

"Kane, this is not helping," Aiden pointed out.

"I think what Gideon is trying to say is that mating a transitioning vampire take time," Dr. Li interjected.

"Exactly," Gideon agreed. "As does the loyalty of a new and possibly unwilling mate. Celeste and her coven would have to locate someplace nearby until his transition was complete and he felt loyalty to his sire."

"He's right," Aiden agreed. "That also means Lily could still be nearby. That still gives us a chance to find her!"

"More than a chance . . ." Dr. Li agreed as he looked at Aiden. "If Lily is with Zane, you may not be able to connect with her by mating yet, but you are able to connect to Zane by shared blood."

Kane smacked Aiden across the shoulder. "That's it, buddy! Connect to Zane, we find your woman, and we save them both. Good thinking, you two! I'll be sure to let The Elder One know what a good job you did in his absence."

"Yes . . ." Gideon began slowly. "I'm sure he will be anxious for your approval when he returns."

Kane grabbed Aiden by the arm and began to haul him out of the room. "You do that. And let him know one more thing: Aiden and I are going to need a couple of personal days to go kick some nightwalking, stiletto-heeled ass. He shouldn't mind when he finds out its Celeste."

"On the contrary, I think he would say it's a foolish idea to go off on your own without a full team in place and a well-thought-out plan."

Kane dismissed the notion altogether, saying, "You're funny, Gids," and kept moving Aiden along.

Aiden stopped just outside the door and turned back for a moment to say, "I haven't said this to either of you, but thank you—for everything." He knew this might be the last time he saw either one of these men, both of whom had been critical to his survival during his transition. Because if he found Lily alive and she would still have him, his home would no longer be at The Oracle.

Gideon seemed to understand that Aiden was implying he would not be returning. "You realize what you're giving up . . .?" he asked, "being the only vampire known in existence free enough to live on sacred ground? It really is quite remarkable."

"No," Aiden replied. "I realize what I'm fighting for."

CHAPTER TWENTY-SEVEN

Two days later, Aiden stood at the edge of an icy cliff and stared out over the enormous glacial lake several thousand feet below him. It had been a hard two-days-worth of climbing with no luck in finding either Lily or Zane. Aiden felt frustrated, more frustrated than he could remember feeling.

"You've barely said a word all day. That's so unlike you," Kane said to him in a voice loaded with plenty of sarcasm. Kane was stoking the small fire that was keeping their temporary camp warm against the freezing temperatures, not that Aiden really noticed the temperature now that he was a vampire. "Normally, I would let you just stew in your own soup until you come out of it, but I'm worried you might boil over this time."

Aiden simply turned and gave his friend a half-hearted smile before returning his stare through the darkness toward the valley below. "You know me better than that."

"I do. But I need you focused."

"I'm focused," Aiden replied sharply. "It's all I can think about."

"That's my point. I think you're so worried about what might be happening to them that you're not allowing your connection to Zane to direct you."

Aiden put his hand to his forehead and sighed. "Kane, I'm telling you, I can't feel anything. We've been roaming these damn mountains for two days and I get no reading on him. Which means he's either dead or Celeste has already taken him out of my sensing range."

"Or . . . there is a third option," Kane offered, ". . . that he's somehow blocked to you."

Aiden considered that for a moment. "That's possible, I suppose, but . . ."

"But what?"

Aiden turned around and walked back toward the fire, which was providing a heat he no longer needed. He was still getting used to all of the changes in his mind, in his senses, in his body, but he just didn't have time to worry about all of that because he had to find Lily. Her separation from him for the past ten days made him feel as if this huge chunk was missing from his life, and he didn't know how to get it back. "I can't feel *her.*"

"Who? Lily? You're not supposed to be able to feel her. You, yourself, said you're not mated yet."

Aiden was shaking his head. "I know, I'm not making any sense . . . You know that feeling in your gut? The one that tells you the person closest to you is alive and breathing? That they are not gone from this world? I don't have that . . . Not even that."

"That doesn't mean anything's happened."

"I hope you're right. With Zane, my connection has been clear. With Lily it feels like an energy that's been there the whole time, deep down, hidden. And now it's just gone?" Aiden turned in frustration and walked back to the cliff's edge. "Maybe I'm imagining things. I'm still trying to get used to all this sensory overload now as a vampire."

"I don't think you're imagining this. I think you've connected to your mate, whether you've finished that connection or not," Kane answered. "When I came face to face with Skye that first time in Yellowknife, you could have taken me a thousand miles away from her in that moment and I still would have found my way back. When you're with the right person in the supernatural world, what's logical and what's true can be two very different things."

Aiden walked back into the firelight and sat down on a boulder next to Kane, clutching in his hand a small vial he'd been carrying with him since they'd left The Oracle two days ago. "What made you think to ask Dr. Li for this?" Kane asked, tapping his finger on the vial. "It's old school."

Aiden stared at the container for a long while. "I don't know. I guess I'm looking for any advantage we can get. I can't stand the thought of not knowing what's happening to her right now."

"She's a vampire, Aiden. She's strong. Hell, she's probably stronger than either you or I. Right now, you need to trust in that strength. And we need to focus on how to help her, which means figuring out what could be blocking you from feeling her."

"You're right . . ."

"Of course I'm right. Now let's go over what we know," he said, stoking the fire once more and watching the sparks shoot skyward. "Fact number 1: If Celeste's plan this whole time has been to turn Zane, it will take time before he's strong enough to move on with her coven, right?"

Aiden nodded in responded, "It's also possible that because he was already in the process of turning, he may be recovering more quickly."

"True . . ."

Aiden quickly scanned the many high peeks around them. "But let's assume, for now, they are here somewhere—why can't I feel them."

Kane appeared to think long and hard for a moment before a smile slid over his lips. "What's the *one* thing we know of that will muddle up those new finely-tuned senses you have?"

Aiden thought about it for a moment. "Sacred ground."

"Exactly."

"But how—?" Aiden suddenly stopped as the answer seemed to come to him as easily as flipping on a light switch. "Davin's Lair . . ."

Davin's Lair was the name The Brethren had given to a cavern in the Rockies that was within a few short miles of where they were currently located. The cavern was surrounded on all sides by a wide trench that had been filled with sacred ground stolen from Oracle lands by Nightwalker Luther Davin. Essentially, the sacred soil circled the cavern, except for a three-foot opening that allowed the vampires to pass through, thus blocking a vampire or Dhampir's senses as well as if they were actually standing on sacred ground.

"I thought Alec ordered that cavern to be cleared out and destroyed."

"He did," Kane replied. "The cave was blasted shut with explosives, but Alec hasn't had the extra manpower to spare to have the trench dug up and removed. That's a massive undertaking. But Celeste knew about the location of the cavern where Luther was holed up. I'd bet my life she and her coven have dug their way right back inside."

Aiden jumped to his feet. "We can reach it in an hour!"

Kane also stood up quickly and braced a hand on Aiden's shoulder. "Hold on there, buddy. It's the middle of the night. You go charging in there now and they'll sense you coming a mile away. She'll have the advantage."

"Her coven will need to feed—possibly even be hunting down in the lowlands. Let's use that to our advantage. We can set up a distraction for the rest that will get them out in the open while I go in and search the cavern."

Kane smiled at him, the firelight revealing an extra twinkle to his eye. "Not a bad plan. Let's see if we can give those blood-thirsty women something nice and juicy to chase, shall we."

***

Lily was determined not to show the toll the past week spent in captivity, being staked against a rock wall like some kind of tortured animal, had taken on her physical strength . . . Or how much Celeste was grating on her nerves.

"What is taking them so long?" the coven leader complained to no one in particular, because all of Lily's coven sisters had been hunting down the mountain for the past couple hours. "I swear, I'm running a coven of nothing but lazy bloodsuckers! What . . .? Am I supposed to get my own dinner?"

Lily was just grateful her sisters were no longer feeding on her. Celeste continued with her mind games. The coven leader allowed the other women to drinking from Lily periodically, a sort of sacrificial punishment, she supposed. Every time she felt the sharp prick of their fangs sinking into her skin she wondered if this would be the moment she would be bled dry. The only thing that had kept her going were her frequent thoughts of Aiden. She knew, by now, his arms would be healed. She just hoped he was near the end of his transition, hating the idea of him still suffering in any way.

"You're being awfully quite, Lillian. Maybe I should send you out to get my dinner," Celeste taunted as she came towards her, forcing Lily to keep her face cast down so Celeste would not see that it had shifted to her vampire form. Despite her weakness, her face had been shifted for the better part of two days. Her *gift* had been blasting a single image into her head. One that she desperately needed to draw. An image that surprised her. But having lost so much blood, she simply didn't have the strength to free her arms and legs from the iron stakes.

"You're not fooling me, you know. I can tell you're suffering. But you brought all this all on yourself. If you would simply—"

"I owe . . . you . . . nothing," Lily croaked, her voice now reduced to a sandpaper whisper.

Celeste's stiletto heels clicked against the ground as she walked slowly toward her captive. "I disagree. I think you owe me an apology. At *least* one. I mean . . . Let's face it—you owe me so many."

"Apology for what?"

"How about for your coven sisters' deaths, Arial and Sherra? That's certainly a big one. Then there's the fact that you deserted your coven to shack up with a genetically engineered freak. Although I must give you props, he's a fine-looking genetic freak. Might have gone after him myself if it hadn't been for fate stepping in and pointing me toward my next mate here," she chortled, glancing toward Zane's figure sitting motionless against the rock wall a few yards away.

Lily had to swallow the bile that had risen in her throat. Celeste was so twisted in her own self-centered thoughts that it would never occur to her that Zane would feel disgusted by her . . . or trapped. The first few days, despite his unrelenting thirst, Zane had showed signs of trying to fight what was happening to him. He would push Celeste away, denying his thirst, but it would never last. He needed the blood too badly. Now he was a rough and ragged shell of his former self as he sat mute in a corner of the cave, and Lily hated seeing it.

Celeste laughed. "And, of course . . . there's your general lack of respect to me. There are a dozen things to apologize to me for, Lillian, and I'm merely asking for one. One little, believable, heartfelt . . . real apology."

Lily still said nothing. The last thing she was worried about was apologizing to Celeste when her brain felt like it was being stabbed over and over again with an image that was trapped in her head. And her sire's pointless chatter was making Lily's anger rise.

"Fine . . . have it your way. I guess I'll just have to find another way to entertain myself." Her heels clicked some more. "Let's see . . . What can I do, what *can* I do . . . Aw, yes—I have a new vampire to mate. Silly of me to forget that one." Celeste turned her back on Lily and walked over toward a very quiet Zane.

Lily snapped her head up. "Celeste, don't do this! He doesn't want this."

Celeste ignored Lily and turned all her attention to Zane. As she approached him, she knelt down just a few feet in front of him. Zane's black eyes were wild with excitement for blood as he rose to his knees, reached forward, and yanked her hard to him. He held her tight as he sank his fangs into her throat and drank freely. But, after a moment, Celeste pulled back from him without warning, then pressed him against the rock wall. He stared back at her with anger and confusion at having had his thirst denied. "You want my blood?" she challenged him. "You want me to feed you . . .? Weaken myself to make you stronger? Then there is a price."

Celeste tore at the fly to his jeans and underneath found him hard and erect, as most male vampires, especially new vampires, often were when they drank. Feeding their blood thirst and sexual gratification were often one in the same to Nightwalkers, because their baser animal instincts were taking over. Lily realized how fortunate she was that even though she was a vampire she still could understand the difference between a purely need-based, sexual act and a truly intimate and connected experience with another man, as she had with Aiden.

Zane was not so fortunate.

Celeste stroked and teased him while he was still trying to reach for her neck. "It's time, dangerous one," Celeste purred to him before mounting his erect cock. She snapped her fangs into his neck; he whipped his head back in pained response. When she'd taken enough blood, Celeste forced his mouth to hers and kissed him almost violently, mixing their blood together on her tongue as she began undulating her hips.

Lily felt sick to her stomach. She saw that Zane wanted to fight, but he didn't have enough strength. There was just a blank look, a numbness that erased everything else in his expression. The whole act she was witnessing was no better than male rape, simply because in these first days Zane would be unable to focus on anything but his thirst. But the sexual charge he would feel from her blood mixing with his own in his system would excite him and leave him craving more. The result would be that he would feel irresistibly connected to Celeste, something most males did not understand as they were becoming a new vampire. Celeste knew that and used it to her advantage, trapping the men to her until such time as she grew bored with them.

And she always grew bored.

Lily had run out of time. She had failed in her promise to Aiden that she would protect Zane. Celeste was mating Zane right in front of her, but with the painful image in her head threatening to split her in half she could barely think. Her body shook even more on the stakes, causing her to bleed again. When she could not hold it in any longer, she let out a long, agonized cry.

Celeste immediately stopped her hips and, bracing a warning hand on Zane's chest to remind him where he was to stay, slowly turned her head to face Lily. "What's your problem?" she asked as she separated her body from Zane and rose smoothly to her feet. "I'm a little busy here."

Lily lowered her head once again to divert her gaze from Celeste, but her sire kept coming towards her. "I asked you a question!"

When Lily still didn't answer her and simply couldn't control the shaking of her body even a little bit, Celeste grabbed the top of her head and yanked it up until Lily was directly facing her. Celeste could have used the situation to put Lily into a trance, but instead, Lily was the one with eyes alight like fire—a brilliant, peacock blue fire . . . and they gave everything away.

"Now I see the problem. You're getting an image. Well, why didn't you say so?" Celeste reached for the hilt of the stake in her left arm and pulled the intruding piece out of the wall with the ease of pulling out an eyelash. Lily's weight suddenly sagged to that side before she felt the two stakes come free from her legs and then the final one from her other arm. Completely free of the wall for the first time, Lily fell forward on her knees to the ground, her shaking refusing to stop. But neither could she stop her gift.

Her hands searched frantically along the ground for any loose chunks of cavern coal, rock or limestone. Once she had gathered several pieces that she could work with, she turned back to the wall that had been her personal prison for a week and began scraping the coal against the rock. She was drawing faster than ever now. Her gift was bursting out of her at incredible speed after having been pent up inside her for two long, endless days.

Zane growled, a horrible, animal-like sound. "Just wait!" Celeste warned him. "You will get your blood." But Zane rose to his feet, quickly now, refusing to be denied any longer the blood he needed from his sire. Celeste swung on her heels and shoved Zane back against the cavern wall, allowing him to get a taste of her blood before cruelly driving one of the iron stakes that had been in her through his shoulder and into the cavern wall, pinning him firmly to the rock. "I said wait!" she hissed at him. Zane snapped his jaw and lethal fangs closed, trying to capture her neck for a second time, but she deftly pulled away and again turned back to Lily, who was now totally pre-occupied with her drawing task.

Seconds ticked by as she worked, then minutes. Lily couldn't be sure how much time had passed. Her body, her mind, and most especially her hands ached as she clawed the coal into the rock in what seemed like random patterns, but they we not at all random.

She stretched her arms and shoulders until they ached, but even that didn't slow her down. "That's it," Celeste laughed with evil glee. "Show me the future."

But as the image became more and more clear, Celeste grew more and more quiet. Lily then turned a piece of coal in her own hand and cut the edge of it across her skin until it began to bleed profusely. She then turned back to the wall and finished the image in her own blood.

"What the hell . . .?" Celeste said, her voice fading as she stood back staring, stock-still at the image.

Lily felt her head swirling out of control as she, too, took several steps back and glimpsed the entire image she had just exhausted every ounce of her energy to get out of her head and onto the wall. The rough wall surface in front of her was carved with an enormous image of Celeste, eerily underscored in shades of black, grays and Lily's own blood. Her skin was deathly pale, much paler than usual, and her body was twisted awkwardly as scarlet blood poured from each eye.

Lily then heard someone charge into the cave behind her, but she couldn't fight off the enveloping dizziness that sent her crashing to the ground and into a quiet blackness.

***

Aiden burst in to the cave like a violent storm, choosing to forgo the element of surprise, only to see Lily collapse to the ground in front of him. "Lily!" She looked as if she'd been in the fight of her life. Her clothing was soiled and bloodied, her skin marred by large, horrendous puncture wounds that were only starting to heal on her arms and legs. The sight of her sent him into a rage as he, now in fully-shifted Vampire form, vaulted at Celeste, shoving the Nightwalker a dozen feet back from where Lily lay.

Celeste appeared caught-off-guard for a moment. It was truly strange. Her hesitation only lasted for a few seconds, however. She recovered quickly, coming right back at him with fangs in full, lethal extension, smashing him flat against the cave wall directly opposite from Lily's picture. Aiden kept his eyes averted from her lavender trap and focused on her fangs, which hovered just above his throat. She then sniffed at his neck. "Your scents nearly match." Celeste forced his jaw still as she held it in one of her hands, then gave Aiden a pouty look as the lavender colored fire dimmed in her eyes. "Aw, you want your mate, don't you, Nightwalker?"

Aiden returned a hard glare before glancing past Celeste's shoulder to Lily who was still lying unconscious on the ground.

"Join us . . .," Celeste whispered, her fangs scratching over his skin just under his ear. "That is the only way I will ever allow you to be with her."

"Never!" he ground out.

Celeste apparently didn't like that answer. She responded by snapping her knife-like fangs into his throat with the force of a blow gun. The strength and speed at which she drank from him jolted his large frame against the rock. And even though he could feel the increased strength in his body, he was not yet a match, strength for strength, with a six-century-old Night-walker.

She jerked him hard to her and threatened to drink him dry in mere seconds if he didn't find a way to get free of her fast. Each second that went by he felt his strength slipping as she continued to attack his throat. The feeling of Celeste drinking from him was something entirely different from what he experienced when he drank from Lily. With Lily, the taking and giving of blood was all about the connection between him and her. It was good. With Celeste, it was cold and malicious—definitely lethal—and his entire body wanted to reject the notion.

This was wrong . . . and it just might kill him.

A deep, animal-like growl blared from beside him. The dangerous sound had been a blessing because it caused Celeste to let go of his throat. Aiden had a precious few seconds to react. "I said wait!" she snapped at the Nightwalker staked to the dark wall in the corner like some sort of animal. Aiden pulled from his pocket the small vial he had been carrying with him for the past two days. He flipped off the cap and threw the clear contents directly into Celeste's eyes as she turned back to him to continue her feeding. The moment the holy water hit her retinas, Celeste cried out in misery, stumbling several feet back from him. The blessed water burned her eyes as violently as hydrochloric acid would a human's. Their lavender color was instantly extinguished and dissolved into a ruddy mix of blood and burned flesh as she covered her face with her hands. She yelled, "My eyes! My eyes!!!"

Aiden reached for his torn throat and glanced back toward the corner to confirm that the Nightwalker who had saved him was Zane. His friend was barely recognizable. His eyes were nothing more than black rage as he worked frantically to pull out the stake that was pinning him to the wall. Aiden knew then that he needed to find a way to get Zane out of this cavern tonight, along with Lily . . . Lily!

"Lily!" Aiden raced to where she still lay motionless on the floor. He slapped lightly at her cheek several times before becoming aware of the image she had drawn on the cavern wall. He glanced back over his shoulder to see Celeste, her body writhing in pain on the ground, twisted up awkwardly as she clawed at her eyes. Then he realized that the scene he was living was the exact duplicate of the image he now recognized on the wall. Lily had seen that this very moment was going to happen and must have kept it to herself, but now she was paying the price for it. "Come on, Lily. Wake up. Wake up," he murmured in her ear.

Lily finally opened her eyes. At first she blinked several times as if she weren't sure what she was seeing was real. "Come on, baby. I need to get you and Zane out of here. Can you walk?"

She nodded and tried to move to her feet, but he held her still. "I can walk . . .," she said, but as Aiden inspected all the bite marks and puncture wounds on her body, he could see she had been staked with the same iron stakes as Zane, and the thought of how much she had suffered over the past week made his blood surge. His future mate had been in the fight of her life. He just wanted to wrap his arms around her and hold her until every mark in her skin was gone. But he wouldn't get that moment.

A second loud growl roared through the cave behind him. Aiden swung around to see Zane finally pull the deep stake from his shoulder, freeing himself from the wall. Those black eyes of his were alight with senseless rage, reflecting a craving for blood that was beyond his control. He charged at Aiden, who was still holding Lily in his arms. As Aiden was preparing to respond to his friend's onslaught, he heard the piercing howl of an Arctic wolf a brief moment before the creature itself blasted through the entry of the cave and forced Zane back. The magnificent silver creature was so large he seemed more a creature of myth or mythology than of the animal world.

It was Kane, the shape-shifter.

"It's about time you showed up," Aiden growled at his friend as he kept Lily close. The wolf simply made a slightly irritated noised that resembled a dog questioning what a human was saying. Aiden knew he would hear an earful from Kane later about his gratitude. "I'm assuming we don't have a lot of time before the others return?"

A second growly sound came from the wolf, a noise that Aiden could easily decipher as something like, "No shit, Sherlock."

"You don't have to fight us . . ." The words surprised Aiden as he turned back to see Lily reaching her hand out toward Zane. "We can still help you. I can feed your thirst. I can make the pain stop." Aiden couldn't prevent the stiffening of his body as Lily made this bold announcement. He would do anything to help Zane right now . . . anything. But letting him drink from the woman he had every intention of mating the second he got a chance to? Well, that was a thought he physically recoiled from.

Lily squeezed Aiden's arm as if to offer him reassurance, but that still wasn't enough to convince Aiden to let her do it. He didn't even recognize Zane in this blood-starved state. He feared that no matter how much they could calm his thirst, even temporarily, Zane would hurt Lily.

Celeste sat there on the cavern floor, her eyes still bleeding. "You're too late, Lillian. He's mine. I've made him mine."

Lily shook her head at Zane. "That's not true. You need a sire to help you through this. I can still be that sire." Remarkably, Aiden saw a flash of recognition, a moment of hope, in Zane's eyes, a signal that he understood and processed what she was saying to him. His friend was still under there somewhere. "Your body will recognize my blood. I can feed you and satisfy your thirst. You just have to choose to leave with us."

"Don't let her fool you," Celeste challenged. "I am your sire. I made you . . . You will die without my blood."

Lily stepped forward and reached her hand out to Zane in offering, and Aiden followed right beside her. "That's not true, Zane. I swear it's not true. You have a choice."

Zane stared at Lily for the longest time, his expression tired but questioning; obviously, he wanted to believe her. That moment gave Aiden hope. "Come with us, brother. Take what she is offering you. I give you my permission."

Those words were the most difficult Aiden had spoken in his life. He had always been a man of few words, but these words had an impact on him. He understood their significance. He understood what he was committing both of them to, and it would be the hardest thing he'd ever done, allowing Lily to sire Zane. But he would do it if there was any chance his friend was still in there.

Zane looked from Lily to Aiden, and Aiden saw his friend, not the new vampire. There was sadness in Zane's eyes, a resignation that scared Aiden to death because he had never seen it in his friend before. Zane was the fighter, the dangerous one. He wouldn't allow the bad things of this world to beat him. He fought them. But right now, he didn't see that in his eyes. "Don't do it . . .," Aiden said to him, shaking his head. "Don't do it, Zane . . ."

Then the moment was gone and the angry hunger had returned to his friend's black eyes. Zane swung around and dropped to his knees behind Celeste, pulling her to him. "No!" Lily cried just before Zane snapped his fangs into Celeste's neck, feeding his thirst as if his sire would never quite be able to satisfy it.

Celeste, still blind from the Holy Water eating away at her eyes, just sat there, a satisfied smile crossing her lips as Zane yanked her roughly to him once more . . . because she knew she had won. Her satisfied cackle could be heard vibrating off the walls of the cave. Aiden felt as if he were stuck in place, unable to move even a single muscle as he watched the friend—the brother—he had just lost continue to quench his thirst upon his enemy.

When Zane had finally drunk enough to be able to tear away from Celeste's throat, leaving her blood streaming in lines down his chin, he looked at Aiden with an expression that said, *'I've made my choice'.* "Go," his raspy voice scraped, ". . . while you can."

"No! I don't accept this!" Aiden's entire body filled with rage. He might not be able to force Zane to come with him, but he sure as hell would not leave him trapped with a blind, six-century-old Nightwalker who'd worn out her welcome on this earth five centuries ago. He would see her destroyed and burned inside the fires of Hell.

"Aiden . . .," Lily said softly, squeezing his arm as if she could read his mind. It refocused him on her. "You can't . . . He will need his sire's blood." It was a warning Aiden understood, and yet he wondered whether Zane had somehow known a long time ago that this moment was coming for both of them. It saddened him to think that he was right. For Zane, even if some day loyal to his new coven, would still be alone.

He was always alone, it seemed.

Aiden pulled Lily behind him and approached Zane, lifting him to his feet and pressing him back against the cavern wall. "Don't you give up!" he growled. "You hear me? You take this!" Aiden pulled his brother Keegan's watch from his wrist, the symbol of the commitment Aiden had sworn to finding his brother. But now it was a symbol to a new brother. He shoved the old tank watch into Zane's hand. "This will remind you of the man I know is still in there. My friend! My brother! We will always be connected by blood. When you're ready . . . I will be there."

Zane appeared to be stunned, and he leaned back against the rock wall, fighting to keep himself erect. Aiden could see that his friend understood every word he was saying. "The same night awaits us all, brother," Aiden said in barely more than a whisper. "How do you choose to face it?"

With Zane still staring at him, Aiden released his friend and turned to Lily. Reaching for her hand, he led her out of the cave as Celeste continued to cackle over her victory. They were leaving, free with their lives and with Lily free of Celeste, but somehow it didn't quite seem like a victory. Every second that passed as Aiden put more distance between himself and Zane, he felt increasingly battered on the inside, in much the same way he had when he lost Keegan. Had he made the wrong choice to leave Zane there?

"The same night awaits us all." It was Zane's voice. Aiden's vampire hearing could detect his friend repeating this short sentence in the distance, and the words pierced his very soul, down to his core. These few words gave him back the hope that some day he could save Zane. Maybe not today . . . but some day . . . when Zane *wanted* to be saved.

Aiden, with Lily at his side and the giant wolf in front of them, kept walking.

CHAPTER TWENTY-EIGHT

Aiden stood at the window, freshly showered with a bath towel wrapped around his waist, staring out toward the mountains from which he, Lily and Kane had just made their escape. Since Lily was not able to return to Oracle grounds, Kane offered the home he shared with his new wife, Skye, as a temporary place for them to stay until they could decide what to do next.

The house was about a half mile from The Oracle property, and Aiden was grateful for a quiet, safe place to bring Lily. She had barely said a word since they had left the cave, but he realized how anxious she was to clean all the blood and grime from her body and to give her wounds a chance to heal after her week in captivity. He gave her some private time to shower using the bath facilities in another guest room, but he hated the separation from her because he wanted nothing more than to hold her in his arms.

There was a light knock on the door. "Come in . . ."

Kane entered, already showered and fully dressed himself. "Lily is settled in the other room," he began with a curious look on his face. "She seems to be doing remarkably well for someone who's been through what she has this week. I think she would probably like to see you." Kane walked in front of him for a few paces, then suddenly and smoothly pivoted toward Aiden. "Which begs the question . . . why are you still in here, asshole?"

Aiden scowled at him. "I was giving her some time to get settled."

"Good plan, buddy," Kane replied dryly. "No wonder you're still single."

"I'm not single! I'm with her."

"Yes, I can see that—except for the long hallway and several rooms between you. What the hell is going on in that noisy head of yours?"

Aiden recognized Kane was right. What *was* he doing in here? Why was he not already with her? His memories of recent events had been crowding his head for the past two hours. "When I found her in that cavern," he began slowly, ". . . seeing her brutalized like that . . . it terrified me. And on our way back down she wouldn't say anything of what had actually happened to her and Zane."

Kane snorted, as if he found that statement amusing. "She's a smart woman."

Aiden didn't see what was amusing about any of this.

"She sees you're worried for her," he continued. "And she knows what it took for you to leave Zane there. My guess is, she's worried you might be suffering from an emotional juggernaut."

"*What?*" Aiden blurted, his head shaking in his confusion.

Kane clamped his hand tightly over Aiden's shoulder while he explained. "Emotional male juggernaut. EMG."

"Not to be confused with, *OMG*, what are you talking about?" Aiden replied sourly.

Kane just ignored him and continued as if he had not been interrupted. "It's the very last moment in a man's frustration before he's about to break something or someone. Think of Clint Eastwood squinting and hissing his final words of warning to the bad guy in any one of his movies; you just know that if one more syllable is spoken someone's dead before the next scene." He removed his hand from Aiden's shoulder and pointed a slow finger at him as if to emphasize the importance of his point.

"Am I Clint Eastwood in this scenario?" Aiden asked him with complete befuddlement. "Are you saying I was a syllable away from killing Lily?"

"No, of course not. I'm saying she knows you well enough to let you work through stuff in your own head. Hold on to that woman, buddy, because I don't think you're going to find another one willing to put up with your over-the-top strong and silent routine."

Aiden, now truly perplexed, could only stare back at his friend. "Where do you come up with this stuff?"

"Pretty good, huh?"

"No, not really."

Kane just smiled. "Look, my point is, Lily's a good woman . . . and she loves you. Don't let all the bad stuff that got you to this point stop you from going forward. You're free, Aiden. You can have whatever life you want now. The transfusions don't matter anymore."

"I'm a vampire now, so it matters some." Aiden argued back at him with a sarcastic smile. "But you're a good friend. Thank you."

"Hey, don't thank me yet. I just spoke with Lucas . . . Alec knows he's alive. The *'Oh, Elder One'* is on his way back to The Oracle as we speak—which means you and I are both in hot water. He's probably already figured out we knew Lucas was alive this whole time and didn't tell him. I mean, it's not going to be hard for him to figure out that Lucas was our Yellowknife Wraith the way he Looney-Toons his way between dimensions."

Aiden rubbed his hands over his face, and said, "Great."

"Exactly . . . But you have enough to figure out with Lily. You let me worry about Alec. Trust me, I have a way of softening him up."

"No, you really don't," Aiden replied back, not at all confident of Kane's powers of persuasion.

"Of course I do. The man practically hinges on every word I say."

"No, he really doesn't."

Kane clamped his hand on Aiden's shoulder one final time. "Whatever. I'm outta here."

But before Kane could leave and shut the door, Aiden said to him. "I should've gotten him out of there."

It wasn't hard to decipher that Aiden was referring to Zane.

"Zane made a choice," Kane replied, stopping in the open doorway. "You and Lily offered him a way out. He chose to stay."

Aiden shook his head. "He didn't choose anything. He stayed because he could see the truth. That, despite what I said, there would have been no way I could've shared Lily as a blood sire with him."

"Probably. Nor should you be expected to!" There was no hesitancy in Kane's response. "Lily's not a sire to you. She's your future mate. That's a whole different ball game. If you asked every other alpha-male vampire out there they would tell you the same thing—'*hands-fucking-off*.'"

"So I just live with it? Live with knowing he's in a world of hell while I'm happy?"

"Yeah, you do." Kane started to close the door behind him, then thought better of it and added, "Zane has to want to fight for what good is left inside of him. You can't do that for him. And today he wasn't ready."

"Will he ever be ready?"

"Some day."

"What makes you so certain?"

"I saw the look in his eyes when you asked him to accept Lily's blood. It meant something to him—that you would sacrifice so much. Let's face it, there probably hasn't been anyone in Zane's life who's ever done that much for him. And his refusal to take it said much more about his allegiance to you than to Celeste."

***

A little while later, dressed only in a tee shirt and pair of loose fitting sweats, his bare feet absolutely silent on the wood floor, Aiden padded down the hall to Lily's room. He knocked gently on the door and let himself in. She was resting, curled up on top of the covers of the queen-sized bed, clad in an oversized tee shirt and some socks.

Lily turned her head to meet his gaze and smiled at him softly. Sometimes—every time she smiled—she was absolutely the most beautiful woman in the world to him. He went straight to the bed and lay down behind her, fitting every curve of his body to every curve of hers, wrapping his arms around her tight and nestling his head into her neck. In the quiet that followed, Aiden carefully inspected her beautiful body, brushing his hand over her neck, breast and belly, remembering all the bite and puncture marks that had been on her arms and legs only a short time ago. The marks were completely healed already and she seemed remarkably relaxed, considering her ordeal. His memory of the marks, though, would not be gone for some time. "I'm OK, Aiden," she whispered to him.

"I see that," he said after a long pause. "Did you get some rest?"

She shook her head. "I was waiting for you."

Aiden teased the fingers of his free hand through her hair and kissed her temple gently, whispering in her ear, "I'm here."

"You *are* here," she said, squeezing her hands over his. "You came for me, even though you knew I could never return with you to The Oracle."

Aiden blinked, surprised that she was even questioning that fact. "Lily, I love you. Where you go, I go. I promised you I would not leave you again . . . and I meant it."

Lily turned herself in his arms and curled her face into his shoulder. After several light kisses on his neck, her fresh, citrus-like scent seemed to embed itself into his brain and he inhaled every bit of it. "I love you, too," she said. "Thank you for coming for me."

"I will always come for you."

She smiled, twining her feet with his long legs at the end of the bed. "So . . . what now?"

Aiden stared at her thoughtfully. "I need to find out what happened to Keegan. Even if it's not the news I'm hoping for . . . I just need closure."

"I want that for you, too. Are you sure you're ready to leave The Oracle?"

Aiden nodded. "I'm just not sure I'm ready to leave Zane with Celeste. I keep hoping, in my connection to him, I will feel he has changed his mind."

"Can you feel him now?"

Aiden's expression turned somber. "Yes, he's moved outside of the cave. Darkness . . . I just feel darkness."

Lily tightened her arms around him. "It will get better. I promise it will get better. He *will* find a way to free himself from Celeste, just like I did. I know he will."

Aiden smiled at her, hoping she was right. "Will you come with me to find Keegan? As long as I have you with me, I can handle what I find."

She kissed him. Then she kissed him several more times along his jaw line and around his neck. There was no way Aiden could hold back the satisfied growl that rumbled in his throat. "I really hope that's a yes . . . and that you intend to do more than just kiss me there."

Lily smoothed her hand over the healed skin where Celeste had tried to rip his throat out, and Aiden could feel the shiver run through her. "Are you all right?" she asked him with quiet concern.

He nodded, bringing her closer and tilting her head to his throat. "I'm fine. But I need my mate to claim what is hers—what is *only* hers." Lily smiled and licked her tongue teasingly across his skin. After a moment he could feel the teasing prick of her fangs on his skin, and now *he* was shivering, but with pleasure. "No more waiting, beauty."

"No more waiting," she repeated softly as she began to remove his tee shirt. Her hands smoothed over his chest and arms. He closed his eyes, succumbing to her skin play, and in a few moments he felt the sharp sensation as her fangs puncture his throat. He jerked and groaned hard, pulling her as close to him as he could get her. She sucked on him and he could feel the blood being pulled through his veins and onto her tongue. He did feel pain, but this was a good kind of pain, a blissful kind of pain. The kind that told him, 'this is the woman with whom I will spend the rest of my immortal days'.

After a few moments, she pulled back and he began drinking from her. The sensation of her blood on his tongue this time was as amazing as it had been the very first time. She was like a life force to him. His mate. The woman he loved. "Make me yours," he murmured, "just yours."

Lily returned her mouth to his, the residue of his blood still on her lips, and kissed him deeply, with a passion that set his body on fire! The moment their blood mixed on each other's tongue he felt ten times stronger, ten times hotter, and ten times more committed to this woman than he had ever thought possible.

He pulled her head back in his hands and could see that familiar 'drugged' look in her bright blue eyes. This was the look of a woman who wanted only him. She pulled his sweats down, revealing the impressive erection that was waiting for her. Aiden could never remember feeling so hard in his life, or needing a woman so much. She stroked him, at first slowly then increasing her pace and the pressure of her grasp, causing him to drop his head back and close his eyes. "I need you, beauty," he said, then rolled her beneath him and lined his body up with hers and pushed inside her slowly. A breathy gasp escaped her lips, and before he was even fully inside her he felt her go off like a firecracker around him.

Oh, damn, he thought. There was no word in the world to describe the energy that was passing between them. Her orgasm was more powerful than any she'd had with him previously, exploding over his cock and drawing him to the deepest depths within her. Then there was a brightness, a light that that seemed to flash in his mind, and he could feel a rush of air pass between them like a physical touch. They were connecting on a level they had never connected on before. He could feel it; she was becoming a part of him and it made him want to roar with pride.

Finally, Lily Abbott was his!

Aiden wrapped her legs around his waist and reached for the headboard to brace both of his arms. He began to thrust hard inside her and quickly could feel her tightening around him. Powerful sensations that shot from the base of his spine threatened to destroy his hold on reality. "*Oh, damn, Lily!*" he gasped, and in the same moment, she cried out, as well.

He fell against the sheets and heard her blissful sigh of his mate beside him.

She was his.

He could feel it in his blood, in his body, and it was the most amazing feeling.

Aiden rolled them both to their sides, facing one another, their eyes meeting and holding, and he kissed her several more times on her cheek. "You're stuck with me now, my beautiful mate."

Lily laughed beside him. "I don't mind being stuck with you, Aiden Rowan. I don't mind at all."

EPILOGUE

"What do you mean, no one's seen Maya in weeks?" Alec Lambert was clearly upset, questioning relentlessly, and demonstrating as much by raking his hand roughly through his hair. This hadn't been the news he'd been expecting in his first hour back at The Oracle after having been gone unexpectedly for weeks. "Then where the hell is she? She left Seattle three weeks ago!"

"That point is not entirely clear . . . but we may have a clue," Gideon Janes replied, displaying the usual inquisitive lift of his brow. "I have something to show you."

Minutes later, Alec found himself standing inside one of the large banquet rooms on the first floor of The Oracle. "Why are we here? I hardly think an empty banquet room holds the key to Maya's disappearance . . ." Alec's word's trailed off as he noticed that Gideon was pointing toward the storage area just off the main room, its double doors ajar and at least a dozen rows of stacked chairs had been shoved quickly out of the way to clear space in front of a wall. As he and Gideon moved closer to the unlit room he could make out an image that, from a distance, was incredible in its detail and color, but as he got closer the brush strokes seemed less defined. "Who did this . . .?" he voiced with wonder as they entered the storage space and turned on the overhead lighting.

"Miss Abbott, sir. We've discovered quite a few surprising things regarding the lady since you have been away. Needless to say, I will need to catch you up on some rather shocking revelations with regard to our understanding of the vampire world. But to answer your current question, Miss Abbott has the ability to see the future . . . well, technically, to draw a future she sees. Do you recall when the guards found her unconscious just outside this room, in the hallway? You had her brought up to your private library for Dr. Li to examine?"

"Yes, but that was weeks ago. You just found this?"

Gideon nodded. "I'm afraid so."

Alec was stopped cold. But the reason wasn't his appreciation for the incredible drawing that appeared to have been created by enormous, sweeping brush strokes, but rather the image within the drawing—a night scene, full of implied threat. A small, slender woman, clad in a long, flowing cloak, was being pelted by a heavy downpour of rain that was puddling at her feet. Despite the apparent calmness of the female image, the woman's circumstance appeared quite grave. She was surrounded on all sides by a dozen or more Lycans, their yellow eyes piercing the darkness, every one focused directly upon her. The woman's back was to the viewer, but Alec recognized her right away.

"Maya."

"Yes," Gideon replied. "I thought so, too. And I would venture to say that if what is in the drawing has happened, this might explain why she has not returned to The Oracle."

"Shit! She's in trouble," Alec cursed as he swung around on his heels and strode right back out of the room.

Gideon, Sampson and about eight other guards in Alec's retinue followed behind him. "Sampson!" commanded Alec, "Find Kane! Now! We are going to need him."

ↂ

ABOUT THE AUTHOR

Christine is a graduate of Washington State University, where she received a BA in Interior Design. And true to form of using mostly her 'right brain', she splits her time between her commercial design career and her imaginary world of writing. She lives in the scenic Pacific Northwest where she enjoys hiking, camping and photographing many of the wonderful places that served as inspiration for her Charmed Trilogy and her current Men of Brahm Hill series. Her biggest reward in life comes on any given day when one of her books connects with a reader because she herself is such a lover of reading. Some of her favorite authors include Jane Austin, Lisa Kleypas and Julia Quinn.

ACKNOWLEDGMENTS

Leaving Lily Behind was one of those writer's journeys that was lengthy, very personal and, at times, difficult, but also incredibly rewarding. You hear authors talk of having writers block . . . Well, this wasn't writers block as much as getting the written characters consistent with the ones I had fallen in love with in my head. If it were not for the contributions and efforts of several others, finishing this wonderful story may not have been possible. So I would like to take a moment to thank them.

When the author's journey is more difficult, invariably that can make the editor's job more difficult. I would like to thank my editor, Paul McNeese, who exercised great patience and allowed me the time to really flesh out these characters who are so dear to me. We have now worked together through six manuscripts and I so appreciate his experience, perspective and the consistent storytelling voice with which he brings to all of my books. Thank you!

I would also like to thank my wonderful Brahm Hill series cover designer, Whitney. We had unique challenges with this cover in that our hero is unusually tall. I wanted his height somehow reflected while staying with our dark, moody theme. Whitney you did an amazing job!

Many thanks to Kirsten, my good friend and medical consultant. Thank you for keeping me on track with what's possible in human anatomy, even in my super-human world.

Lastly, I want to thank my Dad. Your road this past year was difficult, but I love how you stay the course with such a positive mental attitude and true appreciation for nature and life! I love you.